FINDING STEFANIE

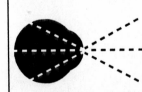

This Large Print Book carries the
Seal of Approval of N.A.V.H.

NOBLE LEGACY, BOOK THREE

FINDING STEFANIE

SUSAN MAY WARREN

THORNDIKE PRESS

A part of Gale, Cengage Learning

GALE
CENGAGE Learning

Detroit • New York • San Francisco • New Haven, Conn • Waterville, Maine • London

GALE
CENGAGE Learning™

LIBRARY OF CONGRESS CATALOGING-IN-PUBLICATION DATA

Warren, Susan May, 1966–
  Finding Stefanie / by Susan May Warren.
    p. cm. — (Thorndike Press large print Christian romance)
  (Noble legacy ; 3)
  ISBN-13: 978-1-4104-2248-4 (alk. paper)
  ISBN-10: 1-4104-2248-8 (alk. paper)
    1. Ranchers—Montana—Fiction. 2. Children of the
rich—Fiction. 3. Actors—Fiction. 4. Montana—Fiction.
5. Domestic fiction. 6. Large type books. I. Title.
PS3623.A865F56 2010
813'.6—dc22   2009046717

Published in 2010 by arrangement with Tyndale House Publishers, Inc.

Printed in the United States of America
1 2 3 4 5 6 7 14 13 12 11 10

For Your glory, Lord

ACKNOWLEDGMENTS

I'm always amazed at the willingness of my friends and family — and even readers — to open their hearts to me. I sometimes ask personal questions, and they offer me advice and guidance to their close-to-the-heart issues in order to help me to write an accurate story. Their trust in me is humbling. My hope is that they believe, along with me, that a fiction story will touch lives and point people to their Savior. Stories of faith could not be told without their honesty and vulnerability, and I'm deeply grateful for their willingness to lay on the altar their personal struggles. May the Lord bless you all more than you can imagine.

Among those who helped me with *Finding Stefanie,* I want to particularly thank the following people: Tim and Michele Nickolay, Allan and Jan Lloyd, Jane Howard, Sharron McCann, Rachel Hauck, Christine Lynxwiler, Susan Downs, my family at First

Baptist Church, Ellen Tarver, Karen Watson, Stephanie Broene, Lorie Popp, Andrew Warren, and especially the Warren kids, who make coming out of my office to greet them after school the best moment of my day.

Thank you all for teaming with me on this book, on this series, and in my life. I'm so grateful for all you do to bless me.

CHAPTER 1

If she could, Stefanie Noble would get on her bay quarter horse, Sunny, ride over the chapped, frozen hills of the Silver Buckle Ranch, and disappear into the horizon. Just keep riding. Because it was only on Sunny that the loneliness and the stress would slough off, and she'd hear the wind, the voice of freedom singing in her ears.

After all, with her brother Nick running the Silver Buckle, she couldn't help but wonder if maybe the ranch didn't need her anymore.

Okay, *sometimes* she wondered. But perhaps not at 5 a.m., smack in the middle of calving season.

Singing — that's what she needed. Something other than the sound of a cow in distress. Her ears ached with the noise as the exhaustion of being up all night pressed down against her, into her bones, her cells.

"C'mon, old cow, push," she groaned,

bracing her feet against the haunches of a weary Black Angus as she pulled on the chains attached to the hooves of a not-yet-born calf.

"She ain't gonna give."

Stefanie glanced behind her. Dutch Johnson, the Silver Buckle's cow boss, looked as tired as Stefanie felt, his face droopy and covered with white whiskers.

"She's hip-locked. We're gonna have to C-section her." He already wore a pair of blue surgical coveralls.

"I can do this." Stefanie's arms shook. "Just give me the puller."

"Stef —"

"It's almost out!" Even as she said it, Stefanie could feel the little calf slide toward her, farther out of the birth canal. "I don't want to lose another cow!"

She refused to let herself feel those words, to remember watching the cow she'd so laboriously raised slip out of life as it bled to death. Stefanie could only blame a month of night calving for her unsteady hands, the way she had perforated the uterus and left a baby without a mother.

"I'm gettin' Nick."

"No!" Stefanie twisted, looking at him. "I don't need Nick. I need the puller. Come over here and lift her leg up, please."

10

Dutch said nothing, just handed her a long bar that looked much like the handle of a rake. Then he grabbed the cow's back leg and lifted it with his tree-limb arms.

Meanwhile, Stefanie affixed the bar across the cow's haunches, hooked on the chains that connected the calf's hooves to the puller, and started to turn the crank, applying pressure.

Slowly the calf emerged. The cow let out a long moan as her baby slipped out into the straw. The little calf didn't move. After-birth glistened in its curly black coat.

"C'mon, baby," Stefanie said, cleaning its face, its mouth. "Breathe. *Please* breathe." She cut the cord, put iodine on it. The calf gasped. "Yes, breathe." She put her hand on its body and began to rub. In a moment, the calf started to take in air.

Stefanie looked up at Dutch. In the shadows of the barn he looked much older than his forty-seven years. But that's what all-night doctoring did. She probably looked about eighty-two instead of what some might call a young twenty-four. Most of the time she sure felt eighty-two.

Dutch gave her a half smile. "I'm going to check the other cows, see if they've dropped their calves yet."

Stefanie sat back in the straw, everything

11

inside her shaking. How she longed for, needed, *thirsted* for freedom. Just one day without . . . *everything.* The weather, the calving, the bills . . . all of it gnawed at her, rubbing her raw with the weight of the shackles.

But this was her life, like it or not.

Although recently, for the first time, she'd begun to think . . . maybe not.

Detaching the hip bar from the cow and the calf, Stefanie watched as the mother turned and slathered her baby with her tongue.

"Good mama," Stefanie said, standing. Grime, sweat, and even blood had long ago seeped into her pores. She reeked of manure and straw, and her hair hung in strings, having escaped her long, dark ponytail. Stretching, she walked past the other stalls, checking the recent mothers and the two heifers who had yet to give birth. Finally, she opened the barn door and slipped outside, letting the wind shear the exhaustion from her face, her limbs.

Behind her, Clancy, their half-shepherd, half-retriever dog, came up and nudged his wet nose into her palm. She smiled at him and rubbed behind his floppy brown ears.

The thaw had tiptoed in this year, haunting the land, giving the air a faint taste of spring, then shirking back, hiding under a blast of north wind and sleet. The pallor of today's sky, stalwart against the encroaching sun, told her that she'd find no hope in the forecast.

No, hope had long ago forsaken this land. Or perhaps it had only forsaken her.

It had returned for her brother Nick and his wife, Piper, now expecting their first child — a girl. And for Maggy and Cole, co-owners of the Silver Buckle, now that Cole had regained his health. And it had certainly found her twin brother, Rafe, recent National GetRowdy Bull Riding Champion. He had never looked so happy as he had at his celebration party when he asked Kat Breckenridge to marry him. They'd probably live happily ever after in her New York penthouse while helping raise money for Kat's charity.

Meanwhile, Stefanie would sleep in the barn and help birth baby cows.

Stefanie, the ranch hand. For some reason, it wasn't at all who she'd expected to be.

Her own smell, as the wind found her, made her wrinkle her nose. The ranch seemed most forlorn at this time of day, most eerie, old ghosts alive in the creak of the barn doors, the low of laboring cows. Sometimes she nearly expected her father's voice to emerge from a hidden stall, calling her to fetch clean water or help him with a calf. For a long time — *too* long — it had been only herself, Dutch, and Bishop, her father, running the Silver Buckle. Somehow even those years hadn't seemed as lonely as having Nick and Rafe return, seeing their lives hook onto their dreams, watching them turn into the men their father had always hoped they'd be, leaving her sorely behind.

It made a girl wonder — who had Daddy hoped *she'd* be? She'd never asked. She always figured she belonged to the land. To the ranch. But with Nick and Piper having a baby, they'd need to move into the house instead of living in the hunting cabin on the hill. And then where exactly would she belong?

She stared out into the horizon, where the outline of the Bighorns barely etched the gunmetal sky.

The horses nickered from the corral across the yard. In the quarantine pen, she noticed that the new quarter horses had huddled up, their noses together as they fought the wind. She'd put them in the shelter last night, but perhaps the draw of hay had lured them out. She should check on Sunny. He'd had a runny nose — a symptom that in other horses wouldn't register a great deal of concern, but in a horse nearly thirty years old, it made her worry.

The horse barn greeted her with a hospitality she craved as she opened the door. Call her strange, but she loved everything about horses, from their expressive eyes to the smell of their manure — so different from that of cows, pigs, or any other ranch animal.

The Buckle's horses stirred little as she entered. The ranch had a small herd of stock horses for riding, but Nick preferred to take his truck out into the field. Stefanie, however, couldn't surrender the nostalgia of working the ranch by hand, just Sunny and her, compatriots.

Perhaps that was where she belonged . . . with Sunny.

Sunny had been the first horse she'd rescued, right about the time her mother lay dying of breast cancer. Stefanie had bought him with a year's worth of chore money after watching him waste away in the backyard of a house just outside Phillips. She'd ached with his neglect, how his ribs sawed through his tan hide, the razor bones of his spinelike spears in his back. He could barely walk when she'd led him to the trailer, and it took a full year before he recovered enough for her to start training

15

him. She probably would have lost hope if it hadn't been for his eyes. They all but begged her to notice him. Begged her to care.

That year she'd brought Sunny back to the beautiful gelding he'd been born to be and discovered that she had a talent. A way of understanding an animal that ministered to both their broken places.

Nick's horse, Pecos, raised his head to stare at her as she walked to the end of the row of stalls. A beautiful black-and-white Overo paint, Pecos had a wild streak that at one time had seemed exactly fitting for her oldest brother. But Nick had worked his wild streak out of his system. As had Rafe.

She always thought she'd been born without the Noble propensity to rebel and wander. So why did she suddenly feel so restless, so unfit for the life she'd always known?

Stefanie flicked on a light midway through the barn, and it pooled on the dirt floor. Funny, she didn't see Sunny standing in his stall. Coming up to the paddock door, she spotted him lying down fully on his side. As if in distress.

"Sunny." She opened the door and crept in. "What's wrong, pal?" She knelt at his side, her hand splaying across his body.

He didn't raise his head, just opened his eye and looked at her a long moment before closing it.

His breathing, under her hand, was labored.

Oh, Lord, please . . . Stefanie ran her hand down Sunny's neck, over his withers. "It'll be okay," she said softly. Had one of her new horses had a contagious disease? She had quarantined them. Still, perhaps Sunny had just developed a cold.

She got up and retrieved her medical kit. Finding a thermometer, she prepared it and took his temperature.

The reading dried her mouth — 105.5.

Sunny began to cough. Then blood dribbled from his mouth into the straw.

Stefanie took one look at the ooze, turned, and ran from the barn. "Dutch!" She bolted across the yard, nearly tripped, then flung herself toward the calving barn. "Dutch!"

He met her at the door, catching her.

Her breath came in gulps of razor-cold air. "It's Sunny. I think he's got — the new flu, the one —"

"Calm down," Dutch said, but he had already started jogging toward the barn. "Call the vet!" he yelled over his shoulder.

Stefanie counted the seconds with her thundering heartbeat as she sprinted inside

17

the house, grabbed the phone, and left a frantic message with the on-call vet's answering service in Phillips. She didn't care that she left a muddy trail across her kitchen floor, a bloody handprint on the phone. Her gaze never left the horse barn door. The message delivered, she dropped the phone onto the cradle and ran back outside across the yard.

Dutch met her as she reached the door, a wall that stopped her cold as he grabbed her arms. "No, Stef, you can't —"

"I have to help him. Let me go!" She yanked out of his grasp.

He stepped in front of her again. "No."

Stefanie looked up at him, her heart choking off the breath in her throat as she read his grim face. Oh. *Oh.* She gasped for air and grabbed for the barn door, missing it and going down hard into the dirt.

Dutch crouched beside her, his big hand on her arm. "I'm sorry. He was probably gone by the time you left the barn."

Gone? *Gone?*

Oh, Lord, please, oh no . . . Her breaths came fast, one on top of another. She clamped her hand over her mouth as if holding in a scream. Only she didn't have one. Instead a ball of pain scoured her throat, falling down into her belly.

Gone?

She couldn't breathe. Couldn't . . . Stefanie moaned, a sound so mournful it made her hurt clear through. She shook free of Dutch and crawled toward the barn. Somehow she found her feet.

Dutch had left the paddock door open, the light on. She stood there for a moment, staring at Sunny, at his beautiful brown hide, his long eyelashes closed over his eyes. He'd always been a magnificent horse in temperament, in form. He possessed an inner strength that had seeped into her soul.

Now he seemed at peace, as if he might be sleeping.

She edged close and dropped to her knees.

She heard Dutch's heavy steps behind her as she laid her hands on Sunny's body. The breath no longer lifted it, but she still felt the warmth of the life that had run through his veins.

"Stefanie . . ."

Her voice emerged just above a whisper. "Once, near the end with Mom, I couldn't take it anymore. It was right after my thirteenth birthday, and I kept thinking, what if she didn't make it till I was fourteen? Everything hurt inside me. I wanted to leave because I couldn't stand to see her suffer, so I packed a backpack and . . . I left. I walked all the way to Cutter's Rock, where it butts up to the Big K, and stood there on the edge of the ravine. I thought that maybe, if I threw myself over, perhaps I could fly. I really thought it. Just fling myself over and fly."

She hiccupped a breath, drawing in another for strength as she opened her eyes. "Sunny found me. I don't know how he got out of the corral, but as I stood there, ready to jump, he appeared, rubbed his nose into my back as if to say, 'Take me with you.'" She stroked his mane.

"Stefanie —"

"Go away, Dutch. Just . . . go." Stefanie ran her hands over Sunny's side. Such a strong animal. How could he be gone so quickly?

Slowly, she climbed over him, lying alongside his back, her head on his neck. Tangling her hands into his mane, she closed her eyes, breathing in his smell, remembering the hours, probably collective years she'd seated herself across his back, trusting him. Talking to him as his ears cocked back, listening.

"I wish I could go with you," she whispered. She turned her head into his neck, letting the sobs rack her body.

The invincible Lincoln Cash — as his press agent called him — had survived jumping out of airplanes, rolling from fiery car crashes, leaping from stampeding horses, and falling from sky-soaring buildings. He'd even weathered bad lines and an occasional tabloid scandal. So it seemed particularly ironic to him that he could be taken out by a button.

Just a simple, pearly tuxedo button, no bigger than his fingernail, one down from his collar, sewn into his designer shirt. He should have ripped it off, made it a part of the scene, but instead he'd fumbled with it as his director, Dex Graves, and beautiful Elise Fontaine looked on with a host of other grips, makeup artists, camera people, and extras.

Watching his career crash into smithereens.

He broke out in a sweat as he tried to open his shirt, and even before Dex called, "Cut," Lincoln knew the charade was over. As silence descended on the closed set, thirty people staring at him, he released the infuriating button and watched his hand shake.

For once, Elise had nothing to say. She sat, her dress up past her knees, her blonde hair tumbled down to her shoulders, and looked at his hand in horror.

The horror that thickened with each thump of his heart.

Lincoln blew out a breath and ran his hand through his hair, then went to shove the offending extremity into his tuxedo pants pocket — only he didn't have a pocket in this costume. So instead, he simply walked off the set and didn't stop until he got into his trailer and locked the door.

He paced in the confined space. He'd had the trailer outfitted with all the comforts of home — two televisions, wireless Internet, a fully stocked fridge with freshly catered food every day. Despite its state-of-the-art gadgetry, the trailer also helped him escape to the hills of Montana, with the dark leather sofa, the panorama picture of the property he'd recently purchased, the lineup of Louis L'Amour Westerns on the bookshelf.

His hand had stopped shaking, and he stared at it, frustrated. Maybe he should quit now, while still at the top of his game.

"Lewis, where are you?" The voice traveled from the places he'd fought to hide it, crept out, and crawled over him. *"Don't you know I'll find you?"* Old, rancid fear prickled Lin-

22

coln's skin; he was ten years old again, skinny and weak.

He'd escaped that life. And never looked back.

He grabbed a towel and brought it to his sticky forehead before he realized he'd be wiping off his makeup. His hand twitched again, and he dropped the towel, grabbing his wrist, holding it still. Pinpricks of a limb just emerging from sleep encased his hand and he tried to shake them away.

Nothing.

Something had to be wrong with him. Dreadfully wrong. To make matters worse, today he'd had to pause, blink, and fight to scrape up the words he'd memorized last night. His short-term memory had never been stellar, but recently it lobbied to expose him.

"Lewis, I'm going to find you."

Banging at the door made him jump.

He opened it, half expecting to see Elise in all her diva glory. She'd been feeding the press juicy nontruths about their so-called torrid backstage relationship and doing her best to make them come true over the past three months. And he would have to be an ice block not to notice her long, tanned legs and perfect curves. But ever since his body had begun to short-circuit on him, fear had driven from him any desire to let someone close enough to discover that he was . . . what?

Lincoln hadn't the faintest idea why he felt as if his body were walking through sludge, always a second or two behind his brain's commands.

Dex, bless him, stood at the door, his baseball hat backward, a slight sweat filming his forehead, to match the tenor of Lincoln's pulse. "You okay?"

"I'm fine," Lincoln snapped.

Thankfully, Dex didn't take it personally. Round and rough around the edges, with hair that looked more like a string mop and enough padding around his waist to evidence his propensity to linger over dinner, usually brainstorming a scene, Dex personified a man who lived for films. He was always rethinking a scene, reshooting with new angles, always reviewing the dailies. He'd known Lincoln since he'd been a fresh-off-the-street extra, had plucked him out of the crowd, shined him up, and made him into a star. Lincoln would do just about anything for Dex — and did, most of the time. Including Dex's crazy stunts that nearly got him killed.

"You sure you're okay?" Dex said, pushing his bulk into the trailer. "Were you out late last night?"

Lincoln hadn't been out late, with anyone, for months. No, last night he'd been locked in his trailer, trying to figure out how to rebuild his life should it all come crashing down around him. How to take care of Alyssa and how to not be a has-been at the age of thirty.

No wonder he looked rough today, according to his makeup artist.

"No," Lincoln said, moving aside for Dex to sit on the leather sofa. "I was working on the script."

"I'd rather you get your rest. I have people to prompt you, you know. I don't know why you push yourself so hard, Linc."

Because he wanted to be known as a professional in the industry? Because he needed this gig more than anyone really knew, and he had to have his game on each and every minute? Because he, better than anyone, knew that fate could turn on him?

Lincoln stared out the window of his air-conditioned trailer at the grips delivering messages and supplies to the various costumers and set designers. "You know why."

Dex was perhaps the only person who knew about his crimes and about the person Lincoln had left behind.

"Listen, I don't know what's wrong, but

you know you can tell me, huh?" Dex said.

Tell Dex that sometimes, when Lincoln got up, the room spun and he found himself face-first on the carpet? Tell Dex that occasionally his vision cut out or got fuzzy around the edges? Tell Dex that the thought of doing his own stunt in the next scene — the one where he was supposed to bail out of a car before it launched off a pier into the ocean — had him cold with fear?

"Please tell me that you're not, uh . . . nervous about your love scene with Elise." Dex gave him a look.

Lincoln answered with a dry smile, but yes. His previous scripts hadn't contained nearly as much skin as this movie — a thriller about a Miami high roller. How he longed for a good Western, where he might strap on a six-shooter, jump on a horse, and chase after the bad guys.

Then again, maybe the people who ran his career knew he needed fast cars and lots of brawls to keep the momentum of his career at a decent clip. If someone got too close, they might actually see that really, he didn't know a thing about acting.

I'll find you, Lewis.

"No, c'mon, of course it's no big deal, Dex." Lincoln laughed and shook his head. "Kissing Elise? I think I can handle it."

"You know, it wouldn't hurt your press to be seen with Elise Fontaine on your arm. She's the next big thing, and I'm fairly sure she has a thing for you."

Maybe, but lately Lincoln had a hard time stomaching the life he'd found so enticing at nineteen. Ten years did that, he supposed. "I'm sure it would." He didn't bother to hide his opinion in his tone. Elise and her flock of paparazzi were the last thing he needed right now.

Dex sighed. "I was thinking that after this, maybe you should take a break. Go somewhere. Go to your new place in Montana. Have you even set foot on the property since you bought it from John?"

Lincoln shook his head. He had met author John Kincaid last summer while taking location shots for the film based on a book Kincaid had written. Lincoln had fallen in love with the land, the smells, the wide-open spaces that allowed him to think, and when Kincaid's ranch came up for sale, he'd bought it on a whim.

"Then maybe it's time." Dex stood. "Let's get through this scene and the final action shot, and then we'll talk about you taking a hiatus." He slapped Lincoln on the shoulder and opened the door. "Five minutes, pal."

"I'll be right out." Lincoln closed the door

behind Dex and let out another long breath, surprised that he'd been holding it. *Get ahold of yourself.* He closed his eyes, tried to center on that place inside him that helped him crawl out of his skin and into the psyche of his character. *Be Barklay Hamilton, multimillionaire, cigarette-boat racer, winner. Be a champion.*

Lincoln needed a drink. Opening the fridge, he took out a glass bottle of energy drink, set it on the counter, and unscrewed the top. His hand had stopped shaking. But he never knew for how long.

"Lewis —"

No. He shrugged the voice away, refusing to listen.

He wasn't Lewis, hadn't been for a decade — more, even. He was Lincoln Cash — superstar, Oscar nominee, winner of the Golden Globe. He was a winner. A man the people respected. A hero.

He reached up and, with a flick of his fingers, opened the button. See, that wasn't so hard. Dex was probably right — he was just tired and needed a vacation.

Lincoln opened the door and stepped out into the sunshine of the lot. The sun baked the pavement, heat radiating into his dress shoes. Cables snaked along the parking lot leading toward the hotel they'd rented for this scene. How he'd rather be on a sound-stage, but no, Dex loved to shoot on location. And this location had to be Miami in March. Thousands of spring breakers lined the set, hoping to ogle him. He waved to his fans as he took a swig of his drink.

The dizziness hit like a bullet. One second he stood vertical, a picture of health. The next he was sprawled on the pavement, the bottle shattered, his body twitching in an all-out seizure.

And he couldn't even scream.

Gideon North begged fate to be gentle with him, to forgive and, just this once, give him a break. Not that he deserved it, but if fate operated on an as-needed basis, he should be at the top of the list.

Especially driving on fumes, an ugly sky in his rearview mirror, with two kid sisters who looked at him as if he might be the bogeyman.

They would be a family again — didn't they see that? Even Macey didn't seem to understand — yet not only was she old enough at fifteen to comprehend responsibility, she'd also been the one to spring this crazy idea. Maybe she hadn't believed that he'd take her suggestion seriously. Maybe her letters had simply been dreams scrawled in desperation. Maybe she believed that he'd abandon her again, the last in a painful line of liars.

But Gideon refused to believe that one drop of his father's blood might be in him, and he'd proven it by doing everything Macey had begged of him. Not only that, but he'd gotten them out of Rapid City, out of the shelter, out of the cycle of foster homes, street living, and hunger.

Gideon turned off the highway and headed west. He glanced at the gas gauge, gripped the wheel of the old Impala wagon he'd boosted, and scanned the darkening land for shelter. He supposed they could sleep in the car, but the way the wind had kicked up, throwing frozen tumbleweeds across the road, he'd prefer shelter. And a fire. And something nourishing in their stomachs.

At least for Haley. . . . He glanced in the rearview mirror at the way she curled into a tiny grubby ball inside a red Goodwill winter jacket two sizes too large for her. One of her pigtails had fallen out, lending her a forlorn, lopsided look. And her eyes screamed hunger. But she didn't speak. Hadn't spoken one word since they left the shelter.

Yep, he was the bogeyman.

"We're going to be okay," he said, because it seemed like the right thing to say. Now that he was eighteen and out of the detention center, wasn't it his responsibility to care for his sisters?

He refused to hear his father's mockery behind his thoughts. Yes, he was going to take care of them. Build them all a place to live. A safe place where they didn't have to hide at night. Where their world wasn't punctuated by cries or people yelling. By Haley's tears.

Gideon's hands, cold as they were, whitened on the steering wheel. His sweatshirt would make poor insulation tonight. He had given his jacket to Macey — she hadn't thought beyond her backpack and shoes when she'd seen him drive up to the emergency foster shelter. She'd just grabbed Haley and run.

Haley had finally stopped crying when they hit the Montana border.

Things would change now, for all of them. He'd make them change.

"Where are we going?" Macey said or rather mumbled into the collar of his jacket. "I'm hungry."

"I know that," he snapped.

She flinched, then glared at him.

Gideon clenched his jaw, wishing that had

come out differently. He wouldn't be like their father — *wouldn't.*

"I'll stop soon," he said, now softer. He'd turned off the highway five miles back, following a sign for a town, hoping for a McDonald's. But as he slowed, those hopes were dashed by the sight of the one-horse rinky-dink spot on the map they'd limped into. A couple of feed stores, a tire shop, a bar, and an old diner that looked like the throwaway back end of a train.

He pulled up just beyond the lights that splashed against the sidewalk. "Stay here," he said, putting the car into park. "I'll be right back."

In the backseat, Haley sat up, her eyes huge. But still, she said nothing.

Macey, too, watched him.

"I'll be right back," he repeated.

Macey gave a stiff nod.

The aroma of hamburgers and french fries made Gideon's empty stomach knot as he shut the door. A trail along the back of the diner led to a row of trash cans and a trailer home. He stood there, staring at the dark windows of the trailer, then at the diner.

Just one more time. Because he had to. Just . . .

He took a deep breath, then crept toward the trailer.

Small towns were easy — people here trusted each other, and he justified himself with the argument that people who left their doors open deserved a lesson on safety. He went inside and looked around.

The owner had milk. And bread and cheese, a jar of mayonnaise, and a box of cereal. All this he scooped into a plastic bag he found on the counter. Shadows pushed into the ancient trailer, over the fraying green sofa, the faux plants, the tattered La-Z-Boy in the corner.

Memory rushed at him, and for a second he was back at Meadow Park, watching television while his mother propped Haley on one hip and fried hot dogs on the stove. Macey was playing with her Barbie dolls on the kitchen table. In Gideon's memory, his mother turned to him and smiled, and something caught in his chest, a vise so tight he couldn't breathe.

Hurry.

He swept the memory away and went to the bedroom, ripping the blankets off the bed. Grabbing two pillows, he shoved everything under his arm.

He was in the car again in under five minutes, cramming everything into the backseat on top of Haley. Then he climbed in and pulled away, easy, as if his heart

33

weren't churning in his chest.

Macey's face had gone hard. She turned away from him, staring out the window.

Gideon said nothing and kept driving, keeping an eye on the gas gauge. The town ended in less than thirty seconds, just past the trailer park, and he followed the road, winding back into the hills, the valleys, the cover he needed to build a new life for them.

He passed miles of barbed wire fencing and dirt driveways that led to tiny box homes with feeble light showing from the windows. He guessed the black humps against the darkening horizon had to be cows or maybe bulls. Here and there the tattered outline of trees edged a hill, boulders lumping in washes.

He would have missed the house entirely if it hadn't been for Macey, who spotted the For Sale sign tangled in the barbed wire fence. She saw it flash against the headlights and said simply, "Hey."

For one short summer he and Macey had made a game of living in vacant for-sale houses. It had been safer than roosting on the streets. Now an old, feeble hope stirred inside him. He turned in to the drive and threaded his way across the land, happening upon the dark compound of a ranch. His headlights skimmed open cattle pens, a vacant barn. The growth of weeds around the front steps evidenced that the house hadn't been lived in for months.

Gideon pulled up and put the car in park but kept it running. "Stay here."

Macey sat up, and for the first time he saw fear flash across her face. She nodded.

He got out, kept the car door open, and sneaked toward the house. The front step gave a predictable groan as he mounted it, and he stopped, his pulse rushing in his ears.

Nothing gave reply but the wind, needling through his sweatshirt and threadbare jeans.

He tried the door. The handle didn't turn. But whoever owned the house had the same blind faith as the inhabitants in town, and the nearest window opened with the smallest effort. He climbed inside.

Gideon landed in a kitchen, barren except for a sink and empty counters, dark and smelling of cold, dust, and neglect. His tennis shoes scuffed on the floor as he went through the small house. An aged shag rug ran into the living room and back to three tiny bedrooms. Foolishly he tried the light, but of course, the electricity had been turned off.

Still, it would do. More than do.

He unlocked the front door and returned to the car. "We'll stay here," he said.

"For how long?" Macey asked, turning to look at Haley.

He followed her gaze, seeing the same question in Haley's blue eyes. How many different beds had his seven-year-old sister slept in during the three years he'd been in jail?

"I don't know. Let's just get out and get warm." He grabbed his loot from the trailer and led the way into the house. "Make Haley a bed," he said to Macey, thrusting the blankets at her. He glanced at the fireplace. "I'm going to see what I can do to get us warm."

Macey went into the dark family room, but Haley hung back, staring up at Gideon. She swallowed, and he had the strongest urge to bend down, put his arms around her, and tell her that it would be okay.

But despite their great luck — the bedding, the food, the car, the house, the absence of flashing red lights and sirens in their wake — and regardless of how much he begged and bargained and even sacrificed, Gideon wasn't sure if fate would be that kind.

CHAPTER 2

"If we don't find a home for them soon, they'll have to be destroyed."

Stefanie barely heard Joe Bob — JB — Denton's words, watching as twenty or so thin and sickly draft horses milled around the holding lot of the Billings fairgrounds. Last month she'd helmed the rescue of thirty-some horses discovered in a dilapidated corral behind an old trailer home on land tucked deep in Custer National Forest. A cross between draft and quarter horses, most of the animals had a chance of survival if they found the right owners.

She'd taken three of them. One carried the flu that had killed Sunny.

She should have quarantined them longer before bringing them home.

Negligent. The word ramrodded through her brain even now as she watched JB's weight shift from one worn boot to the other. He didn't look at her, pulling his battered brown Stetson low over his eyes, hunkering into the wind with his dirty down jacket over his lean, work-toned frame in a posture that screamed hurt. Funny how the recklessness of his bad-boy high school persona had drained from his eyes over the years, leaving only desperation.

She wondered if she bore a similar look.

However, desperation was a poor matchmaker, and Stefanie knew better than to be taken in by JB's smile. Even if he did have a way of making a girl believe she might be lucky to be in his shadow, he also had a jealous streak as wide as Montana. She hadn't given him so much as an encouraging smile lately, but even so, the cowboy seemed to think he had dibs on her — according to the scuttlebutt at Lolly's Diner.

She probably would have never noticed JB's occasional social drive-bys, the once-in-a-while phone calls — albeit for the purpose of rescuing abused horses — or conversations down at Lolly's Diner in town if Rafe hadn't announced his engagement to Katherine Breckenridge after taking home the gold buckle at last year's Get-Rowdy bull riding championship.

Because although Stefanie hadn't finished college, she could do the math. Her mother, at this age, had not only had three children but also had only fifteen more years ahead of her.

"I heard about Sunny," JB said. "I'm sorry, Stef."

She stared at the horses, letting the wind from the north skim off the sudden rush of tears over her loss. "Thank you." She put just enough warmth in her voice to offer peace. Phillips was too small to keep avoiding someone in the canned foods aisle.

Of course, JB, being the cowboy who never quit, took that as a c'mon-over-for-dinner invitation. "So, I was thinking —"

"Forget it." She'd vowed long ago that she'd steer clear of arrogant yet good-looking cowboys. Stefanie didn't need — or want — a man whose ego needed daily feeding.

She did a mental assessment of the lot of horses, of their herd behavior. "I put an announcement about the horses on the Internet. We'll find homes for them."

JB followed her to her truck. "Tell your brother we'll be out to help him with roundup." He spat out chewing tobacco behind him. Nice. "And if he needs any extra hands . . ."

The transient life of a cowhand. Stefanie climbed into her pickup and drove out of the fairgrounds, east toward Phillips.

Nearly a month since Sunny had died, she had yet to find a new horse. Not that she was looking very hard. She'd never find a horse to fill that empty cavern. She'd done a magnificent job of setting up a barbed wire perimeter around her grief, and JB's words had only dug that fencing into her heart. She pressed her hand to her chest through her flannel-lined canvas jacket.

She didn't have time to grieve. Work had to get done. Calves birthed. Cattle fed. Horses checked for the flu. The pickup fixed. Bills paid. Stefanie let work consume her thoughts as she drove. *Vaccinate the new calves. Move the yearlings to the spring field. Start working on backing the new quarter horses. Clean the house. Bring the trash to recycling. Throw out my accumulation of entertainment magazines. . . .*

She admitted that she might have a little obsession going. Ever since meeting Lincoln Cash last summer during those few days he'd been scouting locations for his new movie, she couldn't walk past the grocery store magazine rack and not notice Lincoln's name, not have it jump out at her in glaring black and red, not see issue after issue with pictures of Elise Fontaine wrapped around him.

What was it this week? Oh yeah: "Lincoln

40

Cash Nearly Killed in Death-Defying Stunt."

Nearly killed.

Stefanie probably had a bit of a teenage crush going for the actor. Not enough to sign up for his fan club, but seriously, what wasn't to like? He was a pro at collecting fans. Wooing them with his dangerous smile, a three-day whisker growth, the blond hair that always seemed exactly the same length, right above his shirt collar. He looked like he'd walked off a movie set just in time to put an adolescent skip in her heartbeat.

For two whole hours they'd chatted during the Fourth of July rodeo, and he'd never taken his beautiful blue eyes off hers. He'd even asked about the Silver Buckle Ranch as though he might actually be interested in her and her ho-hum life — *"The truck died. I fixed a water line. We sold a bull."* Still, it didn't mean that she registered on his radar.

Besides, she'd already learned the lesson about falling for gorgeous men. Her heart still bore the scars she'd dragged home from freshman year of college. Sometimes she even saw Doug Carlisle on television, hawking his used cars, a salt-in-the-wounds reminder of her stupidity. She should have realized that the golden boy on campus wouldn't fall for a down-on-the-ranch girl like her.

She glanced at the sky, the clouds bunching beyond the mountains, trapped behind the Bighorns.

Nearly killed. Stefanie wondered how true the tabloid headlines were. Wondered if, indeed, Lincoln Cash had nearly died.

Okay, really, she had work to do. Or at least work to worry about.

The prairie land began to undulate in a rolling landscape of ravines, washes, and hills as she drove east. Overhead the sky evidenced the crisp day — the weather hadn't quite decided if it would surrender to spring. The last two nights had dipped into the thirties, and ice had crusted the puddles in the yard come sunrise. Of course, she'd spent most of the past month in the barn. She should probably put a cot out there.

Stefanie rolled her shoulders, stretching her tired muscles. She hadn't expected to take over the ranch — it had simply fallen to her years ago after Nick and Rafe left. Her father had leaned on her like a son, needing her to take over as his health failed. For a long, long time, his need for her had filled a gap in her, the lonely places that felt so raw they could double her over.

She'd thought Nick's return would be a

balm for those raw spots. Sometimes she wondered if it had only made them worse. Or maybe she realized that the empty places in her life weren't going to be fixed by the triumphant return of the Noble boys to the Silver Buckle Ranch. No, those hollows went much, much deeper.

They would probably never be filled.

Oh, boy, when had she, a girl who had been a Christian most of her life, surrendered to despair? She flipped on the truck's radio, trying to find reception to the local Christian station, and heard only static.

Fine. She hummed a few bars of her favorite song, filled it in with the first stanza, then finished off with the chorus: " 'Fill my cup, Lord, I lift it up, Lord! Come and quench this thirsting of my soul. . . .' "

She'd never been a great singer, but she could hold a tune in the shower and the cab of her own truck, and she bellowed it out now. " 'Bread of heaven, feed me till I want no more. Fill my cup, fill it up and make me whole!' "

Rocks kicked up against the chassis of the truck as Stefanie turned off the highway onto the dirt road that led to the back way to the Silver Buckle, past the Kincaid place. But the words of the song lingered, sinking into her thoughts. Why, if she was a Christian, did life sometimes seem so empty? Why did she still have such hollow places?

Why, when she seemed to have everything she'd ever needed — her ranch, her brothers — did she feel so lost?

"I have learned how to be content with whatever I have." The words of Paul — she must have read them recently — filled her thoughts. Stefanie raised her eyes toward her land, to a horizon already hued with purple twilight, dark wisps of clouds. "Lord, help me learn how to be content. Please fill these empty places. . . ."

Those weren't clouds. As she focused, she saw a trail of black, a glow of orange tufting just over the hills.

The Kincaid place couldn't be on fire, could it? She hadn't checked it recently — especially since the land had stood vacant for nearly a year. She knew John had sold it, although the new owners had yet to arrive. The sky was clear, and she hadn't seen any lightning. She scooped up her cell phone and glared at the no-signal display on her screen.

Slowing at the gate to the Big K, she got out and opened it to let her truck through. She floored her pickup over the ruts and rocks of the two-lane field trail. The orange

44

glow pressed against the encroaching darkness, the black smoke a halo of doom. She
topped the ridge on the back side of the
property, and for a second, her breath left
her. The front half of the house was on fire,
the flames moving quickly toward the back.
Good thing there weren't any people living
there. The place would be engulfed in moments.

She stopped and picked up her phone
again. It registered an analog signal, and
she hit the first entry on her contacts list —
the number to Lolly's Diner, which was
closer to emergency central than the local
dispatch. A voice answered — Stefanie assumed it could only be the new owner of
the diner.

"Missy! There's a fire at the Big K! Round
up the volunteers!" Stefanie hung up and
pressed her speed dial to the Silver Buckle.
Her sister-in-law, Piper, answered and
Stefanie repeated herself.

Then she floored the truck down the hill.
She might not save the house, but she could
at least be a good neighbor and save the
barn for the new owner.

Lincoln had nearly died in Dex's crazy
stunt. He should have known better, should
have paid attention to his face-plant outside

his trailer.

The one his press agent had creatively attributed to fatigue.

And the one that had driven Lincoln, finally, to the doctor.

But like a fool, did Lincoln listen to the diagnosis, pay attention to the flashing red lights put out by his body? No. Instead he'd heard the cheers of fans, the reputation that demanded he do each and every stunt, and climbed into his shiny Aston Martin and proceeded to nearly kill himself. Every movie with Dex included a scene where Lincoln had to bail out of a moving vehicle — the Ditch and Roll. The stunt had become Dex's movie hallmark. Until a few weeks ago, Lincoln could do it in his sleep.

This time, his hands hadn't reacted in time to open the door, and he'd driven right off the pier into the surf and nearly drowned.

Which had finally embedded the truth soundly into Lincoln's brain.

Apparently the doctor *hadn't* been trying to scare him, and over the last month, dread had grown in his throat, so thick it threatened to choke him. Every time Lincoln went to sign an autograph, every time he walked the red carpet, every interview where he lost his train of thought, he waited for the truth to splash across the headlines: "The Invincible Lincoln Cash Has Multiple Sclerosis."

Life just wasn't fair. Lincoln hadn't dreamed that the last movie he'd ever make would be a shallow thriller about a cocky ex–race car driver.

Not his last. No. Yet as he drove north in his new Ford Super Duty 250, out of Wyoming and into eastern Montana, Lincoln knew he'd cheated death for the last time.

If he hoped to have any sort of future, he had to escape, hide, and regroup. And Dex's idea of doing it on his ranch in Montana seemed the best of his options. No way was Lincoln going to check himself into a spa, thank you.

In the deepest places of his heart, the places he didn't share with the media or Barbara Walters or even the Actors Studio, Lincoln Cash had hoped to be more than a movie star. Yes, he had the adoration of fans around the globe, but what he really hoped for, really wanted, was . . . respect. The kind of career that made interviewers pause, made fans look at more than his smile, his physique.

Something that made the world remember Lincoln Cash as more than an actor with a fast car and a James Bond smile.

Of course, he also needed a gig that would keep Alyssa in one of the best rehabilitation homes in the country. Preferably something that didn't require his jumping from moving vehicles.

Headlights from across the highway strobed in his eyes, and he blinked away the surge of panic that his vision would cut out.

"I'll find you, Lewis."

The voices had returned, stalking him as he'd packed up his home in Hollywood. In a previous life, he would have spent the free time after a film shoot hooking up with one of the extras who'd been eyeing him, jetting with her down to Saint Martin.

Even that had lost its luster after his last weekend fling had turned into a full-blown tabloid scandal, complete with threats, property damage, and a restraining order.

No, his best option right now was to find someplace quiet and hide.

He took the turn off the interstate toward Phillips.

On the seat next to him he saw his cell phone reception begin to drop off. Dex had given him time to escape, especially after Lincoln agreed to head to Montana. However, he hadn't exactly told Dex why, which meant that any day, Dex might track him down with a hot new script.

Lincoln tightened his hand on the steering wheel. Dex didn't need to know the truth yet. After all, he could get better, couldn't he?

He *would* get better. And return at the top of his game, like bull rider Rafe Noble had after the car wreck that had nearly killed him.

"Your exacerbations may last up to three months and then vanish completely," his doctor had said in his most optimistic voice during Lincoln's last appointment. "And until the disease progresses, we won't know exactly how your particular symptoms will manifest."

Translation: "We won't know how much your life will change until it already has."

Lincoln had stared at the doctor, wanting to ask a million questions, horrified at the one uppermost on his mind. *Was it genetic? If he had children, would he pass it down to them?*

Not that he had any prospects at the moment. But he'd be a liar if he didn't admit that his thoughts now and again tracked back to meeting Rafe's twin sister, Stefanie, last summer.

Maybe it was the fact that she'd never seen one of his movies or even heard of him, for that matter. Maybe it was the fact that he was a friend of her brother, a man he'd come to admire. Or maybe it was simply her smile and dark, intelligent eyes, her long black hair down over her neck.

Most of all, being around Stefanie for those two hours, Lincoln hadn't felt like a guy trying to keep up with his headlines. He just felt like . . . a guy.

A guy who liked a girl.

Meeting Stefanie had also made him notice that he had no one permanent with whom to share his ten-thousand-square-foot California home, no one on whom he might test new ideas or reveal buried dreams. No one to unload his fears on.

He had plenty of fears now.

But now, of course, it might be too late. His diagnosis might change everything. And like the doctor said, they wouldn't know anything until he didn't get better.

What if he didn't get better?

He had to get better.

Even if his backup plan worked, even if he did turn the Big K Ranch — formerly John Kincaid's place — into a film showcase, Lincoln still had to contend with the truth. Peel away the shine of his persona, and he wasn't sure anyone would like what they found underneath. But maybe it wouldn't come to that. He'd worked too hard to build a life, an identity.

The recent craze for reality shows helped too. According to his agreement with the American Film Institute, his film company would sponsor ten filmmakers. Once a year, the filmmakers would show their projects at Lincoln's festival, the winner bringing home a contract. He hoped that, over time, when critics mentioned his name, it might be in the same breath as Redford and Eastwood and Ron Howard, men who had leveraged their acting careers into behind-the-camera gigs of legendary proportions and into the annals of filmmaking. Maybe he'd even try his hand at directing someday.

As soon as the words *This would be a great place for a film festival* had left Dex's mouth last summer while they'd been shooting location shots in Montana, the idea had taken root in Lincoln's brain. And when the chance to buy the ranch fell into his lap, Lincoln took it as a sign.

A fortuitous sign. The fact that he'd purchased the property months ago, before any hint of his disease, told him that Someone might be looking out for him. Might be on his side.

At least that's what he told himself over and over. What he needed to believe, in fact. Because at this rate, he had only three

51

choices: Ignore God. Blame God. Or need God.

Lincoln wasn't sure exactly which one to choose, but he had a gut feeling that only one would help him figure out how to live his new life.

The new life he meant to find in Montana.

Before it was too late.

Libby Pike didn't care what people said behind her back. She knew she wasn't as pretty as her sister, Missy. Knew she didn't have the curly blonde hair, the smile that made every cowboy in town head to Lolly's Diner after work to get a taste of Missy's homemade pies. But then, she wasn't after the same life Missy desired. She didn't want to own a business or bask in the attention of every eligible bachelor — and that wasn't saying much — of Phillips. She had bigger dreams, overseas dreams. Eternal dreams.

More than anything, Libby Pike wanted to be a missionary. And not just any missionary but the Amy Carmichael, Mother Teresa kind of missionary who comforted the hurting, fed the poor, and poured out her life for the ones the world forgot.

For as long as she could remember, she'd had that dream. Maybe she'd been born with it. And lately, she'd had the opportunity to practice.

She didn't know what the little girl's name was, but she had eyes as big as the sky — haunted eyes — and a ragged stuffed cat and a hunger about her that tore at Libby's heart. She'd first seen the little girl a week ago, standing outside the Laundromat next to the car parts store. She'd been sitting on a bench, looking cold and grimy in a red winter jacket that swallowed her. When Libby walked by, something — maybe the way the little girl didn't meet her eyes — made her stop.

She'd crouched in front of the girl and said, "My name's Libby. Are you out here all alone?"

Which was how she'd met Gideon.

The way he'd appeared, practically materialized, right there on the sidewalk, one would think she was trying to steal the kid. After meeting Gideon, she knew what a terrible mistake that would be. He didn't seem any older than herself, but something in his blue eyes and the scar over his left eye told her that he meant business when he said, "Back off." He'd grabbed the little girl by her jacket and pulled her behind him. She stared at Libby from under her scraggly dark blonde hair.

Libby had looked at him and frowned.

"She's cold. And she looks hungry."

"Who are you, Social Services?" He wore only a sweatshirt and a pair of jeans with a hole in the knee, and she could see that his skin was red, as if he, too, might be cold. With the wind sliding off the hills, it had been in the low forties all week. Not sweatshirt weather. His face was gaunt, sallow, his dark hair long under the hood he'd pulled up.

"No. I just saw her sitting here and thought she might like a cookie." Libby directed those last words at the little girl, smiling. She thought she saw a flicker of life before the girl lowered her eyes.

"She doesn't need a cookie," he said softly, but Libby caught the slightest hitch in his voice. "Thanks anyway."

It was the thanks that had given him away. The reason she couldn't simply dismiss him as rude. That and the way he'd glanced down at his sister, as if he suddenly, desperately, wanted to give her a cookie.

"Stay here. I'll be right back," Libby said. "I'm just going over to the diner —"

"No —"

Only she didn't wait, just jogged past him, ran inside the diner, and grabbed two peanut butter cookies from the glass jar on the counter. "Hey!" Missy yelled as Libby grabbed a napkin and wrapped them inside, before dashing back outside.

The boy and his hungry kid sister had vanished.

But the next day, she'd watched for them. And sure enough, they appeared about dinnertime, just as the shadows grew long between the buildings. Libby noticed the way he slunk inside the Laundromat and reappeared five minutes later.

He certainly wasn't doing his laundry.

But Libby didn't care. She'd figure out his creepy behavior later. She dashed out of the diner in her waitress uniform and caught them as they rounded the corner. She spotted an old, rusty blue Impala parked in the alley between the Buffalo Saloon and the feed store. "Hey! Hey!"

The little girl turned. Then stopped.

Her brother looked back, and for a second Libby saw anger, or perhaps fear, cross his face.

"Go —"

"I brought you cookies. And . . . bread and some leftover meat loaf." She wasn't sure why she'd grabbed all that. But she extended the foil-wrapped package.

The boy stared at it. He glanced at his sister, who held his hand in a white grip, her eyes on the ground. Then he looked at

Libby. "I can't pay right now."

"Oh, for pete's sake, do I look like I want to be paid? They're leftovers. Take them." She thrust the package at him.

He met her eyes. And despite the hard set of his jaw, the muscle that tightened in his neck, everything that poured out of his eyes bespoke gratefulness. He let go of the little girl's hand and took the food.

"My name's Libby," she said softly.

He glanced past her, looked behind him. Then he said, "I'm Gideon."

"You're not from here. Did you just move here?" She ran her hands down her cold arms, shivering slightly.

"You'd better get out of the cold." He lifted the food. "Thank you."

She nodded. "If you . . . I mean, sometimes Missy has leftovers. I can leave them out back, if you . . . you know . . . want to —"

"I could use a job." His tone changed so quickly, from embarrassed to desperate, that Libby's breath caught. But his earnestness vanished in a moment, replaced by hesitation. "I mean, if you . . ."

"I'll ask Missy. Come by tomorrow, okay?"

She had known he would. Or rather, as he gave her the barest hint of a smile, she had hoped it with everything inside her.

A week later, she could hardly believe that the guy doing dishes in the back room was the same boy she'd given a package of meat loaf to. Gideon had showed up, exactly as she'd suggested, and asked her sister for a job — any job.

And Libby could have kissed her beautiful sister for giving him a chance. He'd rolled up his sleeves, plunged his arms deep into the hot soapy water, and scrubbed as if his life, and a flock of other lives, depended on him.

She wanted to ask about his parents, but something inside told her no. That to raise the question might resurrect the wall that she was slowly chipping away.

Libby's persistence, her patience, seemed to be paying off. Gideon even smiled, at least twice, and once after wiping out the sinks, he'd snapped the towel at her. Like he might be trying to make friends.

He had a real nice smile. It lit up his entire face and erased the haunting expression. He had a funny way of flipping his hair back when it hung over his eyes and a deep quietness about him that made her ache to unlock his secrets.

As her father had always said — and she, unlike Missy, actually listened to his sermons — to be a good friend, one only needed to listen.

There were many ways, however, to listen. Now Libby watched as he loaded a tray of dirty dishes, and she couldn't help but notice his arms — strong arms, one of which bore a tattoo right above the wrist. He wore a chain around his neck with something dangling from the end. And, although he obviously had let the holes grow closed, she saw the markings of piercings on his left ear and above and below his eyebrow.

He definitely wasn't from around these parts.

"Can you bus table four?" she asked as he walked past her toward the kitchen. He held the tray of dishes from three tables on his shoulder.

"Yep," he said, glancing at her.

The sun had already begun to dip into the horizon on the back side of the school past Main Street. Libby loved Phillips in the evening, when the streetlamps would flicker on, bathing the street in pools of light. She loved to listen to the jukebox — she remembered when Lolly ran the place and she'd loaded up her favorite fifties tunes.

At closing, music from the Buffalo Saloon, laughter, and sometimes yelling from the parking lot punctuated the air, chorused by Egger Dugan's junkyard dogs in the trailer park behind the diner. Why Missy had moved into Lolly's old trailer, Libby couldn't fathom. Not that she would judge, but just a few weeks ago someone had broken into the trailer and taken blankets and food from the fridge. And it wasn't the first time — a couple of months ago, one of Egger's dogs ended up dead — poisoned, murdered, according to Egger.

Libby would happily let Missy back into the room they'd shared at the parsonage.

"Dinner crowd will be coming in," Missy said, carrying a pie from the kitchen. "Can you check the salt and pepper shakers?"

Libby nodded, heading back toward the kitchen. The phone rang.

"Pick that up, will you, Lib?"

Libby grabbed the phone and tucked it onto her shoulder. "Lolly's —"

"Missy! There's a fire at the Big K! Round up the volunteers!"

"Stefanie?" Libby fumbled with the phone, but it had already been disconnected.

"Who was that?" Missy said, squeezing past her in the door.

"Uh . . ." Libby stared at the phone. "Fire . . . fire at the Big K!"

Missy turned, her mouth open. "Call —"

But Libby couldn't hear her over the crash of dishes as Gideon dropped his tray into the metal sink, turned, and sprinted from the diner.

CHAPTER 3

Fate couldn't be this cruel. The old Impala skidded on the dirt road as Gideon tore toward the ranch — good thing he'd found the name Big K etched into a board in the barn or he wouldn't know that right now his sisters were burning to death in the house he'd found for them. The house he thought would harbor them, keep them warm, safe.

He should have known that it couldn't last — the place to stay, a job with abundant leftovers, even his friendship, or whatever it was, with Libby. All of it seemed too good, too happy for a guy with a past like his.

He deserved this fire.

But his sisters didn't.

Gideon could see the flames from here, a good mile away, clawing at the night sky. Adrenaline mixed with dread, and he thought he might retch.

He'd been careful — *so* careful. Yes, the

house had filled with smoke the first time he lit a fire, but that had been weeks ago. Since then he'd cleaned out the fireplace, opened the flue. And he'd taught Macey how to bank the fire, keep the place warm.

If only they hadn't had the cold snap. . . .

No, if only he hadn't snatched his sisters from the shelter. At least there they'd been fed and warm and . . . alive.

He couldn't breathe. His hand went to his neck, to the chain, traveled down to the cross at the base. He gripped it, letting it bite into his palm, squeezing hard because words couldn't come.

Then he hit the brakes and used both hands to turn the Impala into the Big K drive. A couple of women turned as he skidded into the yard and stumbled out of the car.

Cars and pickups littered the yard, people dousing the blaze with a garden hose, dirt, buckets of water. Flames engulfed the house, a literal furnace of red and orange and yellow consuming the structure, breaking through the windows, curling toward the roof.

His knees nearly buckled. *Macey. Haley.*

"Hey, kid, are you okay?" A tall cowboy with dark hair came toward him, concern on his face.

"Two girls — did you see two girls?" He didn't wait for an answer and ran around to the back of the house.

Haley liked to play in the back bedroom, in the closet, where they'd found a stash of old clothes, shoes, purses, and even a box of ceramic animals.

Gideon shielded his face with his hand as he saw that the flames hadn't yet reached the room. "Haley!" Grabbing a rock, he hurled it at the window. He pulled his hood over his head and sprinted toward the opening. "Haley!"

He felt arms around his waist yanking him back, and he whirled, swinging.

He connected, then couldn't believe it when he saw he'd decked a woman. She winced, stumbling back.

Gideon turned to the house. The heat burned his face and he flinched. But he couldn't — "Macey!" He was crying now; he could feel his body lose control, hear his own agony as he danced there another second, hating himself for his fear. *Help me.* . . . He started for the house.

"No!" Whoever the woman was, she wasn't staying down and she grabbed his arm. "Get back!"

He turned, more angry at himself than at

her, using every ounce of adrenaline as he tried to push her away.

More arms went around him, this time male, and he struggled against them. "Leave me alone!"

"They're out, man! They're out!" The man dragged him away from the flames.

Gideon saw it was the same man he'd spoken to moments earlier. He shoved him hard.

The man seemed to expect it. He didn't respond except to stay on his feet and guard him like a lineman from running toward the burning building.

"Where?" Gideon screamed. *"Where?"*

"Gideon!" He heard Macey then, her surly tone replaced with terror. He turned and she rushed at him, face blackened. He crushed her to himself, probably hurting her, but he didn't have the power to do anything else. His body betrayed him and he fell to his knees, taking her with him. They both landed in a pile. He knew he was crying, but he didn't care. Or maybe he did because one arm locked around her neck and the other hid his face.

His body convulsed, and he became a fool, sitting there on the cold, soggy ground, weeping like a grade-schooler. Macey, for once, kept her mouth shut.

When Gideon wiped his eyes, Haley had joined them, standing a few feet away, tears running down her face. Macey pulled away from him and reached out for her.

A crack sounded from the house. Gideon turned just as the outer wall crashed in. Sparks flew over his head.

"Let's get you out of here," the man said.

The woman Gideon had hit — he easily recognized her from the goose egg on her chin — came up behind him. "Put them in the truck with Piper, Nick." Without even asking, she took Haley's hand.

Haley stared up at her, and then, although Gideon expected her to pull away, she followed.

The man named Nick had Gideon by the arm, and for a second he was again in the past, back at the crash scene, watching the cars burn, being dragged away by the cops. For a moment, it all pummeled him — the tragedy, the blame, the fear.

He couldn't go back to jail. He wasn't worried for himself — he'd survive; he always figured out a way. But Haley needed him, didn't she?

One glance at her as she walked away from him, in the grip of the woman with the long black hair, told him the truth. Maybe she and Macey would be better off if he just disappeared.

The man steered Gideon and Macey toward a black pickup parked safely away from the flames. A woman with blonde hair leaped out, worry on her face. She wore a baggy shirt, but even in the darkness, Gideon could see she was pregnant.

"Is he okay?" the woman asked.

"Shaken," Nick said. "How about you sit in the truck for a while, huh, son?"

Gideon glanced up at the guy, weighing his options. How soon before Nick — who had cop written all over him, from his stance to the accusatory look in his eyes — figured out that Gideon and the girls had been squatting?

Oh, who was he trying to fool? Clearly the guy already knew.

Gideon shrugged out of his grip. "I'll stay out here, thanks."

He looked at Macey, standing with her arms folded across her chest, staring at the chaos he'd brought them to. Just yesterday, as she'd sat with Haley in her arms, he thought he'd seen the flicker of a smile.

Gideon ached with how much he wanted that smile to stay. Because, though Macey didn't know he'd noticed, he'd seen her arms, the marks in different stages of healing, some angry red, the older ones purple, and knew that she'd been cutting herself again.

No. He couldn't leave. Macey needed someone who understood. Who knew what they'd all gone through. Who wouldn't leave them.

But . . . he looked at the house again, felt the heat burning his face. His gut twisted, and again, he had the stupid urge to cry.

"How'd it happen, Mace?" he asked, grabbing her arm. The blonde woman gave him a frown, but he didn't care, just pulled Macey away. "Tell me how it happened."

The fire glowed in Macey's eyes as her face hardened. She yanked her arm away. "Haley was cold. So I stoked the fire. I only left the house for a second — to get more wood — and when I came back, the carpet was on fire. A log had rolled out."

"Why didn't you put the screen on? I told you to —"

"Shut up, Gideon! Why did you bring us here, anyway? We were fine back at the group home!"

"That's not what you told me." He gritted his teeth, lowering his voice as the blonde shot him another look. "You told me to come and get you."

Macey's eyes glistened. "What was I supposed to say? That once we were free from

67

that place, I didn't want you around?" She shrugged, as if to say, *You forced it from me.*

Her words choked him, burning as they fell to his gut. He glanced at Haley, in the cab of the truck, dirty, cold, afraid.

What had he been thinking? That he could somehow make things better? make them a family again? erase his crimes, his mistakes? start over?

He turned away from Macey, from Haley, and stared at the house that he'd thought — what an idiot — he'd make into a home. Another wall fell in, crashing, flames shooting higher into the night. The crowd gasped, stepped back.

Sometimes his naiveté scared even himself.

When he heard another car door slam, Gideon glanced over his shoulder. As if to put a resounding finish on his failure, Libby, cute Libby, stood in the cold night, a sweater wrapped around her waitress uniform.

She came toward him, concern on her face. He liked her eyes the most — hazel, with little flecks of gold around the edges. Although her sister, Missy, had the goods in the looks department, Libby, with her short brown hair and sweet smile, had a kindness about her that made her soft and pretty.

Libby's friendship had dug into the nooks and crannies of a wall he'd thought so solid nothing could break through. And now he knew why he'd erected it. A guy like him didn't deserve a girl like Libby. Liking her, letting her into his life, would only hurt.

Not that he'd entertained any real considerations that she did like him; still, it was hard not to notice her when she stayed late with him to lock up. He'd started to live for her smile, and when she'd laughed when he snapped the towel at her — yeah, his brain had begun dreaming up all sorts of scenarios. He was probably the stupidest guy alive.

Libby approached him, put her hand on his arm. He sucked in a breath and focused on the fire.

"You okay?" she asked.

Gideon made the mistake of looking at her. And then, like the fool he was, he covered his eyes with his hand and, for the first time probably ever, at least for the last five years, answered that question truthfully. "No."

The kid packed a mean punch, even if he didn't intend to. Stefanie watched the boy — more of a man, really, the way he'd tried to fight her and Nick to get into the

69

house after his sisters. In a way, he reminded her of her twin brother, Rafe, back in the days when Rafe had established his iron-clad reputation as the bad boy of Phillips. This young man wore the same external attire — ripped jeans, an old sweatshirt, a shadow that could be more dirt than beard. But different from Rafe, or perhaps more visible, was the desperation, the agony, as he'd collapsed on the ground, holding his sister.

Even now, watching him fight the emotions on his face as he stared at John Kincaid's burning house, Stefanie knew there had to be more to this story than just a kid accidentally setting a house on fire.

A story that included a very frightened little girl. One look at her had turned Stefanie's heart inside out. She needed a bath, a warm meal, and someone to make sure she had a safe place to sleep.

Unfortunately, Phillips didn't have a Social Services department. But it did have the Silver Buckle, and — staring at the two girls, the little one sitting in the cab with Piper where Stefanie had deposited her, the other standing behind the boy and Libby Pike — Stefanie knew in her heart exactly where they'd sleep tonight.

In fact, the idea felt so full, so rich, that

70

she knew it was the perfect answer. The ranch had always been a place of healing — especially the past couple years with Nick and Rafe returning. Perhaps it could be again.

Especially to a young man who needed a break. Her jaw ached where he had walloped her, but given a switch in circumstances, she couldn't say she wouldn't have done the same thing.

Suddenly it hit Stefanie where she'd seen him before. Carrying dishes at Lolly's Diner about three days ago. He'd been busing tables — wearing a white apron and a staid look.

How long had this little family been squatting on John's land? They couldn't be related to the new owners, could they?

The final wall of the house — the back wall — fell in, and then the house was just a pile of fuel, a giant bonfire lighting the night.

Nick was watching the fire with Egger Dugan and the two hands from the Silver Buckle, Andy and Quint, who had wet down the barn. Thankfully the other buildings had all been situated far enough away that the sparks hadn't hit them.

Stefanie walked over to Libby and the boy. "Hey," she said to Libby. She knew the

71

pastor's youngest daughter as well as anyone might know a kid five years younger than herself. She remembered Libby as the one who climbed under the pews and untied worshipers' shoes as her daddy preached. Or maybe that had been her sister, Missy.

At any rate, Libby had grown up. When she turned to Stefanie, she wore compassion in her eyes. "You okay? You've got a quite a bump there."

Stefanie nodded at the boy. "Thanks to Rocky here."

"Gideon North," the boy said, not quite looking at her. "I'm sorry about that."

Stefanie lifted a shoulder. "I'm Stefanie. And it wasn't as bad as being kicked by a horse." She glanced at Piper, who watched Gideon with a guarded look.

"I don't suppose we should ask what you were doing here?" Stefanie glanced at Nick, who was probably listening to their every word. He'd been a cop once, and everyone in town sort of expected him to be one again.

Gideon said nothing. He watched the fire with a wretched look on his face.

His sister leaned against the truck, arms folded, face dirty. She had black hair — so black that Stefanie knew it had to come from a bottle — and a number of piercings

72

up her ears and one over her eye. Whatever makeup she'd once worn, it had trailed down her face, or maybe that was simply soot. She wore a black shirt under her jacket and a pair of black jeans that looked like she'd painted them on.

Stefanie had had a pair of jeans that fit like that once. Caused her more trouble than she wanted to remember.

"What's your name?" she asked the girl.

Her eyes cut to Stefanie, then back to the fire.

"Macey," Gideon said. "Her name's Macey."

"Thanks a lot," Macey snapped.

"Nice to meet you," Stefanie said, although that sounded corny because clearly it wasn't nice at all, for any of them. Not with the inferno in front of them.

"And what's your name, princess?" Stefanie said, leaning toward the little girl, who watched her with wide eyes. She shrank back into the truck.

No one said anything.

"I don't know it either," Libby said quietly. She smiled at Stefanie, and suddenly, strangely, Stefanie felt a kinship with the pastor's daughter. As if Libby knew exactly what Stefanie might be trying to do.

"It's Haley," Macey said, then narrowed

her eyes at Gideon. "She doesn't speak."

"She speaks," Gideon said. "Just not when I'm around."

Ouch. Stefanie tried to read his face. He hadn't even flinched, but she felt something knot inside her chest. Especially when Macey didn't contradict him. "Are your parents around here?"

More silence, long enough for her to know that maybe she shouldn't have asked that question. But she had to be sure before — "Okay, then, tonight you're staying at my ranch. We'll figure out what to do tomorrow."

Macey eyed her, and when Gideon turned, she saw hesitation in the set of his jaw. "No. We can't."

Of course he would say that — after all, she wouldn't say yes to the first stranger that offered a roof over her head. Unless she was broke and had two little sisters to care for and was watching everything she had burn to the ground.

"Listen, don't be stubborn." Stefanie kept her voice deliberately casual, low, easy. "Let me and my family help you, at least for tonight."

Desperation was a tough negotiator. She watched his options play across his face as he glanced at Macey and Haley. Then he sighed, looking at the ground. "Just for to-night."

For starters.

Macey sighed, loud enough to hint at mutiny, but only wrapped her arms around her shivering form.

"Good thing John emptied the propane tanks when he left," Nick said, coming over to join them. Either he'd heard everything and didn't want to interfere or he agreed with her invitation. Regardless, he gave Gideon a nod. "Looks like it might have just been an accident."

Translation: Nick would listen if Gideon wanted to talk. Sometimes, like now, Stefanie got an up-close-and-personal look at the type of man Nick had become, and it filled her with joy.

"Who does this house belong to?" The question came from Macey, who asked it so quietly, it nearly got lost. Stefanie saw how she gave an easy shrug as if not really caring but curious.

"Don't know," Nick said. "Used to belong to a friend of ours, but he sold it. I heard it was purchased, but I don't know by whom."

"Hope they have fire insurance," Libby said.

Gideon gave her a dark look.

"Sorry," she mouthed.

75

Stefanie wondered if Libby's father knew she was here. Because . . . well, Pastor Pike wasn't shy about his expectations where his daughters were concerned. Missy, now that she had her own business, her own house, had made rich fodder for the rumor mill over the past nine months. Apparently her independence made her "headstrong, rebellious, foolish, and just askin' for trouble."

Stefanie had no doubts the same adjectives had been used for her a few years ago, when she'd taken over running the Silver Buckle Ranch.

As for Libby, wasn't she going to be a missionary or something?

Another truck pulled up and Stefanie looked around. A few more onlookers sat in their vehicles, out of the cold, their bright lights illuminating the burning pile of rubble. But from this pickup emerged a group of cowboys from the Double B, the Breckenridge place. Her gaze connected with JB's.

In a way, JB sort of reminded her of how she remembered Lincoln Cash — dark blond hair, a rugged shadow on his chin, penetrating eyes.

JB nodded at her, touching his hat. "Howdy, Stef." He walked by her to stand next to Nick. "Someone torched the old

76

Kincaid place, huh?"

Nick said nothing. Beside her, Gideon shoved his hands in his pockets, his jaw stiff.

"Nick, I think I'm going to take these kids home," Stefanie said softly.

Nick glanced at her, and for a second, argument, or perhaps concern, flashed in his eyes.

She met it with a look of her own. She'd inherited the same Noble spine he had. Besides, one look at Gideon told her that he wasn't a hardened criminal about to make a run for it. This kid had *broken* written all over him.

And if God could change her brother Rafe, maybe He could do the same with Gideon, given enough big sky and patience. The thought made her put on her fight face. If Nick even opened his mouth to argue —

Nick nodded. "I'll stick around here for a bit, but I'll sleep on the foldout tonight."

Stefanie could read between the lines — he wanted to help, but he wasn't letting her stay in the house alone with Gideon and his little flock despite how innocent they looked. "No — it's my idea. I'll sleep on the sofa. You and Piper can have Dad's room."

She reached for Haley, who recoiled. "It's okay," Stefanie said, wondering what had made the girl accept her hand earlier. She kept it outstretched and offered a smile.

Haley scooted out of the truck but didn't take her hand. Instead she reached out for Macey, who pulled her close. Stefanie met Macey's eyes, challenge in their depths.

"There's some chili in the Crock-Pot," Piper said, engulfed in one of Nick's wool-lined denim shirts. She looked tired tonight, her blonde hair down and blowing in the wind.

"Thanks," Stefanie said, pulling out her keys. "Ready to go, Gideon?"

He glanced at Libby, as if needing something from her. Approval? Forgiveness?

"See you tomorrow," Libby said, smiling at him. Was she blushing? Hmm.

A car door slammed, and Stefanie watched another form making its way through the darkness, just outside the glow of light. Apparently Gideon had inadvertently ignited a town meeting. People she didn't even know were emerging from the hills —

Except, she *did* know him. Stefanie stopped swinging her keys as her eyes tried to deceive her, tried to tell her that she recognized Lincoln Cash, in the flesh, walking up the drive of the Big K. All six feet two of him, wearing a leather jacket and jeans, his blond hair just below his ears, sporting his trademark scruffy rub of whis-

78

kers. He shoved his hands into his jacket pockets and seemed mesmerized by the flames. There was a serious, even pained, look on his face, in his blue eyes.

No. She was tired, and the smoke and flames had made her eyes water. Besides, he didn't have an entourage or a curvy blonde on his arm. It couldn't be Lincoln Cash.

He caught her gaze. And in the briefest of moments, something sweet, perhaps a memory, filled his expression.

Could she breathe? She tried it, and her breath came out in a gasp that earned her brother's sharp look. Oh, good grief, now she was acting like a fan, a sappy fan.

She turned away, staring unseeingly at the embers that now glowed, pulsating in the night. "Lincoln Cash is here," she said, more for herself.

But Nick heard it. "What's he doing here?"

Stefanie said nothing, paralyzed. She could even feel Lincoln creeping up on her; the little hairs on the back of her neck had begun to vibrate.

"Hey, Lincoln, remember me?" Nick said. He held out his hand.

Stefanie watched them out of her peripheral vision as Lincoln took it.

"Sure do. Rafe's brother — Nick, right?"

Nick clapped the man on the shoulder. "What brings you to Phillips?"

Lincoln glanced at her. "Hi, Stefanie."

Stefanie managed a smile. A very bad one, lopsided, all teeth. What was wrong with her? "I'm surprised to see you." Her voice was high and squeaky; she sounded like she was about three years old.

And *surprised* might be the understatement of the century. Why on earth would Lincoln Cash simply drop out of the sky to land here, at the Big K, the night the house burned to the ground?

The answer crawled slowly through her chest and made it to her brain by the time he responded.

"This is my property." He looked past Nick to his burning house, then back again. "And I want to know who burned it down."

Silence fell like ashes between them. Lincoln had to know that the entire bunch of them had become liars, accessories to the crime, when no one spoke a word. Until . . .

"I did, Mr. Cash," Gideon said, meeting Lincoln's eyes. He was ashen, rattled by Lincoln's appearance. He wasn't the only one. "It was a mistake," he said quietly.

Good for you, Gideon, Stefanie thought. See, she knew that buried inside this kid lay real potential.

Potential that Lincoln Cash apparently couldn't see, what with the stars of fame and power blinding him, because he looked Gideon up and down before he said, "You're right, kid. A real big mistake."

And as Stefanie stood there, a cold slice of reality spearing through her, Lincoln turned to Nick and said, "Point me in the direction of the sheriff."

Fire. Of course, fire.

Watching from the car as the flames flickered in reflection against the windshield, it all became painfully, gloriously clear.

He would die by fire. He deserved it, really. He'd wiggled out of justice so many times; fire would be slow and painful and the poetic way for him to meet his end.

She leaned her head back on the seat, a wave of relief rushing through her, the adrenaline of the road still buzzing her nerves. She couldn't believe she'd found him — although she'd done her homework, stalked him for so long he'd become almost a part of her. Sometimes they even had conversations in her head. His arrogance often astounded her.

It would be a relief for both of them, probably, when it was over. The waiting, the wondering when exactly it might happen.

She would ache with the loss, but a sweet ache. Nothing like before.

He had done this to her. To himself. Watching him now, standing there, distraught, sated the hunger in her belly.

Time to make him suffer. Just like she had promised herself.

CHAPTER 4

Lincoln had been tired. And crabby. And sore. And mad.

And an Academy Award–worthy jerk. If there might be any confusion in that assessment, in the tally of votes, one look at the expression on Stefanie Noble's face confirmed it.

That and the snarl she'd added to her tone since the last time he'd seen her. He didn't remember a snarl when they'd talked last summer, during the Fourth of July rodeo in Phillips.

"What is your problem, Lincoln? Didn't you hear him? He said he made a mistake! An accident!"

An accident was knocking over someone's planter with a football, maybe banging someone's car with a bike. Lincoln wasn't exactly sure what the word might be for incinerating someone's house, but *accident* didn't come close.

Besides, he'd taken one look at the kid, at the way he shoved his hands in his pockets, at his slouched yet wary pose, the expression of defiance as the boy peered at him through that shaggy hair, and Lincoln had flashed right back to the past, to the trailer park and getting his insides rearranged by just this sort of kid.

The sooner this little arsonist was behind bars, the better off Phillips would be. Lincoln couldn't ignore the flint of disappointment that slivered though him. He'd thought Phillips was safer than this — free from the punks that plagued bigger towns. In fact, he counted on that safety to attract celebrities like himself who needed to hide from the crime that stalked them.

"I heard him loud and clear, thanks. And nice to see you too, Stefanie." He only half meant the sarcasm in his voice. When he'd envisioned this moment — well, not *this* moment, not the moment when he'd watch his only shelter burn to a crisp, but the moment when he'd see Stefanie again — he'd entertained the notion of rekindling the tiny flame he'd started last summer.

Or at least he *thought* he'd started it. One look at her face now — and wow, he'd forgotten how pretty she was with her big brown eyes, that long dark hair, the high cheekbones, the slim, strong, yet graceful aura that she carried in her step — and he wondered if she'd ever liked him at all.

Maybe she'd simply liked the Lincoln persona.

Of course she did. After all, what did he expect?

"Don't 'nice to see you' me," Stefanie said, echoing his sarcasm with deadly accuracy. "Could you just try to be a nice guy? Can't you see that these kids need our help?" She gestured to the kid, whose eyes darkened as he glanced at Stefanie, apparently piqued by her description. No, he wasn't remotely a kid, judging by the scars, the anger on his face. This punk had left "kid" behind at least a decade ago. Which was why Lincoln felt justified in his urge to flatten him.

If he could control his arm enough to swing, that is. And then there was that little issue of his balance. Lincoln was turning back into a hundred-pound weakling, right before his own eyes.

"Don't you think you should be a little more concerned for the victim here? That *is* my house burning down." How would she react if someone set her ranch — her *future* — on fire? "And what do you mean by *mistake?*" he growled at the kid. See, he

85

could be nice. He wasn't yelling, was he?

"I think Gideon was just trying to keep his sisters warm — he built a fire in the fireplace and it got out of hand," Stefanie answered for him.

"Since when did you become the local public defender?" Lincoln snapped, watching her glance back at a girl, a teenager, who stared at Lincoln with eyes that told him his star powers had taken control of her mind. Behind her, another little girl slunk behind her sister's leg, apparently terrified by the mean man.

He really felt like a jerk now. All the same, he couldn't afford to have juvenile delinquents running around Phillips, especially when they left flames and rubble in their wake.

"I'm only defending him because you had to come in swinging. It was an accident — don't you see how hungry and cold they are?" Stefanie answered, even stepping between Lincoln and Gideon, a little bobcat of attitude.

No. All he saw was trouble — past, present, and future. Where was Dex when he needed the guy to yell, "Cut"? This scene hadn't played out at all like Lincoln had hoped.

"Where are their parents?" he asked, trying — *really* trying — to put a soft tone in his voice.

No one said anything.

Swell. "Listen, why am I the bad guy here? I'm just saying, the kid burned down my house. Where I'm from, that's a crime."

"I'll fix it."

This, mumbled from Gideon, hit Lincoln square in the absurd bone. He couldn't help letting out a burst of laughter that didn't in the least resemble humor, expect perhaps a crazed Jack Nicholson — in — *The Shining* kind of humor. Maybe the drugs the doctor had given Lincoln affected his ability to control his emotions, but with everything inside him, he wanted to leap on this skinny kid and strangle him.

"Right," he said instead, ignoring how the kid flinched. "Let me get the tool kit from my luggage. We'll get started on it tonight. Because I forgot my tent and my sleeping bag, thinking that maybe I might have a place to sleep tonight."

Liar. But Lincoln delivered the line with such rancor that even he believed he had intended to bunk down in John Kincaid's three-bedroom modular home, maybe build a campfire in the living room and dine on a package of cold ramen noodles.

"Oh, please," Stefanie sneered, one hand

on her hip, apparently using her killer X-ray vision to see right through him. "Like you were really going to stay here. It doesn't have satin sheets or a mint for your pillow. Oh, and furniture or appliances, for that matter."

And here, when he'd met her, he thought Stefanie Noble quiet. Even docile. Clearly she was the one who deserved the Oscar. If this reception was any indication, he'd read every happy, pleasant vibe he'd picked up last summer entirely wrong.

Fine. He didn't expect *everyone* in the world to love him. Not really. However, even if he had been a little over the top with his response, he didn't deserve *both* barrels. His house was on fire. He had feelings too.

Lincoln folded his arms over his chest, thankful that his hand didn't shake for once. "It's true; I'd forgotten the warm and friendly Phillips hospitality, but obviously the law has changed. What, is this the let-bygones-be-bygones form of justice? Or maybe just, 'Hey, let the rich guy pay for it. He's got the dough.' "

Stefanie also crossed her arms, not rattled in the least by his throwing out the truth. Instead a smile — and he put it solidly in the category of nasty — raised one side of her mouth. "That sounds about right, Mr.

Cash."

Lincoln stared at her, everything inside him hollow. He'd wanted to hide, not be trampled into the soil. So he held up his hands in surrender. "Sorry, sweetheart. My fault for thinking that a guy might get a fair shake here. Sadly, I'm fresh out of fifties. And a house, it looks like. I guess I'll just go find a tree to put my bedroll under."

"Lincoln —," Nick started.

Stefanie cut him off. "I think there's a big cottonwood over in Idaho."

They'd attracted a small crowd. Or, given the population of Phillips, a large one. But enough murmuring and unrest rippled through it to evoke the Old West traditions of lynching and being run out of town on a rail. Lincoln had seen enough Westerns to know that wasn't his preferred method of deportation.

Besides, he needed this town on his side if he hoped to sweet-talk them into spiffing up the place for his purposes. Maybe fixing — or installing — sidewalks, replacing the green road sign that announced Phillips with a real Western-looking carved sign that gave the place some class. Perhaps even adding another restaurant.

Stymied, he turned and surveyed the wreckage of his house. The fire had died to

89

spitting flames and simmering embers. Thankfully the barn, which had been rebuilt less than five years ago, still stood, as did the rest of the outbuildings. He'd already talked to a contractor about revamping the barn to create a theater. He'd have to track the man down and have him rearrange the schedule to work on the house first. Lincoln hadn't seriously planned on living in John's old digs, but he'd slotted the demolition of the house after the building of the theater.

This *accident* might even have saved him a headache. It probably wouldn't hurt him to let go of his anger. Except for the fact that Lincoln knew, better than most, how kids like the one who had torched his house only meant trouble. Trouble and hurt and danger and — most of all — tragedy.

He watched as Stefanie rounded up the two girls, motioned to Gideon, then gave Lincoln a stinging glare as she walked past him, toward a truck sitting not far away on the back side of the property.

Lincoln's gaze fell to the little girl walking hand in hand with her older sister. His gut twisted so tight his eyes began to burn.

The punk belonged in jail. Before he hurt someone else.

Someone like Alyssa.

■ ■ ■ ■

Stefanie still couldn't believe the way she'd treated Lincoln Cash.

Her sarcastic tone, the horrible way she'd reacted to his tragedy. She had overreacted in an epic, live-in-her-nightmares kind of way.

Even if he had been calloused toward the need radiating from the kids or the wretched guilt on Gideon's face, she didn't have to go into she-bear mode.

It was just . . . well, she expected so much more from him — no, *wanted* — more from him. She wanted the charming guy she'd met last summer, the one she'd seen on the big screen, the one who occupied her hopes. Maybe it had been his attitude that set her off, arriving in his shiny luxury rental car with his bad-boy looks, his designer jeans and leather jacket, swaggering in like he owned the place.

Which, apparently, he did.

What was he doing back in Phillips, anyway? The last thing her town needed was his entourage clogging traffic. And where was his arm candy, Elise Fontaine? Stefanie hadn't seen — okay, *purchased* — a magazine in the last six months that didn't have a shot of them together somewhere in the pages, if not on the front cover.

Stefanie ran a hair pick through her wet hair. She'd showered right after showing Gideon to Rafe and Nick's room and getting the two girls settled in her old room. Although she'd purchased a new comforter and pillows, it still felt just as girlie as when her mother had remodeled it the year before she died. Pink roses on the wallpaper, a shelf for knickknacks — mostly Stefanie's horse collection. And a dollhouse her parents had made for her eighth birthday, complete with miniature furniture, set on a table in the corner. Over the years, she'd taken down the posters and the dusty horse-riding trophies, the basket of stuffed animals. But with the white-painted French provincial dresser and desk and matching double bed her parents got on mail order from Montgomery Ward, the room still looked like it might belong to a twelve-year-old. Stefanie hadn't had much time since her thirteenth birthday to do anything but tend to ranch chores.

Besides, sometimes, deep inside, she longed to be twelve again. Longed to be the girl who dreamed of maybe someday raising a herd of horses and using them to help troubled children. She'd even named her dream ranch — Redemption Ranch. She'd rescue horses and children, and just like she and Sunny had, they would heal each other. She hadn't taken those dreams out to scrutinize for . . . years. Definitely not since her mother passed away.

But suddenly, like an echo of an old prayer, those dreams had formed right before her eyes as she'd watched Gideon tumble out of his car and sprint toward Kincaid's burning house. Even after he'd hit her, everything inside her had longed to help him. Especially when he collapsed in the dirt, one hand over his face, trying to hide his tears. She'd have to be made of stone not to see how much he cared about his sisters.

Which, apparently, was the substance of Lincoln's heart. Stone or perhaps granite. So much for his hero image. Heroes didn't kick down-on-their-luck kids in the teeth.

"Since when did you become the local public defender?" She smiled remembering Lincoln's words. That's right. Just call her the Defender of the Oppressed. Besides, someone had to care about these kids.

She snagged her pick in her long hair, and it went flying across the living room. She didn't bother to look for it, just finger-combed the rest. She caught her reflection in the dark window, then got up to check out her bruise.

She bet Elise Fontaine never got a bruise. Elise Fontaine probably didn't wear thermal underwear to bed, probably didn't have makeup from graduation still in her bathroom, half-used, and probably got her hair cut more often than every two years. Stefanie stood at the mirror, smoothing out her thermal jammies, checking out the curves — or lack thereof — sucking in her stomach, straightening her shoulders.

She shook her head. Who was she trying to kid? Lincoln Cash, for all his charm, wouldn't notice a girl like her. She was just a ranch hand. A horse rescuer.

Defender of the Oppressed.

She wasn't sure what identity fit her best. Tonight she'd been proud of herself. For the first time in years, for a second, she'd felt exactly, perfectly right, standing between Gideon and the world.

Toe-to-toe with Lincoln Cash. She thought of her cutting words about his name and cringed. She hoped she hadn't wounded him. Much.

But stars like Lincoln didn't wound easily, did they? After years in the tabloids, he had to have the skin of an armadillo. All the same, she wanted to hide under a rain barrel. Next time she saw him, she'd give him a second chance to be a nice guy.

Stefanie climbed onto the sofa, preferring not to fold it out, and tucked her mother's afghan over her.

A splinter of shame dug deeper as she remembered her parting shot about sleeping in Idaho. She hoped he'd found a place at the Buffalo B and B.

She never should have let Lincoln get under her skin, despite his arrogance. She'd acted about thirteen and like a broken-hearted fan.

She most definitely wasn't a fan anymore.

And she certainly didn't entertain any fantasies of her and the magnificent Lincoln Cash riding off into the sunset together. In fact, she could probably delete any romantic notions of riding off anywhere with anyone. Except maybe JB. But she'd have to be unconscious before that happened.

Most of all, she'd have to remember that movie stars didn't fall for plain ranch girls who knew how to rope cattle but didn't have the first clue how to balance in high heels.

No, she'd be like Dutch. Live forever on the ranch. Single. Alone.

Lord, help me learn to be content. Please fill these empty places. . . .

Upstairs, she heard one of the kids get up,

shuffle into the bathroom, close the door.

Is this an answer to prayer, Lord? She closed her eyes. *Please. Please let them stay.*

"Who is he, Libs?"

Libby took the toast from the toaster, put it on a plate, and skimmed low-fat butter from the tub with her knife. "Who is who, Daddy?"

Her father, Duncan Pike, pastor of Phillips Community Church, pulled out the vinyl-cushioned chair and sat down, reaching for the coffeepot she'd set in the middle of the table. She'd been trying to ease him off fully caffeinated coffee after his mild heart attack a couple years back. Although he had legs that resembled Montana fence posts, the extra helpings of pot roast through the years had settled over his belt, and deep inside, she feared one day coming home to find him dead from a coronary.

Thankfully, she'd tricked him into half-decaf coffee — for all he knew, he drank three cups of fully loaded Colombian roast every morning. It was her little secret.

In fact, the secrets had started to pile up in the last week. Secrets like how she'd begun to care for Gideon. Care in a way she'd never felt before.

"You know who." Her father picked up

the Sheridan paper, reading the headlines.

The dawn poured through the huge picture window that looked out onto the church parking lot from the parsonage, and light puddled on the ancient off-white linoleum floor. The kitchen, built in the fifties, still contained the tiny Formica table and chairs — now a novelty in some catalogs. In fact, the entire two-bedroom house had become accidentally retro, with its green shag carpet and yellow cupboards and counter. Thirty years in one place, with the same furniture, the same flock. No wonder her father seemed stuck in his ways.

There was also the fact that he didn't have anyone to remind him that his girls had become women. Sometimes Libby still found him sitting in the dark in his faded recliner, his Bible in his lap, his hand over his face, praying, as if he was just as overwhelmed as on the day her mother had died.

How exactly was she supposed to leave him in six months for Bible college, all the way in Chicago? As it was, she'd put it off for a year already. She just wasn't sure how to leave him.

Her father spoke into his newspaper. "Clarisse Finny called last night, right before you came home. Said you were out at the Kincaid place, watching the fire.

Claims you were standing next to that new boy, the one Missy has working at her place."

"Standing next to a boy is hardly a crime."

Her father raised his head, a sharp look on his face. "It's exactly that kind of response that might make me think Clarisse is on to something."

Libby sucked in a breath. Her father didn't deserve to be snapped at. He gave her plenty of leash for a man who knew the dangers embedded in a town where the boy-girl population weighed heavily on the male side. Cowboys had emerged from the woodwork right about the time the girls hit adolescence, and her big sister, Missy, had been a sort of magnet for their attention.

Libby had tried to tell her father that she would never, ever share in Missy's . . . problems, but at eighteen she still had a curfew of ten o'clock and had yet to have a date. Even to the senior prom. Her father had made her go with her cousin Willy from Sheridan. What her father would never know is that Willy had snuck in a bottle of schnapps and ended up pickled and throwing up in the back of his car. She'd driven them both home before the dance ended.

"Sorry, Daddy. I'm late for work. And Clarisse is a gossip and a troublemaker."

Her father sipped his coffee, then reached for the bran flakes. He wore a look of agreement but, after a moment of sifting through his thoughts, came back with his judgment of Gideon fortified. "No, I think this kid is trouble. According to Clarisse, he set Big John's place on fire."

Libby set the buttered toast down in front of him. "He had a good reason."

Her father glanced at her as he reached for the milk jug.

"That didn't come out right. He has a couple of kid sisters. I think one of them started the fire."

"What were they doing at John's house, anyway?"

"It's not John's house anymore — it belongs to Lincoln Cash."

Her father's spoon stopped midway to his mouth. "The *actor* Lincoln Cash?"

She nodded. "He showed up last night just after his place caved in. Wanted to send Gideon to jail."

"Maybe that's where he belongs."

Libby opened the fridge and reached in for a yogurt. "Stefanie Noble took him and his sisters to her place. Probably, she'll call Social Services today." The thought had kept her tossing the night away, a sickness in her gut.

Or maybe a little higher, in her heart. The fact was, Libby did like Gideon. Especially when he'd stood up to Lincoln Cash and told the truth. Something like pride had bloomed in her chest, and she'd had the crazy urge to hug him.

She closed the fridge. "Don't worry, Daddy. I'm just his friend." She dabbed a kiss on his weathered cheek.

Her father caught her hand, pulled her closer, and returned the kiss. "You just make sure that bleeding heart of yours doesn't go too far." When she met his eyes, she saw more than a sermon there. "I don't want you getting hurt."

She smiled at him but couldn't help but wonder if his warnings might already be too late.

CHAPTER 5

Gideon had died and gone to paradise. Only, he knew he didn't deserve paradise, so perhaps this was simply a dream. Or maybe just an old Western movie, because everything about this place screamed cowboys and horses and one of the *Lone Ranger* episodes he'd seen in juvie hall. From the warm, dry single bed with the wool, red-and-black-checkered blanket, to a bull-riding poster on the wall and a coiled rope hanging on the bedpost of the other single bed, to roping trophies on the opposite dresser. Whoever had lived here had *cowboy* written all over him.

Gideon lay in bed, rested for the first time in . . . He did the mental math and couldn't remember the last time he hadn't slept with one eye open, waiting for the nightmares, both real and imagined.

No nightmares last night. Except, of course, the big one — the fact that he'd burned down the house of megarich mega-star Lincoln Cash. Yes, that should make the news and send the cops running in his direction. Apparently he still had a knack for knowing how to really blow it — big-time. Gideon's eyes had nearly fallen from their sockets when he'd seen the movie star walk up. In fact, he would have considered brain-altering smoke inhalation before he believed that Lincoln Cash owned the house he'd commandeered and, by accessory, incinerated. But Stefanie Noble and her big brother Nick, the guy who had probably saved his life, had no problem identifying the actor.

He wasn't sure what he'd done to deserve Stefanie's loaded-shotgun defense; he'd expected to be led off in handcuffs, right back to jail. He made a mental note never to cross Stefanie Noble.

Although it felt good — way too good — to have someone on his side. Especially when she offered him a place to stay. As much as he hated to say yes, he knew that Haley and Macey needed someplace warm. One night, he'd told himself. One safe, quiet night. And tomorrow he'd hike back to the ranch, fetch the Impala, pile his sisters inside, and head . . . somewhere.

Macey's voice razored into his thoughts:

"Why did you bring us here anyway?"

His throat burned, his stomach empty and clenching. He hated the fact that he'd broken down last night. In front of Macey.

And Libby.

Gideon couldn't believe she'd come to the fire. Couldn't believe she'd stood by him. He should stop thinking about her, about her smile and those pretty eyes, the way she'd touched his arm as he turned to leave.

Stop thinking about her.

He sat up and took a deep breath, listening. He could hear voices downstairs — yes, Macey's voice. Not Haley's, of course.

Macey had told him that Haley stopped talking right before his trial, but he'd traced his thoughts back and couldn't remember her doing anything but babbling. Then again, she'd only been three at the time of the accident. Truthfully, he hadn't been around much even before that, and by the time Haley had appeared on the scene, things had fallen apart in their family enough to make any toddler clam up, hold the pain inside.

That's what he wanted to do. Should have done. Instead he'd run — straight into trouble. And look where it had gotten him. In smoky-smelling clothes, with greasy hair and another crime hanging over his head.

Even if he didn't get charged with arson, how about kidnapping? or breaking and entering?

Laughter drifted from the kitchen. Was that Haley?

Gideon stood, grabbed his jeans, and shucked them on. Then he crept toward the door. The aroma of breakfast — eggs and sausage? — roped him in, and he pulled on his shirt as he edged out into the hall.

"I put a pair of Rafe's old jeans and a shirt in the bathroom. You can take a shower and help yourself, if you want." The voice came from behind him, and he turned. Stefanie was pulling a towel from the closet. As she handed it to him, he noticed her jaw had begun to purple.

"I'm really sorry about that." He nodded at the bruise.

"Don't worry about it. Get cleaned up. Breakfast is almost ready."

She had pretty eyes — dark, yet they bore kindness. She didn't look that much older than him — with her long dark hair and her pink T-shirt under a brown corduroy shirt, her low-rider jeans. Yet something about her made her seem . . . wise, maybe.

He took the towel. "Thanks. We'll be out of your way in a —"

"Uh, no, I don't think so." Her smile

vanished, and for a second, he saw the scene last night and the way she'd dismantled Lincoln Cash with her bare hands.

Gideon stepped back, toward the bathroom and refuge.

"Unless I'm reading the situation wrong, you have little money, an old car, no place to stay, and two sisters to care for. You're either runaways or homeless, and my guess is that if you leave, you'll simply drive until you find another vacant house and squat there for a while until some other disaster happens."

"We'd make do."

"Oh yeah, eating out of garbage cans. Stealing. Sleeping in the car. How long before something happens to Macey or Haley while you're out 'making do'? And what, exactly, will you have to do to 'make do,' Gideon? Because you're not in jail now, but from my vantage point, you might as well start forwarding your mail."

He already knew she didn't pull her punches, and he wondered now if he might be bleeding. "Hey, I have a job. And I'm taking care of them."

She held up her hand. He noticed the calluses. "Hold up. I'm not saying you aren't trying. But is it the best life for them?"

He clenched his teeth, looked away. What

did she know? "Just stay out of it. I never should have come here."

Stefanie stepped to block his entrance into the bathroom. "You absolutely should have."

With her tilted head, the way she folded her arms over her chest, she didn't look easily moved. For a second, relief streaked through him. He'd hate for anyone to know how much he longed to stay.

Which was why his "What do you want from me?" came out less caustic than it could have.

Her eyes gentled. He felt like a piece of cellophane. If he didn't watch it, he'd start bawling again. He looked away.

"Okay, the truth is, I want to help." She looked down at her stocking feet, then back up, wearing a smile. "I know this is going to sound strange, but in a way, I think you're sort of an answer to prayer. I'd like to help you and your sisters, if you'll let me."

Why would — oh, of course. Haley. Everyone loved Haley, with her big, innocent eyes. In fact, it had been Social Services' decision to list Haley for adoption that prompted Macey's panic and their subsequent escape from the group home.

This woman wanted Haley. She'd probably give Gideon and Macey a full tank of gas and a bag lunch if they'd agree to leave

Haley behind.

Sorry, but he hadn't boosted a car and committed a couple of misdemeanors and probably a felony for this know-it-all woman to swoop in and steal his sister.

"I don't need your charity," Gideon snapped and shoved the towel back at her. He thumped down the stairs and through the living room, his chest tight. He stalked through a nice-looking family room — leather chairs, stone fireplace, lots of homey, sweet family pictures on the wall — and into the kitchen.

Haley sat at a wooden table, clutching that grimy stuffed cat with one hand and scooping cereal into her mouth with the other. Macey sat beside her, eating an apple. Although Haley wore a clean shirt over her grubby pants, Macey still wore her black I-hate-the-world uniform, the sleeves of her pullover yanked down over her hands, her thumbs sticking out of holes she'd made in the cuffs. She looked at Gideon but didn't smile.

Piper, the pregnant woman he'd seen last night, stood at the stove, scrambling eggs. She glanced at him. "Morning."

He said nothing as he went over to Haley and pulled her to her feet. "We're leaving, Mace. Now."

Her jaw tightened, but for once she didn't argue. She stood and grabbed another apple, sticking it in her pocket.

"Gideon!" Stefanie came barreling into the room.

He didn't turn, even with Haley's hand limp in his. "Thanks for the hospitality," he said, not nicely.

"At least eat something."

For a second, a crazy impulse inside screamed, *Stay! Stay here and see what this woman, this family, has to offer.* He looked down at Haley, and her eyes had widened, her face pale.

Stay . . . so they could call Social Services, maybe even the cops, and have him hauled away, back to prison. Only this time he'd go to adult lockup. He couldn't deny the fear that snaked through him.

"C'mon, Haley," Gideon said, tugging her.

Idiot. The word pulsed in his mind as he opened the door and walked out into the brisk air. The sky seemed to have collected the smoke from the night before, gunmetal gray in tone. It mirrored the misery that Macey and Haley wore on their faces. The wind swirled up dirt, spit it at him as he walked past the corral of horses, the pickups in the yard, down the drive. Off in the distance, he could hear cows mooing.

"Gideon!"

He didn't turn at the voice, refusing to even let it slow his step.

"Where are we going, Gideon?" Macey said morosely.

He didn't answer.

Smoke rose like fingers toward the heavens, some embers still glowing from under charred beams. Lincoln stood in the yard of his new ranch in quiet disbelief.

Last night, staring at the antler chandelier in the bedroom of the Buffalo B and B, acceptance had come easier, what with Mrs. Charles leaving out a piece of blueberry pie and milk and fixing him up in the best room — the one with the attached bathroom. The other bathrooms in the B and B were shared among all the other guests. Lincoln had needed all the privacy he could get trying to wrestle his body out of bed this morning. Thankfully, the Novantrone treatments he took might be starting to work; this morning one leg hadn't felt two feet longer than the other, and even his hand felt more alive, and the trembling seemed to have stopped.

He just might pull off keeping his condition a secret.

Now, how might he go about building a film dynasty? Especially with a group of teenage vandals running around, burning houses to the ground? That might be something he should leave out of his travel brochure.

He'd certainly made a stellar impression on Stefanie. So much for letting his star status wow her. She'd hardly held herself back from leaping into his arms.

Okay, that fantasy might have been over the top, but it had been years since he'd had to work up more than a smile to attract a woman's attention.

Not that he wanted hers. Maybe he should amend his dreams of a real relationship with someone who would know him and believe in him despite his dark places. After the bruising Stefanie had done to his ego last night, he'd appreciate a few lies thrown his direction.

He held his cell phone up. He got one blip on analog. The wind scoured up ashes, flinging them onto the trampled, yellow grass around the house.

Perfect. Maybe he could start a grass fire, burn the entire county down.

He stuck his cell back into his pocket.

He'd spent the morning on the phone, first with his insurance agent, who promised to hurry on the claim but didn't make any guarantees. Lincoln wasn't sure the payoff

110

would compensate for the time wasted. Then he'd connected with Delia, his assistant back in LA. Between barking at the movers, who were probably breaking his stuff, and listing his phone messages, she sounded like she hadn't caught the fact that there'd be nowhere for her to live once she arrived. Good thing the B and B wasn't full. He'd have to buy out the place for the next three months to house his crew. Or find a hotel in Billings.

He'd already told the contractor to bring in his house, which he'd ordered months ago when he'd closed on the property. A log home on a truck. He'd always wanted a log home, but knowing the cost of wood in Montana, he'd opted for a system used to truck in the wood. He'd picked out a spot on the hill above John's house, and he had planned to use the old house as a visitor/reception center. Maybe he could have barbecues, invite all the local youths instead.

He let his mouth slide up on one side. This wasn't Dallas. He didn't have to panic about being overrun by delinquents in Phillips. In fact, once he placed a call to the Social Services office in Billings, he'd probably never see the kid again.

He should assume, then, that he wouldn't see Stefanie Noble either, based on her overprotective reaction last night. Did she always have such a soft spot for troublemakers?

Oh yeah, he'd forgotten about her brother Rafe. Maybe with him headed on the straight and narrow, she needed a new project.

Pulling out his cell phone again, Lincoln walked up the hill, checking the signal. He allowed himself to rest a couple of times, and by the time he reached the top, he had full reception. But before he called his agent, he stood for just a moment and breathed.

The crisp air in Montana always smelled of freedom. Of wide-open spaces, grasses, and flowers, of animals and the wind off the western mountains, and today a tinge of smoke from last night's inferno. Healing air seeped into his lungs, filled them, and he let out the slightest breath, then inhaled deep . . . deeper . . . holding it.

Letting it fill his lungs, his hollow places.

From this vantage point, he could make out the hazy purple of the Bighorns in the west, the rolling green hills cut away as if with a giant spoon, leaving ragged ravines and drying streambeds littered with boulders.

As if resenting his moment of quiet, the

phone rang in his hand. He looked at the display. Elise.

Yippee.

He opened it, already pursing his lips. "Elise."

"Oh, Linc, where did you run to? We had the most rockin' party last night — I totally missed you."

"Thanks. But I'm involved in a project right now, and I have to focus all my attention on it."

"Oh, I love projects! Are you writing a screenplay? Let me help. I've always wanted to write a film. Please. Besides, I miss you."

"No . . . no. This is something I have to do by myself." Not including the demolition team and a cleanup crew and a team of builders, due to arrive later this week with Delia. If Elise showed up, he'd have a three-ring circus — caterers, builders, press . . . and an illness that wouldn't stay quiet for long.

But making Elise angry wouldn't do him any favors either. She had a way of landing in the tabloids and dragging everyone else with her. "Listen, I miss you too. But you . . . you need to move on."

He heard silence at the other end, could see Elise's pretty face tighten in a scowl.

"I'll call you . . . when . . . I'm finished

with my project." Now he was the one making a face, but he still had the acting chops to add earnestness to his voice. "I promise."

Elise gave a deep sigh, one she should have reserved for the set. "Okay. I'll be waiting." She hung up.

Yeah, sure. She'd pine away for him while shopping on the Sunset Strip and eating dinner at Spago and hanging out with her A-list cronies. It would be tough.

Lincoln fielded a call from his agent. He'd been through five agents since Dex had cast him for his first two-bit gig. This latest guy had been in the industry for thirty years and promised to help him transition from action flicks to drama, but so far, he'd only racked up an expense sheet of dinners with directors and producers. As usual, his agent had a lineup of action scripts for Lincoln's consideration.

Lincoln turned him down, then scrolled through his voice mail. His contractor had called, returning Lincoln's message from last night, and Alyssa's nurse, Nellie, had left her usual day-end report. Lincoln had long ago stopped asking the doctors to call and simply put one of the day nurses on the lookout for Alyssa, in exchange for a monthly check. It was a win-win. According to Nellie, Alyssa had begun to have night terrors. Lincoln scrubbed his hand down his face. Were the memories finally starting to surface after a decade?

Deleting the messages, he stood there overlooking his land, in his mind seeing the house, the stables, the fresh start.

Seeing everything he'd dreamed about, way back when he'd cut through the junk-yard on his way home from school, hiding behind old washing machines and cars from E-bro Quesada, the local gangbanger who had his sights on Lincoln. Lincoln wasn't sure exactly why E-bro had picked him to torture. Maybe because they were neighbors or because Lincoln — Lewis — had run the first time E-bro knocked him off his bike.

In a way, Lincoln had been running ever since.

Speaking of junk — what was that rusty Impala doing in his drive?

Lincoln hiked down to it and peered in the window. A couple of empty soda bottles, paper, and a bag from McDonald's lay crushed on the floor. He reached for the handle and slid inside, into a memory so rich he could have been back at the trailer park, sitting in his mother's beater Volkswagen, hot-wiring it for a Friday night joy-ride.

In fact . . . yes, wires dangled below the steering wheel as if it had been transported through time. Or across state lines, because he'd noticed the South Dakota plates on the car. The kid should have known to switch them out with a different car's first chance he got. Lincoln only assumed the car belonged to the punk from last night, but he felt secure in that assumption. Secure enough that nausea crept through him, remembering how Stefanie had taken the lot home with her last night.

So they could cut her throat while she slept. Perfect.

He couldn't dismiss the image of Stefanie Noble taking him out last night, those dark eyes turning him into rubble, that feisty mouth telling him exactly where he could take his pomp and circumstance.

Now, clear of the pain, he had to admit that she intrigued him. And in a way, she'd earned his respect.

The sooner he got this car back to her troublemaking houseguest, the sooner they could leave. And then he didn't have to be the bad guy and call Social Services.

He grabbed the wires and had the car started in moments, the talent easily returning. He'd have to ask Stefanie for a ride back, but, well . . . He smiled and turned

116

around in the drive, heading for the Silver Buckle.

He could be a hero. She just needed to give him a chance.

"Are you just going to let them go?" Piper stood at the door, one eyebrow raised at Stefanie as Gideon and his little family hiked down the driveway.

What was Stefanie supposed to do? Chase after them, throw a rope around them, hogtie them, and drag them back to the house? Gideon obviously didn't want their help . . . but maybe it wasn't up to him.

She and Nick and Piper had had a little chat this morning. Apparently, despite Nick's willingness to take in Gideon and his sisters after the fire, he didn't like the idea of letting a group of strangers in the house permanently. Still, he could read the desperation in their postures and had agreed to move with Piper into the house — a move that Stefanie had been anticipating.

She'd happily take the sofa forever or even move to the hunting cabin if . . . if Gideon just turned around.

Maybe she should call Social Services. Get them into the system, a real home. Only, as she let that thought settle, she hated it. Really hated it.

Or maybe she just hated herself for buying into the insane idea that she could make a difference in their lives. She was idealistic — Rafe and Nick had always called her a dreamer. But how could she fight the broken look on Gideon's face, like one of the quarter horses she'd rescued, afraid to trust, too much history in his eyes to let her help him? She loved working with hurting animals, seeing their trust, their hope restored . . . and everything inside her longed to reach out to this family and give them a safe place.

Macey had the look of a scared filly, the way she nearly drew into herself, encased in black, from her hair to her toes. Stefanie ached just looking at her.

And then there was Haley. Under all that dirt a look of starvation leeched from her eyes and from the way she clutched that ragged cat. It was all Stefanie could do not to scoop her up and tuck her head under her chin and hold her until the hunger in her expression vanished.

"Gideon!" Stefanie launched off the porch, ran down the road. Gideon didn't turn, just kept walking. "Gideon, c'mon! Don't go."

She saw his head begin to hang, his shoulders tense. If he were a horse, he'd be turned from her and running round and round in the ring. And if he were a horse, she'd wait until he figured out he had nowhere to run.

But maybe Gideon had already figured that out because his step slowed.

She caught up to him, noticing the whitened grip on Haley's hand. The little girl had tears dripping off her chin. Macey didn't look at Stefanie as she stood behind Gideon.

"Listen, Gideon. Don't go. You can stay here. I know you're on the run —"

"We're not runaways. We're just traveling; that's all." He pulled Haley close to him, putting his arm around her.

Okay, so they were all going to dodge the truth for a while. "Well, you probably need some cash, then. I could use a hand." Stefanie gestured to the corral, toward her new quarter horses. "I have three horses I need to train and a bunch of calves that need branding and tagging, and of course, there're always jobs to be done around here —"

"I got a job." He wasn't going to make this easy.

"Yes, I know you do. But maybe you might like another —"

"I'll do it." Macey didn't even lift her head

as she spoke but sighed, looking at the horses. "I'll work for you."

She had the posture of an indentured servant. Stefanie felt like a slave trader. But she also didn't have a plethora of options. "Uh . . . that would be great, Macey. I could sure use your help."

Macey lifted a shoulder, as if she didn't care one way or another.

"I don't want any trouble," Gideon said.

For a second, those words coming from him, a guy who'd burned down a house just twelve hours ago, made Stefanie want to laugh. But she managed a straight face and nodded. "No trouble."

"Don't go calling Social Services or anything."

Oh, *that* kind of trouble. Her humor vanished. "Where are you from?"

"We don't have parents to worry about us, if that's what you're asking," Gideon said, lifting his chin a little and meeting her eyes. His arm went tighter around Haley. "But . . . you can't have Haley."

Stefanie felt as if he'd hit her again, except low, right in the gut. She looked at the little girl, at the way she curled into her brother, even if she didn't put her arm around him. Had someone threatened to take Haley away from them? She put a rein on her emotions when she said, "No, Gideon, I won't take Haley."

Gideon said nothing, drawing a breath, glancing down at his younger sister, then around at the ranch. Stefanie smiled at him, but he didn't meet her eyes.

She heard a motor behind him and looked over his shoulder. An old blue station wagon came into view, and it took a moment for her brain to register who was driving.

It couldn't possibly be Lincoln in that beater, could it? She folded her arms across her chest, everything inside her tensing, not sure exactly what to say to him . . . or how.

The car stopped, and yes, Lincoln got out, awash in his movie star glow. He wore a pair of dark glasses — though the sun had yet to make a decent appearance today — a leather jacket, faded jeans, and cowboy boots. He didn't smile as he approached Gideon. "This your car, kid?"

Gideon glared at him. "Might be."

Lincoln gave a huff that Stefanie read as annoyance. "Well, I got a proposition for you. I won't call the law if you and your sisters get in it and leave. Right now." He reached into his back pocket and took out his wallet. "In fact, here's some traveling money." He pulled out what looked like

121

three hundred-dollar bills.

Then, although Stefanie had lost the power of speech, even her ability to move left her when he looked at her and flashed a smile. "See, I can be a nice guy."

For a moment, she choked, really felt the oxygen cutting off as she saw herself mentally leaping at him and squeezing both hands around his neck.

Stefanie glanced at Gideon, hoping that maybe he'd gone deaf, but no, he was staring at the money in Lincoln's hand as if he might actually be considering Lincoln's offer.

That was *enough*. "What is your problem?"

Lincoln had the audacity to look at her, his mouth open. "Hey, I'm trying to help —"

"And exactly where are they going to go?" Stefanie had balled her fists at her sides, but she wanted to use them on his astonished expression. "But you don't really care, do you?"

"They could get to Sheridan or Billings, hole up in an apartment. He could find a job —"

"He *has* a job! At Lolly's. And he doesn't need your money!"

Although, based on the hungry look in

122

Gideon's eye, maybe that wasn't exactly accurate.

"Listen —" Lincoln grabbed Stefanie's arm, pulling her away. "You do *not* want these kids around."

She yanked her arm away from his grip so hard that she saw him wobble. "What, I lost the power to think for myself? When did you decide you knew what was best for me . . . or even know me? I hardly remember you, Mr. Cash. And now suddenly you want to decide who my friends are?"

"These kids aren't your friends, and yes, I do." He kept his voice low, but she detected something desperate simmering in his tone. Not only that, but the way he said it . . . sort of protective and caring . . .

She needed a good shake. "Look, I'm not afraid of giving someone a chance. Of letting them into my life, my world. Of trusting them until they can prove their trust and investing myself, regardless of their past. These kids need someone, and that's all I care about."

Stefanie wasn't sure where all that came from, but the look on Lincoln's face went from worried to . . . strange. He just stared at her while Haley sniffed and Gideon glared at them.

Finally Lincoln shook his head, but his

voice gentled. As if there might be a human under those rugged good looks after all. "Listen, this isn't a good idea. You haven't been around kids like these. I'm telling you, Stefanie — you're in over your head."

Aside from the way his words stirred up questions, she couldn't ignore the meaning: *You're not tough enough for these kids.* Apparently he hadn't been paying attention to the life she lived. Tough was her middle name.

"What are you doing here, anyway? Why don't you go back to saving your pretend worlds and leave the real stuff to the little people." She put the end of her sentence in finger quotes.

A muscle in his jaw tensed. "I'm here because I'm going to do something good for this town. Because Phillips is a great place, and I'd like to be a part of it."

"Oh, great job. Winning friends already. Wait, I think I hear the Welcome Wagon ringing your doorbell. . . ." Stefanie put her hand to her mouth. "Oh, whoops, you don't have a doorbell, do you?"

His eyes narrowed. "That was mean, even for you."

"You don't think I can be mean? I'm just a cowgirl, you know. I've been around these bulls a long time. Maybe I've forgotten how to be nice."

For a second she even believed herself. Because something about being around Lincoln Cash made her into a person she didn't recognize.

His voice seemed to come from a place of hurt. "That's not true. I think I met the real Stefanie Noble last summer, and this isn't her."

That only made it worse. She ignored the sting of his words lest her emotions spiral off and she do something embarrassing like burst into tears.

"How do you know who the real Stefanie Noble is?" The question lingered there, and suddenly it felt raw, as if he'd forced way too much from her. A burn rushed into her face, yet she rallied. "It's my decision to invite these kids to stay, and that's what I'm doing. You don't have to approve. In fact, hmm . . . that's strange. I ran my life for years without your intervention. I think — uh, yep, I'm *sure* — I can make a decision without you. Amazing, the world runs without Lincoln Cash's say-so."

She knew her words had made a hit because his mouth closed and his face darkened. "Fine." He turned to Gideon. "This is the last chance, kid. Take it or leave it."

Gideon's face had hardened, and for an agonizing moment, Stefanie thought that he might actually grab the money and run. *Please, Lord . . .*

"No. I think we'll . . . um, stay here for a little while."

Lincoln frowned at him, obviously not used to having his brilliant ideas rejected twice. Then he folded the money, slipped it into his wallet, shoved it back into his jeans, and stared at Gideon as if trying to find the right epitaph.

Silence stretched between them. Stefanie could nearly hear Gideon's heartbeat in the wind, in time with her own. *Please, Cash, don't wreck this. . . .*

"Okay, kid, listen up. You remember that this family helped you out. They took a chance on you, and if you so much as look at Miss Stefanie, or anyone else here, the wrong way, I guarantee that I will not only call Social Services but do everything in my power — and don't underestimate me — to make sure you spend the rest of your days regretting your mistakes."

He didn't wait for Gideon to reply, just turned to Stefanie. "I need a ride back to my ranch." Clearly Lincoln wanted her to give it.

She said nothing. She might be stubborn,

126

but she wasn't stupid. She'd seen one of his movies. Knew that ten minutes in the presence of his charm could wrap a girl's brain into knots, and despite the fact that she'd rather ride next to a basket of rattlers, she knew that if she didn't watch it, soon she'd be laughing at his jokes and becoming downright neighborly or something.

Besides, she'd made the mistake of falling for a charmer before and still bore the scars.

She wouldn't be loaning *this* neighbor any sugar.

"I'll drive you back." Nick's voice came from behind Stefanie, and she turned, surprised that her big brother had been listening. Apparently he'd already been out working because he wore his scarred gloves and his brown canvas jacket, his white Stetson over his dark hair. He glanced at Stefanie, but his eyes betrayed nothing.

"Thanks, Nick," Lincoln said and brushed past her.

"Least I can do for a neighbor," Nick said.

Stefanie shook her head.

Gideon winced, looking as if he'd been beaten up.

"C'mon. Piper made eggs," Stefanie said to the little group, starting back toward the house.

As she passed Lincoln and Nick getting

127

into Nick's truck, she met Lincoln's eyes. Neither of them smiled.

Suddenly she felt a touch. Stefanie's heart soared as she closed her fingers around Haley's cold little hand.

CHAPTER 6

Libby had never been one to swoon over movie stars. While Missy had hung posters of Brad Pitt and Leonardo DiCaprio on the walls on her side of the room, Libby had admired people like Elisabeth Elliot, the famous missionary who'd lost her husband in Ecuador so many years ago. Libby wanted to be someone who changed lives, not because of her money or looks but because she showed the love of Christ.

Although sometimes, admittedly, she couldn't rightly tell whether her smile for Gideon grew from her desire to love him to salvation or just . . . love him.

She watched him pile dishes into the dishwashing tray, spraying them with the long hose. He'd seemed quieter this past week, more withdrawn. And harder working. Every morning, she found him waiting on the back step as she opened the restaurant; every night he left last, watching her as she got into her car to drive home.

He looked at her now and gave her the slightest smile. "Lincoln Cash still out there?"

She didn't know why, but she'd noticed that every time Cash came into the diner, Gideon hid in the back room until he left. Which didn't seem very Gideon-like at all. Unless she remembered the way Cash had raked him over the night of the fire. It had taken Libby a few days to forgive the actor for that — despite his smile, the way he complimented her service, even his gigantic tips.

Yet with Cash's long stretches of campouts at Lolly's Diner — Missy had yet to change the name — Gideon couldn't dodge the man forever.

"He's just finishing his pie," she said. "I don't know why he insists on staying until closing every night. You'd think he'd be tired of this place after eating lunch here every day. And most of the time he takes a bag dinner too. But it looks like he's nearly done. You're almost in the clear." She slid her tray of dishes onto the counter next to him. "I'll give you the high sign."

He held up the sprayer, as if he might actually shower her. She wrinkled her nose at him.

"Missy, this is just about the best banana cream pie I've ever eaten." The actor's voice filtered through to the back room.

Gideon's smile disappeared, and he turned back to the dishes.

Libby heard Missy's giggle and knew that her sister, like the rest of the population of Phillips, had fallen under the charm of their local celebrity. Admittedly, he'd turned out to be the town's benefactor as he sold the idea for a film festival to be held in this little pocket of the world. The way he painted it, movie stars and celebrities from around the globe would saturate their little town, drawn here by the charm, the authenticity, and the safety it offered. Lincoln Cash had even established business grants for anyone who wanted to open a restaurant — which made Missy *ever* so happy — or a hotel.

Libby knew from the influx of breakfast and dinner customers that something akin to a barn raising was happening out at the Big K. Gideon hadn't said much, but rumor had it that Cash had a virtual army out on the property, building a house and a theater and who knew what else.

The entire town seemed beside themselves with excitement. After Cash assured her that he'd make sure to endorse her diner, Missy had named no less than three dishes after

131

him — the Lincoln Burger, Eggs and Cash-browns, and a Cashapalooza, which was just a mash of ice cream and hot fudge and caramel she'd asked him to concoct. Currently it was their number-one seller.

Libby had to admit, as she came out of the kitchen and saw him sitting there on the stool — the night backdropping him, one hand holding the newspaper, the other lifting a coffee mug — that he had brought charm to their town. He wore a light brown denim shirt today, sleeves rolled up just below his elbows, a black Stetson, and jeans. When he smiled at her, she identified definite swooning inside.

"Libby, great coffee tonight. I can't believe this is decaf — delicious." He lifted his cup, and she grabbed the pot, filling it.

Missy looked up from where she was wiping tables. "Hey, Lib, would you mind closing up for me tonight?" She balled the rag up and tossed it into a bucket.

Libby nodded. "Gideon's still here too."

"Thanks." She walked by Libby, taking off her apron. "See you in the morning."

Libby collected Cash's plate and set it on a tray of dirty dishes. "Mr. Cash, do you mind if I ask you a question?"

He put down his paper and looked at her. "Go for it."

"Do you go to church?"

He seemed to ponder that. "I used to, once upon a time. Maybe it's time to go, huh?"

Libby tore off his check, putting it face-down in front of him. "Do you consider yourself a good man?"

Cash frowned at her. "I guess I do."

"You seem like one, with all the stuff you're doing around town. I just wanted to make sure it wasn't wasted."

He picked up the check, stared at it for a minute. "I don't understand."

"Coffee and pie —"

"No, I mean, what do you mean, wasted? Isn't doing good a good thing?" He pulled out a ten and pushed it toward her. "Keep the change."

Libby smiled. "Thanks." Another 60 percent tip. "The thing is, being good is fine, but all that goodness isn't going to get you anywhere but farther from God. See, we can do all the good we want, but if we're not saved, it just masks our need for a Savior. Good isn't going to get anyone to heaven. Only realizing we need Jesus, and being forgiven, is going to matter."

"Are you saying that anything good I do without God isn't really good at all?"

"Not in God's economy. The only good

we do that counts with God is the good we do in faith, in cooperation with Him."

He got up. "I'd like to think I'm cooperating with God."

Libby opened the cash register, deposited the cash, drew out the change, and slipped it into her pocket. "I'm sure you do. So maybe going to church might help you figure out what that means."

Cash touched his hat, giving her a wink. "Then I'll see you there." The door jangled as he exited.

She smiled. That was easy. Maybe she did have a knack, just like her mama had said. Ever since she was young, she'd been inviting friends, neighbors, even strangers, to church. Janie Pike had called her the "littlest missionary." How she ached to have her mother's prophecies come true.

"Is he gone?" Gideon stuck his head out of the kitchen. She noticed his apron was wet down the front.

She giggled. "Yeah, big bad Cash has left for the night."

Gideon came out, wiping his hands on a towel. "He's got it in for me; I know it. That's why he's here every night. He thinks I'm going to do something bad — maybe steal money from the till or set the diner on fire."

134

Libby took Cash's coffee cup and put it in with the dirty dishes. "I doubt that. He's just hungry."

"Every night? During closing time?"

"Wait, is that him, sitting outside the door with a six-shooter?" She cupped her hands above her eyes as if peering outside. "No, he's looking in here with binoculars. Duck!"

"Stop." Gideon didn't look amused. "He doesn't like me."

"You got off on the wrong foot with him is all."

He gave an incredulous huff. "I burned his house down, Lib." He looked so wretched when he said it, his hair over his eyes, leaning against the doorframe.

Libby turned her tone soft. "Everyone knows it was an accident, Gideon. Really."

He shrugged, then brushed past her to pick up the last tray of dishes. She stepped back to let him pass but reached out to touch his arm to stop him. He jumped as if she'd shocked him.

"You know, you don't have to live as if the world hates you. You have a fresh start here in Phillips."

An expression so raw came over his face, everything inside her stilled. Then he shook his head. "There are no fresh starts for me. Just . . . moving on."

135

"So, you move on."

He gave her the smallest smile. "Right. Moving on into the kitchen now." He winked, and although the man voted one of America's sexiest men had just done that without causing the slightest reaction from her, this from Gideon had her body suddenly alive, every nerve tingling. She swallowed as he disappeared into the kitchen.

She should lock up and go home.

Taking a spray bottle, she sanitized the counter, found a couple of dirty cups left behind, then switched off the front light, locked the front door, turned off the diner lights, and went to the back.

Gideon had just begun to spray down the dishes he'd placed on the tray in anticipation of loading them into the dishwasher.

Libby reached around him to put the cups on the tray and bumped his arm. Water sprayed down the front of him.

"Hey!" The strangest look came over his face.

And then, she didn't know why, but she shrugged as if she didn't care in the least that he was saturated. "Sorry."

She saw her mistake a split second later as a smile, a dangerous one that she'd never seen before, crawled up his face.

He turned the hose on her and depressed

the sprayer.

Warm water soaked her — her hair, her face, her pink T-shirt under the white apron, the black uniform pants, her white tennis shoes. She screeched and turned to protect herself, but he didn't stop, just sprayed her down the back.

"Stop!" Libby accompanied her cry with a lunge for the sprayer and must have taken him by surprise because she not only got her hands on it but turned it back on him, drenching his face, his hair, his clothes.

Gideon wrapped one arm around her waist, pulling her away, wrenching the sprayer from her grasp.

They were both breathing hard, laughing, dripping onto the floor. He had a nice laugh, deep and full, and she hadn't really heard it, ever. It made everything inside her feel warm. He still had his arm around her waist, and as she wiped her face with her hands, she noticed how tall he was, nearly a half head taller than her. And strong — one-handed he'd muscled the sprayer from her without hurting her. But with his black T-shirt plastered to his body, she realized that he wasn't nearly as skinny as he was fit.

He still wore the smile as he let her go and ran a hand down his face. He gave her a look, half disbelief, half mischief, shaking his head. "I should have known you were trouble."

Her mouth gaped in mock indignation, but she never got a word out. Before she could blink, before she could catch her breath, before she could even think, he leaned down and kissed her.

It might have been a quick kiss, just for fun, but she leaned in and kissed him back. He tasted of water and something tangy, like soda. He moved right into the kiss, putting his arm around her waist again and pulling her to him.

Everything inside her simply exploded. She felt sensations she'd never experienced before — her heart racing, and fear, too, only with a sweetness that started in her toes and moved upward, toward her heart. She'd never been kissed before. Her arms went around his neck, and she lifted her face and loved the feelings that went through her. Not that she'd been dreaming of kissing Gideon — she'd tried not to think about it, actually. But now, everything that she felt about him, although new, she poured right into that kiss. And he kissed her back, as if he might be feeling exactly the same way.

Gideon pulled away. His smile had vanished. His hand came up and touched her face, as if he might be in shock, with his eyes wide. He swallowed, and a small smile began to curve his mouth. "I really like you, Libby. I really, really like you."

Her breath caught, and for a second, although she knew he meant it in every good way, she felt sick, right in the pit of her stomach.

What was she doing? She forced a smile, stepping back from him, disentangling herself from his arms. She pressed her stomach, mostly to keep the churning inside. "Yeah. Okay. I . . . uh, I gotta go."

He looked like he'd been slapped. "What . . . what did I do? What's the matter?"

Libby turned, wiping a silly tear away. What was wrong with her? She hadn't really expected words of undying love, had she?

No. But the reality of how far she'd let herself fall from her own standards rushed over her. She'd wanted to save her first kiss until she met *the* boy . . . and that wasn't supposed to happen until after she had been a missionary for a good long time.

Not only that, but what was she doing kissing, of all boys, Gideon — who probably had a world of experience kissing girls?

"Nothing. You didn't do anything wrong."

She felt his hand on her arm, but she

couldn't face him. He hadn't done anything, not really. But she should have known better than to . . .

She was turning into one of those girls at school who hung around the boys' locker room.

Some missionary she'd make. She would bet they didn't teach this method of evangelism at Bible college.

Libby pulled away from him and shucked the tears off her cheeks. "It's nothing. I'm just wet, and it's late. . . ."

He stood there, quiet, beside her — so quiet that she thought he hadn't heard her. She glanced up at him.

He looked as if he'd just run over her pet dog or maybe seen someone die. Horrified. "I didn't mean to hurt you," he said, his voice shaky. "I . . . you were . . ."

A wave of sympathy poured through her. She held up a hand. "No, it's my fault. I gave you the wrong impression. I shouldn't have . . ." She swallowed and looked at the floor. "I gotta go."

"Libby —"

"Please, Gideon. I'll see you tomorrow, I guess. Can you lock the back door when you leave?"

He nodded. But she felt his eyes on her as she got her coat, put it over her wet clothes, and closed the door behind her.

As she stood there in the cold, her heart still thundering in her chest, calling herself an idiot, swirling all the crazy feelings inside into a hard ball of shame, she noticed a truck parked in the street, a figure sitting inside.

It sped away just as she stepped into the alley.

All Lincoln had wanted to do was protect her. To keep Stefanie from making a mistake that could hurt her in more ways than she could ever imagine. And the fact that he'd tried to send Gideon off with a pocketful of cash should have been a good thing, should have counted for something.

But as Lincoln had watched his great plans disintegrate in the heat of Stefanie Noble's anger, he'd actually been conjuring up old movie lines, trying to figure out which one might turn the moment from agonizing to charming.

"Frankly, my dear . . ." No, that wouldn't work.

"As you wish . . ." Too over-the-top.

And then she'd zinged him with, *"How do you know who the real Stefanie Noble is?"* Her question hit way too close to his own issues and irked him, even a week later. No, he didn't know her. Not really. He could correctly tag her as intelligent and strong and maybe a bit naive, the twin sister of his tough-as-grit friend Rafe, but beyond that . . . no. Lincoln didn't know her.

But he wanted to. Before, she'd been a curiosity. Now Stefanie Noble had become a challenge. He hadn't had someone so vehemently dislike him in years.

She'd actually called him a despot looking for a kingdom at the recent Phillips town meeting, where he'd floated his idea along with his grant program and his desire to help put Phillips on the map.

He'd never been a pariah before. Thankfully, Stefanie's protests had fallen on deaf ears, but the icy look she'd given him two days ago as she entered the diner still made him want to grab a wool jacket and a scarf.

And to make matters worse, he hadn't the faintest idea how to get back on her good side. Or at least convince her that he wasn't evil incarnate. Sitting outside Lolly's Diner watching Gideon leave, somehow he knew that kid held the key.

Lincoln had watched as the lights went off in the diner earlier — in fact, he'd been hanging around all week, somehow drawn here, a gut feeling inside compelling him to remind Gideon, if only by his presence, to toe the line.

Also, Lincoln simply couldn't shake the mental snapshot of the little girl at the fire, looking at Gideon as if he might be her only hold on life. She reminded him so much of Alyssa that it had taken his breath away.

Hence the parking space outside Lolly's.

He watched as Gideon locked the door and pulled his sweatshirt hood up over his head. He ran out to the ancient Impala and got in. Lincoln saw the taillights flicker on, heard the engine fight for life. As Gideon pulled away, Lincoln put his own truck into gear. He normally didn't follow the kid home, but something inside him told him to trail Gideon, at least until he reached the Big K.

Lincoln didn't know what else to call his new ranch. He'd thrown out character names of heroes he'd played — Redford had used up that option — and anything with the name Cash felt arrogant, especially after his go-round with Stefanie. At the time he'd picked it, the name had made him feel strong. Important. Now it seemed to mock him.

He kept far enough behind Gideon that the Impala's taillights vanished behind dips and curves in the road. Overhead, a cloudy sky obscured the stars, making the night

143

inky and dangerous.

Lincoln tested his hand. The feeling had returned slowly, and his gait held no limp — signs that this exacerbation might be healing. But he lived each day in a sort of what-if mode, not wanting to push too far, get his hopes up. Where would he be if he didn't have the disease pushing against his dreams, hovering over his future?

He refused to let those thoughts dig into him.

He'd inadvertently caught up to Gideon. Or . . . no. The Impala wasn't moving. On the side of the road, it looked as if it had simply died and coasted into the ditch.

Gideon stood over the car, the hood open, staring at the engine as if he might have night vision and be able to decipher the tangle of greasy hoses and wires.

Lincoln slowed, drove by, and stopped in front of the Impala. He dug a flashlight from the glove box and opened his door. "Hey there," he said, keeping his voice friendly.

He didn't exactly expect Gideon to break into cheers, but the look of mistrust that filled his eyes as he put his hand up to shield himself from the light speared Lincoln through the heart. Maybe Stefanie had been right in her abysmal opinion of him. He lowered the light but not before he noticed

Gideon's wet hair and the fact that he shivered. What, did he shower at the diner?

"What happened?"

Gideon regarded Lincoln as he came over to stand by the car. "What do you want?"

Lincoln wasn't sure why he'd stopped, but he suddenly wanted to make amends for the way he'd treated the kid. According to his own observation of the teenager, he was a hard worker, kept his head down, and tried to be polite to the people around him. Lincoln had heard him treat Missy and Libby with respect and noted that the couple of nights Gideon had locked up with Libby, he'd waited on the street until she got into her car and drove away.

As if he might be watching over her.

It had nudged Lincoln's stereotype of thug off its footing. Which was why he turned to Gideon now and injected kindness into his voice. "Nothing. I saw your car, and . . . well, I thought I could help." Lincoln flashed his light over the engine. He didn't know a distributor cap from a spark plug, but he gave a good show of it.

Gideon's expression lost its hard edge, just for a moment. "I think it's the carburetor, but I don't know. It's too dark. I have to look at it in the light."

Lincoln nodded, as though it might be

145

exactly that. Then he took a deep breath and said, "Kid, listen. I came down too hard on you last week. I'm sorry."

Gideon didn't meet Lincoln's eyes, but Lincoln saw his defenses kick down a notch. "Uh, yeah . . . well . . . I'm sorry about your house, Mr. Cash."

"Can I give you a lift home?"

Gideon gave one last forlorn look at the car before he reached up and closed the hood. "Better than walking, I guess."

The Ford still bore the new truck smell, and Gideon noticed. "Nice ride."

"Thanks. I just got it."

Gideon ran his hand over the leather bench seat.

"I always wanted a pickup," Lincoln added for some reason. Instead he'd driven sports cars all his life. Because that's what Lincoln Cash did. He sat back, turning the heat up. "How's work at the diner?"

Gideon gave him a quick look. "You're there every day. You should know."

"I like the pie."

"I get the feeling you're there to make sure I don't snatch anything from the till."

Lincoln cut him a look. "Should I be worried?"

"No. Missy's been real nice to me. I wouldn't steal from her."

"And what about Libby? Seems to me you two are becoming friends."

Gideon turned toward the window.

Lincoln had a strange feeling in his gut. He'd been eighteen once and knew how a pretty girl with a nice smile could get inside a guy's head. "Gideon?"

"Yeah, she's nice too. Real nice."

Lincoln trilled his fingers on the steering wheel, wading through the layers of concern. They passed the Big K in silence. The bright lights of the construction project on the hill lit up the log home as if it might be the president's digs. He'd hired a small army to construct his house, yet he could hardly believe how quickly they'd cleared a foundation and erected the walls, the roof. They'd also had to dig a septic system, run power and phone from the road, drill a new well, and install a propane tank. He'd learned so much about construction this past week, he could probably play the part of a disgruntled contractor who went after the town council and held them hostage for permits. Thankfully, his little pep talk at the school had impressed the powers that be, and according to his timetable and his contractor, he'd be in the house within the month.

"Nice house," Gideon said quietly.

Lincoln looked at him. "Yeah, well, I didn't start out like this. It took years of hard work." He didn't know why he said that or why he suddenly had the urge to tell Gideon more, that he'd been more like Gideon than he cared to admit — desperate and on the run.

"Someday I'm going to have a house," Gideon said almost under his breath. "Me and Macey and Haley."

Lincoln had made the same promise to himself and even to Alyssa long ago.

He'd kept only half that promise.

"My dad used to . . . well, that was a long time ago, but he built houses." Gideon's voice turned lean. "Got laid off in the winter, though. Not much building in snow."

"You want to be a builder like your dad?" Lincoln asked.

Gideon's posture remained set on slouch. Out of Lincoln's peripheral vision, he saw Gideon's jaw tighten. "I don't want to be anything like him. He was a drunk and a liar. He beat my mom and me, and the happiest day of my life was when they put him away."

Lincoln blew out a breath, aware of how closely Gideon's words echoed his own once upon a time. In fact, looking at him, Lincoln suddenly had a picture of himself, thin and desperate but driven. He didn't have a sister, but he knew what it felt like to bear the burden of taking care of someone else.

He should help the kid. More than just by giving him a lift home. The thought jolted Lincoln but sunk in and made sense. Not only did Gideon deserve a chance, but maybe Stefanie would start to forgive him. He took a breath, dug deep, and kept his voice casual. "How would you like a job on my crew?"

Gideon glanced at him, that mistrust back in his eyes.

"I know you can't be making much at the diner. And you work all the time. I've got a summer of big projects ahead of me, and I could use someone as hardworking as you. I'll pay you the same money the standard carpenters are earning. What are you making at Lolly's?"

Gideon mumbled something about minimum wage.

"I'll triple that."

He could hear Gideon breathe in, the sound of disbelief and hope. "Why? Why would you do that for me? A week ago you were throwing money at me to make me leave town. What are you trying to pull?"

"I know, and I'm sorry. But this is legit; I

promise. It wasn't right, what I did, and I'm trying to make up for it."

Gideon had stopped shivering, and now he looked down at his hands, still wrinkled, probably from the dishwater. "Yeah, okay. I guess that's a good idea."

Attaboy, Gideon.

When they reached the Silver Buckle drive, Lincoln pulled in real slow. "You like staying here?"

Every time he saw the Nobles' ranch, it reminded him of a movie set out of an old Western. The two-story homesteaded log home with the front porch and the assortment of outbuildings had found a way into Lincoln's daydreams. He wondered what it might be like to carve out a life on the land with his bare hands, powered by sweat and character and determination. . . . The notion lodged deep inside and started to germinate.

"Yeah. Nick and Piper are great. Haley really likes Piper. She's going to be a mom, so I s'pose she's figuring out how to do the mom thing with Haley, but she reads to her, and Haley's got a real kitten now that she drags around. Macey likes working with Stefanie. They're training some of the new quarter horses they just got. Macey's been learning how to groom them, and yesterday she was in the corral with one, doing something with a rope."

"You going to learn to ride?"

Gideon gave a sharp laugh. "Nope. I don't ride horses."

Lincoln wasn't sure what to make of that. "Do you ride?"

"Had to learn how for . . . work."

"You ride horses in your movies?"

Lincoln glanced over at him. Could it be that this kid hadn't seen one of his movies? "Yep. And drive cars and boats and once I even jumped from an airplane."

"That's bad."

Lincoln nodded. "You get to do a lot of cool things when you're an actor."

"I thought it was just for show. You know, the stuntmen doing all the fighting."

"Not in my movies," Lincoln said. And not just because the films were always on tight budgets. Because something inside Lincoln — especially in the early days — compelled him to prove himself, if not to his audience, to himself. Over and over.

Until, apparently, it really *would* kill him.

As if he were reading Lincoln's mind, Gideon asked, "Did you ever get hurt?"

Lincoln flexed his hand and put it in his lap. "Nearly got killed."

"That's twisted."

Yeah, he'd have to be half-crazy to do the things he watched himself do. "You have no idea."

"You got horses on your new ranch?"

"I will. Maybe."

"You should ask Stefanie to train them. She's really good."

Lincoln stared at Gideon and felt a smile start deep and spread through him. They stopped in the Silver Buckle yard. "I'll be out early in the morning, so I'll swing by and pick you up for work. We'll figure out a ride after that, okay?"

Something much like relief, or maybe gratitude, crossed Gideon's face. It tore at Lincoln. For a second he saw himself the first time Dex had asked him to read for a part. What Gideon didn't know was that Lincoln knew exactly how it felt to have raw, wet, chapped hands from washing dishes for ten hours. How it felt to have to decide between feeding yourself or finding a place to sleep. How it felt to want something so badly it gnawed at your insides.

Sometimes it still gnawed at him.

"Thanks, Mr. Cash."

"Call me Lincoln. And you're welcome, Gideon. See you tomorrow."

CHAPTER 7

"I'm here because I'm going to do something good for this town. Because Phillips is a great place, and I'd like to be a part of it."

Lincoln Cash was haunting her. In the tabloids, in her small town, and now, at her own home.

And he looked good doing it too. Stefanie stood in the kitchen, watching as the man she kept trying to forget got out of a fancy black pickup and sauntered toward her house. He wore a pair of faded jeans, black cowboy boots, a deep blue cotton shirt that probably matched his eyes, and a brown bomber jacket.

He had the aura of a man who knew the world loved him. She was surprised he didn't have a trail of press behind him.

Well, he usually did.

And that was the last thing she needed in her life, especially with three runaways stashed at her house. And she wasn't going to let them go without a fight. Even if she had to take on Lincoln Cash.

Why did he insist on returning to the scene of his crimes? Couldn't he see that he had no fans at the Silver Buckle? Except for Clancy, that is, who got up from the porch and greeted Lincoln, shoving his nose into Lincoln's hand. Lincoln crouched down and rubbed the dog behind both ears.

Traitor. Stefanie shook her head.

Haley sat on the floor with a former barn kitten, now bathed and de-fleaed, curled on her lap. Haley herself had been bathed by Macey, her hair shampooed, her face scrubbed, and her clothes washed — although Stefanie had wanted to burn them. Piper had gone into Sheridan early in the week and returned with three bags of clothes from Wal-Mart. She'd spent the afternoon showing Haley her new attire.

Piper had managed to coax a smile from the little girl, but they all ached to hear her voice, the one that matched her beautiful eyes, the tawny blonde hair, the gap-toothed smile. Haley had a gentleness about her, evident in the way she cared for her new kitten. And the way she'd begun to warm to Gideon, sometimes even waiting for him outside his room until he dragged in from work, had affected her older brother.

Seeing him take his little sister in his arms, hug her with his eyes closed, even tuck her into bed at night made Stefanie's throat ache every time.

She worried about Gideon too. He seemed ragged to the bone, and last night he'd trudged in cold and wet. She didn't ask but simply knocked on his door with a pile of Rafe's clothes and gave him a don't-mess-with-me look.

When Gideon had come down the stairs this morning for breakfast, she was glad to see that he wore a pair of jeans and a thermal shirt under a red flannel work shirt. Rafe had worn that outfit about six years ago, and in a way, Gideon looked so much like her reckless twin brother that it scared her a little.

Please, Lord, don't let Gideon make the same mistakes Rafe did.

She'd stopped feeling guilty about not calling Social Services . . . mostly because, with Piper and Nick now living in the house, it seemed a million times better than anything Social Services might offer, especially short-term. It had also made the inevitable decision about Stefanie moving to the hunting cabin easier — they'd all simply focused on practicality.

It didn't make the nights any less lonely.

But it did give her a good reason to get up early and head down to the house.

Evidently, in time to greet Lincoln as he climbed onto the porch and knocked on the door.

At Lincoln's knock, Macey looked up from her cereal and met Stefanie's eyes. Macey had surprised her the last few days. Despite her dark exterior, the multiple piercings, the sullen set of her jaw that suggested attitude, she'd worked without complaining, mucking out the barn and grooming the horses. The quarter horses that Stefanie had purchased from the herd still held at the fairgrounds were young, most of them just over three, and unbacked. They were all thin and wary, candidates for compassion. Just like Macey.

Stefanie had known Macey would be the right fit when she'd handed the teen a brush and led her to a sorrel that stood nearly fourteen hands. As Macey had quietly groomed him, he'd stood perfectly still, sensing perhaps that she was new and probably afraid of his size. She'd shucked off his winter coat, causing the sorrel's hide underneath to glisten, shining under the sun.

It had reminded Stefanie so much of Sunny, of watching him bloom under her care, that she hadn't been able to speak.

156

She just sat on the rail and watched as Macey combed out the sorrel's mane, then his tail.

It was as Macey rolled up her sleeves to wash him that Stefanie saw the cuts on her arms. Deep red, some of them. Others faded. But so evident of abuse — whether self-inflicted or otherwise — that Stefanie had to climb down off the rail and hide in the barn until she scraped up control.

Stefanie didn't care what it took; she wasn't going to let anyone hurt these kids.

Which was why she pursed her lips and gave Macey a solemn don't-worry look as she opened the door to Lincoln.

He swept his hat off his head and gave her a smile that probably netted him a million dollars in one sitting. "Hey, Stefanie."

She clamped one hand on her hip. "What do you want?"

"I'm here to give Gideon a ride to work." He peered inside, nodding at Gideon.

Stefanie followed his gaze. "What are you talking about?"

"Gideon's coming to work for me. On my house." He winked at Gideon. "No more washing dishes, huh?"

When Gideon acknowledged Lincoln with a shy grin, someone could have knocked her over with a housefly. Since when were they best pals?

As if to rub salt into her wounds, Cash flashed another smug million-dollar grin at her.

She didn't trust him as far as she could throw him. And, even as strong as she was, she didn't expect it to be farther than the porch. Still, he had the unnerving ability to knock all her expectations off-kilter. Clenching her jaw, she opened the screen door. "Well, you might as well come in, then, and let him finish his breakfast." She turned to Gideon. "You need a lunch?"

Gideon shook his head, and she wondered if he ever ate lunch.

Lincoln must have read her mind. "We have lunch catered at the ranch. He'll be fine."

Okay, whoever he was, this guy had stolen Lincoln's body and wore it just as well. She studied him, trying to shake down the invader. "I don't know what you're up to, but . . ."

His expression said that he hadn't a clue what she might be referring to. Actor, indeed.

She shook her head, turning away. Then she heard him sigh.

"I'll be outside on the porch. Take your time, Gideon."

Take his time? She assumed that a big star like Lincoln would live by his watch, his schedules, his phone calls.

As if her legs thought for themselves, she followed him out on the porch. "I don't get it. A week ago, you're trying to bribe them to leave. Now you're Gideon's best friend?"

"Maybe I'm just trying to be a nice guy." He raised his eyebrows as if to say, *See, you judged me wrong.* "I'm really pretty decent if you get to know me."

"Well, that's the point, isn't it? I don't know you at all."

"What are you talking about? We met last summer. Had a perfectly decent conversation."

"Yeah, let's see. You told me about your house and your collection of cars and how you and Rafe fought over the same makeup artist during one of your film shoots. You signed four autographs, posed for three pictures, and extolled the virtues of caviar, which I have never eaten nor wanted to."

He had the decency to turn red.

"None of that information was anything more than what I could have seen on a Biography Channel episode. So, no . . . I don't know you, Lincoln. And frankly, I'm not sure I want to."

His smile vanished. "I don't know what I

159

did to put a burr under your saddle —"

"Excuse me —"

"I agree that I didn't have my happy face on when I rolled up to find my ranch burning, but I'm trying to make that right. However, you don't seem to want to give me a chance. Which makes me wonder about the impression I made and what happened to the girl I met last summer."

Lincoln held up his hand as she made to speak. "I know we didn't talk long, but at the time, you seemed to enjoy our conversation, and although your impression of our chat seems less than stellar, let me tell you *my* experience." His voice softened. "I spent time with a beautiful girl who has an interesting life. I listened to her tell me about her love for horses and her ranch, with so much magic in her voice that it made me fall in love with the place too. She made me laugh at her expression when I described fish eggs, and she was patient enough to let me sign a few autographs when I should have given her my undivided attention. That's the conversation I remember. But now, you look like you'd rather spend time with a cactus than with me."

Stefanie folded her arms across her chest, but his words had unseated her. Perhaps she was being too hard on him.

160

"What did I do, Stefanie?"

She looked away. The sun had come up, burning off the last of the clouds, and spring filled the air with the scent of grass coming back to life, the sound of a meadowlark in the field. "I'm just not your type, Lincoln."

The look on his face spoke confusion and a hint of hurt. *Oh, please.* Like that truth wasn't screaming from her ancient frayed jean jacket right down to her old boots covered with manure. On the contrary, his boots looked fresh out of the box — or better, off some handcrafter's shelf. She put on her armor, refusing to be swayed by his pout. He was just looking for a distraction while he did whatever he was doing here in Phillips.

"Or maybe you're not *my* type. I can't keep up with you. I don't have the hair or the wardrobe —"

"There's nothing wrong with your wardrobe —"

"For a girl who works with cattle all day, yes, but not for . . . well, whatever works in your world."

"I don't have that world anymore."

Stefanie rolled her eyes. "I know you're probably trying to be nice, but let me save you the trouble. This is about as dressed up as I get. I don't have designer dresses in my

161

wardrobe, and I've never had a manicure. I am not a girl who would fit into your world."

He opened his mouth, but she stopped him. "Don't. We're just too different." She lifted her shoulder and injected as much nonchalance into her tone as she could muster. Never mind that her stomach couldn't get any tighter, her throat more dry.

She gestured to the corrals, the barns, the fields. "This is my life and all it's ever going to be." She swallowed, then forced a smile. "But I am glad to see your change of heart about the kids."

"Just give me a chance to show you that maybe you're wrong about us. We're not so different, really."

For a split second, Stefanie almost believed him, almost said yes. Almost bought into the fantasy that rose in her mind, the one where she was inside those incredible arms, the recipient of his 100 percent breathtaking attention.

She'd spent enough time analyzing her reaction to their conversation last summer to know it wasn't the clothes or the fancy cars or even the celebrity status that made him a star. He might have been showing off, trying to make her like him, but he couldn't help it. Fans loved him because he had a lethal charisma that poured off the screen and into their hearts. A girl couldn't be in a room with him for ten seconds without turning his direction, being hypnotized by his charm.

Except her, thankfully. She knew the devastating effects of that kind of charm, knew better than to fall for a golden boy with a Texas swagger and a heartbreaking smile. Especially if she wanted to keep her pride intact. Still, if Lincoln Cash planned on sticking around Phillips, it would behoove her to stay far away from his smile. Because this time she had nowhere to run.

"No, Lincoln, there are no more chances. I would appreciate, however, if you wouldn't do anything to jeopardize these kids. They're doing okay here. And I want it to stay that way."

He sighed, looked away from her. If she didn't know him better, she would think that was real regret she saw on his face. But he was an actor, a very good actor.

And he certainly wouldn't feel any real regret about not wooing her. Didn't he see that she was making it easier for him? Now maybe they could pass each other on the street without inducing a cold snap and killing the flowers.

Gideon came out on the porch.

"C'mon, kid. Let's get to work." Lincoln started to follow Gideon down the steps. Then, to her surprise, he turned, and a smile came over his face, as if he hadn't heard a word that she'd said. "See you round, neighbor."

It hit Stefanie that that was exactly what she was afraid of.

Gideon couldn't get Libby off his mind. It had been a week since he'd quit his job at Lolly's. That was a difficult conversation he'd never expected to have. To quit one job because he'd found a better one? To have a decent wage and work hard enough to feel exhausted, yet happy at the end of every day? He could hardly believe his good fortune.

Of course, he'd had to admit to himself that more money and outdoor work had nothing to do with why he'd left the diner. No, shame and confusion led that list, a list that ended with not wanting to get into more trouble than he already had.

Lincoln had turned out to be a decent guy under all those expensive clothes. He treated everyone like they might be his best friend, remembering not only their names but their kids' names and even their favorite sandwiches, which he ordered every day from

Missy and passed out on the job site.

Libby had delivered them yesterday. Gideon hadn't seen her arrive, and when he walked into Lincoln's nearly finished living room and spotted her unloading the bags onto a sheet of plywood over the sawhorses they'd been using for a table, he nearly tripped over the cord of a Skilsaw.

She just might be prettier than he remembered; it had only been six days, so his memory wasn't that fuzzy. More than that, he relived the moment in the diner over and over, trying to figure out exactly where he'd gone wrong.

Sometimes he could even taste her soft mouth on his, kissing him back, and feel her arms around him. He'd never quite felt the way he had when he'd kissed Libby. He'd kissed girls before — well, at least before jail — but this kiss had made him believe he could fly.

Weren't guys supposed to be cool about this sort of thing? All the guys he'd been with in juvie hall had already dated a lot of girls, had acted like it was no big deal not only to kiss a girl but to do more. He was ashamed now to think about the way he'd talked and acted, pretending that he knew exactly what they meant.

Deep inside, in the place beyond desire,

he couldn't help but think it was supposed to be this way, that kissing the right girl should feel like flying or maybe singing — something perfect and warm and right.

Which was what Gideon had been trying to tell Libby before he'd completely messed everything up. He kept going back to that moment when he had Libby's face in his hands, staring into her eyes, and couldn't think of anything more clever to say than "*I really like you.*" He'd thought about it for hours as he laid flooring, painted walls, and helped build a deck and finally decided that what he should have said was *Libby, I can't think straight around you. All I care about is seeing your smile and knowing that I helped put it there. If that's love, then I guess . . . I'm falling in love with you.* Yeah, that's what he would have said.

Those words ran through his mind in a blinding second as he saw Libby again, standing there in the living room with the sun pouring through the window. She had on a pink T-shirt, the same one she'd worn that night at the diner, and her hair was up in a cute ponytail. She set the sandwiches out and didn't look at him . . . not once.

It made him hurt all the way through. He reached for a sandwich but couldn't walk away. Not when he saw something on her face that looked like pain.

"Libby?" He came around to stand beside her. She said nothing but glanced at him.

Actually, she glanced at the steel-toe work boots Lincoln had given him. He even wore a tool belt, just like the rest of the guys. In fact, he'd made a few friends with the locals, especially a cowboy named Luther and another named JB, who worked on a nearby ranch and had shown up for the great pay and short-term work before roundup.

Gideon wished he hadn't spotted Luther lifting some of the tools off the site. The guy had even bragged about it a couple times. Gideon still wasn't sure what to do about it, but it made him sick to his stomach, especially after the second chance Lincoln had given him.

"Libby, how are you?" Gideon asked quietly.

She breathed in deep; then, though he could tell it took effort, she forced herself to look at him and work up a smile.

He wanted to kiss her again. But something in her eyes, a sort of nervousness, made his breath hitch. "Do I owe you an apology?" he asked softly. "I'm . . . sorry. I . . . don't know . . ."

Whatever the look had been, it drained as compassion filled her pretty eyes. He recog-

167

nized it so easily that the knotting in his stomach eased even as the ache inside him grew.

"It's okay, Gideon. It's good to see you." She handed him a Coke. "Do you like your new job?"

Their friendship came flooding back to him. He remembered the way she'd stood beside him only two weeks ago as he watched his life turn to ash, so scared he wanted to — did — cry. And not once had she uttered a word of ridicule or blame.

"Wanna share my sandwich?" he blurted. *Oh, how lame.*

"I gotta get back," she said, that hurt look again on her face.

Gideon couldn't bear to think that he'd put it there. "Five minutes. Let me show you around. It's a great house."

That hooked her. He carried his unopened sandwich around the house as he showed her Lincoln's massive digs. He had a huge kitchen with a limestone floor quarried from some Montana mine. The alder cupboards and center island with a granite top filled a kitchen that could probably seat a small army. From the kitchen, the house sprawled out to a huge family room — the carpet would be laid later this week — and a two-story stone fireplace. Palladian windows looked out both sides, with a view of the Bighorn Mountains to the west and the sprawling Big K land on the east. A deck, with a yet-to-be-installed hot tub, jutted out the back.

"Gorgeous. I've never seen a house so big," Libby said.

"Yeah, it even has a maid's quarters on the other end of the house. And you should see the plans for the movie theater. He's going to make over the barn into this huge theater. It'll house, like, a couple hundred people."

"We've never even had a movie theater in Phillips."

"Let me show you the upstairs." Gideon led her up a curving staircase with hand-hewn pine spindles and a knotty pine rail. He showed her the master bedroom, which he'd help paint sky blue, and the master bathroom with the two sinks, the two-person soaking tub, and the giant, two-headed shower. He wasn't sure whom Lincoln might be sharing this with, but whoever the lady was, Gideon knew she'd like it from the way Libby's eyes widened.

He suddenly wished, with everything inside him, that he could give her a house like this.

He showed her the four other bedrooms,

and for a moment she stood in the northernmost room and stared toward Phillips. "My entire house would probably fit in the kitchen." She shoved her hands in her pockets. "The place is huge."

Gideon opened his sandwich and offered some to her, but she shook her head. He took a bite. "I know. We could fit my mom's trailer in his bedroom. And back at juvie, they'd put about fifteen guys in a room this size."

The bread seemed to thicken into paste in his mouth as he realized what he'd said. He couldn't look at her.

"You were in jail?"

He swallowed the lump in his mouth. "Yeah." He wished she wouldn't look at him like that, all shocked and even a little sad. "I . . . uh . . ." He was sick of lying. Of hiding. Of the guilt that chewed at him. Besides, Libby wore that compassion again in her eyes, and it made his brain turn right off, made him react completely on desperation. "Actually, Libby, I killed somebody."

Had he really said that? He groaned as the air seemed to be sucked out of the room. He expected her to gasp or maybe look at him with accusation, but when he glanced at her, she'd leaned against the wall, frowning.

"What happened?"

Gideon blew out a breath, but it was too late to stop now. "Well, in case you're thinking it, it wasn't murder or anything. I didn't shoot someone or anything like that."

Nothing in her eyes changed, as if she wasn't surprised by his lack of violence. "I was out with some of my boys — joyriding in a car I boosted. The guy driving had been drinking, but we all were sorta . . . well, drunk. I don't know how it happened, but the car went out of control. It jumped the median and hit an oncoming car."

As he spoke, he was right back there — squealing tires, metal slamming against metal as the car rolled over and over. He heard the screams as he pulled himself out through the jagged windshield, covered in blood. He felt again the heat as the car and then the van that lay on its side exploded in flames. He even tasted his bile as he remembered retching onto the grass.

"Both my friends and the passengers in the van died — a man and his kid. The driver lived, but she was pretty banged up. I don't know what happened to her. There wasn't even a trial. I just pled guilty. Even though I wasn't driving, I'd stolen the car. . . . It was my fault. I've never figured out how to say I'm sorry to the victims."

Libby said nothing.

"While I was in lockup, my mom got sick. They said it was the flu, but I don't know." He shrugged, hating how his voice sounded like he was talking through a tunnel, dark and hollow. "She passed away, and Macey and Haley went into foster care."

"What about your dad?"

Gideon crumpled the sandwich wrapper into a tight ball. "My dad is in lockup down in Kansas. I'm hoping I get lucky and never see him again." He didn't care that Libby flinched at his words. She probably didn't have a dad who took out his frustration on his kid. "Macey wrote to me, told me what was happening with her and Haley. Right before I got out, she said that Social Services was putting Haley up for adoption. I got them both out as soon as I could."

"Which is how you ended up here in Phillips."

He nodded and finished his sandwich, although it felt like clay in his mouth. "I guess it was fate."

"I don't believe in fate, Gideon. I know God has a plan for everything. Even the bad things."

Did He have a plan for Gideon's heart to stop beating right here in the middle of Lincoln's magnificent house? Because that's

172

how he felt as Libby stepped toward him. He could hardly breathe when she simply put her arms around him, laying her head on his chest.

"I'm so sorry for all you went through," she said softly.

He closed his eyes, hating how they burned, and listened to his heart thunder in his chest, knowing that all the words he dreamed of saying to her were absolutely, without a doubt, true.

He was falling in love with her.

She had to find a way to get in that house. Or at least get close enough to him to watch and wait. And she could wait. Now that she'd found him, she'd bide her time, scout out the perfect angle, wheedle close to him.

Plan the finale.

She watched him survey the house, like he was some sort of king on his royal land. He didn't deserve this fresh start.

Especially after what he'd done to her.

For two weeks she'd hung around this town, watching, planning. Twice she'd almost gotten close enough to inflict damage. But she didn't want to wreck it, didn't want to risk not being able to finish the job.

She backed her car out of the driveway, thankful that so many cars and trailers and people milling around hid her surveillance.

It wouldn't be long now. No, not long at all.

CHAPTER 8

"Maybe you're not my type."

There had to be something crazy wrong with Lincoln because Stefanie's words burned a hole through him, infecting his brain, driving him insane in the dark hours of the night.

What was that supposed to mean? He'd made a career of adapting, of being someone's type.

Not her type?

Well, he could become her type. A cowboy, complete with a Western drawl, a slow smile, the ability to rope, and a herd of beautiful horses. He was an actor, and he could slip into the role of cowboy like a second skin.

Yeah, he could become Stefanie Noble's type. Prove to her that he was exactly the kind of man she needed in her life.

Especially since he had this disease licked. Lincoln was starting to even wonder at the diagnosis. His hand felt fine — *he* felt fine.

No more memory loss or vision flashes, no more limping. Maybe he'd just been tired — his grueling production schedule had sucked the energy from him, and at thirty, he wasn't the same man he'd been at eighteen, able to recover from, say, nearly drowning, like he once had. But now he felt whole and strong and back to his invincible self.

He'd known that the Big Sky air would snap him out of it.

Lincoln felt so good that he'd even come up with a brilliant plan. He finished buttoning the starched white dress shirt and tucked it into a pair of black suit pants, then buckled his snakeskin belt. He'd put on weight this month — something he'd fix starting tomorrow in the weight room downstairs. The house seemed oddly quiet this morning, thanks to the exodus of half his construction crew. The half that remained would start remodeling the new barn into a grand movie theater, holding two hundred, as well as landscaping the grounds.

He'd finally put his finger on the restlessness inside him. Despite the crowd of people working on his house for the past month, he was lonely. The kind of lonely that he couldn't salve with gourmet dinners and beautiful wannabe costars. He even missed Dex. The closest thing he had to a friend lately was Gideon, whom he drove back and forth to the Silver Buckle every day.

But hopefully, after today, he'd fix the gap in his social life.

The smell of eggs and bacon drifted from the kitchen, and he blessed Delia for finding Karen, a live-in cook/housekeeper. Not that he couldn't survive on Missy's food for the next decade, but after watching the way Gideon looked at Libby every time she delivered lunch, he'd decided he'd have to figure out a way to dump water on any flames of romance.

Didn't Gideon know that Libby was the pastor's daughter? A little fact he'd discovered when Pastor Pike had stopped by a couple days ago — probably sent on a divine mission by his evangelist daughter — and invited Lincoln to church. He wasn't so stupid he couldn't figure out that Pike had also hung around until he'd gotten a good look at Gideon.

Despite being a man who supposedly lived for forgiveness and grace, Pastor Pike didn't look the least bit grace-filled about his daughter's choice of friends.

It had churned up a strange feeling in Lincoln, one that made him mention to Pike that Gideon was one of the hardest workers he'd ever met. He hadn't been lying. Hiring Gideon had probably been one of the smartest moves Lincoln had ever made. First, the generous gesture had endeared Gideon to him for life. Plus, he'd inadvertently put a watchdog in with the crew. It was Gideon who'd reluctantly told him about Luther and his sticky hands on the power tools.

Hiring Gideon had also scored points with Stefanie. She'd actually lifted a finger in a wave two days ago as he passed her on the road into Phillips. And last night, when she'd come out onto the front porch as he dropped off Gideon, he saw the faintest glimmer of a smile in his direction. He fully planned on cultivating that relationship, thanks to Pastor Pike and the dropped tidbit of information that the Noble family attended Phillips Community Church.

And now, so did Lincoln Cash.

He grabbed his new black snakeskin boots and went down the stairs in his stocking feet.

Karen turned and piled eggs onto a plate. "Good morning, Mr. Cash."

He sat at one of the wrought iron high-top stools and pulled the plate toward him.

"Is this turkey bacon?"

"Yes, sir," she said.

According to Delia, Karen had recently moved to Phillips and came with glowing references. Delia knew how important a good cook was — Lincoln could barely make toast, and he was always on the lookout for someone who could whip up a decent pie. Maybe Karen would be his culinary savior. With a quiet demeanor and a hesitant smile, she seemed exactly the type to keep his secrets and make sure the house would stay immaculate.

Between Karen and Lolly's Diner deliveries, he might live.

He'd have to remember to send Delia some roses when she got back to her home in LA. It felt strange to be without her at the helm of his household. A widow in her late fifties, she'd taken on running Lincoln's house, his correspondence, even his finances, six years ago, when his name became known in faraway places like Russia and Japan.

Delia had even investigated and found the right doctors for Alyssa, and she was currently researching the background to Alyssa's experimental medicine. According to the nurses, her night terrors had worsened, and she'd begun to withdraw and stare listlessly out the window.

If he hadn't left Texas when he did, he would probably be doing the same thing right now.

He hoped Delia would agree to move to Phillips permanently, but in her absence, Karen seemed a good replacement.

"Are you getting settled in okay?" He took the eggs, pouring ketchup on the plate. "Anything you need?"

"No, sir."

"If you do, give Delia a call. She'll make sure you have everything you need."

"Yes, sir," Karen said, turning back to the stove.

"So, where are you from?" He skated his forkful of eggs through the ketchup.

"Oh, not far from here." She didn't look at him.

"Do you have a family?"

"No. I . . . don't have a family." She sounded as if her voice caught on the answer.

"It's pretty rare to find someone with your talents way out here in the middle of nowhere."

When Karen turned, he noticed she had a pretty, if tired, face, guarded eyes. He placed her at about thirty-five, although she might be younger. The wisp of white in her dark hair, right along the brow line, made her seem older, he guessed.

"I needed a job, and this is what I was looking for. I'm very pleased to work for you, Mr. Cash." She barely lifted her eyes to him.

He finished his bacon and eggs, then pushed the plate toward her. "Thanks," he said.

Karen took the plate and gave him a hint of a smile. She was singing to herself when he left a few minutes later.

The sky overhead sang of spring as he drove his pickup into Phillips. He could smell summer in the air, the freshness of the ground awakening. He had overheard that some of the ranches had already started roundup. He had an itch to see one and even asked JB if he could hang out at the Double B when the Breckenridge place held theirs.

He would be a cowboy, a real cowboy.

Phillips Community Church had to be straight out of an old movie. Goodness and righteousness were embodied in the white steeple and stained-glass windows.

Organ music spilled out of the red double door as Lincoln parked in the gravel parking lot, next to dirty pickups and a few dusty sedans. Opening the door, he slipped into the back of the church.

A few heads turned, but the singing muffled any murmuring or conversation about his arrival. He spotted an empty seat a few pews up on the left and scooted in, smiling as the woman next to him, dressed in her Sunday best from the early eighties, handed him an open hymnal, pointing to the right stanza.

He stared at the song and opened his mouth, but as if a hand had reached up and grabbed his throat, nothing emerged.

He'd suddenly been sucked back in time. Sweat beaded along his spine, and he felt as if he might be again standing in the front pew, knees shaking, staring at an open casket, listening to the hum of accusation behind him.

He needed to leave. But now, like then, his feet were rooted to the spot and it was all he could do to breathe, to stand there and dumbly move his mouth, to fake calm when everything within him felt as if it had been churned up and stuffed inside.

But he was an actor. So he gritted his teeth, smiled, and shook hands when the hymn ended and Pastor Pike invited them to greet one another. He even said the requisite "Jesus loves you," as instructed. He clutched the hymnal with white hands, however, as he sat down.

He'd make a point of never making this mistake again.

Pastor Pike opened the Bible and began to read, but Lincoln was aware of nothing but his heartbeat in his ears, the sweat sliding down his back. What did he think would happen? That God would reach out of heaven and zap him?

Uh, *yes.*

Lincoln slipped the hymnal into the holder at the front of the pew and ran his wet hands along his legs. The church had to be eighty years old, but with the bloodred carpet and finished pine paneling, it looked like it had been updated in the early sixties. Pastor Pike stood on a platform behind a simple podium, now getting warmed up for his sermon. Lincoln tuned him out. He didn't need the hell-and-damnation message — he already knew where he was going.

Apparently church attendance was a part of this town's social makeup, because as his gaze scanned the room, he noticed faces and profiles of most of the people he'd seen in Phillips. Missy and Libby were in the front row, and there was the guy who ran the hardware store down the row from him, and JB was two rows up on the right. He looked for the Nobles but didn't see them, and a pang of disappointment went through him.

Next time Lincoln put his life in jeopardy, he would make sure his sacrifice panned out. What had he been thinking, coming to church? He'd believed too much of his press again, thinking he was untouchable. His head began to throb.

" 'As Jesus was walking along,' " the pastor read.

Lincoln glanced at the open Bible on the lap next to him. John 9.

" '. . . he saw a man who had been blind from birth. "Rabbi," his disciples asked him, "why was this man born blind? Was it because of his own sins or his parents' sins?" ' "

Both, of course. Although Lincoln had never met his real father, he knew that the man had hightailed it toward the Texas line when he'd discovered Lincoln's mother was expecting. The next "dad" had stuck around all of two years. Then one day Lincoln came home to find all their belongings gone. Then again, the relief of never having to dodge the man's anger had made up for having to sleep on the bare floor.

Lincoln placed the blame of growing up on food stamps and sleeping on the sofa in a rickety trailer soundly on his deadbeat dads.

Pastor Pike's reading interrupted Lincoln's dark memories. " ' "It was not because of his sins or his parents' sins," Jesus answered. "This happened so the power of God could be seen in him." ' "

Lincoln wondered if Pastor Pike could feel his glare from where he was sitting.

"See, the Pharisees wanted to blame the man's ailments on something he did or the sins of his parents. Because if they could, they could insulate themselves from the pain of this world. If they simply didn't sin, then they wouldn't experience blindness or sickness or anything else they considered a punishment of sin."

Pike seemed to look right at Lincoln. "But it doesn't work that way. We can't behave our way out of accidents or sickness or dark circumstances. This man wasn't blind because he was a sinner. And the evidence of his blindness didn't convict him as a sinner. That was the condition of his heart, regardless of his ability to see. But God used the man's blindness to bring him to Jesus. To healing. And He'll do the same in our lives."

Okay, Lincoln was out of here. He checked his watch.

"If we let our situation define us instead

of lead us to God, then there is no victory."

What victory could there be in losing his body? his career? everything he'd worked for? Lincoln tested his hand just to make sure it felt fine.

"Consider Hebrews 12. God says that we are to endure divine discipline, remembering that God is treating us as His children."

Yeah, that sounded about right. Lincoln had grown up with exactly that image of God, based on his stepfather's fists.

"Not every suffering is discipline from God, but we can react as if it were — allowing Him to use it for good in our lives, producing a harvest of trusting God in all situations. We don't have to let circumstances define us, but we can let them produce definition in us. Circumstances can bring you to God so He can teach you how to grow in the character of Christ."

Lincoln didn't want definition or character from God. He wanted healing. But he knew better than to ask. Just like he knew better than to stick around and get beat over the head with a sermon. Besides, he didn't agree with Pastor Pike. Not at all. God wasn't disciplining Lincoln because He loved him. Lincoln was being punished. For both his parents' sins . . . and his own. He knew exactly why he'd been afflicted, why

186

his body was giving out on him.

He got up, and although he knew everyone in town would watch and that news of his cold and barren heart would be fodder for Phillips gossip for days, he ducked his head and stalked out.

Maybe Stefanie had been right. He wasn't her type at all.

Because her type wasn't a man who had gotten his mother murdered.

Stefanie watched Lincoln leave and sat there on the far edge of the back row, something hot and painful in her chest. Could it be that she actually felt sorry for him?

A man didn't walk out on a sermon without having a burr in his soul.

He'd looked forlorn or even pained by Pastor Pike's words. Words that she probably should have been paying attention to, but dragging her attention off Lincoln as he'd strolled into church and slid into the pew next to Clarisse Finney had proven to be more than a girl could manage. Especially a girl who couldn't get the supposedly nice Lincoln Cash off her mind.

Besides, deep down inside, she was starting to believe his claim of being a good man. Or at least she wanted to. Gideon returned home every night with a new report from the work site of how Lincoln bought lunch for the workers, told them stories over break time, and brought Gideon a soda. Clearly, the actor had Gideon awed.

Lincoln could start his very own fan club — or at least another chapter — right here in Phillips, complete with membership badges and den meetings.

Not that she'd sign up or anything.

The door closed softly behind Lincoln, while Stefanie listened to Pastor Pike finish his point from Hebrews 12. " 'Look after each other so that none of you fails to receive the grace of God. Watch out that no poisonous root of bitterness grows up to trouble you, corrupting many.' "

Stefanie bowed her head, nearly choking on the words and on the rampant thistle of bitterness that she'd let twine around her heart and choke out every attempt by Lincoln to be her friend.

She hadn't exactly been nice to him. Maybe she'd let him provoke her into behaving in ways she'd never thought possible. She'd been downright cruel to him. And for a terrible, evil moment, she'd felt justified. That probably made her feel the most shame.

No, he wasn't her type. But maybe, despite his apparent throng of fans, he could use a friend. A neighbor.

She remembered last summer when she'd believed they'd had the beginnings of a friendship. For some crazy reason, she'd thought she'd sneaked past the glitter to the real Lincoln Cash and found a guy who really liked her. Who was really interested in knowing her and her life.

His description of their conversation filled her mind: *"I spent time with a beautiful girl who has an interesting life."* Sure, and in the next breath he'd try to tell her that he wanted to move to Montana, settle down, start a family. Regardless of the truth, she had the distinct feeling that she had somehow cut off grace from his life, at least the grace she could give him.

The grace he was so apparently trying to earn.

As the congregation stood to sing the final hymn, she slipped out of the back pew and out the door.

Lincoln was climbing into his truck.

"Lincoln!"

He turned, and the expression on his face looked so wretched, so torn, it stopped her midway down the steps.

"Wait!"

He seemed to hesitate. Maybe she really *had* hurt him, gotten through that perfect exterior and wounded something inside.

No, that was just too hard to fathom.

Yet, as if he knew she'd seen his agony, or maybe just because he couldn't let someone see inside to the real Lincoln, he manufactured a smile and raised his hand. "Hey, Stefanie."

She walked across the gravel lot. "I thought I saw you here."

He came around the truck, fiddling with his keys. My, he cleaned up well for church, in his white shirt, black pants, and shiny boots. His shaggy hair and not-so-clean-shaven whiskers only added wildness to the rather tame attire. Always ready for a photo shoot.

She leaned against the truck. "You okay? You ran outta church pretty fast."

He put on his sunglasses. "I'm just fine. Thanks." He didn't offer more, his I-am-a-star demeanor solidly back in place now.

"You sure? Because, you know, if you want to talk —"

"Nope. I'm just . . . not in the mood for church." He flashed another smile, but she read ever so clearly the warning in his voice: *Back away from the church topic.*

Being a pure Montana girl, she hadn't been born with a tendency to spook. But she also knew when to let something go. "I hear your house is done, that you moved in."

"Finished about three days ago." He glanced past her toward the church. "How about you come over and let me show you around?"

Now that would be a colossally bad idea. Because even as he said it, his mouth slid into a slow, devastating smile, and he pulled his glasses down, letting her see the twinkle in his blue eyes.

Her gullible heart, which apparently didn't listen to the warnings in her brain, began to gallop in her chest. "Uh, I don't think —"

"C'mon, Stefanie. Let me be neighborly."

Neighborly? Was that what he was calling this waterfall of charm? "I don't think so."

"The entire family can come — Macey and —"

"I'm not sure that's a great idea. Haley is just starting to get used to being with us, and I don't want to put her into a new situation, and even Macey isn't thrilled about leaving the ranch yet."

"Then just you. I promise to be on my best behavior." If she were on a movie set, she would have thought he'd rehearsed the way he tilted his chin to look right into her eyes, the tenor of his voice husky and low.

191

"Please?"

Please? Oh, brother, was that all it took? A steamy look, a wicked smile? She disgusted herself.

Don't let him miss the grace. She pursed her lips.

"Besides, I need your help."

Yeah, sure, to do what? Pick out curtains?

The congregation had begun to spill out of church. A few people looked their way, and she greeted them with an overly wide smile. JB saw her, and along with his lifted hand, she noted a frown.

"How so?" she asked, looking back at Lincoln. For a second, she wished that one of the kids or Nick or Piper had come to church today. She could use the rescue. But no one was ready for the nosy questions, and although Gideon had asked about attending, when she'd knocked on his door this morning, all she'd gotten was a sleepy grunt.

"I recall you telling me how good you are with horses."

"I didn't say that. I said I *trained* horses." But the fact that he remembered their conversation sent another blow to her defenses.

"Well, that's good enough for me." He twirled his keys around his finger. They glinted in the sun. "I need to get horses for the ranch, and I was wondering if you'd help me pick some."

He wanted horses? As he said it, an idea — a *magnificent* idea — filled Stefanie's thoughts, slid right into those nooks and crannies of frustration she'd been nursing ever since she'd rescued her recent quarter horses.

Just yesterday, JB had called her again with the final number of remaining horses. She'd spent most of the night downstairs in front of the fire in their massive stone fireplace, curled up on the leather sofa, casting her prayers toward heaven. *"Don't worry about anything; instead, pray about everything. Tell God what you need, and thank him for all he has done. Then you will experience God's peace, which exceeds anything we can understand. His peace will guard your hearts and minds."*

Lord, could this be Your peace?

Admittedly, she didn't love Lincoln's idea about filling Phillips with celebrities. The minute movie stars and notables flooded the town, they'd also have obnoxious tourists who parked on the sidewalks, ridiculed their food, and generally made Phillips feel like a throwback to the forties. Everything decent and ordinary and safe would vanish.

193

However, if she could get Lincoln to embrace his new ranch life, maybe he could see past his big dreams for glory and do something to really help this community.

"I'm really a nice guy when you get to know me."

Yeah, prove it.

"Sure, I'll help you." Stefanie smiled up at Lincoln, past the glasses and the swagger, trying desperately to glimpse the potential inside. "I'll be by tomorrow. I think I know just what you're looking for."

CHAPTER 9

"These are horses?"

That hadn't come out quite like he'd meant it. Especially not how he'd hoped. Lincoln had been nearly holding his breath for the past twenty-four hours, counting the moments until he could get Stefanie alone and maybe prove to her that he wasn't the guy she so easily mistrusted.

But if she really wanted to make him suffer, really wanted to put his nice-guy claim to the test, then she'd picked exactly the right herd of horses.

These were not the horses he would have chosen for a Lincoln Cash herd. These horses were . . . ugly. Big and clumsy and bony. Could a person even ride them?

"Yes, they're horses," Stefanie said, and judging by her tone, he'd made her mad. "They're Clydesdales."

She looked especially fetching today in a pair of dark jeans, her long hair captured under a brown Stetson, wearing a faded brown leather jacket and a pair of work gloves. Practical yet pretty. The real deal.

Lincoln felt overdressed in designer jeans, the shiny snakeskin boots, and his brown calf-hair blazer that would be more appropriate while enjoying a chardonnay at Morrell on Rockefeller Plaza than in the middle of a muddy fairgrounds pen inspecting a motley herd of skeletal animals that looked like fodder for a glue factory.

He wasn't about to say that, though. Not with Stefanie looking at him with her best X-ray vision.

"Clydesdales?"

"You know, like the Budweiser horses?"

He surveyed the animals and did a quick mental comparison. "I don't think so. These animals don't look anything like those horses that pull the Budweiser wagon."

"They're draft horses, or quarter horse–draft crosses bred for their size. The smaller ones of the lot and a number of quarter horses have already been purchased. These mares were rescued a year ago from a PMU farm in Canada. They were bought by a couple who wanted to start a herd, but as you can see, they did a pitiful job."

Indeed. Although they might have been beautiful once, or maybe could be someday, these horses had suffered something terrible, attacks that could only be described as feral, with some of them nursing gashes and wounds that would disfigure their hides forever. They had empty eyes and milled about as if confused, afraid. Lincoln had ridden many horses, but he'd never seen any so skittish.

"What's a PMU farm?"

"Pregnant mare urine." Stefanie held a burlap bag and now opened it, stepping up to the corral and digging out what looked like a dried piece of manure. "It's used to create a hormone replacement therapy drug as well as over-the-counter antiaging drugs."

"You mean like face creams?"

"Among other things, yes." A large black horse was eyeing Stefanie's outstretched hand and the apparently yummy manure ball she held.

"Why would anyone want to put horse urine on their face?"

Stefanie's attention was on the black mare, which had started to walk her direction. "Vanity. Apparently it's more important to look good on the outside than to care for God's creatures."

Lincoln noticed the animal step near Stefanie. The horse was so big that despite its clear lack of nutrition, Lincoln had the sudden urge to pull Stefanie back.

But she didn't move, just kept her hand out. Clearly she wasn't made of meek stuff.

"What's that?"

"An alfalfa ball. It's a treat for the horses."

The horse stretched out her neck, ever so far, and licked up the ball. Lincoln expected Stefanie to move, maybe rub the mare's nose, but she stayed completely still.

The horse took another step toward her.

"So, what happened to these horses? They look so beat-up."

Stefanie lowered her voice, her tone soothing, her gaze on the creature. "The PMU horses are constantly being bred because it's only when they're pregnant that their urine is useful. They're kept in these tiny 'collection' stalls, where they can't move or lie down flat for long stretches of time — like six months. So they don't get any exercise and are very weak."

The horse took another tentative step and, this time, touched her nose to Stefanie's hand. Stefanie rubbed the horse's nose gently, then traveled up her face, petting. The horse took a final step until her head was over Stefanie's shoulder. Stefanie reached along her neck, ran her hand over her withers.

Lincoln held his breath and wondered if

he'd ever seen anything so beautiful. It churned up a feeling that he couldn't place, a softness inside him or maybe a longing. Stefanie had patience and authenticity that . . . well . . . scared him. He wasn't used to women not caring if they wore makeup or stepped in manure, wasn't used to women seeing beyond the obvious to something beautiful inside.

The more he got to know her, the more Stefanie Noble intrigued him.

The more he wanted her to like him.

"Recent discoveries of synthetic drugs have dropped the demand for these horses, and they were headed for the slaughter-house," she continued, oblivious to his eyes on her. "Obviously they weren't worth much, and their previous owners saw an opportunity to create a number of dude strings, horses for dude ranches."

"These horses? To ride? They're so big!"

"But they have wonderful temperaments." She laid her head against the black neck of the horse. "They are incredibly versatile, making great trail and pack horses."

She'd attracted attention, and another horse, this time a bay, edged toward her.

"Unfortunately, these horses were moved here to a ranch located near the Bighorn Mountains. Because they'd been kept in such confinement, they weren't prepared to react when cougars and even bears preyed on them. When our group found them, the pasture was littered with the carcasses of foals and mares, and most of the surviving horses had terrible wounds."

The second horse had wandered up, but Stefanie didn't reach out to her. Lincoln watched, a slow smile flooding through him as the bay acted jealous, like a child on a playground wanting a piece of candy also. She nudged Stefanie, who smiled and handed the horse an alfalfa treat from the bag she carried.

"Hey there, pretty," she said, rubbing the horse's nose. "Want to come and live on Mr. Cash's ranch? He'll take good care of you."

He would? Her words ignited something warm inside him. Yes, he would take care of them. Lincoln moved closer to Stefanie, his hand out, wanting to pet the horse. But the animal stepped back, shying away.

"Let her come to you, Lincoln." Stefanie handed him an alfalfa ball. "Just stand here, and let her trust you." She gave him a smile, one so full of confidence that he took the treat and held it out.

He'd probably get his hand bitten off.

Standing next to her, waiting for the horse

to respond as Stefanie spoke in low tones to the animal she embraced, Lincoln felt a wave of shame sweep through him. "I'm sorry I called them ugly," he said quietly.

"I know. You just had to know their story, and suddenly they became beautiful, didn't they?"

He looked at the herd, the bays and blacks and roans, their strength and size, and especially the way all of them seemed to have at least one ear perked in his direction. As if waiting for his response.

"Yes."

Stefanie smiled at him so sweetly that he felt as if he might be in high school for the way his heart exploded. "Look. You made a friend."

The bay had hesitantly decided to give him another chance. Not unlike, he hoped, Stefanie. When the horse nipped at his hand, Lincoln instinctively recoiled.

"She's not going to hurt you," Stefanie said, putting her hand under his, amusement in her eyes. "Lincoln Cash isn't afraid, is he?"

"Listen, Dances with Horses, not everyone can talk to the animals. Besides, she's got awfully big teeth."

"All the better to eat you with." She lifted his hand toward the animal. "Don't move,

Superhero."

He sort of liked the new nickname.

With her hand still under his, he waited. Sure enough, the horse moved closer, nudging him for his touch.

"Horses are really like giant dogs."

"I don't see these dogs wanting to fetch my slippers."

"When they don't feel threatened, they want to reach out. They want to connect."

Lincoln looked at her, something about her words tugging at him. She met his gaze. She had such gorgeous eyes, dark and mysterious. Yet today, full of forgiveness.

"Can I ask you a question, Lincoln?"

He rubbed the horse's nose. "Does it have to do with my purchasing the population of a dog pound?"

She laughed. "Why did you come to Montana? to Phillips?"

He ran his hand down the horse's neck, mimicking Stefanie. "To start a film festival." That answer felt strangely hollow, so he tried again, putting more charm, more drawl into his voice. "And, of course, for the neighborhood."

She rolled her eyes, and he laughed.

"You know what's most interesting about these horses? They grew a winter coat, and it covered up all these scars you see now.

We wouldn't even have seen many of them if we hadn't been grooming off their winter coats. But by the time we saw the scars, we had already recognized how precious and alive and worth saving these horses were. And it didn't matter how they'd been hurt. We already loved them." Stefanie stepped away from the horse and headed toward the truck.

The horse she'd left stayed at the rail, nickering after her. Needing her, it seemed.

Lincoln followed Stefanie, aware that he might have more in common with his new herd than he wanted to let on.

Libby had been on the verge of tears all day. She couldn't look at her sister, could hardly pour coffee, and mostly just wanted to hide in the bathroom and sob.

"Libby, I don't want you hanging around that boy anymore." Her father had been judgmental, condescending, chauvinistic, and downright unreasonable.

She'd stared at him as she set his toast down in front of him this morning, a hundred words rising to the surface. She wasn't a child anymore — she had turned nineteen four months ago. Where was the Christian love and acceptance he'd raised her to have? And what about Missy? She had a corral of boyfriends, from Luther McKinney to Andy Rider from the Silver Buckle, and her father hadn't uttered a murmur of complaint. Not only that, but ever since that kiss at the diner, and even when she'd hugged Gideon at Lincoln Cash's house, he hadn't made the slightest attempt to kiss her.

Even if she sometimes wanted him to.

She'd watched her father ladle sweetener into his decaf coffee and add nonfat milk to his oatmeal, then sank down into a chair, her hand flat against the checked orange and yellow, flannel-backed plastic table-cloth, and schooled her voice. "Daddy, Gideon is a nice guy. He wouldn't hurt me."

Her father glanced at her. "I'm sure you believe that, honey. But I've seen boys like him before, and I don't think he's the one for you." He picked up his spoon. "Besides, with you leaving for college in the fall, don't you think it's better if you keep things at a distance between you?"

She looked down, running her finger along the tablecloth. She couldn't tell him that she'd been thinking of not going to Bible college. Maybe staying here in Phillips . . . with . . . Gideon.

Libby got up, that realization hot in her chest. She poured herself a cup of coffee. "He's my friend. And he'll notice if I stop coming around."

"You don't have to be unfriendly to him. Just . . . don't go out to Mr. Cash's place. Gideon will get the message. I'm sure it's not the first time."

"That's not fair. He's gotten a lot of raw deals in his life."

"Like jail?" Her father lifted his gaze to hers.

"The apostle Paul went to jail," she said softly, not looking at him as she said it.

Her father had seen right through her comment and given her a small shake of his head.

She closed her eyes, feeling raw. She didn't want to admit that she lived for lunchtime, for that hour every day when she and Gideon walked around the Big K as he told her about his life back in Rapid City before his imprisonment and after. His confession to her had opened a door to trust, and although some of his stories made her want to cry — and more than once she had broken down on the way back to the diner — every day he seemed a little happier. A little less broken.

And she fell for him a little bit more.

She loved him for the gentleness he'd shown his sisters and the way he threw himself into every project Lincoln gave him.

She loved him for the way he looked at life, despite being beaten by it, and because he believed, truly believed, he could make something of himself. She loved how he talked to her quietly, watching for her reactions, as if he didn't want to hurt her. And she loved how he looked at her, all his emotions in his eyes, even if he didn't voice them.

He loved her too. She knew it, and the fact that he hadn't even tried to hold her hand made her love him more.

Finally she'd given in to that truth and embraced it. Maybe, if he saw her love for him, her compassion, her acceptance, he'd see Christ's love there too. At least that's what she told herself.

"Daddy —"

"Let Missy take the lunch today." He'd set his coffee down and given her a sad smile. "Trust me, will you?"

She put her hand over her mouth, because everything inside her wanted to cry out in pain, and nodded.

Lincoln Cash had a sweetness about him that could get a girl into big trouble. Stefanie added another log to her glowing fire in the hunting cabin fireplace. The night air bore a briskness in its touch, the way it snuck under the door.

She'd arrived home from her day with Lincoln to find the cabin chilly and eerily quiet. And hearing Lincoln's drawl, his laughter and teasing still in her ears.

Yes, the man could be very dangerous, especially when he smiled at her in that eye-twinkling, lopsided way, the wind drifting his scent — a rich cologne — her direction. Stefanie could hardly believe she'd spent the afternoon with him and hadn't wanted to strangle him once.

Well, maybe once. But he'd backpedaled quickly after his comment about the condition of the horses, and when he wrote a check to purchase the entire herd, he'd etched a foothold in her heart.

Especially after looking scared — and she'd seen scared in the eyes of people she'd trained to work with horses enough to recognize it. After all, despite their own fear, horses could hurt or even kill a person without realizing it. Yes, Lincoln had been nervous, at the very least.

She had to like a man who knew he wasn't made of steel.

Which made calling him Superhero that much more delightful.

Dances with Horses. She smiled at that memory, then opened a jar of peanut butter, took out a spoon, and dug out a heaping tablespoon of creamy dessert. She liked the name nearly as much as Defender of the Oppressed. It felt a thousand times better than Ranch Hand.

Standing at the door, she looked down at the house. Dinner had been quiet tonight. Gideon spoke little about what he did at Lincoln's, although Stefanie had seen him wearing a tool belt and carrying boards to the barn as she unloaded the horses from the trailer into Lincoln's corral. She'd agreed — admittedly without much coercion — to return to Lincoln's ranch tomorrow and teach him how to care for the horses. She should also help him track down a wrangler.

In fact, the day had stirred up all sorts of ideas. Like the fact that Lincoln Cash wasn't the only celebrity buying up property and moving to Montana to start a ranch. She'd read about others too. Other wannabe cowboys who needed people like her — real ranchers — to teach them how to ride and care for their animals, how to run a ranch.

Staring out at the lime green grass, the fields dotted by lazy cattle, she wondered if perhaps helping Lincoln care for his animals might be an opportunity from God.

There she went again, dreaming of what she didn't have, kindling the fires of discontentment. What was she thinking? She'd always be a ranch hand, the Noble who stayed behind, birthed the cows, shod the horses. And she should be happy — seeing Macey and Haley and Gideon living out of their car should have given her a hard shake. Why couldn't she open her eyes and see what she had here — a family, land, a purpose, and now an opportunity to help Gideon and his sisters.

When had the ranch turned from refuge to prison?

She tossed the spoon into the sink. Piper and Nick had updated the cabin with contemporary artwork Piper brought from Kalispell, which went oddly well with the vintage fifties-style fridge and white Formica countertops and table. Although small — with only two bedrooms off the living area, separated by a tiny bath — the cabin had absorbed the love Piper and Nick had brought into their first home, and Stefanie felt like an intruder. Piper's towering stack of books beside the worn leather sofa and a Bible on the round pine table next to an empty stone coaster betrayed a passion for reading so much like Stefanie's father, Bishop, had had. No wonder Stefanie leaned on Piper more and more for wisdom.

Piper had become the sister Stefanie had always longed for. Why couldn't she have arrived ten years earlier?

Then again, if she had, Nick wouldn't have been ready to let go of his past and embrace the future God had for him.

Stefanie wondered when she might be ready too. She sank into an overstuffed chair before the ledgestone fireplace, watching the flames, listening to the crackling. How many hours had she sat in front of the fire, listening to the quiet house, when she'd come home from college halfway through her freshman year? Her father had tried to pry from her the reason for her early return, but she'd wound it so tightly inside her, shoving it into the darkness, that she couldn't bear to unravel it.

She could still feel it sometimes — the hard coil of pain deep inside. A pain that stung and left a harsh taste in her mouth.

A bitter root.

A verse from Pastor Pike's sermon slunk into her thoughts: *"Look after each other so that none of you fails to receive the grace of God. Watch out that no poisonous root of bitterness grows up to trouble you, corrupting many."*

Stefanie rubbed her hands on her thermal

shirt, then reached for a plaid fringed afghan. Maybe she did have a bitter root. Something embedded and stubborn and poisonous inside her. Tears bit into her eyes. She didn't want to be bitter, but as she remembered her tone with Lincoln when he'd first arrived, it sounded . . .

Bitter.

How could she be bitter? Yet the past oozed into her mind, and she felt again the fist of betrayal as she watched her boyfriend — had Doug ever been her boyfriend or was he just the man who had used her? — draw another woman into his embrace. She saw herself hide in the bathroom, pulling herself together, aware that she had turned into someone she didn't know. Someone who had given the best parts of herself to a man who didn't cherish them.

And to think she'd believed that when he invited her out for a fancy dinner at a nice hotel, he'd had candlelight and dinner on his mind.

Apparently not with her.

She closed her eyes against the voices, the ones inside that called her a tramp. Dirty.

A voice that said she had betrayed everything she believed in. Betrayed herself.

Maybe she did have a root of bitterness inside her, poisoning her. Poisoning her relationships with men. Poisoning her ability to be content. Poisoning her ability to trust.

How did one yank out the root of bitterness?

Stefanie winced and reached for Piper's Bible, looking up the verse in Hebrews 12. Her gaze went to the first part of verse 15. "Look after each other so that none of you fails to receive the grace of God." She'd thought God had been speaking to her on Lincoln's behalf so that he wouldn't miss out on His grace.

What if He'd also been speaking on her behalf? What if God had brought Lincoln here . . . for her? to show her His grace?

The fire crackled as a log fell in the hearth and sent out a spray of sparks.

Stefanie pressed a hand to her heart, remembering Lincoln's smile, the easiness between them today, and realized she wanted to give Lincoln a chance to be a friend.

And not only for his sake.

But for hers.

CHAPTER 10

"Aren't you hot stuff!" Piper set her magazine aside as Stefanie came down the stairs, barefoot and carrying a pair of spiky black boots. Piper sat in the chair Stefanie's father had always occupied in the family room of their house, back in the corner, where he could survey the room, the stone fireplace, the leather sofa, the passage to the kitchen. Bishop Noble's stack of books and his Bible still occupied the table; even after two years, no one had moved them.

"Who?" Stefanie stopped at the bottom of the stairs and glanced at Macey, who'd sprawled on the sofa, reading one of Stefanie's ancient Nancy Drew books. Apparently mysteries never went out of style. Haley had built a house for her kitten with blankets and pillows and was playing on the wool braided carpet in front of the fire. She looked up as Stefanie entered and smiled.

How Stefanie longed to hear words from

Haley. But the fact that the little girl now climbed onto her lap freely or occasionally gave her a hug seemed words enough.

"You, silly," Piper said, one eyebrow tilted up at Stefanie's attire.

So she wore a little black dress. What else did a girl wear to dinner? She wanted to look nice for him. Just a little. He'd been on extraspecial nice-guy behavior all week.

"Lincoln's making me dinner," Stefanie said. "It's just dinner. We're going to talk about his new horses, and he wants to show me his house. It's nothing."

Piper smiled, one hand on her growing belly. "Yeah. I know exactly where making dinner leads."

Stefanie laughed. Two years ago, Piper had hired on as a so-called cook even though she hadn't a clue how to boil water. As an undercover reporter, she'd been hunting for clues to a crime. Along the way, she'd had her heart stolen by her chief suspect. Yes, dinner could be a dangerous thing.

Stefanie, however, wouldn't be taken in by Lincoln's charm. He'd taken a chance on her pick of horses and had even listened to her advice, but she'd successfully calloused herself against his devastating smile, his lethal charisma. She could learn from the mistakes of her youth.

"We're neighbors, Piper. That's it. Nothing more. Really. Yes, he's nice. And what's not to like? Smart, handsome. And he's incredible with the horses we bought."

"We?"

"I helped." She finger-combed her dark hair. She'd let it down tonight, but it always had a mind of its own. "I can't believe I actually talked him into buying the entire herd — all ten horses — but he's great with them. He's bonding with a few of his favorites. He's actually been out in the barn, spending hours grooming them, feeding them, even learning how to handle them."

"Maybe he's more of a cowboy than you thought."

"Oh, he's got cowboy in him all right. From his Stetson to his snakeskin boots, although I'm not sure how much is the real deal and how much is an act. But he's still not my type."

"What do you mean he's not your type? You have something against tall, blond, and heartbreakingly handsome?"

Stefanie laughed. "Not in the least. From a distance. But I've been there, done that. . . ."

Stefanie's humor vanished. Sometimes her mouth ran ahead of her brain. But she'd been privy to a few of Piper's darkest moments, namely when she tried to run out on Nick in his hour of need, so . . .

"In college, I sort of fell for the campus jock. He was a football star, a senior, and gorgeous. His father owned the local car dealership, so he was a bit of a star on campus too." She had long since tucked Doug back in her mind, but now his laughter, the way he'd two-stepped up to her at a dance that first night on campus, twined through her memories.

"I thought he loved me. . . ." She gave a halfhearted shrug and smiled at Macey, who put down her book and looked at her curiously. "I guess he got bored. Or . . . I don't know. We dated for three months, but it ended when I found him with another woman."

Piper glanced at Macey and stood, waddling over to Stefanie. With the baby due in less than two months, she looked like the fun had long since vanished from her pregnancy.

She hooked Stefanie by the arm, drawing her into the kitchen. "He cheated on you?" she whispered.

"I'm not sure he'd consider it cheating. Now that I think about it, he took great pains to hide our . . . whatever it was. We spent a lot of time indoors . . . if you know what I mean."

Apparently Piper knew exactly what she meant. She gave her a soft smile. "We've all made mistakes."

"Yeah, well, in my book, this was a big one. And to make it worse, I thought he'd planned this romantic getaway. . . . I got dressed up." She sighed, seeing herself young and naive. "I probably made more of it than it was. But I was pretty ashamed of myself. I finally quit school at the end of the semester and came back to the Buckle."

Piper wore a murderous look. "Did Nick know?"

"No — I didn't need my big brother fighting my battles for me. Besides, he was . . ." Well, he'd disappeared from the ranch by then, and none of her letters were answered. "Out of the house."

Piper knew enough of Nick's past to give an understanding nod. "So now, what, you swear off all good-looking men?"

"Yep. Just the dogs for me." Her little joke fell flat. "Listen, Lincoln Cash isn't my type because I'm not *his* type. Yes, he's gorgeous, but I don't swoon when he walks into the room —"

"No, you just get mean."

"That's not true. I've been really nice. Overly nice. But the biggest reason is that

I'm not going to be Lincoln Cash's Montana distraction. He has a life, and it's not here. Mine is. As soon as Lincoln lands another great movie role, he's moving back to Hollywood. I can feel it in my bones. He's here for fun, to pass time, or maybe even to try and pull off his film festival. But it won't last, because despite his smile and the fact that he spent this week doing a stellar impression of a normal guy, I can't help but think Lincoln can't live without his fancy cars, his gourmet restaurants, and his gaggle of beautiful women. It's only a matter of time."

Piper had obviously been practicing her wise-mother look because she used it on Stefanie now. Pretty well, in fact. "I think you might need to look beyond what you see. Give him a chance."

Stefanie held up her hand. "Don't even go there. I'm not looking to repeat my mistakes. We're just neighbors, and I promise you, that's all we'll ever be."

"Neighbors. Sure." Piper went over to the fridge and opened it, then closed it with a huff. "Why is it that whenever I want something good to eat, it's never there?"

"Want to come with me? I think we're having steak."

"I wouldn't dream of tagging along. By

the way, where's Gideon? I didn't see him come home."

Stefanie sat down, pulling on the expensive black boots she'd worn in New York City last fall at one of Rafe's GetRowdy bull-riding charity events. She figured wearing them again helped justify the expense. Besides, there weren't too many places in Phillips where she could get dressed up without igniting a maelstrom of "high-and-mighty" comments.

She zipped into the boots. "He's upstairs, lying on his bed. Seems to me that something is eating at him — he's been chewing on something distasteful for the last three days, by the look on his face."

"He definitely has a lot on his plate." Piper opened the fridge again and took out a bag of baby carrots. "All of us do." She looked up, crunching.

It suddenly occurred to Stefanie that maybe . . . what if Piper and Nick didn't want the kids around? Yes, they'd been supportive, and Piper had clearly fallen in love with Haley, but once their own child arrived, how anxious would they be to invest in three runaways who needed their full attention?

Haley wouldn't talk, and no one could ignore Macey's damaged arms. It looked as

219

though her cutting had stopped, the last marks having turned pink and healing, but if they went back into the system, who knew what might happen?

In one short month, these kids had filled up so many empty places inside Stefanie, it took her breath away. She remembered how hollow her life had been without them.

Stefanie grabbed the long trench coat she wore for church. "We're doing the right thing. They need us."

"Mmm-hmm." Piper nodded. "Be safe."

Stefanie didn't know exactly what Piper meant by that, but she gave her a nod and headed out the door. Clancy met her on the porch, tail wagging, and followed her to the truck. "No, pal. You can't go with me. I know you love Lincoln —"

Everyone, it seemed, loved Lincoln. He had hypnotized the entire town with his plans — and his money — but like she'd said to Piper, she knew how to stay out of the vortex of his charm.

See, just neighbors.

As she drove up to John Kincaid's old ranch, Stefanie had to admit that Lincoln had done an incredible job of sprucing up the neighborhood. His massive log home fairly glittered against the night, with its sprawling two stories totaling over four thousand square feet, the massive wrap-around porch, the two fireplaces. She could hardly believe that just over a month ago he'd arrived to find his home in flames.

The new house overlooked the foundation where the old modular home once stood. The rubble had long since been bulldozed away, and construction workers had resealed the cement floor, ready to rebuild. The barn, which had been gutted and re-sided, had been remodeled, and the plans included a huge movie screen, floor and balcony seating, and even a café. Everything someone needed to fully experience a Lincoln Cash epic.

She felt as if she were watching one live, right before her eyes.

Across the yard, he'd expanded the livestock barn, although he'd kept the original doors and siding, and had enlarged Kincaid's corral. Inside, the ten horses he'd rescued were probably enjoying fresh hay. He'd also taken her advice and let them out to pasture during the day. Beyond the new livery stable, a pole barn housed the tractor, his pickup, and a four-wheeler.

Next to Lincoln Cash's operation, which had shot up like a boomtown, the Silver Buckle seemed downright decrepit.

Stefanie drove up the drive toward the

house, parked her pickup in front, and got out. The wide porch held two huge pots of geraniums and a swing, which swayed in the wind.

She raised her hand to ring the bell, but the door opened, as if sensing her presence. Lincoln stood there in his stocking feet, a pair of very faded jeans, and an orange pullover. He held a glass of what looked like Coke in his hand.

She gulped, feeling very overdressed in her black dress and spike heels. She squelched the urge to turn and run.

"You look incredible."

"For a girl who hangs out with horses all day?"

"Hey, Horse Girl, you know how to clean up." He gave her a blatant perusal, then ended it with a wink. "Do the other cowboys in Phillips know you have legs?"

Stefanie could feel her face flame. *Just neighbors!*

He grinned, the scoundrel. "I promise not to tell anyone," he said, moving aside to let her in.

"I'm going to hold you to that." Good grief, even she could hear the delight in her voice. She stepped into the house. The beauty of the foyer took her breath away, and for a moment, she completely forgot herself. "Wow. This is amazing."

A giant antler chandelier hung from a two-story entry, lights embedded in the crannies of the horns. The floor was dark — darker than any wood she'd ever seen — and contrasted with the gorgeous wood of the pine logs. A staircase wound upward, with what looked like hand-tooled spindles and banister. The place even smelled new, like varnish, only tempered with the delicious smells of what she assumed was supper.

Her stomach offered a little growl.

"Perfect," Lincoln said, setting down his drink on a rough-hewn bench in the hall. Probably cost a couple thousand, easily. "I like a girl who's hungry." He reached for her coat, and she let it slide off her into his hands.

"I can't believe you built this in a month," she said, reaching to pull off her boots.

He caught her arm. "Keep them on. They look nice on you."

She eyed the white carpet that started in the next room. "They could be muddy."

"I'll get the carpets cleaned. I just never see you in anything . . . daring. I like it."

Stefanie's stomach did something she hadn't felt in . . . well, she couldn't remember the last time. Maybe she should take her boots off anyway, but with Lincoln smil-

223

ing down at her . . .

She smoothed her dress, took a breath.

"I feel way out of my league." He wore the slightest smile, and if he meant to tease, she saw nothing of it in his eyes. "Come in. Let me show you around."

Although her home was made of logs — cut down from Silver Buckle property back when the place had been homesteaded by her great-grandfather — those logs didn't in the least resemble the ones used for Lincoln's house. Snug, clean, and bright, these logs looked as if they grew that way. The foyer opened into a two-story family room, with beams running the width of the house and a Montana-quarried flagstone fireplace jutting to the ceiling. Giant windows overlooked a lighted deck that most likely viewed the Bighorn Mountains during the daytime. On the other side of the stairs was a grand kitchen with dark cabinets and dark marble counters fit for some five-star chef.

Indeed, Lincoln had a chef in the kitchen right now, a woman with dark hair who looked up and flashed Stefanie a smile.

She managed one back.

"The house is actually a kit," Lincoln said. "They truck in the pieces, and it's like putting together giant LEGOs. Just follow the instructions."

Oh yeah, just like LEGOs. "But you had to have an army of people here to accomplish this."

Lincoln shrugged. "I wanted a place to get away, and this was the time to do it. Now that I'm here, I'm thinking of selling my place in California."

He was thinking of selling his house?

"It's not completely done yet, though. I still have to finish the library, and there's no furniture in the upstairs bedrooms, except the master. I focused on the essential areas and my office. I hope to finish it all soon. Would you like something to drink?" He raised his glass. "Diet Coke. I'm an addict."

Stefanie shook her head. "Water, later, will be fine."

Whoever had designed the place had expertly mixed the Old West with new styles — wrought iron and leather furniture, paintings by Montana painter C. M. Russell, nubby llama wool blankets draped over furniture, mica-paper light fixtures. . . . With everything inside her, Stefanie wanted to plop into one of his overstuffed chairs and bury herself in a book. "Who did your interior design?" she asked.

Lincoln took a sip of his Diet Coke. "Me."

Stefanie tried not to let surprise show on

her face. Honestly, she would have expected to see his movie posters, maybe memorabilia from his various action movies, gaudy black leather, and leopard prints on the floor. Instead the place was styled with elegance, with an eye toward fitting into the Montana landscape. Who was this man? "Beautiful" was all she could say.

"We have some time before dinner. Let me show you the rest of the house."

She followed him through the kitchen to a formal dining room, complete with a hand-carved table made of more of the dark wood, and into another room that made her smile. "I've never seen a personal movie theater in a house."

Lincoln flicked on the lights. "It's a media room. Lots of houses have them nowadays. Mine only holds nine people, so it's small."

It didn't look small. A huge screen, bracketed by black curtains, took up one entire wall. The room sloped down, like one of the theaters in Sheridan, only this room had three rows of plush black leather recliners — she'd known she'd find it somewhere — complete with cup holders and little tables that she guessed would hold more than popcorn. "So this is where you watch your massive collection of Lincoln Cash movies?"

He gave her a smile, but it didn't reach his eyes. "I don't suppose you want to see the electronics for this room?"

"Did you design them?"

The slightest hue of red in his face indicated that yes, he'd probably put the entire thing together. She didn't know why she was surprised.

"Where do you keep your movie collection?"

He gestured to a door — which seemed right, because a man like him would probably have every movie ever made — but when she opened it, she found a shallow closet with just two rows of DVDs.

DVDs of Lincoln Cash movies. And every one of them still in the package.

She picked one up. "They're not opened. I suppose you don't need to watch them to know what they're about."

Disinterest showed on his face. "I don't watch my movies."

Her smile vanished. "What?"

Lincoln took the movie from her hand and slid it back on the shelf. "There's more house."

He pointed out the view from the back deck, showed her how to use the remote control for the outside lights that lined the driveway, how to run the ceiling fans, and how to control the music piped through the house.

Through it all, she kept hearing, *"I don't watch my movies."*

Why not? Even she knew that making a movie was hard work — she had listened to John Kincaid's stories of watching his book *Unshackled* being made into a movie. Why wouldn't Lincoln want to enjoy his efforts?

He finally led her back to the foyer and a room leading off from it. "This is my office."

Stefanie found herself drawn into this little room with the mocha-colored walls, various Stetsons hanging behind the desk, the wall of books — she noted that he had Louis L'Amour's entire leather-bound collection — and the pictures on his dark wooden credenza. A laptop was closed on top of the desk. Yet, not one movie poster, not even a wallet-size celebrity vanity picture.

And if he were to have them, they'd be here.

She walked over to the collection of photos on the credenza behind his desk. She recognized Lincoln and Dex Graves, the director of *Unshackled,* in what looked like a shot taken on this land, perhaps in this very place. "This was when you were working on the movie last summer, wasn't it?"

He nodded, and for a second, she was again sitting next to him on the bleachers at the Fourth of July rodeo, listening to him tell stories of life on the set. She'd thought, even then, that he had a magic about him. And that magic showed in every photo — the one of John and Lincoln in costume, and in another, of a young woman with a wide smile and unfocused eyes. Stefanie picked it up. "Old girlfriend?"

Lincoln took it from her. "No." He touched her elbow, steering her out of the office. "Karen made some artichoke dip for an appetizer. I promise, you'll love it. She's a great cook."

Stefanie had the definite impression that she'd asked the wrong question. "Did I offend you?"

"Nope." He walked into the kitchen. "We'll be on the deck," he said to Karen.

Wasn't it freezing out there? Although it was mid-May, Montana's nights still required a jacket or sweater. But Lincoln grabbed neither as he opened the French doors. "Join me?"

Stefanie gave him a dubious look, then stepped outside.

The warmth hit her like a summer night. Even though the deck overlooked a vast ocean of crisp darkness, the eating area — a deliciously set table for two — seemed to be in its own pocket of warmth. As Lincoln pulled out her chair, Stefanie saw why. Four outside heaters that looked like trees blew heat toward the dining area. July, in his backyard.

"This is incredible."

He smiled. "Welcome to my housewarming party."

Karen came out and set a chafing dish of bubbling dip between them, then a basket of tortilla chips.

"Thank you, Karen," Lincoln said.

Stefanie saw by her smile that she, too, had been infected by the Lincoln Cash charm. But, really, how could Stefanie blame her? It would be nearly impossible to be around all this 24-7 without letting it test your resolve. Except, of course, for a girl like Stefanie.

She took a chip and dipped it into the gooey cheese. "I see I'm the only one at your party."

Lincoln sat back in his chair. "I'm just getting to know my neighbors."

She crunched her chip, savoring the perfectly blended flavors. She'd have to get the recipe for Piper. "That's not what I see. I think there's a petition in town to make you our first mayor and rename Main Street after you."

He laughed at her jest, but she could see the thought pleased him. As if he had any doubts?

"Would you sign the petition?"

She shrugged, reaching for another chip. "Depends on the other candidates. Besides, you don't need my vote."

"Yours is the only one I care about."

The chip got caught in her throat. She coughed and reached for a glass of water, drinking it down.

Lincoln sat there, grinning.

Not quite, mister. She wasn't the same stupid, starstruck girl she'd been in college, dating the campus hotshot. And she wouldn't let Lincoln into her heart to wreak the same damage.

But despite her words, she couldn't help feeling that, given the chance, she'd vote for him sticking around Phillips. . . . After all, he made a very good neighbor.

Stefanie Noble had the power to leave Lincoln's head spinning, throwing fuel on the fire he'd been trying to bank for a week, ever since they'd brought home his new herd. It wasn't easy to be around her every day, or rather, it wasn't easy to be around her and not want to touch that silky dark

231

hair, maybe take her in his arms and kiss those lips that seemed to have an opinion about everything.

He'd never dated such a bossy, strong woman. Most of the women he knew not only asked how high when he suggested "jump" but did their homework to know his favorite food and perfume and wasted no time in telling him how lucky they were to be with him.

Except, he wasn't exactly dating Stefanie. And she kept him at bullwhip distance, doing nothing to impress him, not once sidling up to him to ask for his help, not once giving him a look that suggested her mind lingered on anything but teaching him how to groom and rein-train his horses.

Until tonight.

Until she'd worn a little black dress. It wasn't even a low-cut, thigh-high, barely there kind of dress. It was simple, with a wide neck, and draping to her knees. On any other woman it might have been unnoticeable. But with all that dark hair down and blowing slightly in the breeze, those equally dark eyes, and a slight blush on her face — residue from the way she'd reacted to his flirting — he'd never seen anyone so beautiful.

He needed to keep his wits about him and

keep in mind that he was trying to be her kind of man.

Although, frankly, he was having a hard time figuring out what that might be. Because the man who had concocted this evening wasn't the same guy who endured the smell of manure, who spent hours getting greasy horsehair on him. Yet it was only as that man that he'd gotten a reaction from her.

"You're doing a great job with the horses," Stefanie said now as she scooped into the artichoke dip.

"I have to admit they do have a certain elegance despite their brokenness," he said, standing at the grill, his back to her, cooking steaks and foil-wrapped asparagus.

"Mmm," she said. "Reminds me, in a way, of Gideon. All he needed was a chance."

Lincoln didn't turn for fear the truth might be written all over his face. The fear that his second chance might be too late.

He'd woken this morning with that pins-and-needles stinging sensation, this time in his right leg. He'd been trying all day not to panic, but it wasn't easy to hide his returning limp. Or the fact that earlier tonight, for no reason at all, the room had tilted and he'd found himself facedown on his bedroom carpet.

He hadn't dodged the MS bullet after all. It had resurfaced just in time to mock him. Especially when it took him nearly thirty minutes to button his shirt, and by that time, he'd worked up such a sweat that he'd had to change it. He chose a pullover the second time around. Which meant he had to change into jeans.

And she'd shown up in a dress. He felt like a jerk.

But he wasn't about to cancel dinner.

"I love what you've done to the Big K," Stefanie said, sitting back in her chair at the table. She'd finally decided on raspberry iced tea and sipped it from a tall crystal-cut glass.

"Thanks. I had my eye on it ever since last summer."

"When does *Unshackled* come out?"

"The premiere is in late June. It's supposed to be a Fourth of July movie, something that touches the heart of freedom and the Old West. I think it's the token Western for the summer."

She turned her glass in her hand, staring at it, and he suddenly had an image of her in a long silky dress, her hair piled up with tendrils spilling over her shoulders, her arm tucked through his as they climbed out of the limousine at the premiere.

No. That life was over. He needed to get that reality through his hard head.

He turned back to the steaks. "So, how's Rafe?" He'd been following this year's exploits of her bull-riding brother and knew he was high in the standings for the Get-Rowdy bull riders, if not first.

"He finally proposed to Kat."

Something thick filled Lincoln's throat; he might even name it jealousy. Unlike his own so-called torrid romances, Rafe and Kat had the real deal going on.

He scooped the meat onto a serving platter, then grabbed the tinfoil and slid it onto the plate. He touched his mouth to soothe the burning as he brought the plate to the table. "You probably have steak all the time —"

"No, actually, we're more of a spaghetti family." Stefanie held up her plate while he forked a steak onto it. "So this is a treat."

He sat and served himself and was just about to lift his Diet Coke in a toast when she smiled at him and said, "Can we pray?"

Pray? "Of course," he said, but he kept his eyes open, watching her as she bowed her head and prayed out loud.

He might be in real trouble. Apparently, to be Stefanie Noble's type, he'd also have to return to the little white church. He fabricated a smile and a heartfelt "Amen," but everything inside him had started to churn.

"How are the kids?" The question came out so . . . so domestic and homey that he couldn't help but make a face. "I didn't quite mean that the way it sounded."

Stefanie wore another cute blush but kept her head down, cutting her meat. "They're fine. Macey is almost as good with a horse as you are."

"I'm sure she could teach me a few things."

"She reminds me of me when I was a kid."

Lincoln noticed how she poured steak sauce over her meat, and it made him smile. He would bet she'd eat the entire portion too. He hadn't seen a woman eat an entire meal since . . . well, probably since back in Texas. "You wore all black and looked like you wanted to beat up the world?"

She gave him a look of confusion.

"Macey," he said and winked.

"Oh. No . . . I liked horses, just like her. When I was young, I wanted to start a dude ranch — only for lost kids, sort of like Macey and Gideon." She glanced up at him through those dark lashes, as if testing his reaction.

"I think you'd be great at that."

He felt her smile all the way to his heart.

"I grew up in Dallas, wondering what it would be like to ride a horse," he said, cutting his asparagus. He didn't tell her that he was so uncowboy in his core that he still fought fear every time he got near the big animals. Or that for his first movie, he'd been so afraid that Dex had to find an animal practically as old as Methuselah before Lincoln would ride it. Those secrets could stay buried.

"I'll bet you're a natural."

He gave a laugh that was half embarrassment, half dismay. "Not at all. I wish I had half the horse sense you do. Did you go to school or something to learn? Maybe college?"

Stefanie cut another piece of meat. "I went to Montana State for one semester."

"Why only one semester?"

He'd been an actor long enough to see when someone faked their answer. She wouldn't win any Academy Awards for her sudden fidget-with-her-food performance.

"Came home to run the ranch."

Hmm. He watched her put her drink down and wipe her mouth.

The phone rang in the kitchen. Thankfully, he'd asked Karen to stay, and she answered it.

Lincoln leaned forward, lowering his voice. "Wanna know a secret?"

Her fork stopped halfway to her mouth. She gave him a small smile and put it down. "Sure."

"I never went to college."

Stefanie looked truly surprised. "But you have a degree, don't you? Didn't I see a college certificate — ?"

"It's an honorary degree. From USC. I taught a couple classes there and spoke at their film school graduation, and they gave me a diploma."

Her mouth opened, then closed, and she gave him a disgusted look.

He grinned at her.

"Mr. Cash?" Karen stood in the doorway, holding the phone, one hand over the mouthpiece. "It's someone from a hospital in Texas. They said they need to talk to you — that it's urgent. Something about Alyssa?"

He glanced at Stefanie and knew that the blood was draining from his face. He had momentarily lost any composure he might have and swallowed before answering. "I'll take it in my study. Thank you." He wiped his mouth. "I'll be right back."

Stefanie gave him a look he couldn't, and didn't have time to, interpret.

As he expected, it was the night nurse, giving her daily report. The situation with Alyssa had escalated. Not only was she experiencing night terrors, but they'd spilled out into day terrors also, and she was slipping in and out of mild seizures. The doctors wanted to prescribe a benzodiazepine drug, a sleep aid.

Lincoln listened as the nurse listed the side effects, wincing at more seizures, hysteria, and coma. He'd sunk into his desk chair and, long after he'd hung up, sat there, his head in his hands, thinking.

"Linc, are you okay?"

He hadn't heard Stefanie come in, but there she stood, outlined by the door. She padded into the room and slid onto the desk by his chair. Her pretty bare feet dangled down. Apparently she'd taken off her boots anyway.

"You want to talk about it?"

No. He didn't. What he wanted, what he *really* wanted, was to forget everything, forget the mistakes he'd made, forget the dismal future that hovered like a guillotine, even forget for a second that he had responsibility hanging around his neck, and take Stefanie Noble in his arms. He wanted her to think about him, dream about him like he dreamed of her. He wanted to see stars in her eyes — not the kind he saw in his fans' eyes, but real stars, the kind based on . . . what? He wasn't even sure who the real Lincoln was after all these years.

Mostly, as he'd watched her this past week, the way she worked so patiently with his horses, he ached to be the type of guy that might make Stefanie Noble proud.

But no matter how hard he tried, he couldn't figure out a way to impress her, didn't even know if he should try. What kind of future could a guy like him give her? He'd practically heard his own voice mocking him when she'd picked up one of his movies. No, he didn't watch his own films — even at premieres, it was sheer agony. Because all he saw on the screen was Lewis Carter, a guy who'd faked his way to being a hero.

Lincoln wasn't invincible. And as he sat there, cradling his head in his hands, he knew that he was tired of trying.

But the last thing Stefanie Noble would respect was a weak man. A man who couldn't saddle a horse or rope a calf. A man who might someday need a wheelchair to get around. The fact that every patient was different, every case of MS individualized, only scared him more. He might have finite, manageable symptoms . . . or not. In the end, however, his nerves were still breaking down, his body slowly decaying.

"Linc?"

He looked up at Stefanie and forced a smile. "That was . . ."

"Is someone hurt?"

He sighed, staring at the phone. Maybe it was her tone — full of compassion and trust — but he suddenly, desperately, needed to tell someone . . . no, *her.* "It's someone I've been looking after. She's having seizures, and they want to put her on some pretty strong meds."

"Does she have epilepsy?" Stefanie scooted closer, put her feet on his chair.

"No, she was in an accident. Head trauma."

"Oh, I'm sorry. When did it happen?"

"A long time ago, when I was about seventeen. She got caught in a drive-by shooting, got shot in the head." He glanced at the phone.

Stefanie's mouth opened, and she didn't try to conceal her shock. "I'm so sorry."

He took a breath, blew it out. "It was the same shooting that killed my mother."

Out of the corner of his eye — because he couldn't look at her horror straight on — he saw her cover her mouth with her hand. He closed his eyes as her other hand

241

touched his shoulder.

In the movies, he might take this moment and use it to turn her into his arms. For a second, the bad Lincoln, the one who'd once lived for beautiful women, even considered it.

Instead, the man who wanted to let her see the real Lincoln — whoever that was — got up and walked away from her. He stared out the window.

"I'm so glad you weren't hurt," she said softly.

Lincoln fought the burn in his throat, the way it wanted to close up, cut off his breathing. He leaned his forehead on the cool pane of the window. "No, actually, I wouldn't have been." He turned to her, and before he could stop himself — maybe because he wanted the purging, someone to confess to — he said, "Because, you see, I was in the car."

CHAPTER 11

Stefanie stared at Lincoln Cash — incredible, beautiful Lincoln Cash — and couldn't breathe.

"What?" she managed to say, but it didn't seem that he heard her because he covered his eyes with his hand, shaking his head as if he'd been sucked into some memory that overwhelmed him.

The memory of killing his mother?

"Oh," he said, and it sounded more like a groan than anything. "I don't know why I . . ."

Stefanie slipped off the desk. And then suddenly she had her arms around his neck, pulling him down to her, wrapping him tight. Holding him. Because, although this night had started out with her feeling completely out of her element, wondering why she'd agreed to dinner, wondering how to fortify her heart, right now, in this moment, she knew she had to be more than a

243

neighbor. Lincoln needed a friend. "Linc . . . shhh."

His arms went around her; his head touched her shoulder. He was shaking a little and holding on to her tight, like he meant it.

Like he needed her.

She closed her eyes, laying her head against his chest, breathing in the smell of his freshly laundered shirt, his cologne, and the musky scent of the outdoors. "What happened?" she whispered.

He said nothing for a long time. Then he took a deep breath and moved back.

She searched his eyes, but he turned his anguish away from her.

"What happened?" She kept her voice gentle and slid onto the desk again.

He sighed as if expelling pain. "I was . . . so . . . stupid." The way he said it, like he was spitting, made her heart ache. She knew exactly the kind of stupid that elicited that tone.

He braced his hand against the wall and stared out the window. "There was this kid where I grew up. His name was E-bro —"

"E-bro?"

"It was a gang name — and his favorite sport was . . . well, let's say I learned how to take the hits I do on the screen from real-life tutoring, thanks to E-bro and my step-dad."

Stefanie clenched her jaw against that visual.

"E-bro was a couple years older than me in school and one of those kids that had been born with a beard and a mean streak. He thought I'd be a good target for torture, so I spent most of my school years running home, in hopes I'd get there before he did. When I didn't, I'd hide out in the junkyard near our trailer park."

Admittedly, Stefanie had a hard time getting her brain around Lincoln hiding, his knees knocking. But she didn't say that, because the look of agony on his face as he turned to her confirmed his words.

"Later on, when I was fifteen and sixteen, I just learned to take the lumps. But I wanted so desperately to be strong and maybe pay him back, so I —" he shook his head — "I joined another gang."

"A rival gang?"

"Yep." Lincoln sat down in the desk chair, pulling her foot onto his knee. He had his hand around her ankle and now rubbed his thumb along it, almost absently.

She tried to focus on his words.

"My new brothers decided to pay E-bro back for everything he'd done to me, so we

245

piled into a car and headed to his house."

Stefanie could almost see that night playing in his eyes, the fear and anger that would drive him to vengeance. She knew what it felt like to hurt and even be so angry that you might do something you'd regret.

"But the problem was E-bro lived beside me, in the next trailer over, which was probably why he'd picked me to torture in the first place. . . . It's hard to be accurate with a MAC-10 submachine gun." Lincoln's voice tightened, and he closed his eyes. "Of course, E-bro wasn't home, even though the shooter decimated his trailer, but the worst part was that some of the shots went wide."

"And hit your mom," she whispered.

"Yeah. And . . . the little neighbor girl. Alyssa was about six years old. She was like a little sister to me. She'd come over a lot, especially when her mom worked late, and that night, she was over. . . ." He hung his head, his dark blond hair falling over his face. Was he trying not to cry?

She put her hand on his shoulder. "What happened next?"

He shook his head, as if unable to talk.

So she waited, letting the silence and her touch speak patience and compassion.

Finally he said, "I was sick. Literally. They dumped me off at the hospital, but I spent

246

the night retching, horrified, as they operated on Alyssa to save her life." Even now, his voice sounded like he might be choking. He sat back with an expression of self-loathing so wretched that she knew it came from a place of honesty. "I couldn't live with myself, so I turned myself in. The cops had been trying to get a hook into these guys — the shooter and the driver — for months, and they offered to dismiss all charges if I testified."

"You testified."

Lincoln nodded. "I went to my mother's funeral, stuck around long enough to see them go to jail, feeling like I should be right there with them, and left town."

"And went to California?"

He released her foot, got up, and walked again to the window. "I changed my name and got a job as an extra on a Dex Graves movie." Turning then, he cocked his head, a wry, mocking smile on his face, and held out his hands. "Behold, the invincible Lincoln Cash. Are you impressed?"

Stefanie slid off the desk and caught his hand, squeezing it. "Actually, yes. I think it took a lot of courage to testify against those guys. They could have come after you. And it's clear to me that you're still looking after your neighbor."

247

The look he gave her, as if he might be peering right through her, right to her soul, desperately testing her words, turned her inside out, sweeping away her defenses.

Which was probably why she stood on her tiptoes, put a hand around his neck, and kissed him.

He stayed completely still, his mouth soft on hers and tasting faintly salty like tears.

What was she doing? She didn't love Lincoln, did she? Perhaps it was compassion or even concern . . .

No. In this moment, she loved the part of Lincoln Cash she'd just seen.

Suddenly he moved, curling his arm around her, holding her tight against him. His hand went to her cheek and finally — *finally* — he kissed her back.

In fact, instead of holding her, Lincoln ran his hand behind her neck and kissed her like she'd never been kissed before. Not neighborly at all.

When he pulled away, she held his wrist, her heart thumping through her chest — so much that she wondered if he could see it.

Lincoln angled his forehead to hers, touching it. "Wow . . . I don't know what to say. . . ."

She smiled at him gently, not sure what to say either. Her mouth, however, apparently had a mind of its own. "It's better than in the movies."

He swallowed, and then a smile broke out across his face, something honest and perfect. "Really?"

He seemed as nervous as she was, and that — only that — stopped her from leaping from his arms and running back to the Silver Buckle. Gathering her breath, she managed a soft smile, praying she wasn't the most gullible person on earth. She ran her hand down his face. "Oh yes, Superhero. Oh yes."

This couldn't be any better. With him distracted, probably with that girl, he wouldn't suspect it coming, wouldn't know what had happened until his new life was shattered right before his eyes.

Just like he'd done to others.

Done to her.

With so many people around, it had been difficult to get close to him, but perseverance had paid off. Now it would simply be one of many choices, one of many opportunities.

And if fate stepped in, perhaps he wouldn't be the only one who suffered. It seemed that justice, or perhaps irony, might be that kind.

This, my love, is for you.

The engine turned over and the car backed down the drive quietly, without the lights.

For the third day in a row, Gideon had ended up with a corned beef on rye and hated it. He sat away from the group on a boulder at the edge of the yard — especially away from JB, who seemed to hold him personally responsible for Lincoln firing Luther. But after all the actor had done for Gideon — and mostly because he didn't want to get blamed — he'd had to tell Lincoln about the tools Luther had been taking home from the work site.

And it had stirred something unfamiliar inside Gideon when Lincoln believed him. Even thanked him.

Sometimes Lincoln came down to sit with Gideon at lunch. He told him about movie stunts, like the Dex Ditch and Roll, which sounded so cool that Gideon thought he should probably try it.

Maybe it would take his mind off the fact that Libby had failed to show up for lunch all week. He bit into his sandwich, nearly gagging on the spices in the bread, and washed it down with a cold soda. He put the sandwich back in the paper and folded it up. He didn't care how hungry he got.

He couldn't help a wry shake of his head. Less than two months ago he had been digging out of garbage cans, stealing food, or raiding the Laundromat, hunting for petty change, hoping for enough quarters to feed his sisters, himself. Now he had a car, or a wreck of a car, but a job and regular meals and a sort-of . . . family.

He liked Nick and Piper and especially Stefanie, who had moved out of her own house for him. He hadn't been able to look her in the eye for about a week because of that. But the way she paid attention to Macey — his sister gobbled it up, the need in her eyes painful for Gideon to watch. At least she'd stopped cutting herself.

He'd followed her out to the stable a couple nights back to have that conversation. Macey had been feeding one of the horses, and he'd seen then, for the first time, how much she resembled their mother. The way Macey stroked the horse's blaze, spoke in soft tones, Gideon heard his mother and the way she'd told him everything would be okay. The way she'd tried to calm his fears.

He'd stood in the shadows, watching, feeling about ten years old, until Macey heard him. And then he'd poured all his fraying emotions into picking a fight with her, forcing her to show him her arms.

After Macey had left in a huff, he'd sat in the silence, listening to the horses eat, smelling the hay, the layer of animal sweat, and wished he could live here at the Silver Buckle forever.

He'd do just about anything to stay.

Even if Libby never came back, even if he'd scared her away — and that thought burned inside him because of how much he missed her — he wanted to stay at the Buckle more than breathing.

"I don't believe in fate," Libby had said.

As Gideon got up to throw away his sandwich and soda bottle, he didn't want to either.

He wanted to believe that someone out there cared about him.

Enough to give him — them all — a home.

CHAPTER 12

"I know that look." Piper stood in the kitchen, cutting the crusts off a peanut butter and jelly sandwich. "I wore it right after the roundup with Nick when I knew I'd lost my heart forever."

"I haven't lost my heart," Stefanie said, draping her coat over a kitchen chair. She opened the refrigerator and grabbed the juice carton.

"Let's see, this is week number two that you've gone over there? I hope he's paying you for all your expertise."

Stefanie must have worn a look of horror because Piper burst into laughter. "Okay, now I really need to know what you're doing over at Lincoln Cash's place, because with a look like —" Her mouth opened. "You kissed him!"

Stefanie poured herself a glass of juice and put the container back, then took a drink.

"You kissed him!" Piper grabbed Stefanie's arm and pulled her toward the dining room. The sun strode in across the giant oak table, through the faux tulip centerpiece. "You kissed Lincoln Cash?"

Stefanie ran her finger around the lip of the glass, a smile building. Yeah, she'd kissed him. And now she couldn't get the feel of his strong arms around her, the smell of his cologne, the taste of his kiss from her mind. She nodded and glanced at Piper.

Piper's mouth opened a long time before words emerged. "What was it like?"

"Piper!"

"Hey! I don't have to read it in the tabloids — I get the firsthand account. I want details."

"No. You're terrible."

"He's a good kisser, isn't he? Did you hear movie music? Was there swooning?"

Stefanie made a face. "Oh, come on. Yes, an entire orchestra broke into a sweeping soundtrack." Although . . . if she thought hard, maybe there had been music. . . . "I'm not talking about this." She cleared her throat, keeping a straight face. "Let's just say that I now believe every movie kiss he's ever given. And am insanely jealous of all his previous leading ladies."

"So, are you his current leading lady?" Piper leaned one shoulder against the wall.

Lincoln Cash's leading lady? Stefanie took a breath as those words sank in. She wasn't . . . hadn't thought . . . oh, boy. Her smile faded. "I don't know. We're . . ." They couldn't be just neighbors or just friends either, because . . . well, she didn't kiss her friends.

Piper raised one blonde eyebrow, waiting. "He's just . . . I mean . . . I don't know."

Piper put a hand on Stefanie's arm. "Listen, I know you well enough to know that this is a big deal in your life. However, I'm not sure I can say the same for Lincoln. Are you sure you want to be . . . kissing him?"

Stefanie took another sip of juice. Friday night, and the few days since then that she'd been working with his motley herd of horses, had felt a little like a fairy tale — a sappy love story from the Lifetime channel.

She remembered how Lincoln had watched her yesterday as she worked with a little foal to take a halter.

"When did you learn how to work with horses?" he'd asked. He sat on the top rail of the fence, looking every inch like a movie poster, with his shaggy hair blowing in the wind, wearing a T-shirt under a jean jacket with a pair of faded jeans and boots.

Thankfully, she'd been back in her regular

skin, wearing a brown cowboy hat, her long hair tied in a low ponytail that ran down her back. Her canvas jacket and jeans were covered with a fine film of dust, and she hadn't bothered to put on makeup.

She wasn't sure she wouldn't get a bacterial infection from the dried-up mascara she'd used Friday night anyway. What *was* the shelf life on makeup?

She'd kept her gaze on the animal, moving the halter over his face. "When I was about twelve." She put her hand over the horse's face, rubbing as she brought the halter slowly over his nose. "I saw a horse in a field not far from school. He was horribly neglected and starving, and I knew I had to buy him. So I saved up my chore money and rescued him from the owners." She moved the halter deftly behind the foal's ears, letting the animal bounce his head, all the time keeping her voice soft.

"His name was Sunny," she'd said, aware that the words came out less painfully than she'd thought they would. She stepped close to the foal, running her hands over him, not looking at Lincoln as she took a breath. "He died a few months ago from a flu he picked up. We think it was from the quarter horses I rescued. I didn't know, and by the time we discovered it, I couldn't save him."

There was more, of course. The guilt of knowing that she might have saved him if she'd taken better precautions.

She'd snuck a glance at Lincoln.

He was staring at her with compassion on his face, as if everything inside him wanted to come over to her, take her in his arms.

For a second, she longed for it too.

"I'm sorry," he said instead, and his tone was enough.

She blinked away the wetness in her eyes. "It's probably not healthy to have a horse as a best friend." She moved away from the foal, holding the lead. "There's only one doing the talking."

Lincoln's voice was gentle. "I could listen to you talk all day, Horse Girl."

She hated to admit how much she liked it when he called her a nickname. But her face gave her away.

"So, what did you and Sunny talk about?"

As she'd predicted, the foal had begun to pull on the lead. Stefanie picked up a long stick onto which she'd tied a white handkerchief. She now held the foal's lead and gently ran the handkerchief over his body, then tickled his back end. The foal moved his hindquarters, causing the pressure to lessen on his lead.

Immediately she dropped the rope and

scratched his forehead, cooing sweetly. A little kindness went a long way with the foal and apparently with her, too, because she heard herself talking before she could rein in her mouth. "Mostly I talked about my mom and then my brothers and finally my father. My world wasn't very big at the time."

"Rafe told me your dad died a few years ago. He never mentioned your mom."

Stefanie repeated the technique, and the foal responded again. She dropped the lead and rubbed his forehead. "She died when Rafe and I were thirteen. Breast cancer." She didn't look at him, leaning into the animal. "She fought for about three years before it took her."

A fence creaked in the silence that followed. The wind snatched a tumbleweed and threw it into the corral.

Lincoln had slid off the fence and slowly walked over to her. She appreciated his efforts not to scare the foal. He reached out and pulled her to him, not unlike she'd done for him. He tipped her hat off her head, letting it dangle down her back by its strings, and his lips moved against her hair. "I'm so sorry, Stef."

Lifetime movie indeed. She had probably fallen for him right then, just like the foal

258

that followed her around the pen.

But eventually reality would move in, wouldn't it? Despite his words, she didn't really believe that Lincoln would stick around, and she'd all but given him her heart to stomp on. Not only that, he was an actor, an award-winning actor. He knew how to woo a woman's brain — and heart — into knots.

She might be the most gullible person on the planet.

"Hey," Piper said softly, bringing Stefanie back to the present and breakfast and reality. "I'm not saying Lincoln's not a keeper. I'm just . . . I don't want you to get hurt."

Yeah. Her either. Lincoln Cash's leading lady. Oh, brother. Maybe going over to his ranch again today was an exceptionally bad idea. She nodded to Piper and returned to the kitchen, putting the glass in the sink.

Macey had already gone outside. Stefanie saw her through the kitchen window, standing at the corral, watching the horses they'd been working with. She wore some of Stefanie's old clothes and had her foot up on one rail, her chin braced on her hands, leaning on another rail. The pose reminded Stefanie of many she'd struck as she had watched the horses, either learning their behavior or lost in a world of her own mak-

259

ing, one that had her mother's voice, her mother's smile.

The memory drove her outside and into the yard. "Hey, Mace," she said.

Macey gave the barest hint of a smile. Stefanie noticed she'd wiped all the makeup from her face. Probably ran out of black liner. But without it, Macey looked fifteen and surprisingly innocent.

"Did you notice how Orlando's inside ear is locked toward me?" she said.

Not only had Macey named the horses — Stefanie assumed after her favorite actors — but she'd begun to work on getting them to join up, to overcome their natural flight tendency and see Macey as their friend. The reward of watching the horses follow Macey around the pen, waiting for her response — a scratch on the forehead — made Stefanie's heart do a little dance every time.

Please, God, let Macey see that she's lovable.

"That's because he knows you're here. Talk to him and see what he does."

Macey spoke softly, calling him, and sure enough — Stefanie wanted to hug the beautiful buckskin for his response — Orlando turned and looked at her.

Macey climbed up to the top rung and leaned over, holding an alfalfa treat. Orlando trotted over and licked it from her hand. She petted his forehead. "I think he likes me."

"He loves you. He knows you're his friend, and he's your friend for life."

Stefanie saw Macey's face harden, as if she might be fighting tears. She climbed up beside the teen and gently put her arm around her. To her surprise, Macey didn't shrug it away. "You know, God loves you too, Macey. He made this horse just for you to know that. He loves you, and He's not going to forget about you, just like you're not going to forget about Orlando."

Macey looked away, pain on her face. "I don't want to leave here."

Stefanie's throat burned. "I don't want you to either."

Macey sighed and stuck her hand in her jacket for another treat. "Gideon said that one of the guys at Lincoln Cash's place was saying the town wants to get rid of us. That the people met and they were going to send the pastor out to tell Lincoln to fire Gideon."

"Who would want — ?"

"Everyone hates us. Even Libby won't talk to Gideon anymore."

Well, that explained a lot about Gideon's recent sullenness. "The pastor isn't going to

tell Lincoln to fire Gideon. And maybe Libby's just been busy —"

"Gideon really liked her!"

"No one wants you to leave," Stefanie
said.

"Lincoln Cash does. He didn't want us
here, remember?" Macey's eyes filled, and
despite her hard-jawed efforts to stop them,
tears rolled down her cheeks. "He even tried
to give Gideon money to make us leave."

"He didn't know what he was saying."
Lincoln had made such an about-face in his
actions, it had nearly knocked Stefanie over.
He wouldn't be getting close to her in hopes
of talking her into getting rid of — ?

"Clancy!" Macey hopped off the fence.

Stefanie spun, watching as the girl ran
across the yard to where Clancy had fallen.
The animal heaved, but Stefanie could see
that nothing but bile emerged from his dripping jowls. She ran over to him.

Macey knelt before him, her hand on his
body. "What's wrong?"

Stefanie bent over the dog, checking his
eyes. Piper came out on the porch. "Call
Dutch or Nick!" Stefanie said, feeling for
Clancy's pulse. Thready and weak, the pulse
accompanied the dog's labored breathing.

Clancy stared up at Stefanie, his glassy
brown eyes pleading for her to help.

"Help me get him in the truck," she said to Macey. "Hurry."

Deep inside, Lincoln knew he should have expected a visit from the pastor. Not only had he run out on Pastor Pike's sermon — a reason for any pastor to come a-callin' — but Lincoln probably needed a visit from the representative of divine holiness. As a man who'd played fast and loose with God's laws for over a decade, Lincoln knew he shouldn't be having the thoughts about Stefanie Noble he was having.

He couldn't believe she'd kissed him. Not that he hadn't been thinking — or hoping — that he might get his arms around her last Friday night, but after he'd told her about his sins, the last thing he'd expected was her arms around him.

He shouldn't have been surprised. Everything about Stefanie spoke of giving and patience and acceptance, from the way she embraced three runaway kids and the gentleness she had with his broken animals to the way she looked at him and the smile she had in her dark, pretty eyes. That little smile produced a feeling inside him he couldn't quite name.

Fear, perhaps? Stefanie now knew him better than any other woman anywhere. In fact, she knew enough about him to really hurt him.

But it wasn't exactly fear. . . . For the first time in . . . well, he knew he'd never felt this kind of alive before. A sort of energy infused with hope, perhaps.

Until, of course, the local clergyman came knocking. Now he just felt dread.

"Mr. Cash?" Pastor Pike stood at the door, lean despite the paunch and stern in a pair of black cowboy boots, pressed dark jeans, a button-front dress shirt, and a long wool jacket. He reminded Lincoln of an Old West sheriff — all he lacked was a six-gun. "Can I come in?"

Lincoln held open the door, wondering if Pastor Pike could sense the fact that Lincoln had held Stefanie in a lingering clinch right here in the foyer only a few days ago before sending her out the door with a container of leftovers Karen had packed up for the kids.

"Sure, Pastor," Lincoln said, shuffling back, hating how this morning, his foot had shown signs of spasticity, sliding instead of lifting as he drew it along the floor. "Take a seat in the family room." He extended his hand, thankful when the pastor walked in front of him.

A pastor wouldn't betray his secrets,

would he?

Secrets that were getting harder to hide.

Thankfully, Stefanie hadn't found him lying in the muck in the middle of his barn yesterday morning, or he'd have some explaining to do. And the fact that he spent most of his time sitting on the sidelines this week had more to do with his increasing fatigue than a desire to let Stefanie do all the work.

He slid his hand from his pocket, tightened it into a fist. His left hand had continued to worsen, and this morning, like before, his vision blurred around the edges. Still, his doctor had been reluctant to put him back on his previous medicine or start him on a round of anything else. Charting his exacerbations, as the doctor called his flare-ups, would help them know how to treat him in the future.

He was his own walking guinea pig. Perfect.

Lincoln perched on the edge of a chair — it was easier to get up that way. He braced himself, much like he might if Dex told him he was cutting a scene or even a role.

Pastor Pike took a deep breath, as if whatever he had to say might be difficult. "Mr. Cash, everyone in town is excited about your plans. I talked to Rolly, and your loan to spruce up his B and B is just what he's been praying for. And I know that although my daughter is in a snarl about Denny McFarland's plans to open a steak house, I for one can't wait for a decent porterhouse." He smiled.

Lincoln's mind went to the steaks left uneaten last Friday night.

"We're all gung ho, but —" Pastor Pike looked out the windows toward the view of the Bighorns — "we've run up against a problem that we thought someone should bring to your attention."

Lincoln didn't move. "Go on."

"It seems there's been a rash of trouble in town these past couple months. Someone broke into the Laundromat and emptied out the quarters from the machines; there's been vandalism at the school — graffiti — and hot-rodding down Main Street that broke a streetlamp; and Frank over at the hardware store said that someone stole a display of lawn art."

Lincoln folded his arms across his chest, tucking in the hand that still trembled. "I'm not sure what this has to do with —"

"Everyone knows that you're friends with the Noble family. Clarisse Finney has threatened to call Social Services about the kids, but I thought . . . well, we were hoping you might just have a conversation with Stefanie."

"You think Gideon is responsible," Lincoln said, barely keeping his voice civil. "You think he's behind the stealing, the vandalism."

Pastor Pike wore a grim expression. "We haven't had this sort of trouble for years." He shook his head. "Frankly, the last troublemaker we had in Phillips was Rafe Noble."

Lincoln hid a smile at this. He knew Rafe well enough to know that Pastor Pike spoke the truth. "It's not Gideon. He's a good kid. Hard worker. And his car is a wreck. I think it's currently rusting away in the Nobles' yard."

The pastor nodded as if he was listening but said, "I think everyone in town would feel a whole lot better if Stefanie sent those kids on their way."

"To where? They don't have anyplace to go —"

Pastor Pike raised a shoulder. Lincoln had the feeling that the shrug contained inferences about his cash flow and a suggestion to share it. Lincoln said nothing — too stymied by not only the pastor's implication that he should shove a wad of cash in the kids' hands and send them down the road to their next gig but also the fact that he'd already done it once, to his great shame.

Pike finally said, "How about calling Social Services? That's what they're there for."

"No." Lincoln found his voice, pulled it out of his shame, felt it build in strength. "I'll tell you what Social Services will do. They'll take those kids and slap Macey in a shelter or a temporary group home. Haley will be sent out to some nice foster family who will want to adopt her, and Gideon might even go to jail for kidnapping. They'll never see each other again."

He remembered the conversation he'd had with Stefanie about losing her mother and her comment about Macey being a lot like her in her love of horses. It occurred to him that perhaps she had more in common with Macey than she let on. He imagined Stefanie at thirteen — long skinny legs, scraggly hair, hiding out in the barn with her horse, trying to cope with the grief of losing a mother. How did a teenage girl survive losing the one person who might help her navigate through life?

No wonder Stefanie had become a pro at handling horses and even the North kids. Nurturing them gave her the chance to experience the nurturing she'd never had from her own mother. As he'd watched her train the foal yesterday, always repeating the reward of the soothing touch, Lincoln ached for the little girl who had lost so much of herself so early.

Everything she'd done to protect the North kids — including her claws-out reaction when he'd accused Gideon of starting the fire — made perfect sense. Because she knew exactly how it felt to be alone.

And he wasn't going to let her go through that again.

"No, Pastor, I won't talk to Stefanie about giving up her kids."

"They're not her kids." The pastor spoke quietly. "They're runaways, and they don't belong in Phillips."

Then Lincoln might not belong in Phillips either. The words were nearly on his lips. But from the distance, the sound of a Skilsaw and hammering filtered into the house as his crew finished the inside of his movie theater. Next week the electrical equipment would arrive, and after that, the interior, the seating.

And just this morning, he'd started to believe that he might pull this off. The festival, hiding his MS, and even having Stefanie Noble as a permanent fixture in his life.

Pastor Pike must have sensed his indecision — apparently Lincoln had lost the ability to conceal his emotions. The pastor stood and held out his hand. "I think, if you mull on it for a while, you'll see that this is the best option for all of us."

Lincoln never thought he'd see the day when a man of the cloth threatened him, but as Pike held out his hand, that's exactly what Lincoln saw in the gesture. *Help . . . or we don't help you.*

The feeling left him hollow as he showed Pike to the door.

CHAPTER 13

This couldn't be happening again. Stefanie sat in her truck, outside the home of the make-do vet's office in Phillips.

Poisoned. Clancy had been poisoned. Maybe in his food, the vet said, although with the mounds of scraps and other ranch debris the dog snacked on, who knew? Besides, all of Stefanie's hearing had been cut off after Clancy's heart had stopped.

Thankfully, Piper had taken Macey and Haley back to the ranch hours ago, before they could watch Clancy suffer.

Someone had *poisoned* their dog. Stefanie cupped her hands over her face, pushing the heels into her eyes, fighting to hold back the tears, but it didn't matter.

Someone had killed their dog. And she hadn't been able to do a thing about it. Hadn't even recognized it. How long had Clancy been sick? If she'd stayed in school, become the veterinarian she'd hoped to be, then maybe . . . well, maybe she would have seen the signs. Could have saved Clancy.

And Sunny.

And her dreams.

Maybe she wouldn't be stuck on a ranch watching life pass her by.

It didn't matter that Clancy hadn't been around for long, that Nick had brought him home from the pound a year ago; she still loved the mongrel Labrador-shepherd mix. His death stirred up the voices she'd kept buried so long.

Quitter. Failure. Nobody.

Then she heard the echo of Macey's words drilling into her brain: *"Lincoln Cash does. He didn't want us here, remember?"*

Lincoln wouldn't hurt her dog, would he? She felt nearly sick as she pressed her hands to her stomach. Why would he? Unless he wanted her to think that perhaps one of the kids had done it. Unless he still wanted Gideon and the kids to leave. . . .

She spun gravel as she backed the pickup out of the lot and onto the dirt road. She could see Lincoln's glowing monstrosity on the hill, a garish display of wealth and arrogance. Dusk had long passed, and twilight hovered on the horizon, backdropping Lincoln's house in a final ta-da. That she hadn't arrived to help him today should have elicited at least a phone call, but of course, Lincoln wasn't about to chase her. After all, he was the movie star, the hot commodity.

All this time had he been lying to her, using her? Maybe not like she'd been lied to and used in college, but using her all the same.

Defender of the Oppressed.

Dances with Horses.

Cash's Leading Lady.

She'd believed these names a little too much. Now they told her who she really was. A fool.

She was just a back-hills girl from eastern Montana. He was probably surprised she could speak in full sentences. Oh, boy, she really had fooled herself. What had she been thinking? She could see the headlines now: "Lincoln Cash's Latest Fling Is a Hick."

She turned into the Big K and floored it up the driveway. The lights from the house fractured the growing darkness, and she saw more light coming from the theater — aka Cathedral to Lincoln Cash — as she drove by.

Braking, she slammed the truck into park, turned it off, and launched herself from the seat. Tears stung her eyes, and she bolted toward the house. Not even bothering to knock, she barreled inside and caught Lincoln in his kitchen, sitting on a stool. He half rose, shock on his face.

"Are you still trying to get rid of Gideon and his sisters? Macey told me that Gideon thinks the pastor is going to ask you to fire him. Is it true? Did Pastor Pike tell you to get rid of Gideon?" She stood there, waiting for an answer, reading it all in his expression.

Lincoln's jaw tightened, and he glanced at Karen. "Let's talk in my office." He reached for her, but she yanked away from him. She must have been a little more forceful than she'd thought because he fell forward, catching himself on a chair. But he deserved it, the jerk, the arrogant, two-faced —

"Yes, Pike was here. And, yes, he asked me to get rid of Gideon." Lincoln's voice emerged in a low growl. He seemed to be breathing harder than her slight expression of violence merited. He spoke through gritted teeth. "Can we please go into my office?"

"No!" Stefanie whirled, intending to make an escape before she heard one more suave Lincoln Cash word. "I don't want to talk to —"

His arm curled around her again, a grip that seemed more desperate than strong. "Please, Karen, will you excuse us?"

Karen turned off the heat for whatever she stirred on the stove and walked away.

Stefanie waited until she was out of the room, then rounded on Lincoln, her emotions catching up to her, hot and full. "You . . . lied to me. I can't believe I fell for it again, this hypnotic Lincoln charm that makes a girl believe in —"

"What did I do?"

"And to think I thought it was real, that you really liked me."

"I do really like you!"

He had both his hands on her arms now, and she hit him hard in the chest. For such a tough guy, he winced, but it didn't remotely match the pain in her chest.

"Stef, stop it!"

She broke away from him again with a little shove. This time he went down, catching his chin on the edge of the chair.

She stared in horror as he landed on the floor, blood spurting from his cut chin. He clamped a hand over it and closed his eyes.

The air went out of her anger. "Linc— oh, I'm sorry. I didn't mean —"

"Forget it." He grabbed the chair, using it to pull himself off the floor, still holding his chin. She watched as he limped over to the sink — wow, she'd really hurt him — and pressed a wet towel against his chin.

Everything inside her grew cold. "I'm sorry."

Lincoln held up a hand, turning away from her. She watched his wide back, those strong shoulders rising and falling as he gazed out into the darkness. She could see his reflection in the window, and something about his expression scared her. Resignation. Even . . . regret?

What if . . . what if she was right? What if he *didn't* want her? She had come here hoping he'd deny her accusations, but seeing the look on his face, as if he'd made a colossal mistake letting her into his life . . .

She moved around the counter and stood beside him, putting her hand on his strong arm. "Someone poisoned my dog."

He glanced down at her, and what seemed like real concern filled his eyes. But he said nothing.

"I thought . . . well, Macey said that some people in town wanted to get rid of Gideon and that you might do it." Stefanie put her hand on her head. "I'm sorry. I don't know what I was thinking. I guess I just let my fears run away with my brain. I thought . . ." She couldn't tell him what she thought. Couldn't admit that an old shame had swept over her, and her anger at herself had combined with her grief to cause her to ac-

276

cuse Lincoln of something she knew he'd never do.

Lincoln's expression softened. "Thought what?"

She bent her head and, to her horror, began to sob. Loud, unbecoming sobs. She turned but felt Lincoln's arm around her shoulder, pulling her back to him.

His face came near hers. "Shh. Thought what?"

"I gotta go." Her voice sounded as if it might be caught in a vise. More than anything she wanted to stay. Needed to stay.

Stefanie bowed her head and felt Lincoln's lips on her hair. Then he took her hand and led her to the sofa in the family room, settling her down beside him, turning her so that she nestled in his arms.

"Okay, Slugger, now that I'm not going to hit any sharp objects, go ahead and unload."

She turned into his chest and let herself cry.

Gideon sat in his beat-up clunker and called himself a fool. Everything inside him hurt — his bones, his eyes, especially his heart — as he watched Libby serve the last of the patrons in the diner. He'd fixed his car a couple of days ago — the only decent skill his father had ever taught him — using the money he'd earned from Lincoln. He'd spent the last two nights sitting outside Lolly's Diner, trying to scrounge up the courage to ask Libby what he'd done to make her angry.

With Libby, for the first time, he felt like someone . . . worthwhile. If a girl like Libby could like him, could see that he wasn't the guy everyone labeled him, then maybe he didn't have to live with those labels.

But in the end, she didn't want him either.

He could see her through the glass, wearing a brown shirt to match her hair, and his chest clenched as she smiled at Luther and JB. That Luther was trouble. Thanks to his father, Gideon could spot a guy who wouldn't hesitate to beat a woman. When Luther began making rude comments about Libby at the work site, it had taken everything inside Gideon not to go after the man with a nail gun. He'd thought, when Luther got fired, that maybe he and Libby had escaped him, until JB mentioned that they'd been hanging out at the diner. Probably just to torment Gideon, but it had all his protective instincts firing.

He'd just sit in the car and make sure that Libby got home okay. Every night, if he had to.

Libby had braided her hair tonight, two

pokey braids that stuck out from behind her ears. And her smile — she put everything into her smile, her eyes, her posture. He ached for that smile.

He could even imagine her laughter. He fought the swell of envy, focusing on the sound of her giggle in his memory, the way it had made him feel as if he were soaring.

Thirty minutes later, he watched as Libby finished serving Luther and JB, then began to close for the night. JB strutted out to his truck and roared away. Luther sauntered over to the Buffalo Saloon.

Gideon kept an eye on the saloon as Libby turned off the Open sign, mopped the floor, flipped off the lights, and disappeared into the back room.

Moments later, he saw her appear outside in the alley. She had her sweater wrapped around her, and now, instead of getting into a car, she strolled down the street in the direction of the church and the parsonage. It being a cool night and a short stroll, Gideon imagined that she'd walked to work.

He intended to wait until she was down a block to turn on his car. To his shock, she crossed the street right toward him, opened his door, and slid inside.

His heart, his breath, stopped right there as she turned to him, a soft smile on her face. "Stalking me?"

Gideon barely managed a nod.

She laughed. "I saw you out here last night too. Why don't you come in?"

He gripped the steering wheel, everything inside him going still. Why had he thought she couldn't take care of herself? Apparently Libby had no qualms about walking home late at night. He'd been overreacting, of course.

"I'm sorry. . . . I was just worried." He made a face. "Sometimes some of the guys at the work site say things. . . ."

"They're guys." She shrugged. "I'm used to cowboys."

This kind of talk could hardly be limited to cowboys, but Gideon said nothing.

"But you're very sweet," Libby said with that entire-body smile.

Great. Just what he'd hoped to be. Sweet. "I'll drive you home." He reached to start the car.

But she put a hand on his arm. "No, you can't do that." Her voice held a hint of sadness. "My dad —"

"He doesn't like me."

"He doesn't know you."

"Maybe if he got —"

She put her hand on his mouth. "Shh." As he watched, frozen, she leaned over and, taking his hand from the steering wheel, put it on her waist. Then, because he still couldn't move, she kissed him. Softly. Perfectly.

He wanted to pull her to himself and touch those cute braids and kiss her like he'd been dreaming of kissing her since that day in the diner, but something inside him held him back.

Maybe it was her hand on his chest, exerting just enough pressure to warn him off. Or maybe it was the way her other hand held his, not letting it roam. Or perhaps the innocence in her eyes as she backed away from him.

"That was just to let you know that it's not you, Gideon."

What wasn't him? That she couldn't see him? Because it *felt* like him. If he was some hick cowboy who had grown up in this town, her father would let her see him. Then the pastor wouldn't even blink an eye about him driving up to her house, knocking on the front door, and picking her up for a date, would he? Gideon tried to deny the taste of resentment in his throat, but he couldn't swallow it away.

Libby touched his face. "I miss you too."

He looked away from her, out the window. "It's not the right timing. I'm going away to college in the fall — to be a missionary. And my dad's right. It's not fair to either of us to let our feelings spiral out of control."

Oh, his emotions had already run off into the hills. He hadn't a prayer of getting them under control. "That's no big deal."

His words wounded her — he could tell by the way she frowned — but she recovered quickly and nodded. "Yeah . . . no big deal." She'd seen right through him.

He took her hand and kissed it. "I'm going to make sure you get home okay."

"I figured." Libby slid out of the car, slammed the door, and headed down the street toward the lit church and tiny parsonage. But every few feet, she'd look over her shoulder and smile.

CHAPTER 14

After everything else he'd done to make God mad, Lincoln wondered why he hadn't ended up as a pile of ash right there on the sidewalk in Phillips. Because, any way he looked at it, he'd threatened the pastor.

And meant it.

"I want a list of everyone who wants Gideon out of town." Lincoln had stood at the door of the parsonage, the motor of his pickup still running, one arm braced on the doorframe as Pastor Pike stared at him. He'd gone there after tossing the night away, remembering how Stefanie cried in his arms. It burned a hole right through him.

Lincoln wasn't exactly sure what had happened to him last night, as he'd held a rag to his bleeding chin, terrified that Stefanie had seen him stumble, had discovered his secret, only to have her turn into his arms and sob, but he'd felt something shift inside him.

A feeling of tenderness that he hadn't known for years.

Maybe never.

She'd sobbed long and hard, and he saw her embarrassment in her eyes as she pulled away. She touched his wounded chin, and it was then, *right then,* that he nearly told her. Nearly confessed that it wasn't her fault he'd fallen. That in fact, he wasn't the man she supposed him to be but someone who wasn't a hero, someone who had nothing but frustration ahead of him. But the words glued to his chest. She wasn't in the mood to talk either, so he simply drew her close and turned down the lights, used his remote control to turn on some country music, and watched the stars through his giant windows.

He had a feeling her tears had to do with the more gargantuan losses in her life than just Clancy, but the fact that someone had killed her dog made the boy inside Lincoln who had once been weak and small rise up in fury. Someone had gone too far. Someone mean and vindictive.

That injustice had driven Lincoln to the door of the pastor at nine this morning, demanding a list of suspects.

"Excuse me?" Pike retorted. Attired in a

friendly sweater and suit pants, with his perfect pastor smile, the close-cropped hair, looking proper and upright, he didn't resemble in the least the kind of man who had leveled a threat at Lincoln only a day earlier.

"You know what I'm talking about." Lincoln opened the screen door and barged in. He took off his sunglasses and rounded on the pastor, spotting a curtain fall from one of the windows in the bungalow across the street.

"Please, come in," Pastor Pike's voice said, even if his body stayed near the door.

"I want to know who killed Stefanie Noble's dog."

The pastor shook his head, and Lincoln had the crazy urge to knock it right off his shoulders. But that would only compound his crimes with the Almighty, wouldn't it? Moreover, he wasn't entirely sure that he wouldn't be run out of town if he decked the local cloth.

"Maybe you should try looking closer to home."

"Gideon would never hurt Stefanie —"

"I'm not talking about Gideon, although I wouldn't put it past him." Pike strode over to a sofa, where last Sunday's newspaper lay in a mess. The entire little house looked like it had been caught in a time warp, stuck in the early seventies. Green shag carpet that smelled as if it might have grown there ran through the family room and up the stairs. Family pictures of two little girls and an adoring wife — the ideal family — patterned the wall, and a milk-glass vase with faux flowers sat on the scratched coffee table. A macramé pillow, in the same shade of green as the carpet, decorated the sagging gold sofa.

The entire scene conjured up memories of Lincoln's trailer home back in Dallas. He could almost hear his mother calling him inside for dinner.

"I'm talking about this blast from your past, Mr. Cash." Pastor Pike thrust a section of the newspaper at Lincoln. "Maybe it's you we should be asking to leave."

What? Lincoln looked at the page that had been turned open to the entertainment news. The Hollywood rap sheet listed the various misdemeanors.

"Middle of the page, halfway down."

Oh. Gina Burney was out of jail. The same Gina Burney who had broken the restraining order Lincoln had taken out against her one too many times and who had been in county lockup for the last six months. The same woman who had tried to run him off the road and set his mailbox on fire. The woman who had once, not so long ago, been an extra on one of his movies, with whom he had had a brief fling.

She probably had good reasons for never forgiving him. He tasted acid in the back of his throat. "Gina Burney is out of jail."

"Mmm-hmm. Not that I keep track of your life, Lincoln, but that little gem in last week's paper made me wonder exactly what someone might do to get close to you. Or hurt those who are."

Lincoln folded the paper. It would have been nice if his agent had let him know that the woman who had once told him she would make sure he never hurt another woman — and then gone into vivid detail as to how she would prevent that — had been released. He hoped his restraining order crossed state lines.

"Gina is a sick woman, but she wouldn't come to Montana. Besides, she's been getting help." Some of which he'd anonymously paid for. Because he'd never felt right about the way he'd treated her. Had he known ten years ago that the sins he committed might haunt him, he might have lived for wisdom and not pleasure. "Why would she come all the way to Montana, get into my life again, when she could start over?"

"Maybe she knows something we don't." Pike stood there, a pillar of righteousness, of judgment.

Lincoln simply . . . well, lost it. "This isn't my fault. And it's not Gideon's fault. I want you to find out who poisoned Stefanie's dog."

"What do you want me to do? Resurrect the inquisition? Maybe build a pyre in the middle of Main Street?"

Wow. Pastor Pike had more spur in him than Lincoln expected. Well, so did Lincoln. "If that's what it takes. Start with Clarisse Finney."

"Clarisse?"

"Yes, Clarisse and her history of killing animals, namely Dugan's junkyard dog."

"How'd you hear that?"

"Interesting what a guy picks up sitting at Lolly's for hours on end. I know more about the people in this town than you'd think." His eyes traveled to the pictures on the wall, and his voice dropped a notch. "I was sorry to hear about your wife."

Pike took a step back, the air out of his sails. "Thank you." For a moment he stared at Lincoln, a mix of strange emotions flitting across his face. "Clarisse is an interesting lady, but she's not a killer. She's our resident hippie, has a strange mix of beliefs, from New Age mysticism to a Baptist-style upbringing. Makes wind chimes and sells them on the Internet. On a windy day, you can hear them all the way down Main Street. She's got the morals of a saloon girl and the mouth of an outlaw, but I don't think she'd kill a dog."

"I heard she told the sheriff that she suspected Gideon of stealing from the Laundromat. I'm thinking that's where you got your suspicions. Way to assume the best about people, *Pastor*."

Pike actually turned ashen as Lincoln watched the last of the fight go out of him.

"Maybe I shouldn't have jumped to conclusions, but . . . well, you know kids who come from the inner city. They've got a rough side —"

"Yeah, I do, actually, and Gideon is the last person who would kill Stefanie's dog. He loves the Noble family. After what they've done for him, after giving him a chance and believing in him, he's not going to wreck that by betraying them."

"I know Gideon might be a perfectly nice —"

"Spare me. You don't think that for a second. You see his long hair and pierced ear and rusty wheels and instantly peg him as a kid who will get your daughter in

289

trouble, which, by the way, doesn't say much for her judgment."

"I admit it's easy to give grace to people when it doesn't affect your life. But try doing it when it means you have to trust them with something or someone who means more to you . . ." Pike sighed, running his hand over his forehead. "Okay, so maybe I shouldn't have let my fears do my speaking for me. I'm sorry I . . . uh . . ."

"Threatened me?" Lincoln let the words be sharper than he meant.

He could see argument rise in Pike's eyes. Then the man nodded.

"Listen — just find out who killed the dog, okay? And stop blaming me and my friends." Lincoln turned to leave, then rounded on the pastor one final time, saying what he should have said yesterday, when he'd been too shocked to respond. "In case you're wondering, no, I'm not asking Gideon to leave town. Frankly, I think Libby could do worse." He crunched the newspaper in his hand. "I'm keeping this."

Lincoln stormed back to his pickup, anger churning inside, feeling so helpless he wanted to scream. He threw the crumpled paper on the seat, grabbing the steering wheel with both hands.

What was Gina doing out of jail?

And could she have found him?

"You're pretty. Like my mom." Macey stood at the door, wearing a short-sleeved shirt and a pair of jeans. Stefanie noticed that she'd stopped working so hard to hide her arms, and the few times she'd rolled up her sleeves, Stefanie saw no new marks. It made her want to sing.

Stefanie stood in the bathroom, blow-drying her hair. Thanks to a miscalculation about one of her new quarter horses, she'd taken a painful spill into the dirt, smearing mud into her hair and down her chin. Although she slept up at the hunting cabin, she'd left most of her wardrobe back at the house.

Most of the time she didn't know where she belonged anyway. Or even who she was.

For the first time in years, she'd rushed a horse, made him skittish. Scared him. All because she couldn't get her brain off last night. And the way she'd hidden in Lincoln's arms.

She couldn't believe she'd nearly dragged Lincoln right into her past, her mistakes, her broken places. She didn't realize she was there, back in the shame of her freshman year in college, until the words had tumbled out and suddenly she'd teetered on the cusp of letting him inside, letting him see her wounds.

But after her tough-girl act last night — and she had to admit liking her newest nickname, Slugger — she couldn't bear to let Lincoln know how much he meant to her. Or after he'd held her like he did, that she'd actually thought he was just using her.

She'd managed to keep her wits about her. Lincoln did have great arms, though. Big enough, it seemed, for her grief.

But now, it seemed that in becoming whoever she was in his eyes, she'd confused the woman she'd always been.

She flipped her hair back, staring at herself in the mirror as Macey came in and sat down on the closed toilet seat. "My mom had long black hair like yours, only she wasn't quite as skinny."

Stefanie supposed, in girlspeak, this might be a compliment. But as she ran the blower under her hair, she couldn't help but compare her figure with the ones Lincoln usually spent his time with. She certainly didn't have leading-lady curves like his most recent costar, Elise Fontaine.

But Lincoln hadn't been holding Elise Fontaine in his arms last night, had he?

She refused to listen to the voice that told her he was just bored and used to having a woman in his life, even if he had to troll the local horse barns to get her.

"Gideon told me your mother died. I'm so sorry," Stefanie said, glancing in the mirror as Macey chewed her fingernails down past the quick. She remembered a not-so-long-ago time when she'd done the same thing. "My mom died when I was about your age too. I still really miss her."

Macey nodded, chewing a hangnail. "She worked as a waitress. But she loved horses. Had pictures of them up on the walls of our trailer. Sometimes she would crawl in bed with me at night and tell me stories of growing up on her ranch."

"Your mom grew up on a ranch?"

"Yeah, in South Dakota. Until she met my dad. He was a builder and worked construction. They traveled a lot, went where he could find work. Until he got injured. Then we just stayed in Rapid City."

"Gideon didn't mention your dad."

Macey shrugged. "He's in jail. For life. Robbed a liquor store and killed someone."

Stefanie suspected there was more to that story . . . as with every story. But she finger-combed her hair and didn't press.

Macey rested her chin on her knees, her voice dropping. "He was pretty rough on Gideon."

Stefanie held back a wince.

"The thing is, with Gideon around, Dad mostly went after him. Not Mom or me or Haley."

How awful to feel safer because someone else was getting the blame. However, hadn't Stefanie felt some relief when her father focused on Nick's absence and worried over Rafe's career? With his attention on her brothers, he couldn't ask the hard questions: Why his only daughter had quit school halfway through her freshman year. Why she'd returned to the ranch, thrown her life into training rescued horses and running cattle. Why she hadn't followed her dreams of being a veterinarian. For a long time, she didn't care that he didn't inquire . . . just felt glad she could hide. After a while, especially when he'd gotten so sick, the questions didn't matter anymore.

"Gideon says that we can start over here." Macey looked up at her as if waiting for confirmation.

Stefanie sat on the edge of the tub. "My dad used to say that you have a new chance to change your world every day. It's actually a verse in the Bible — Lamentations 3:23. God's mercies are new every morning." She took Macey's hand. "Hey, how about we put some nail polish on."

Macey shrugged.

Stefanie hadn't worn nail polish in years . . . maybe since she'd been Macey's age. But she must have picked up a bottle along the way because she found some bright pink polish in the bottom of the drawer. She shook the bottle, raising one eyebrow.

Macey put down her knees and held out her ravaged fingers. "I'm really sorry about Clancy," she said as Stefanie put on the polish. "Do you think someone did it because of us?"

Stefanie didn't answer right away. She wasn't even going to think those thoughts — or at least, had been trying not to. But the fact that someone might come after their family because of . . . what? Fear? Prejudice? It made everything inside her coil in fury. "It doesn't matter. You and your family are staying."

Macey remained silent for a moment as she watched Stefanie brush on the polish. The smell filled the tiny bathroom.

"I never thought Gideon would actually come for us." She spoke so quietly that Stefanie practically held her breath to hear her. "I wrote to him over and over, and I couldn't believe he actually came to the home to get us, like I asked him to."

"Gideon's a pretty great brother."

"It wasn't his fault — what happened. He didn't do it."

Stefanie blew on the first hand.

"He hadn't even wanted to boost that car. But his friends did it, and he got dragged along."

Stefanie stilled. She hadn't heard the entire story, just bits and pieces from Gideon — like the fact that he'd been in juvenile lockup. She'd spent more time focusing on who he was now. She didn't look at Macey as she took her other hand, straightening out her fingers. "People do things they regret when they want someone to like them." She ran her finger over Macey's chewed nails. "Or when they're hurting."

Then she dipped the small brush in the polish and began to paint them. "Let them grow, and in no time, they'll be healed."

Macey lifted her fingers and blew on them. She looked at Stefanie and smiled. "Yeah, you're a lot like my mom."

Stefanie wasn't sure why, but the words found tender places she didn't know existed. She finished a second layer on Macey's fingers. "Beautiful."

Macey rolled her eyes. "I'm not really a pink girl," she said, though something in her voice suggested otherwise. "But thanks."

She got up, blowing on her fingers as she left the bathroom.

"People do things they regret when they want someone to like them." Stefanie's own words lingered as she gathered her wet towel, hanging it on the rack. Was she being naive with Lincoln? letting him inside her heart to ravage it, just like . . . just like Doug Carlisle had done so many years ago?

What was it about her that made her fall for the wrong kind of man? the kind of man she so clearly didn't belong with? One look in the mirror, at her straight-as-a-fence-post figure, her lifeless hair, her drab eyes, told her that Lincoln was just playing games with her heart. He'd toss her aside, just like Doug had, when he got bored with her.

She closed her eyes, hating the voices inside that told her — even if they were right — that she didn't deserve a love story.

Not, at least, with a leading man like Lincoln.

God's mercies were new every morning. Except for girls like her.

CHAPTER 15

He was having a Lincoln Cash the Invincible day. He'd started naming his days. Some were weak days, when the fatigue or numbness or dizziness or even his own fears crawled over him. Those were the days he drove the four-wheeler, which he kept parked near the house, down to the work site to direct traffic or over to the corral to watch Stefanie, who spent more and more of her time here, training the animals she'd talked him into buying. She'd showed him how to teach a horse to join up — that miraculous moment when a horse knows you're his friend and will bond with you, follow you everywhere.

He wasn't sure who had joined up with whom, but he had begun to believe that he, too, might follow Stefanie anywhere. He had imagined her smile on him when he'd marched into Pastor Pike's house and told him not to even consider Gideon a suspect.

The North kids weren't the only ones who'd started to feel like they'd finally found a home in Phillips. Until the crumpled Hollywood insider report, Lincoln hadn't given a thought to the tabloids or his agent or even his upcoming movie premiere of *Unshackled*. Dex had left a cryptic message on his voice mail a few days ago mentioning the event, but Lincoln still had a month before he had to make an appearance — however brief.

It felt light-years away.

Which, hopefully, was where Gina the stalker was also. He'd spent roughly three days on the phone with Delia and his other representatives, tracking down Gina and her whereabouts. According to a local PI he'd used a few times, Gina had vanished shortly after she'd walked out of the county jail after serving her time. Which meant she could be anywhere . . . including Phillips, Montana.

Perfect.

Lincoln was trying to forget about Gina and her threats, however, at least for the moment, and focus now on choosing between a springer-spaniel mix and a fuzzy-looking thing he might call a sheepdog. Around him, in the Sheridan pound, dogs of all sizes barked at him, each one fighting for attention, some jumping up and pawing at their cage doors, others simply staring at him with eyes that begged him to take them home. One basset hound lay on the floor, looking up at him with what resembled tears filling his eyes.

Thanks to Stefanie's influence, Lincoln felt despicable for not adopting the entire lot.

He picked the sheepdog and waited while the pound managers cleaned him and updated the animal on shots and papers. The dog — he had to still be a puppy for his friskiness and the way he licked Lincoln's face and neck — had big brown eyes and brown and white stringy fur, not unlike a mop. Lincoln also bought a cage and put the dog inside with about a year's supply of biscuits. He secured the cage beside him on the truck seat.

Lincoln hoped bringing Stefanie a new dog less than a week after her other dog had died wasn't excessive. But he couldn't help it. It seemed that lately everything inside him wanted to make Stefanie smile.

He was a man living on borrowed time. Any moment, this happiness could burst and rain down pain. And he knew this because he had never felt so free, so hopeful . . . so himself.

He'd tucked Lewis Carter so far into the past, mostly because of the memories, but also because Lewis had been the person inside who had wanted a home and a dog and maybe a wife and someday a family. And Lewis came storming right out of hiding when Stefanie looked his way.

Sometimes Lincoln caught himself wondering what it might be like to let her inside his life — really inside, to look at all his weaknesses and even the ugly future before him. But maybe also to wake up to her smile and someday have kids, if the doctors said it would be okay, each one of them with dark hair and matching dark eyes and a smile that could light up his universe.

He put his fingers through the cage, and the dog licked them. "I sure hope she likes you."

The Buckle was quiet when he pulled up, the sun sinking behind the log house. He got out of the truck, leaving the door open, and breathed in the cool near-summer air, smelling the life blooming from the prairie grass, the blossoming hills. He knew that Nick and Cole St. John, with whom Nick ran the Silver Buckle, had held a roundup two weeks ago, so most of the cattle were on a faraway pasture. Still, two large bulls lounged in the field behind the house.

Climbing back into the truck, Lincoln opened the cage and released the squirming dog. He'd also purchased a collar and a leash, which he put on the puppy before letting him down to sniff.

He was negotiating the porch steps when he heard laughter spilling out from the front door. It sounded like Stefanie and perhaps Piper.

"Are you saying you're falling for him?"

"I don't know. Maybe. What's not to love?" Stefanie's voice, full of just enough honesty, stopped Lincoln on the porch. He could barely hear above the sudden rushing of his heartbeat.

"You can't be serious," Nick said. "Aside from the fact that you aren't leaving the ranch and that he'll someday return to his life in Hollywood, he's not a Christian, is he? That thought alone should make you put on the brakes."

Lincoln wasn't a Christian? He thought he was a Christian — hadn't he gone to church when he was a kid? That counted, didn't it? Nick's words made him bristle.

"I'm not sure he *isn't* a Christian. A man doesn't act like he did at church without having something between him and God, even if it might be fractured."

Thank you, Stefanie.

302

Only, her words made Lincoln squirm. He hadn't exactly turned around to confront the feelings Pastor Pike's words had stirred up: *"If we let our situation define us instead of lead us to God, then there is no victory."*

Frankly, considering the source made it that much easier for Lincoln to push the words into the dark recesses of his mind. But even more than that . . . the words frightened him. Because if God was using Lincoln's circumstances to mold him, he just might fold.

"But don't panic," Stefanie was saying. "I'm not saying I love him. I just . . . really like him."

Lincoln looked down at the dog, who had chosen now to piddle on the porch, guilt raking over him for eavesdropping. But he couldn't seem to move, yearning to know . . .

"I've never seen you this happy. I don't want you to get hurt again — especially if he doesn't turn out to be the guy you're hoping for."

Please, let her say that he was her type. That he was exactly the guy she was hoping for. That he'd proven something to her. . . .

And what did Piper mean by the words *get hurt again?*

Did this have anything to do with the

mysterious something Stefanie had mentioned but never elaborated on, the something that had her swinging like Babe Ruth?

Of course, the tattler on the other end of the leash barked, just as Lincoln would have given his right leg or maybe his new pickup to discover Stefanie's answer.

But suddenly it didn't matter because when Stefanie opened the door, those beautiful eyes grew wide, and her hands covered her mouth. She looked up at Lincoln even as she crouched. "Who is this?"

"He's your new dog if you want him."

As if the animal had already confirmed the answer, he leaped into Stefanie's arms. She giggled — a sound that went right to the center of Lincoln's body and warmed him clear through. She carried him into the kitchen, grinning.

Feet pounded down the stairs, and in a moment, Macey had the dog in her arms, laughing as he licked her face. The puppy's entire body wriggled with joy, his tail moving so fast that it caught Haley, who had come down the stairs with Macey, in the face, and even as she blinked, she laughed.

Then the dog turned to Haley and launched. Haley went down, giggling, petting, closing her eyes as the animal bathed her ears, her cheeks, her eyes. "Stop! Stop!"

she said.

The entire room went still. Piper and Stefanie gasped, and even Nick didn't move.

Haley lay on the floor, still giggling, the dog now over her, licking her ear.

Macey wore a look of triumph and grinned at Stefanie. "See, I told you she could talk."

Haley didn't seem to notice that everyone was staring at her, wearing funny faces. She wrapped her arms around the dog and buried her face in the animal's fur.

Stefanie stood and took Lincoln's hand. "What's his name?"

"Bill? You know, sorta because it was a guy named Cash who found him?"

"Bill," she repeated, and something sweet entered her eyes. "I like it." She looked at him, and he knew her words before she spoke them. "You did good, Superhero."

In that moment, he knew for sure that today could only be called a Lincoln Cash the Invincible day.

"I'm not saying I love him. I just . . . really like him."

Those words throbbed in Stefanie's mind as she wrapped her arms around Lincoln's waist and let him drive them over the hills of the Big K. She thought he'd want to explore his land on horseback, but sitting behind him on the four-wheeler made her feel modern and fun, the air in her hair, the motor drowning out words. Not that she needed to talk. Probably she shouldn't.

Lincoln had bought a dog for her yesterday. An adorable dog with brown eyes and curly fur and the tendency to want to sit in her lap and lick her hands. She'd never had such a crazy, extravagant, thoughtful gift in all her life.

Not that men were in the habit of giving her gifts, but . . . a *dog.*

It had made her wish she'd told him exactly what had been on her mind the night he'd split his gorgeous chin open. That she'd been so utterly wrong about him. He wasn't at all like Doug Carlisle, the man who had made her believe in her foolish eighteen-year-old heart that he'd loved her, that he wanted to marry her. That she should give him her body as well as her heart.

Sometimes she still saw Doug on commercials for his family's car dealership branches, paunchier but still dazzling with his blue-eyed, golden-haired, local-boy-turns-star glory.

But his radiance didn't have a prayer of brilliance next to Lincoln's supernova shine.

Which had Stefanie scared to death. Despite the gift of Bill the dog. If her heart didn't watch out, it would fall right out of her chest and into Lincoln's strong arms.

But before she did that — or hopefully before her feelings moved one more inch in the direction of no return — she planned on getting to the bottom of his relationship, or lack thereof, with God. Nick was right: she had no business falling for a guy who didn't share her beliefs. But she couldn't get past the sense that deep inside, Lincoln longed for redemption — and just didn't know how to ask. If she could, she wanted to help him ask.

With the picnic lunch strapped behind her on the four-wheeler, the day had all the makings of romance — in the wind-stirred cirrus clouds, the way the grass greened under the grooming of the sun, the hint of summer in the fragrance of lupine and primrose in the air. The Big K seemed lonely without the cattle, and she noted a couple of fences — especially the ones that bordered Silver Buckle property — that needed mending. Lincoln drove her through gullies and ravines and even over a small jump. A thrill of fear tornadoed in her stomach.

Not unlike the one in her heart. What on

earth was she doing?

They finally stopped at the top of Cutter's Rock, right where it connected to Silver Buckle land. From this vantage point, she could look west to the Bighorn Mountains, or east, where the parallel tire tracks headed toward the homesteaded Noble house. She got off, staring at her land as Lincoln untied the picnic basket.

"My great-grandfather first lived in a house just over that hill," she said, pointing. "An old log cabin."

Lincoln set the basket down and pulled out a blanket. "When I looked at a map of the property, I saw that this place might overlook your property." He peered over the edge of the ridge into the canyon below. "Good thing Dex never saw this. He'd turn it into one of his classic Dex Ditch and Roll escapes."

"What's that?" She grabbed the end of the blanket and helped him lay it out. "Is it painful?"

"Yes, very." When he grinned at her, she felt another swirl in her stomach. "Dex does it in all his movies — I have to jump out of a moving vehicle. Mostly you just launch off, roll, and land in the padding the stunt guys put out."

"Is that how you were nearly killed in your

last movie?"

The look he gave her was immediately shrouded with something unfamiliar and scary. "How did you know about that?"

Stefanie felt a blush press her face and didn't answer, making a note to self to dispose of any magazines before she invited him to the Silver Buckle. Apparently her brain had already invited him inside her life. She fingered the edge of the blanket. "I have a confession to make."

Lincoln looked downright magnificent today in a cream-colored shirt rolled up at the sleeves and a pair of faded jeans and boots. He even wore a cowboy hat over all that blond hair. It seemed a crime for a man to be that handsome. What kind of fairy tale had she landed in?

"Yes?" he asked, kneeling on the blanket and opening the basket.

"I've seen only one Lincoln Cash movie."

"Only one?" He wore the strangest smile, one side quirked up, as if this amused him.

"We don't have any movie theaters around here, so . . ."

He laughed, taking out a cellophane-wrapped sub sandwich. "What kind of movies do you like?"

She shrugged. "Romance. Chick flicks."

He handed her a sandwich. "I've never

been in a chick flick. I tend to do movies that are pure adrenaline. Which means that once you've seen one Lincoln Cash movie, you've seen them all. There're bad guys and lots of explosions, and I always manage to save the girl."

"There's nothing wrong with saving the girl." She smiled. "Besides, I'm sure your movies are great. Maybe you can loan me a DVD. Or better yet, we could try out your new media room."

His smile fell as he pulled out two cans of Diet Coke. "Remember, I don't watch my own movies."

Until now, she hadn't been sure if he had been kidding or not. "Really? I don't understand why not."

Lincoln made a face as if he'd eaten something sour. "I know too much about them to . . . I just don't like it."

"That's crazy. All your hard work and you don't watch them?"

"Nope." He held his soda as if contemplating opening it, then put it down and sat beside her.

She opened hers. "Then here's to us watching one together."

He didn't smile but simply leaned over and kissed her. "Maybe."

Stefanie opened her sandwich. "Karen

310

made these?"

"Yep. I let her have the day off."

"You're lucky that someone would move all the way here from LA to cook for you."

He took a bite of his sandwich. "I found her here — or at least my assistant did. She just showed up looking for a job. I figured she was a local."

"Never seen her before. But I'm sure word leaked that the legendary Lincoln Cash needed help."

Lincoln didn't smile at this, as if she'd somehow hurt him.

"How's Alyssa?"

Lincoln hadn't said anything about his young former neighbor since the night he told Stefanie about the accident, and now the way his head came up and a pained look entered his eyes, she wished — or almost wished — that she hadn't mentioned it.

Finally he sighed and nodded. "Better, I guess. Only, I think the medicine has made her a bit catatonic." He shook his head. "I should go see her, but . . ." He looked out toward the horizon. "I'm not that strong."

"You're one of the strongest guys I know," Stefanie said, realizing that she meant it. And she knew strong men. Her brother Rafe rode bulls for a living, and Nick, like their father, had *bullheaded* written all over him, from his backbone to his attitude. But Lincoln was strong in a different but just as important way — in his determination and his kindness toward Gideon and the horses and in his thoughtfulness and even his dreams for his ranch.

Lincoln sighed. "Actually . . . there's probably something you should know about me."

"It's about church, isn't it?"

He looked at her, confusion streaking through his eyes.

"When you walked out." His broken expression had been bothering her since that day.

He pursed his lips. "You know, in case you were wondering, I do consider myself a Christian. I went to church when I was a kid. I even got baptized. Maybe I've strayed now and then over the years, but I've always tried to do good things. Doesn't that count?"

Stefanie's mind traced back to Nick's words. She didn't mean to make him feel uncomfortable. . . . Well, maybe she did. "It looked like you had something between you and God . . . and if you want, I'll listen."

He considered her a moment. Then he put down his sandwich and wiped his hands, his mouth. "Okay, here's the deal. I asked God for something a long, long time ago."

He picked up his unopened soda can. "And He didn't answer."

"And you haven't asked Him for anything since."

Lincoln tapped the soda on the blanket. "That pastor's sermon, about God disciplining us like He would a son, it just . . . I don't want to talk about it."

Stefanie saw him then, a kid like he'd described, afraid and thin and knocked around by his stepfather, and everything inside her ached. Didn't men know that the way they treated their sons and daughters forever imprinted on them a picture of God, good or bad? It made her profoundly glad to have grown up with a father who loved God and lived it out as best he could.

"Besides, you can only ask God for something so many times before you realize He's not going to give it."

"So you quit asking."

He shrugged.

But she recognized the look. She'd been asking God for something for nearly six years. First, forgiveness. Then, peace. And most recently, contentment.

She touched Lincoln's hand. "I'll tell you what. How about I ask for you, and you ask for me?"

Lincoln stared at her, a smile inching up

his face. "And what do you want from God, Stefanie Noble?"

What did she want from God? It felt like a question she didn't deserve to answer, didn't know how to answer. She had so much — a family, a home, land that spoke to her soul. She had her horses and now the North kids, whom she loved more and more every day. She didn't need more, right?

Him. She wanted him. But she wanted a Lincoln who wanted her just as much. And she wanted a Lincoln who was free of the secrets that hid in the back of his eyes, the ones he thought she didn't notice. But she couldn't say that out loud, could she?

"I want something in my life that is more than cattle and land. I want something meaningful and lasting."

He reached over, wound his fingers through her hair. "Like giving Gideon and his family a home?"

Now how did he know that? The fact that he'd guessed made her wonder just how easily he read her. "A few years ago, I even tried opening a dude ranch, but it didn't work. And last year, Rafe was going to do this fund-raising thing on our ranch. But ever since the North kids arrived, I've seen the ranch in a new way. Maybe . . . Nick would never go for it, but when I was little,

I used to dream of opening a ranch for kids — foster kids or maybe disabled kids. Kids who needed the healing that being around horses and the outdoors brings. Sort of a horse whisperer for kids, maybe."

Lincoln was looking at her in a way that made her body feel as if it might be giving off a glow. "I've loved that idea ever since you mentioned it."

Stefanie could barely swallow, and she looked away. He remembered that?

He put his hand on her cheek. "You should do it."

Oh, brother, now real tears filled her eyes. She wiped them with her hand. "I'm sorry. I don't know why I'm so gooey about this."

Lincoln thumbed away a tear. "I could completely see you being a mom to a bunch of kids, foster or otherwise. You're so patient and giving, and you believe in people."

"I didn't believe in you. I thought you were selfish. And a jerk."

He made a wry face. "Except for that glaring mistake, yes."

"I've decided that you are a nice guy, by the way."

"Oh," he said, lifting her chin, his mouth close to hers. "I'm glad you finally caught on."

He leaned down to kiss her, but suddenly,

well . . . "Linc, you need to know that . . . I'm not . . . I'm not going to . . . you know."

"Huh?"

He was already on the way to stealing her heart — after all, there it was lying right on the checkerboard blanket they were sitting on, ready for him to scoop up — but she couldn't let him walk away with it without knowing the ground rules.

"You know what I'm talking about."

Lincoln stared at her, as if she might be speaking Swahili.

"I'm not the kind of girl you normally . . . date, okay? You need to know that."

"Know . . . what?"

"Listen, I'm not . . . going to do the things that you might normally expect. . . ."

Lincoln stilled, his smile falling, his forehead creasing to a frown.

Stefanie felt an arrow to her gut. Why did he look so confused? "It's just . . . I know that maybe you're used to . . . you know. And it's not like I'm a prude or anything, but I've made some mistakes, and I'm not going to go down that road again."

"Oh?"

It might possibly be that her lungs had simply stopped working. She felt like a fish, gasping for air. But she wanted more from their relationship than whatever Lincoln was

316

used to having.

"I don't know what you think —"

"You just need to know that I've got standards. Rules. Beliefs —"

"Stop." In his tone was something sharp and even hurt. "I can't believe you'd even think that I'd expect —"

"You're a movie star, aren't you?"

"Oh, that's kind." Lincoln backed away from her.

"I didn't mean it like that. It's just that people expect —"

"Promiscuity from movie stars?"

Stefanie met his eyes, finding not humor but the strangest hue of frustration. "You sound like an old-time preacher."

"I told you I went to church when I was a kid." Something stirred in his eyes. "I can't believe you'd think I'd . . . What kind of morals do you think I have?"

She wasn't sure where to begin to answer him, but a burning had started in her gut.

Lincoln held up his hand. "Don't answer that." He sighed, shook his head, and looked away. "I came here to Montana to leave all that behind. I kind of thought I could, with you."

Oh.

Stefanie reached out to him.

But he moved away from her. "Maybe I

317

should take you home."

"I'm sorry. It's just that the last guy I dated, well, he wasn't like you. He . . . had expectations." She felt a burn on her face, the shame of her past roiling through her. "Expectations I wish I hadn't given in to."

Now she wanted to go home.

"I'm sorry."

He took her hand and held it in the silence as the trees collected the breeze, a hawk circled in the sky.

"I was in college. Freshman year. I fell hard for the campus hotshot, a guy named Doug Carlisle. Ironically, he's on television now, in cheesy car dealership commercials." Stefanie desperately needed Lincoln to laugh. Just to get the air flowing between them again.

"See, I knew it. You're a groupie at heart."

She hit him in the chest but took a full breath.

"Careful, Slugger, you have a wicked punch," he said.

"I wasn't a groupie. But I did think he loved me."

All the teasing vanished from his face. "He didn't." It wasn't a question, more of a groan.

Stefanie shivered against the memory of the party after the football game, the cold seat of the car against her back, the icy shame that entered her heart.

"We dated for three months. I was hopelessly in love with him, but he didn't share my feelings. He made reservations for dinner at an expensive hotel. Or at least I thought they were for us. I saw it in his planner, and I assumed — well, I was naive and thought he might be proposing or something. I even bought . . ." She hung her head, but Lincoln's hand cupped her chin, lifting it. "A dress. A golden dress — it was beautiful." She wrinkled her nose. "You know I'm not a dress girl."

"I completely disagree." He ran his finger down the tip of her nose.

Stefanie closed her eyes, fighting a new kind of emotion. "I waited for him to pick me up. I actually called the hotel to confirm, and yes, he was there. I grabbed my own taxi, thinking that I was supposed to meet him there, thinking it was my fault." She didn't want to see what she remembered behind her closed eyes, but now, suddenly, Doug's betrayal didn't feel as sharp, and her shame didn't close in on her like a fist. "He *had* made plans. . . . Except not for us. Or rather, not with me."

Lincoln's thumb trailed down her cheekbone.

She opened her eyes, and to her surprise, he looked wounded. *Please don't let him be acting.*

Something terrible ranged over his face. "Guys can really be jerks." The sorrow in his eyes tightened her throat. "On behalf of all men who have been jerks to you, I apologize."

"Oh, Linc—"

"Let me finish." He swallowed. "I have this incredibly sick feeling that I've behaved like Doug Carlisle in my life, and I want to tell you that I'm sorry. More sorry than you can ever imagine." He turned away as if to gather his emotions.

It hit her then — full-on, like the hooves of a horse but without the bruising, the tearing of cartilage, the breaking of bones — that she could love Lincoln Cash. Really love him, with the kind of love that believed in him and wanted to know him, his dark sides and his joys, his fears and his triumphs. She could love him for his transparency and despite his arrogance, for his gentleness and his strength. She already loved him for the fact that he couldn't watch his own movies and that he took care of Alyssa. And because he'd given her a puppy named Bill.

Mostly because when she was with him, the look in his eyes made her feel beautiful and strong.

Whole.

And wasn't that some sort of miracle? Maybe it wasn't her actions that made her empty but her anger. Her shame.

Her unforgiveness.

Lincoln took her hands in his, ran his thumbs over the tops, saying nothing. As if waiting for her response.

Waiting for her forgiveness. Not that he needed it, but Doug did. Or rather, she needed to give it. Perhaps forgiveness was the first step to ripping the bitter root from her heart.

"I forgive you, Linc, on behalf of all the girls you've hurt."

When he met her gaze, the bleak look in his eyes began to drain.

She smiled.

When he reached for her, his fingers in her hair, she kissed him without hearing one voice from the past calling her names.

After all this time tracking him down, nudging herself into his life, everything had backfired.

She would blame the woman, the one who'd edged her way into his life, thwarting her plans. Didn't Stefanie Noble know that he would only bring her trouble? only destroy everything?

That's what people like him did — lived life without regard for those they hurt. Those whose lives they destroyed.

She watched him every day, her anger festering inside her, rooting, turning every thought into poison. How she wanted him to hurt like she had. How she wanted to turn his life inside out and make him cry out in pain.

She wanted everyone to know it, to feel with her what he'd stolen. To see how his choices had cost her. People — fans — across the world would applaud her for her courage. For her strength. For standing up and taking back her life.

The life he stole.

And as opportunity would have it, she knew exactly how to make it happen.

CHAPTER 16

It was only a matter of time before Lincoln's world imploded. Not only could his private investigator not find Gina, not only had he woken up this morning with invisible weights attached to his arms and legs, and not only had Dex called again last night, wanting to talk to him, but this morning, Nick Noble had appeared, looking like a man with a bone to pick.

Nick had gotten out of his truck, stared at Lincoln's house, then ambled over and stood at the corral, one leg up on the bottom rail, hands dangling over the top rail.

Lincoln figured it was an invitation to join him down at the O.K. Corral. He tried to push the word *showdown* out of his head, but it was right there, thundering as Lincoln pulled on his boots and grabbed his cowboy hat. He sort of sauntered/limped out of the house and rode the four-wheeler down the hill.

Not that Lincoln had anything to feel guilty about. After his picnic with Stefanie two days ago, he'd been feeling like a man with a second chance. A second chance to treat a woman with respect. Until, of course, Nick Noble came around, looking every inch the big brother.

Nick Noble had been born in this rugged country, probably with a rope in one hand and a branding iron in the other. He looked as natural standing there, the worn good-guy white Stetson on his head, as the tumbleweed did rolling across the prairie.

"Hey, Nick," Lincoln said, climbing off his four-wheeler.

Nick regarded Lincoln with a look that might have rattled a lesser man. "I'll get to the point."

Lincoln braced himself. Out here, a man didn't get to the point until after he talked about his cattle and the weather and his new machinery and probably the local politics.

"What are your intentions regarding my sister?"

Oh, boy. Lincoln stood against the fence, watching his horses. Stefanie had taught Gideon how to feed them and let them out for exercise every day. More and more, Lincoln wondered what he'd do without Gideon.

And without Stefanie. She'd crawled into his heart in a way that he hadn't expected. Sure, he'd wanted to earn her respect, maybe even prove he was her kind of man, but he hadn't been prepared for how complete she made him feel. As if he no longer had to be in the room when she was there; he could just enjoy himself, lose himself in her smile. She had a strength about her that made him strong.

Or at least feel strong.

Lincoln swallowed, letting the wind and the beautiful Montana day fill the silence. He'd started to watch the sky like the cowboys, hoping for rain, worried that it might be another drought season.

It seemed that Nick would wait him out.

Lincoln sighed, not sure how to put what Stefanie made him feel into words. "I don't know."

Nick angled a look at him; clearly the answer wasn't what Nick had hoped for.

Lincoln stared down at his boots. "I don't know, okay?"

"Do you love her?"

Lincoln glanced at him, his face twitching.

Nick's face broke into a slow smile. Then he pushed back his hat and laughed. "Okay, that's enough of a yes for me." He shook his head. "In case you're wondering, if she makes you want to be a better guy and you think you might just stop breathing when you're around her and your head won't stop spinning — that feeling there is called love." Nick clapped him on the shoulder. "Just in case you were confused."

Lincoln nodded, not quite sure what to say and wondering how Nick had gotten inside his head.

Nick's smile fell. "But let me be perfectly clear. You hurt her, and I promise you there won't be any stuntmen around to take your fall for you." He flashed Lincoln another smile. "Have a good day."

Lincoln watched him go, a cold knot in his chest.

If Nick's description was right, he just might be falling in love with Stefanie.

But he had to face the truth: his disease most definitely wasn't going to go quietly into the night. Someday, maybe not far away, he might even need help to get out of bed, to get into his wheelchair. To eat.

Yeah, he'd be a real catch for a woman like Stefanie.

Lincoln thought he might be ill. How was he supposed to tell Stefanie that he wasn't at all the man she saw? wasn't anything like the man she expected in her life?

326

"Good morning." Gideon came out of the barn, holding a bucket of grain. "You want me to put the horses into the pasture after I'm done feeding them?"

Lincoln nodded, unable to speak.

Gideon opened the corral gate, went in, and filled the feed trough. Lincoln's herd of horses had begun to heal nicely, their coats starting to glisten in the sunlight. Stefanie had been right — they were beautiful animals. He wished he could ride one, but he knew in his condition that might never be a reality.

Gideon looked like a *Cowboy U* contestant gone wrong this morning with his black hair sticking out of a baseball cap plunked on backwards, and his ancient thermal shirt, worn cowboy boots, and ripped jeans. Still, as he moved through the horses, it seemed he'd inherited Stefanie's magic with them, a gentleness in his touch that seemed to emanate from inside him. With the right environment and a little support, Gideon would turn out just fine.

Lincoln tilted his hat up. "How are things with you and Libby?"

Gideon looked at him. "What do you mean?"

"I thought you two were friends."

"We are, but . . ." He gave a shrug that

327

looked anything but nonchalant.

Lincoln had studied body language enough to read the signs of rejection. "I'm sorry, pal."

Gideon walked toward him, shaking his head. "Naw, we're not right for each other. She's . . . too good for me. Besides, she has big plans for her life. Going off to college this fall."

"What about you — don't you want to go to college?"

"Me?" Gideon laughed. "I didn't even finish high school. Got my GED in jail."

"That counts."

Gideon came out of the corral and closed the gate. "Yeah, well, I got my sisters to look after."

"What if you had someone else to look after them? What if they were cared for and safe?"

"I don't know."

"Don't you ever dream of doing anything with your life? What do you want to be?" Lincoln saw hesitation in Gideon's posture and leaped for it. "What, Gideon?"

"I . . . sorta started thinking about being a vet."

"You'd make a killer vet — no pun intended."

Gideon's blue eyes shone up at him.

"See, you could very well be college material. And I think you should tell Libby that."

"No, I'm bad news for her."

Lincoln frowned. "What do you mean by that?"

Gideon started to turn away, but Lincoln grabbed his arm. It cost him and he nearly fell. He made a grab for the rail. Gideon gave him a funny look.

"What do you mean you're bad news?" Lincoln repeated, hoping to deflect Gideon's curiosity.

"I'm not . . . in her league. I'm not her type."

"Is that what she said?"

Gideon pursed his lips, as if Lincoln had pried from him his darkest secret.

"Don't you think she should have the right to decide that?"

Gideon shook his head and moved away, clearly already having made up his mind.

But Lincoln's own words thumped inside him all day, like an old rap song. Didn't Stefanie have the right to decide how she felt about his disease?

He spent the day in his office, sorting through the movie scripts piling up on his desk. A number of them caught his attention, even rattled him. Like the film script titled *The Last Ride.* It began at the moment a man died and unwound all the way back to the place where his life had started to derail. It illustrated the passion of a life driven by desperation. However, the dark ending — or rather beginning — unnerved him.

Lincoln easily remembered the day his life had derailed and, more recently, the moment with Stefanie when he thought he heard it clicking back into place.

He set the script aside and picked up another one.

"Finding any good ones?" He had his door open and was surprised to see Karen standing at the door, a basket of his laundry on her hip. She had her hair up, and when she wore it high, with wisps curling around her face, she looked much younger than her thirty-plus years that Lincoln imagined. But of course, Lincoln didn't ask. The few times he tried to inquire about her life, her family, she'd retreated into silence, and he wasn't so thickheaded that he couldn't figure out that she wasn't the chatty type.

"A few. There's a lot of talent out there."

"I've always wanted to write a screenplay, maybe be a filmmaker."

He thumbed through the pages of the screenplay in front of him. "Why don't you try it? You never know what you can do if you don't give it a shot."

His words seemed to encourage her, and she smiled. "By the way, I found this on your office floor. I wasn't sure if it was something you needed." She held up a piece of paper. Lincoln recognized it as the aerial map of the Big K he'd copied before he took Stefanie on the picnic. "No, I have others. Thanks."

"Could I keep it? Just in case I might want to go exploring someday, if that's okay?"

Lincoln nodded, and as Karen left, he looked back down at the script in his hand. It pulled him in, but he decided it was more of a Hallmark movie than a Lincoln Cash project. He became so absorbed that he didn't notice how the shadows edged the room. His attention was jerked away when he heard what sounded like a gunshot.

He was on his feet faster than he would've thought possible. No, not a gunshot. A backfire. Lincoln looked out his window and spotted Gideon standing under the open hood of his car. The kid didn't look happy.

Shadows ringed the hall; the kitchen was dark. Either Karen had already prepared his dinner and put it in the refrigerator or he was flying solo tonight. The smallest itch of irritation nudged him as he flung open the door and limped outside.

Lincoln motored down the hill on his four-wheeler and stopped beside Gideon's car. "What's up?"

"I think the distributor cap is cracked."

"Will it start?"

Gideon shut the hood and wiped his hands on his jeans. "I guess I'm walking home."

"I'll give you a lift," Lincoln said. "My keys are in my truck."

But the truck wouldn't turn over. It gave the smallest rev of life but refused to catch.

"Sounds like your battery's dead," Gideon said, jumping out.

"This is a brand-new truck." Lincoln popped the hood, but aside from knowing how to hotwire a car from his days in Dallas, he was about as useless under the hood as a monkey with a socket wrench.

"Everything looks fine to me," Gideon said, staring into the tangle of hoses. He closed the hood. "Thanks anyway."

"We'll take the four-wheeler," Lincoln said. "Hop on the back."

Gideon sat behind him, holding on to the back of the seat. The sun had fallen to the edge of the western rim, the slightest sizzle of heat remaining in the day. Shadows washed the gullies, darkened the grassland as Lincoln drove Gideon to the Silver Buckle. He flipped on his light as night crested over them, the hum of the motor drowning out any conversation.

When headlights appeared behind him, Lincoln moved to one side, giving the car berth. It passed them, kicking up dirt.

Lincoln was pulling back to the middle when he heard, rather than saw, the next vehicle. He glanced behind him.

A truck. He edged over, but the vehicle followed. Lincoln lifted his arm, waving at the vehicle to pass.

He heard the truck accelerate a second before it slammed into the four-wheeler. What — ?

The machine skidded toward the ditch as Lincoln squeezed the brakes.

The truck hit him again. Lincoln had a second of instinct as the machine hurtled into the gully on the side of the road. "Jump, Gideon!" He sprang off the careening machine, tucked, and landed in the grass.

For a long moment Lincoln lay there, breathing hard, listening to his heartbeat in his chest. Had someone really just tried to run them off the road?

The four-wheeler lay upended in the ditch, motor running.

Gideon. Lincoln opened his mouth to call the boy's name, but he couldn't move. It was as if his limbs had been staked to the ground, and a blinding pain moved up his arms, his legs. Something unseen now weighted his chest. He couldn't . . . breathe. Couldn't . . .

Gideon!

Darkness splintered his vision.

Help!

This could not be happening again. Gideon staggered to his feet, trying to orient himself, blinking back the strobes of white light that cut through his eyes.

The world spun and he felt woozy. He bent over, holding his pounding head in his hands.

Something hummed right behind his ears, hurting. He sank to his knees in the cool grass. His hands felt wet and he wiped them on his pants.

The four-wheeler. A pickup . . .

"Lincoln!" Gideon scrabbled along the ditch, separating shadow from fear. The machine lay upside down, the motor still running. Gideon stumbled past it.

Lincoln's body was jerking, ferocious and violent, thrashing and thumping on the ground.

Gideon stood over him, panic slicing off his breath. "Oh . . . uh . . ." He held his hands out, trying to remember what they said in school about seizures. *Put a pencil in his mouth — no, no pencil. Hold him down . . . or a pillow?* Gideon shucked off his thermal shirt and tried to shove it under Lincoln's head. He stepped back.

And then, because he didn't know what else to do, because inside he knew that somehow he'd be blamed again, because he'd tried so hard to make everything right and now it had all gone horribly wrong, he ran.

Lights were on at the Silver Buckle. He raced for the house with everything inside him. Ran until his breath scorched his lungs, until his legs turned to rubber, until his eyes started to tear. Ran from the old fear that had, despite his dodging, despite his hard work, found him.

Gideon burst into the house. "Help!" He braced his hands on the kitchen table, hauling in breaths.

Piper and Nick were in the kitchen, and Nick bounded to his feet.

"Lincoln . . . he . . . accident . . . hurt . . ." Gideon backed toward the door, beckoning Nick to follow him outside.

Nick grabbed Gideon by the arm as he

reached the porch.

Gideon harbored a healthy fear of Nick, not because he'd been unkind but because everything that shimmered off Nick screamed *protector,* and he just reminded Gideon too much of a prison guard. Now he froze.

"You're bleeding, kid."

For the first time, Gideon looked at his hands. Blood pressed into the creases, the pores. His knees went out from under him.

"Piper, bring a towel!"

Gideon's head started to spin. He reached for the porch rail and missed.

Nick caught him. "Take it easy." He grabbed the towel from Piper's hand and pressed it against Gideon's forehead.

The urge to throw up rushed over Gideon. He groaned.

"Stay here," Nick told him, then motioned for Piper to hold the towel. "I'll find Lincoln."

"Wait. Lincoln's hurt. He's having a seizure or something. Call 911."

Phillips was a town of pickups. Everyone worth his salt owned at least a half-ton, usually a Ford. Which meant that, according to Gideon's description, almost everyone could be a suspect, even if they narrowed it down to a dark-colored pickup — a description that Nick the former cop challenged out of the gate, thanks to the starless night.

It didn't help that Lincoln had decided not to report the attack. Stefanie couldn't decide if that frustrated her or made her profoundly grateful. Any attention on Gideon would only alert Social Services and fracture the delicate peace they'd all found at the Silver Buckle.

But it didn't stop Stefanie from doing some sleuthing on her own. She decided it might be better to start with a narrower approach — a list of candidates who might want to hurt Lincoln.

Barring the nonfans she'd found on the Internet — mainly men who were tired of the macho persona and told him to get a life — Stefanie racked her brain for someone closer to home who might want to hurt him.

She'd scraped up only one name and felt sick for even thinking it. But JB Denton did have a pickup, a mean streak, and an old-fashioned way of thinking that said Stefanie was his girl. Could she have been the cause of Gideon's cut and Lincoln's concussion?

Thankfully, by the time Nick had arrived on the scene, Lincoln had been sitting up — disoriented, yes, but aware of his surroundings. He'd called his own doctor, who'd flown in from Hollywood, and then he'd barricaded himself in his ranch.

Now Lincoln had been avoiding Stefanie for over a week. She knew it was personal because Gideon had no problem getting through those electric gates he'd installed at the foot of his drive. Maybe Lincoln had given him the code. However, every time she called to request entrance, his housekeeper/pit bull, Karen, told Stefanie he was resting.

Resting, her eye. Avoiding her, more like. Stefanie tried to tell herself that it was about the accident and not because he'd been offended by her assumptions at the picnic, that he'd expected more from her than she would give. But it felt like something had changed between them.

At the time, she'd thought it was a good change.

Apparently she read people a whole lot worse than she read horses.

But Stefanie hadn't been born with even the tiniest amount of quit in her. Even if it got her kicked in the teeth and despite her inner flagman warning her off, she'd finally had it.

The sun seemed to agree with everyone but her this morning, hiding behind a wash of clouds that in every other state would hint at rain. Coward.

Gideon had been using her truck to drive back and forth to the Big K, but today Stefanie waited until he had finished his cereal before she grabbed her keys off the hook and marched out to the porch. Gideon said nothing as she led the way to the truck, but just to save on trouble, she gave him a just-try-and-stop-me look as she scooted in behind the wheel.

This morning, Gideon had tied a bandanna over his head instead of wearing his baseball cap. He was starting to get a farmer's tan on his arms and today wore a short-sleeved shirt with a GetRowdy emblem on the front — one that Rafe had left behind.

Gideon had said little since the accident — other than giving Nick a rundown of the events — but Stefanie knew his cut and Lincoln's seizure had scared him. Macey mentioned something about an accident before but stopped when Gideon gave her a stony look from across the room.

Now he stared out the passenger window, in a half slouch that she supposed he hoped screamed, *suit yourself.*

But she knew better. Gideon had suddenly decided to become Lincoln's bodyguard because he'd clammed up when he returned home every night. Even to Nick and Piper's best cop and journalist ploys.

Yep, Lincoln was avoiding her and had enlisted reinforcements.

A meadowlark took flight as she turned off the road and into the Big K. She noticed that above the drive, someone had erected a new sign, along with fancy electric gadgetry.

Spotlight Ranch.

So, Lincoln had renamed the place. A pang of sadness went through her as she realized the transformation was complete. The Big K was gone. Lincoln Cash had changed everything.

Even the way she thought about herself. He made her believe that she was beautiful and worthy and had the right to be in the arms of a man like him, whose dazzling smile was hers alone. He'd looked her in the eyes and without words told her that he might even be falling in love with her.

And that gave her the courage to announce into the security speaker box that she was bringing Gideon to work.

The gate opened.

Stefanie drove Gideon up to the corral, where he hopped out and slammed the door without saying a word to her. His Chevy Impala sat on the side of the yard, awaiting the arrival of a new distributor cap.

She turned off the truck, got out, and debated.

"He's in the theater." Gideon had stopped halfway to the barn. He wore misery on his face. "Don't tell him I told you."

"The theater?"

Gideon jerked his chin toward the old barn, now with a fresh coat of appropriately red paint. And new weathered doors with iron hinges. The picture of the perfect ranch building.

"Thanks," she said, but he turned away and slouched toward the horse barn, looking like he'd just sold out his best friend.

Hmm. Why would he automatically assume that Lincoln was in the theater? Unless that had been his hideout for the last week.

She opened the door to the barn, and the smell of new construction — carpet and wood and flooring — rushed over her. The place was dark. She blinked as her eyes adjusted to the light of the foyer, which looked like an old-fashioned theater entrance. The marquee over the doors was lit, blank but awaiting the name of the movie showing. Framed movie posters — *Gone with the Wind, Casablanca, Planet of the Apes, Star Wars* — ringed the room, bracketing the two red-painted doors.

She'd entered a new world. The world of entertainment and fantasy. The world of Lincoln Cash.

Voices curled out from under the doors as she crept forward and opened them.

Voices . . . and music and laughter. A movie played on a giant screen at the front of the room. She didn't recognize the movie, but she knew the face on the screen, the devilishly handsome smile, the precisely groomed two-day stubble, the blond hair that hung just below his ears. Oh, boy, did Lincoln Cash look good twenty feet tall.

Plush movie seats ran in rows of ten — maybe ten on each side toward the front. Darkness bathed the room, yet as she stood there, scanning the rows, she saw no one. "Linc?"

No one responded.

Apparently Gideon had guessed wrong about Lincoln's whereabouts.

Stefanie turned to leave and spotted him. Sitting in the back row at the far corner. Watching his movie.

Her eyes had adjusted, and with everything inside her she wanted to cry. He looked really rough. His beard hadn't been trimmed in days and now ran toward the side of scraggly. He wore a rumpled T-shirt and a pair of jeans and had his bare feet propped up on the arm of the seat in front of him.

He didn't even look at her as she scooted in beside him. "Go away, Stefanie."

His voice didn't change inflection. She could have been the maid for all the passion he put into the way his eyes finally flicked over at her.

On the screen, Lincoln was engaged in a fast action chase. The comparison with the sullen man in the dark rocked her.

"No. I don't think I will." She sat and put her feet up next to his. "Why have you been avoiding me since the accident? I was thinking it might have been JB. If so, I'm sorry. I didn't know that JB could be so . . . possessive."

"It wasn't one of your old boyfriends who did this."

Stefanie ignored the stab of indignation she felt. Why not? Because JB had nothing to be jealous of? She kept her voice tight. "Then who was it?"

"An ex-girlfriend drove me and Gideon off the road. I have a private investigator who's taking care of it, and she won't be bothering us. . . . You don't have to worry about Gideon."

An ex-girlfriend? "Who would follow you here to Montana?" Besides, it wasn't only

343

Gideon she was worried about.

"It doesn't matter. Not anymore. She got what she wanted — my life is over."

"You're being a little overdramatic, don't you think?" She was unable to keep the absurdity of his words from leeching out through her voice.

Lincoln shrugged.

Why did she have the eerie feeling that he wasn't referring to the accident or even the movie? that he was really talking about his life? She injected a light tone into her voice. "I thought you didn't watch your movies."

"I hate them." His voice didn't sound at all kidding.

"And yet, here you are."

"I don't want you here."

She glanced at him, refusing to be offended. "We don't always get what we want. I don't know what's eating at you, but friends don't let friends watch Cash movies alone. What's happening?"

"You don't want to be with me, Stef. I'm not good company."

"Sure you are. Look, you're just about ready to — yes, I think that girl on the screen must think you're excellent company." In fact, watching him wrap his arms around the brunette made her stomach curl in a way that had everything to do with

344

personal experience. She watched it like someone might watch a traffic accident, eyes wide. For a second, she even forgot that he was there.

"He's not real."

"Oh, I think he is," Stefanie said. She most definitely knew what it felt like to be kissed like the woman on the screen. Which made her staying right here, next to him in the dark theater, a certainty.

"No. What you see is a fake. There is no such thing as Lincoln Cash. He doesn't exist."

Something about his voice, the derision at the end of his last statement, made her turn. He didn't wear even a hint of a smile.

Now she was really worried. She touched his arm, took his hand. It was sweaty. She ran her other hand down his face, leaning close to kiss him.

He pulled away. "What are you doing?"

What *was* she doing? "Listen, I agree that I thought Lincoln Cash was some sort of dream, but when I got up close, I found that, yep, you were pretty real." She smiled, wrinkling her nose. "And today, not smelling so good."

He had an icy look in his eyes.

Apparently his sense of humor had vanished too. "I think maybe you hit your head

harder than we thought on that road, because maybe you're right — I don't recognize the Lincoln Cash I see in front of me.
The one I know is just as charming and
sweet and strong and —"

"I'm not strong."

Her hand traveled up his arm as if to make
a point. He jerked away, taking his hand
from hers.

"Okay. Wow." Stefanie looked at the
screen. "I thought movies were supposed to
cheer people up." She settled back in the
seat. "I hope this ends well."

"It doesn't."

"What, Lincoln Cash doesn't save the
day?" She winced at the sarcasm in her
voice. Clearly she wasn't as good as she had
hoped at hiding her hurt. Maybe she *should*
leave.

"Not this time. Not ever again."

"Lincoln, what's the problem?" This time
she hoped he'd hear real concern. She
regretted being so flippant earlier. She took
his hand again.

To her surprise, his fingers closed around
hers. Then, despite the volume on the
screen, she heard him say, "My name's not
Lincoln. It's Lewis. Lewis Carter."

She glanced at him, fighting the burble of
laughter that wanted to force through.

Lewis? But even in the darkness, his face betrayed no humor.

"And Lewis Carter isn't strong. Or brave. Or even that charming."

She held his hand tighter because he suddenly tried to pull it away. He closed his eyes as if in pain.

"I don't understand."

"Lincoln Cash doesn't exist anymore. Only Lewis." He opened his eyes, and the look in them told her he'd lost some kind of battle. It made everything inside her tighten. "And Lewis has multiple sclerosis."

CHAPTER 17

Lincoln could see the horror in Stefanie's eyes. The spark, that little flame of fire, blinked out as she stared at him, and he wanted to slink down and let his anger, his despair, consume him. Especially with the invincible Lincoln Cash taking out the villain on the giant screen in front of them. He wasn't sure why he'd broken open the movies, perhaps something about needing to wallow in his misery, but ever since he'd woken up on the side of the road, soiled and with the keen awareness of the dismal life in front of him, all he'd wanted to do was hide.

And three days of watching Lincoln Cash take on the world had only made him sick to his stomach. He'd been thrilled about having his own theater. . . . Now it felt like a monument to a joke. He'd become a spectator in his own miserable life.

Thankfully, Nick had said nothing about

how he'd found Lincoln, dirty and broken in the ditch. If Nick even suspected his true situation, well, maybe Lincoln could put him on the payroll and buy his silence. Or probably not. It hadn't worked with Gideon, who told him he couldn't put a price on loyalty.

Gideon was sticking to Lincoln's story of a concussion; that was the story Lincoln planned on going with. But Stefanie had a way of tugging the truth out. The real him out . . . Lewis.

Lewis the wimp.

"Please, God, make me strong." The prayer, spoken years ago through trembling, bleeding lips as he'd hidden from E-bro in his hiding place under a rattletrap car, came back to Lincoln now. Only then, he'd meant it in a turn-me-into-the-Hulk kind of way so he could metamorphose and hurt E-bro like the bully had hurt him. Now he just wanted to be able to stand. To eat on his own.

To not let Stefanie see him crumple in defeat.

"Multiple sclerosis," Stefanie said, and hearing it from her lips sounded like a death sentence. Like he'd told her he had the bubonic plague — a foreign, deathly sounding disease. Although MS wasn't usually fatal, life as he knew it most certainly had perished. "How long have you known?"

"I was diagnosed before I came here. Only . . ." Only he hadn't believed it. Not really. He'd gotten over his first attack so quickly, and it just didn't seem fair, after all he'd been through, that God would mock his prayers with such a vengeance.

"Not every suffering is discipline from God, but we can react as if it were — allowing Him to use it for good in our lives, producing a harvest of trusting God in all situations. We don't have to let circumstances define us, but we can let them produce definition in us." Pastor Pike's words had haunted him since he'd walked out of church. All Lincoln could think was, what kind of God took away a man's dreams? his life? This wasn't discipline. It was a punishment for causing what had happened to his mother and Alyssa. And perhaps also for the way he'd treated women, a truth that he'd only begun to accept.

He deserved to be taken down by his own body.

"I wish you'd told me sooner, Linc. It's not something you have to be ashamed about. I admit I don't know a lot about it, but it seems that a lot of people have MS and live with it." Stefanie had turned toward

350

him, compassion on her face that he didn't deserve after the way he'd lashed out at her. Especially after her attempts to cheer him up.

But he didn't have anyone else sitting here with him in the dark, did he?

"It's basically an autoimmune disease where my white blood cells attack the nerve sheaths on my spinal cord, blocking the nerve signals that control muscle coordination, strength, feeling, and vision. And yes, a lot of people live with it . . . but not people who roll out of cars and beat up people for a living. And . . . the name is Lewis."

"I'm not calling you Lewis. And in case you're confused, the person who jumps from moving vehicles is your movie character. The real Lincoln doesn't have to do any of those things. You can show up and smile, and the fans will love you."

Yes, but will you? The question almost made it out of his mouth, but he hurt enough for today. He shook his head. "I've always done my own stunts, always done my own fight scenes. I can't stop now."

"Wait — don't tell me — you actually *believe* everything you see on the screen." She turned to the movie. "Of course! Because you can truly dangle from a helicopter with one hand and fight the bad guy with

351

the other. You *are* truly superhuman."

She didn't need to add the sarcasm. He got it. They'd filmed that shot on a sound-stage in front of a blue screen, two ropes dangling from a beam overhead. "You know what I mean."

"No, I don't. I don't get why you'd believe that something like MS might destroy the man you are."

"Because the man I am isn't real. He's a fake. Haven't you been paying attention?"

"Oh yes I have. Believe me, I have." She got up, standing in front of him, blocking his view of the movie. Without the glow from the screen on her face, he could only judge her words by the tone of her voice. Which sounded a lot like what she might use with a scared horse.

Perfect.

"The guy I know, the real guy, is kind and generous. He's got a good heart and is will-ing to give people — and horses — a chance. He's brave and compassionate, and some-one . . ." She sounded as if she might be crying. "And he makes a girl feel beautiful."

He couldn't speak. Especially when she touched his face. He put his hand over hers. "That's because she *is* beautiful."

"In fact, the Lincoln I know is exactly the kind of guy I'd like to have in my life."

He closed his eyes, savoring her words for a moment, wishing — *how* he wished — they might even be close to the truth.

"No, he's not, Stef." He pushed her hand away. "I'm not your type of guy at all. The kind of guy you deserve isn't a has-been actor, someone who's made his career by pretending. By using people. By thinking he's a hotshot. The very fact that you felt compelled to tell me about your . . . situation in college when I didn't blink twice about my own behavior tells me that no, I don't have a prayer of being in your league."

Stefanie sat back down in the chair beside him. The movie was playing the credits. A sort of pictorial metaphor to the end of their relationship. The light cascaded over her face, and tears glistened on her cheeks. He wanted to reach up and brush them away, but that would only make him want to slide his fingers through her long hair, pull her toward himself, pretend that this day, this life, didn't exist. Because that was what he was good at. Pretending.

Not anymore.

Stefanie's voice shook, and a hint of real anger came into it. "You think you have the world fooled, but you don't. I've figured you out."

"Yeah?" Lincoln didn't even try to mask

the derision in his voice. Maybe she'd get the hint and leave.

"I think you *don't want* to be in my league. That you're afraid of what it might be like to share yourself with a woman — all of yourself, not just your house or your cars or your horses or your fame, but all of you, your fears and hopes and dark places. Because that's the kind of man I want, and you know it."

He stared at her, at her intensity and frustration, a little scared to speak.

"You think your dark places are so much worse than everyone else's. You think that it makes you weak to be honest and real. But it doesn't. In fact, it only makes you stronger." She touched his jaw. "You know why you're a star? Not because you're, well, way too good-looking for your own good, and not because you're so invincible, but because you're not. I've read your reviews. . . . Okay, I admit it; I've even read the tabloids. The fascination isn't your romances and your near-death experiences — and if I ever hear of you doing that stuff again, I'm going to kill you *myself* — but because on the screen, you make *us* feel strong."

Lincoln took her hand from his face and held it, feasting on her words. He admitted, when he played Lincoln Cash — not only the movie roles, but the real-life Lincoln Cash — he did feel strong.

And so gloriously apart from the Lewis he'd been.

But she wasn't finished. "People go to movies to dream big and hope big and feel big. You bring to life all the dreams and hopes of your characters so well that it makes us feel that we know you and that we can be like you. You make us feel that we, too, can overcome those things in our lives that scare us. And you know what? That's not pretending at all. You couldn't portray that without tapping into a real place inside you."

He knew that longing filled his eyes, knew that he might even be shaking a bit, because her voice softened, and a sweet sadness entered her tone. "It's not an act . . . and possibly you're the only one who doesn't see that."

He wondered what magical powers she had to look inside his soul and make him believe that everything would be okay.

"I figured out what you prayed for that you didn't get, Linc."

He stared at her, remembering their conversation. *"How about I ask for you, and you ask for me?"*

"You prayed that God would make you

tough — that nothing could hurt you."

Close enough. "How did you know that?" His voice barely edged over a whisper.

"You're not so mysterious, Lincoln Cash. A girl can figure you out if she looks hard enough. What you don't realize is that maybe God has already answered your prayer. Because strength isn't in your arms but inside." She touched his chest. "Strength is in who you are. And I promise, the man I know — Lewis *or* Lincoln — is a man of strength."

How he longed to believe her words, to lean into them and let them pour over him. To see himself as she saw him. But with the images of the man he'd been, at least to the rest of the world, still playing in his mind, he only saw the man he couldn't be.

"What would I do without you?" he said, drawing her into his lap, wanting more than anything to forget the past week, the future that loomed over him, and to live in the right now.

"Oh, I think you'd find some other neighbor to fill your life, Superhero."

He forced a smile. "I'm not sure I'd call you just a neighbor." His hand — thankfully today it had stopped trembling — went around her neck, wove into her hair, and tugged her down.

She smiled. "What would you call me then?"

He didn't answer, just kissed her in the darkened back row of his movie theater.

Gideon's car was gone by the time Stefanie headed back to the Silver Buckle. They'd watched a couple more movies and talked for hours, holding hands in the theater. She made sure the horses were put up for the night. Karen had made dinner, and Stefanie stayed for stir-fry, then a cup of coffee while staring at the stars over Spotlight Ranch.

She kissed Lincoln good night at the door and drove home under the silky spray of the Milky Way and the free fall of stars. The smell of grass and an occasional whiff of manure tinged the air, and a tumbleweed skittered across the dirt road as she replayed the evening in her head.

Multiple sclerosis.

The words dug into her brain, and although she wanted to keep the questions from her eyes and look at Lincoln exactly the same as she had this morning, everything suddenly filtered through that truth.

She hated that. Hated the barrage of questions, hated the pity that rose, despite her best efforts. Hated the fact that inside her favorite superhero, his body conspired against him to destroy the life he knew. The life he loved.

She'd meant what she said — that his strength, his so-called invincibility, came from inside. But she wondered how he'd live without Lincoln Cash at the helm. Hadn't that identity made him the man he'd become?

But maybe now, this disease would give him a new identity.

She turned into the Silver Buckle drive. The moonlight washed the house in pale light, and she noted the absence of Clancy on the porch. Nick's truck sat in the yard next to her father's old red Ford. A slight wind bullied a pot of geraniums on the porch as Stefanie slowed and pulled up to the house. A rectangle of light from the kitchen window shone on the ground, and she heard Haley's laughter streaming from the open screen door. Warmth curled inside her. Haley had turned into a regular chatterbox since that breakthrough day.

All because of Lincoln.

The fact that he'd told her this secret that issued from him like a leeching of blood made her ever more aware of the effect he had on her.

She was falling for Lincoln Cash, or Lewis, or whatever he called himself.

She stood on the porch, wishing that she might help him see his strength, might somehow give him a perspective through her eyes. *Lord, make me a blessing in his life. Help me to be someone he needs.*

She let the door bang behind her as the smell of a pot roast coaxed her inside, as Haley looked up, cookie crumbs on her mouth, as Macey turned from a sink full of dishes.

A swell of contentment, even happiness, nearly took her breath away and made her ache. Maybe, after all this time, this was exactly where she was supposed to be. On the Silver Buckle, helping Gideon, Macey, Haley, and even Lincoln heal.

"I'm not sure I'd call you just a neighbor." Lincoln's words found her as she toed off her boots, the depths of realization sweeping through her.

As she took a cookie and sat down beside Haley, a hundred other names drifted through her mind.

Not one of them was *neighbor.*

Libby had looked for Gideon every night this past week. She missed the discussions they had in his car after she got off work, the ones when he told her about his day, when she laughed at his stories of Lincoln and Stefanie and the new horses he was working with. They'd talk for five minutes or so; then she'd get out, and he'd watch as she walked home.

Her knight. Only, he hadn't been there for nearly a week. So when she came out of the diner and saw the old Impala sitting on the street, bathed in streetlights, dusty and battered, to her, it looked like her fairy-tale coach, complete with four white horses and a prince at the helm.

She got in and frowned at the butterfly bandages over his eye. "That from the accident? Are you okay?" She'd heard the account of Lincoln and Gideon being run off the road through the conversations at the diner.

Gideon nodded, but he kept his hands on the steering wheel, staring ahead. She reached out to touch the bandage, but he jerked away.

"Sorry," Libby said.

He sighed, shaking his head. "I don't like doing this."

"Doing what?" Her chest tightened at his tone. He sounded as if she'd asked him to break into the local convenience store.

"I want to be your boyfriend, not your . . . bodyguard." He turned to her, and something in his eyes — desperation, maybe —

made her want to cry. "I like you, Libby. Really like you. And it's not just because you're nice to me, but because you're nice to everybody. I watch you at night as you close up, and you don't rush anybody; you even give Dugan extra pieces of pie —"

"That's because they're leftover."

"No, it's because you're nice. And you always let Missy leave early."

"Because you're waiting for me," she said.

"But you're not just nice. You trust people. I know you called the Buckle a few days ago — Piper told me."

"I wanted to see how you were."

"I'm not good."

Her gaze went to his head, but he grabbed her hand. "I want to go out with you. On a real date. Someplace nice, where I can treat you like you've treated me."

Libby stared at his hand. Over the last two months, the flesh had become chapped and blistered, toughened.

His thumb ran over the top of her hand. "And by the way, I know why you . . . said we could only be friends."

Her throat tightened. She wanted that date too, more than she could bear to let herself dream about. Why couldn't her father see what she saw? Gideon deserved a chance.

"Because I don't go to church."

"That's not exactly why. . . ."

"Here's what you don't know. I did go to church. Back at juvie, I went, and I even went to the altar and asked Jesus to forgive me and everything. I've broken a few rules since then — and maybe that's what's kept me from seeing it — but I've been thinking . . . maybe you're right. Maybe God brought me here."

She closed her eyes, hating how much hope she drew from his words.

"Yeah. He brought me out here to meet you."

"I'm not sure He works like that, Gideon."

"Why not? Why can't I get something good in my life? Why can't I have you?"

Libby let go of his hand. "I don't know. I don't know." She was crying now, her face in her hands. She felt him move across the seat, put his arm around her.

"Shh . . . shh. Stop. Please stop crying."

She couldn't help it. She was trying to do everything right, trying to honor her father and become a good missionary, but Gideon's words hurt. Why? Why couldn't she have him? She was so confused . . . so . . .

She turned in his arms and looked up at him. He thumbed away a tear from her cheek. The streetlight touched his face, made his dark eyes glisten, and she couldn't help it. "I want . . . you to be my boyfriend too. . . ."

His hand went behind her neck, but his eyes stayed on her. He tried a smile, but it came out lopsided and funny. "Can I . . . do you think . . . ?" He swallowed. "I'd really like to kiss you, Libby."

She nodded, and there was a real smile on his face a second before he kissed her gently on the lips. It was everything she'd hoped for, everything she'd remembered. A thread of sweet pleasure twined around her heart with his touch, so Gideon-like — kind and protective and tender. She wound her hands into his T-shirt and let herself kiss him back. He smelled so good, of the outdoors and hard work. He was her best friend; his was the smile she longed for at the end of the day. Gideon. How did she expect to leave him at the end . . . ?

She pulled away. "I still have to leave for college."

He touched his forehead to hers. "Yeah, I know. But three months is a long time. And maybe I might surprise you. Maybe I'll go away to college too."

He kissed her again, wrapping his arms around her. But the bath of light in the street reminded her that anyone could be watching. In fact, her father could be standing at his window down the street. Wouldn't that be a fun conversation to have? So she pulled away again. "I gotta go."

Gideon nodded and blew out a breath, scooting away from her. "I'm going to ask your dad."

She stopped with her hand on the door latch. "Ask . . . ?"

"If I can take you out on a date."

Oh. "Maybe you should go to church first."

Gideon smiled. "See you Sunday. And then I'll ask him."

Libby nearly floated as she got out of the car. Certainly her father would say yes if he met Gideon, really saw his heart. *Please, God, can't You make that happen?*

She looked over her shoulder twice and saw Gideon sitting there as she walked from the pool of light toward her house. She heard his car start up and pull away but didn't turn because he was behind her and she knew he'd follow her.

She was nearly to her alley when she heard the car pull up behind her quickly, the door opening. Suddenly a hand clamped over her mouth, stifling her scream and pulling her backward. What — Gideon?

She tried to turn, managing a kick to his

shin, but he pulled her back, and she fell with him into the backseat.

She bit hard into the hand, and whoever had her swore and slapped her. Then, as he held her arms behind her back, the car peeled out, away from town, into the night.

"Gideon!"

CHAPTER 18

Gideon couldn't remember a time when he'd felt this happy, this right about anything. He'd thought that the mistakes he made would haunt him forever. But fate — no, maybe God, like he'd told Libby — had helped him escape it. These past two months had set him free from all the refuse that cluttered his life. For the first time he had a home and people who believed in him. He had a good job and was learning to take care of animals and people. Macey had stopped cutting herself, and Haley had begun to speak, even to him.

Last night Haley had climbed onto the sofa beside him, leaned over, and kissed his bandage. Like his mother might have done. The act had left him without words, his throat so full he thought he might cry.

Gideon watched Libby now as she disappeared down the street, then tried to start his car. The engine didn't roll over right away. This stupid car. When he'd seen it on the road, it had been marked for towing, abandoned, he thought, because of its downright ugliness. He should probably put the sign back on it. He saw another car drive by him. Libby had disappeared into the darkness between town and her house. "C'mon!"

The engine finally turned over, and he put the car into drive. He didn't really think that anything would ever happen to Libby; after all, Phillips was about the safest place he'd ever been. He just liked her smile to be the last thing he saw every day, to take it home with him in his chest.

Still, as he drove closer, something irked him about the way the car that had just passed him tore away from . . . Libby's house.

A scream. Gideon's lights flashed against the back window of the sedan and he saw bodies. One of them struggling.

He choked on his panic as he drew closer, honking. *Libby?*

His infuriating Impala coughed, refusing to respond. "Please, please, don't die on me!"

He gunned the gas, and his lights scraped the back end of the car before it edged ahead of him and blinked out completely in the dark. Why was it driving without its lights?

The night seemed to swallow the landscape, the car, everything. *Please . . . God. Please!* He hadn't lied when he told Libby he'd attended church in jail, had even begun wearing a cross around his neck as a sort of hope in what he'd learned, the faith he tried to have in the Savior he'd met. He especially hadn't lied when he told her he'd attend now, but as he floored the gas pedal, he made every promise he could think of. *Please, God!*

The road cut to the left, and he nearly careened off it into one of the fields, but he knew the route well enough to react. The Impala spun out and stopped in a puff of dust. As it cleared, as his heart thundered in his throat, he saw the briefest flash of lights on a side road behind him.

A car door opening?

Libby!

He floored it back to the road and discovered a rutted track over a cow gate leading off into a field. He cut his lights and prayed that he didn't bottom out or go over a gully. God gave him enough light from the moon to see the silvery grass. He rolled down his window. And heard screams.

Everything inside him began to boil. By

368

the time he spotted the car, he was halfway out of his own. He hit the ground running, letting his Impala, engine still running, roll toward the brown sedan that he recognized now from Lincoln's work site.

Luther.

The sounds of scuffling, of pain, erupted from a gully, and he launched himself right off the edge of it, landing on JB Denton. Gideon hit his chin on a rock and tasted blood in his mouth, but he came up swinging. JB had seemed twice his size and tough as a bull at the work site, but he went down when Gideon unloaded on him. Gideon spotted Luther coming at him but kept his attention on JB and finding a home for his fist right in the center of JB's nose. JB went down, blood spurting through his fingers.

Gideon turned to meet Luther, but he was already in midair. He tackled Gideon; they crashed into the rocky bed. Something inside Gideon cracked, and pain speared through him, but he sent his elbow into Luther's ear, his nose, his eye. Luther rolled off him, and Gideon bounced up, hesitating between sending his boot into Luther's gut or going to Libby.

Libby sat in a ball, rolled into herself, hand over her bleeding mouth as she stared at Gideon.

Gideon sent a final "stay down" message to Luther with his boot, then ran to Libby, hauling her up by her elbows. "Libby!"

She seemed dazed and looked at him as though she didn't know him.

"Are you okay? Did they hurt you?" He knew that was the stupidest question ever — of course they'd hurt her. Her shirt was torn, her mouth was bleeding, and by the looks of her bloodied fists, she'd put up a fight.

"Oh, Libby . . ." Without looking back, he lifted her into his arms. She didn't move, didn't cling to him, didn't cry.

He didn't know if that was a bad thing or not. Or where to take her.

He put her in the Impala, which had slammed into the sedan, and backed away from the crash, then turned the car around.

Libby watched him with wide, glassy eyes. "Please . . ." Was he too late? He reached out to take her hand, but it was cold and limp.

He didn't know where to go, so, afraid and panicked, he drove to the closest ranch. The home of Lincoln Cash.

Lincoln leaned back in his chair, listening to the nurse's assessment of Alyssa's condition. They had stabilized her night terrors, and the frequency of her seizures had lessened. But she was still largely catatonic, unresponsive to the world.

"Perhaps if you came to visit," the nurse said, referring to the way Alyssa had reacted to Lincoln's visit six-plus months ago. Her response — the way her eyes lit up as if recognizing his voice — had made him vow to return more often. A vow he had forgotten, being too consumed with his own terrors to keep that one.

He clenched his fist, watching it tremble just slightly. "Yes," he said. "I'll see what I can do."

He hung up and sat in his dark office. He wondered if that was how his disease would crawl over him, making him unable to react to the world, overwhelming him until it trapped him in a dark, terrifying place.

He'd been having his own version of night terrors.

Only tonight, for the first time in a week, he didn't see his life spiraling away, out of his reach. No, he'd had a nice dinner with Stefanie, listened to her talk about Macey and Haley and their recent training efforts with Bill. He'd laughed at her sorry efforts to use chopsticks and lingered after she'd kissed him good night at the door, thinking about Nick's definition of love.

He'd sat in his office a long time wondering if this was how his life could look. He might be okay after all.

Lights skimmed his windows, and he heard a horn honking as tires skidded to a halt on the gravel drive.

Lincoln was just finding his feet when Gideon roared in through his front door, looking like he'd done a few rounds in a Lincoln Cash movie.

"Help! Please help!" Gideon whirled and ran back outside.

Lincoln followed him down the front steps and peered in the open door of the rusty Impala. Libby Pike sat curled in the front seat, bleeding from her mouth.

Something sick went through Lincoln. He rounded on Gideon, everything inside him boiling. "What the — ?"

"It wasn't me, dude! I wouldn't hurt her!" A broken look came over his face, a sort of desperation. "I swear I didn't hurt her. It was Luther and JB."

And just like that, Lincoln believed him. He'd had a look not unlike Gideon's once — horror at seeing someone he cared about hurt, possibly because of him. On that long-ago day, Lincoln had watched his countenance in the hospital windows morph from revenge to disbelief to remorse. He wasn't sure if his expression had ever really changed.

"What happened to her?" Lincoln climbed into the driver's seat. "Are you okay?" he asked Libby.

Libby lost it, starting to cry and shake.

Lincoln reached out for her. She recoiled. "Libby, let me help you," Lincoln said, but she was curled into a ball, and he knew he couldn't possibly move her. "Gideon, go around to the passenger side; lift her out."

After Gideon carried her into the house, Lincoln debated only a half second before he got on the phone to the sheriff.

Sorry, Gideon.

When he hung up, he went upstairs to where Gideon sat with the sobbing girl. Gideon was crying a little too, and from the looks of his busted face and the way he'd winced when he carried Libby up the stairs, Lincoln knew there was more to his hurt than Libby's wounds.

"Gideon, I had to call the sheriff," he finally said.

Gideon sat on the bed, holding Libby, smoothing her hair. He looked over the top of her head and nodded. The look on his face told Lincoln that he didn't care if Social Services found him and hauled him and even his sisters back to whatever group home they'd escaped from.

"And I think you both need to see a doctor."

Gideon nodded again.

Then Lincoln went back downstairs and called the pastor.

He was standing in the living room when Pike arrived, and he blocked the stairway before the pastor could go upstairs. "What you see isn't Gideon's fault," he said, but Pike pushed past him.

Lincoln winced at Pike's sharp intake of breath when he saw Libby, at the pain he saw in the pastor's eyes.

Lincoln had studied characters for years, and he supposed he might look exactly the same way if someone he loved had been hurt like Libby. He might even turn on the person he blamed, his hands fisted, as if he'd like to use them, just like Pastor Pike rounded on Gideon.

"What did you do?" Pike roared.

Lincoln had to give the pastor credit for not diving at Gideon's throat, even though the evidence on Gideon's face suggested that the boy had done battle saving Libby's honor . . . maybe even her life.

She hadn't stopped crying.

Gideon stared at Pike, eyes wide, everything on his face screaming guilt. "I'm

374

sorry," he said, which might have been the worst possible thing to say because the pastor had a nearly rabid look on his face. Gideon followed up fast with, "I tried to protect her."

"You did this to her —"

"No!" Gideon shook his head, defending himself even as Pike yanked his grip from his daughter, pushed him onto the floor. "I didn't hurt her. I'd never hurt her."

"C'mon, Libby," Pike said, scooping her into his arms. She curled into his chest, still crying. He cast a look loaded with fire and brimstone at Gideon and carried her toward the stairs.

"She needs to go to the hospital."

"I know!" Pike snapped. "I'll take her."

"I think Gideon needs to go too," Lincoln said softly. In fact, Gideon wasn't looking good at all. "But I called the cops."

"Then you wait for them. I don't care. I'm taking Libby." He looked back at Gideon. "You'd better be out of this town by the time I get back from Sheridan."

Lincoln opened his mouth, then closed it and glanced at Gideon.

The look on his face told Lincoln that Pike could likely expect exactly that. *Don't go, kid. Don't run.* Years ago, Lincoln had hit the road, putting as much distance between his mistakes and himself as he could. And he'd never figured out how to return.

He had to give Gideon points for courage, however, because he stuck around, groaning as a deputy showed up and took his statement. Lincoln asked if he should call Stefanie, but Gideon looked at him with such despair that he decided it could wait.

Gideon was eighteen. And apparently old enough to look after himself.

With his eyesight still occasionally cutting out, the fact that his foot felt sluggish on the gas, and the memory of his recent accident in his mind, the last thing Lincoln wanted to do was climb behind the wheel of Gideon's clunker. But with his truck still dead in the garage, waiting to be hauled in for repairs, and Gideon doubled over in pain, Lincoln had little choice. "Hang in there, Gideon. We'll get there."

By the time they pulled into the emergency entrance, Gideon's skin was ashen, and last time he'd coughed, blood had come up.

Lincoln got out, grabbed a wheelchair, and pulled it up to the car, his hands shaking, only this time he had to believe it was the adrenaline pouring through his body and not a flare-up. The trembling didn't stop, though, even after they wheeled Gideon away, even after Lincoln signed the papers saying he'd be responsible for the kid's medical expenses.

By the time Lincoln had gotten the paperwork processed, they'd already taken Gideon to surgery to stop the internal bleeding his broken rib had caused.

Lincoln dialed Stefanie's number and listened to the phone ring, each drone a moan of dread until she picked up. Then he explained quietly, in a voice he'd heard her use.

"Don't let him die, Linc," she said, as if he had some magical power to stop their worst fears. He could already hear her jangling her car keys.

Like a fool he answered, "No, I won't."

He felt folded inside out, all his raw and ugly edges showing as he considered the orange molded waiting room chairs. Why couldn't waiting rooms be filled with soft lights, soothing music, leather sofas? Lincoln wandered the halls. At 4 a.m., the hospital was a lonely place.

Lincoln found Pastor Pike shortly before dawn sitting at the end of the hall on the second floor, his hands over his face. He stood there at the apex between two hallways, caught in indecision.

The pastor met Lincoln's eyes with such a

look of sorrow that Lincoln moved in his direction. He wasn't sure how he felt about Pike's treatment of Gideon, but he was remembering a scene he'd done in *Unshackled,* where the hero, unable to help the person he loved, had poured out his helplessness by splitting wood. As that scene rushed back to him, he saw the same frustration on Pike's face. He'd like to be splitting wood . . . if not something else.

"You know he didn't do it," Lincoln said, sitting.

Pike didn't need a name. "He probably saved her life."

"Was she raped?"

"No." Pike covered his forehead with his hand. "No, thank God."

"And thank Gideon."

Pike looked up at him. "And Gideon."

"He really loves Libby, you know. Maybe he deserves a second chance."

Pike leaned back, his head against the window. Darkness still shrouded the Bighorn Mountains, although the slightest filter of gray had begun to lighten the gullies, dissipate the lights in the parking lot.

Pike spoke quietly, not to Lincoln, it seemed, although he was the only one in the hall. "It's not easy to raise two daughters alone. I gave myself excuses for how I protected them, even how I judged the people they spent time with. Missy was always so opinionated and strong, and she knew exactly what she wanted. But Libby is softer. More gullible."

"Maybe she saw something in Gideon the rest of us couldn't see."

"You saw it." Pike's tone held self-recrimination.

No, Lincoln mostly saw himself in Gideon. But he didn't say that. "You said something in a service I attended —"

"The *only* service you attended. I don't remember what the sermon was about."

"About letting circumstances define you. Make your decisions for you. You said that God wants to use our circumstances to make us into people of character."

Pike braced his elbows on his knees, running his hands over his hair. "I remember now."

"Do you believe that?"

"Hebrews 12 says, 'Look after each other so that none of you fails to receive the grace of God. Watch out that no poisonous root of bitterness grows up to trouble you, corrupting many.'" He closed his eyes, sighing. "I'm sorry, Lincoln."

Lincoln didn't know what to say.

"I've been so bitter over my wife's passing, over having to parent alone, that I've completely missed the grace of having Libby and Missy around. I've boxed Libby in, afraid that I might lose her too. Afraid that God couldn't take care of her like I could. Afraid that His plans for her might be different from mine."

Lincoln stared at his hands. They continued to tremble. He clasped them together. "What does it mean . . . to 'fail to receive the grace of God'?"

"It means that God is in our lives, giving us moments and people and situations to remind us of His power and love. They aren't always what we expect, or even want, but God does it so that we might grow, not only as people but in our relationship with Him. God doesn't promise that everything is going to be good." Pike's gaze traveled to Libby's closed hospital door. "But He does promise to be with us and hold us up through it all. That's what Paul means when he says in every situation he can be content — at peace — because God can give him strength for everything he needs to endure."

Pike nodded, as if he'd been speaking to himself. "Even this." He glanced at Lincoln. "Making sure that no one fails to receive grace means making sure we recognize God at work in all circumstances. Sometimes even I underestimate how important our eternity is to God." He stood and held out his hand. "Thank you, Lincoln. Thank you for everything."

Lincoln took his hand, amazed at how firm his grip was.

He watched as Pike went in, leaving the door open, and sat beside his daughter's bed. Libby had obviously been given a sedative because she slept soundly. Her father took her hand and bent his head to pray.

"What you don't realize is that maybe God has already answered your prayer."

Lincoln turned and stared out at the Bighorns. *God, is that true?* How could that be true? He hadn't even been able to lift Libby from the car.

But maybe . . . He pressed his hand against the cold glass, and the tremor stopped. He watched the faintest gold of the dawn seeping through his fingers as it reflected off the mountain. Maybe all these years he'd been trying to fill his life with things that made him look strong. Perhaps strength *did* come from inside.

Strength was in his mother, working hard to create a life for him. In Dex, believing in Lincoln when he was a runt kid needing a job. In Stefanie's seeing good in his broken horses. In Libby, who gently reminded Gideon that he was worth loving. And in Nick, asking Lincoln to take care with his sister.

Strength was even in him . . . earning all their trust enough that in Gideon's hour of darkness, he had come to Lincoln.

Yes, Lincoln had money and pull and status . . . but even that, God had given to him. Maybe for this very reason.

"Linc?" Stefanie's voice came from behind him, and he turned. She looked rough, disheveled, with half-moons of exhaustion under her eyes. But the look of need on her face undid him, and he thought he'd never seen anyone quite so beautiful.

"Gideon's still in surgery," Lincoln said.

She buried herself in his arms, her cheek against his chest. He leaned down, breathed in her scent. She molded against him so perfectly it seemed as if she'd always been there.

He walked with her, hand in hand, to the waiting room, where Nick and Piper sat in the orange chairs. Macey had her back to them, staring at her own reflection in the darkened panes of glass. Haley sat in Piper's lap, her eyes wide as she watched Lincoln.

For the first time in hours, he became aware that he was limping slightly.

Two policemen were standing at the counter, and now they approached him.

"Lincoln Cash?" one asked, as if there might be some confusion. He did look a little like a car-crash victim in his blood-stained jeans and jacket. He must have gotten blood on him from Gideon's head wound.

He nodded.

"The hospital says you brought in Gideon North?"

Lincoln glanced at Stefanie, who'd gone a shade whiter. He squeezed her hand. "That's right."

"We have some questions to ask you about the kidnapping of Macey and Haley North."

Lincoln could have kicked himself when he shot a look at Macey, who'd turned from the window when she heard her name. After all his years as an actor, he should have done a much better job of not giving away the ending.

He winced when one of the cops turned and walked toward her.

And when Stefanie looked up at him with an expression of pain, it tore clear through him.

As if she might be watching some eight-millimeter homemade movie, Stefanie saw the events reel out in jerky, painful, warped bits of action.

"What's going on here?" Nick demanded, even as Macey pulled her arm away from the reach of the cop who went after her as if she might be a fugitive. Piper held Haley in her arms, wearing her fight face.

Behind the shouting in her mind, Stefanie faintly heard Lincoln's voice, low and all business. "Gideon didn't kidnap anyone. Those are his sisters, and he thought Haley was going to be adopted."

Apparently that meant nothing to the first cop, who was already recognizing Haley, already preparing to take the little girl away from her life at the Silver Buckle.

Away from the Noble family.

Stefanie let go of Lincoln's hand and pushed past the cop, holding out her arms to Haley, who sprang into them, burying her face in Stefanie's neck, shaking. Her thin legs clamped tight around Stefanie, hanging on with all she had. Stefanie held her fiercely, smoothing her hair, fighting the urge to do just as Gideon had done a couple of months ago. Run.

Please, God, don't take these kids away from us. Let them have a family.

Macey stood at the window, arms folded, glaring at all of them, as if they'd somehow betrayed her.

"That kid's a hero," Lincoln was saying,

telling how Gideon had saved Libby. "You can't seriously think he'd be a danger to his siblings."

His voice, so calm, so determined, wove a thread through Stefanie that held her together. He glanced at her now and again as if to say, "Don't worry."

Except he couldn't hold back the hand of Social Services. Less than two hours later, as a nurse came to inform them that Gideon was beginning to wake, a sleepy caseworker strode through the hospital entrance.

Morning followed the woman in, a cascade of sunlight that seemed to mock them as she questioned Nick and Piper and Stefanie about the past two months. Dread crept in as Stefanie spoke quietly, explaining why they hadn't called Social Services, explaining why she'd thought life on the Silver Buckle might be a better choice, a new beginning for the kids.

After all, she'd begun to believe it too.

Haley had finally gone to sleep, collapsing in Stefanie's arms, and when the social worker reached for her, Lincoln intercepted the woman and led her over to one of the officers.

Stefanie longed to listen in on the huddle of caseworker, cop, and superhero. When the caseworker nodded, agreeing to something, hope lit inside her.

Until the woman returned and motioned for Stefanie to give Haley to her.

"No," Stefanie said, her eyes filling. "Please."

"You have no right to these children," the social worker said, tucking her hands under Haley.

The girl stirred, and when she opened her eyes, she let out a scream.

"Haley, listen to me," Stefanie said, speaking over her screams. "It's going to be okay."

It wasn't, though, and Stefanie wept as Haley thrashed in the woman's arms, fighting. Macey came to the rescue, practically wrestling the caseworker for her little sister. Haley calmed in Macey's arms.

But Stefanie was still screaming inside.

Lincoln leaned against a far wall, his expression grim.

Stefanie watched them go, Haley's eyes, full of fear, holding hers. Accusing. Alone.

Stefanie sank down into the plastic orange chair, sank her head in her hands, and felt everything inside her begin to shatter.

CHAPTER 19

"We'll get them back." Lincoln didn't know what else to say, feeling as if he was even lying to himself. Even with his arsenal of lawyers, the charge of kidnapping against Gideon might stick. Despite Gideon's status as Haley and Macey's brother, he not only did not have custody, but he'd taken them across state lines — a felony offense according to the law.

Lincoln's best cajoling, his charm on overdrive, had only been able to convince the social worker to list him as one of Macey and Haley's approved visitors. She had been inclined to put Stefanie and the rest of the Nobles on the no-contact list.

But he didn't tell Stefanie that. Especially since he'd finally gotten her to stop crying. To pile insult on top of her pain, she wasn't allowed to sit by Gideon's bed in ICU because she wasn't listed as family, so Lincoln was camped out with her here in the waiting room. He'd passed the time by calling his lawyer, who had contacted a local attorney and retained him to plead Gideon's case.

Now Stefanie got up from where she sat in the waiting room, looking thin and tired as she stared out the window. "Thank you," she said softly, giving him a pained smile.

Lincoln nodded and scrubbed his hand over his face. He'd liked the person he'd been as he stood up for the kids as if he might be an uncle or . . . a father. The image of Stefanie holding Haley, her eyes pleading with him to save the day, had found fertile soil and seeded all sorts of thoughts. What might it be like to have children with long dark hair, teasing dark eyes?

He stood and walked over to Stefanie, putting his hand on the small of her back.

"I don't know what I was thinking," she said in a voice he didn't recognize. "Why didn't I call Social Services the first day?"

"Stef —"

"No!" Her eyes glistened with unshed tears. "I always do this — I think I can change things or help or even be something I'm not. I'm not their mother, and I should have seen that. I'm nobody, and now I've lost the kids and gotten Piper and Nick into big trouble."

His attention had caught on the word *nobody*. She was hardly nobody. Even he, a recent observer of life on the Silver Buckle, could see that she held the ranch together, that without her in their lives — in his life — everything would unravel.

But he didn't know how to say that, nor did he know how to soothe the terrible pain in her eyes or the roaring of hurt inside, so instead he pulled her tightly to him. Holding her with every ounce of invincibility he had. "It'll be okay." He'd make *sure* it was okay.

Stefanie wrapped her arms around him, leaning against him.

"Isn't this sweet?" The voice came from behind him.

Stefanie disentangled herself as Lincoln turned.

Elise Fontaine, dressed in black leggings, a printed white cotton baby doll dress, and a short jean jacket, held her sunglasses in one hand and gave a smile that he'd heard some producer had lately paid her a seven-digit contract to flash.

She looked good too, tan and glowing, as if she'd just breezed in from a week at an elite spa. She cocked her head. "You're a hard man to track down, Lincoln Cash.

Don't you answer your cell phone? I had to call Delia, who told me you were in the emergency room! Are you okay?"

He'd erred on the side of secretive about his reasons for needing to contact his lawyer when he tracked down Delia in the wee hours this morning. He glanced at Stefanie, who had edged away from him.

She stared at him a second, then wiped her face and turned to Elise. "Hello," she said, forcing a smile.

Next to Elise, Stefanie had a poise about her that made her seem regal. He didn't know why he hadn't seen it before, but Elise looked downright . . . trampy.

Dex came through the waiting room door before Lincoln could think to introduce anyone. "Finally. I can't believe I have to trek halfway across the planet, or at least Montana, to find you." The man was always moving, energizing every room he entered. But now he had a windblown look, his hair disheveled, a hint of dust on his leather jacket.

"We stopped by the ranch — what a place, Linc! Love it. When you said you were building a theater, I had no idea. It's going to be the go-to spot for everyone in the industry. I already have my marketing people working on a magazine, an insider's view of Cash Productions and the Spotlight Ranch."

Trust Dex to always be one step ahead of him.

Lincoln still had today's emotions to contend with. "What are you doing here?" His words came out harsher than he intended, and he noticed Stefanie frowning at him.

Dex clamped Lincoln's arm. "When someone says hospital and my number-one star in the same sentence, I start to get worried."

"And *I* missed you." Elise wiggled up to him and put her hands on his face, giving him a kiss.

Stefanie watched her without blinking.

Lincoln caught Elise's forearms. "Nice to see you too."

"Didn't you get my messages?" Dex said. "I told you I was coming to check out your ranch." His voice lowered as he looked at their attentive waiting room audience. "What *are* you doing here?"

He needed a cup of coffee. "It's complicated," Lincoln said.

"Well, you don't look so good. And you'd better get your game face on. I saw a news crew not far behind me."

Lincoln didn't answer, but he noticed

391

Stefanie inching toward the door. *Wait.*

"Dex has a great idea," Elise said, looping her arm through Dex's. "We're going to have the premiere for *Unshackled* on your ranch!"

"What?"

"I need a soda or something," Elise said. She turned to Stefanie. "Be a sweetheart and fetch me something cold to drink, will you?"

Stefanie glanced at Lincoln, but his brain wasn't working quite right and he wasn't sure what to respond to first. A premiere . . . in Phillips? And Stefanie wasn't the help. . . . "She doesn't work for me," he finally said.

Elise appeared surprised — Lincoln had been hoping for ashamed. "Really. I'm sorry. And who are you?"

Lincoln stared at Stefanie, opened his mouth, but the right answer refused to emerge. She was his friend? his girlfriend? the woman he loved? The names bundled up in his chest, refusing to untangle. And unfortunately the wrong answer tumbled out. "She's my neighbor."

Stefanie looked as if he'd struck her. Then she swallowed, and he knew he was truly the king of the jerks. "That's right. We're just neighbors." Then she nodded at Lincoln as if confirming something she'd always known. "I'll see you back at the ranch."

"Stef —"

But she'd already brushed past Elise and Dex and ducked through the door.

It was then that the camera flash went off. And his life came crashing back around him.

Could Stefanie be any more of a fool? *Just the neighbor.*

He could have answered anything. *Slugger. Horse Girl.* Even *friend.*

Instead he'd picked the one word guaranteed to skewer her. Stefanie actually thought she might heave, woozy as she felt climbing into her truck. Thankfully, she'd driven separately from Piper and Nick, not sure when she might leave, and now she pulled out of the parking lot, nearly sideswiping a rental car.

She wanted to scream, thinking of Gideon lying there in the ICU, alone. He certainly couldn't count on Lincoln, could he?

She clenched her jaw so tight she thought her molars might crack. That wasn't fair. Lincoln had been a friend to her, to all of them, the last few hours. A very good neighbor, as it turned out.

Besides, she *was* nobody to Gideon. Not

on his list of family. Not even allowed to see him.

Or Macey.

Or Haley.

Her stomach writhed, and again she thought she might be ill.

If she never saw another movie, another tabloid, another hint of Lincoln Cash and his ilk again, it would be too soon.

She wrapped her hands around the steering wheel of her truck, fighting the trembling that shook down her arms, hating the slick of tears in her eyes.

She had really made a fool of herself this time. Had it been only yesterday that she'd practically told him he was her hero, given him a rousing speech about his inner strength, his ability to inspire?

After all that, he'd just stood there and told her exactly what she meant to him.

Nothing.

She floored it out to the road and fishtailed as she turned right.

Slow down. She pictured herself bleeding and lying wheels-side-up on the side of the road.

The entire scene with Lincoln felt so frighteningly familiar it stole her breath. She'd given a part of herself away again. And gotten it stomped on. Maybe not her body this time but her heart for sure, and lots of her closely guarded hope. She'd even given him a piece of her dreams, the ones that included Gideon's sisters and others like them.

Stefanie used her palm to whisk away her tears. How she longed for a ride on Sunny. The thought filled her throat. If only she hadn't been so foolish with Doug, she would have finished school, gotten her vet degree, done something with her life. She never would have had to return to the ranch out of desperation, been trapped there. She probably wouldn't have been around to see Lincoln Cash move into the neighborhood, bringing along his parade of gorgeous women.

She never would've had to feel this horrible roaring inside her heart.

Stefanie turned off the interstate, grinding up dust on the back road, not slowing, her hands white on the wheel, heading straight for the Silver Buckle. To the land, the house, the memories, the safety, the past, and the future, right back to her new home — her lonely, dismal, cold digs.

After all, where else did she have to run?

Libby felt as if she'd been trampled by a herd of horses. She opened her eyes and groaned. What was — ?

Panic reached up and she started to wheeze. A hospital room, complete with a hanging pink curtain and an IV in her arm. Her father sitting on one side, his head on the bed, and Missy asleep on the other side. What had happened? What — she remembered . . . *what did she remember?*

Luther and JB . . .

She gasped, putting her hands over her mouth. "What — ?"

"Shh, honey. Shh." Her father raised his head, blinking, apparently exhausted or at least groggy. "You're okay."

She put her hand to her head and felt a stitch; her mouth tasted funny and her tongue felt big. "What . . . did Luther and JB . . ." She swallowed, feeling sick. "I remember them hitting me, and then Luther — but he didn't. Someone . . ."

"Yes, they've been arrested."

She was staring at her father, at his pained expression, when memory whooshed back, and suddenly she saw it all on fast-forward. Gideon tackling JB and then getting kicked, and Luther jumping on him, and — "Daddy, what about Gideon? Is he — did they hurt him?"

Missy was awake now and she stood up. "Gideon's going to be okay. He got out of

396

surgery a couple hours ago."

Her father fired Missy an age-old look that he used from the pulpit when he wanted them to sit still and be quiet.

"Surgery?" Libby heard the shrill note of panic in her voice. "Why — how bad?"

Her father took her hand. "He had some internal bleeding from a broken rib. But I think he's going to be okay."

"I want to see him."

"I don't think — ," her father started.

"Right now, Daddy. *Right* now." She threw back her covers and swung her legs over the bed on the side of the IV cradle. "Now."

Missy held out her hand. Libby heard her father sigh. "You're not the only one who has to talk to him," he said in a tone that made Libby wonder what had transpired between these two men in her life.

Gideon had just been transferred from ICU, but it still rattled Libby to see him in the bed, a tube in his arm, an oxygen cannula under his nose. His purple eye was nearly swollen shut. His head had a line of stitches.

Beside him sat Lincoln, looking as concerned as if he might be Gideon's lost brother. And sprawled, sleeping, on the other bed was . . .

"Who is that?" Libby stared at the blonde.

She glanced at Lincoln.

"Elise Fontaine. She's a . . . coworker." He gave Libby a small smile, his voice low. "She's had a long morning, and she's hiding from the press, so don't speak too loudly."

"There's press here?"

He made a face. "In force."

"How is he?"

"I think he's going to make it." Lincoln looked at Gideon with such fondness that Libby wanted to hug him.

Gideon stirred and opened his good eye. His gaze fixed on Libby. "Hey there," he whispered between parched lips.

Libby wanted to soar, but when Lincoln offered her his chair, she moved stiffly into it.

"I think I'll stand guard in the hall," he said.

Libby took Gideon's hand, but before she could speak, her father interrupted. "I owe you an apology, Gideon."

Gideon's expression tightened, the smallest movement of his mouth that spoke of stress. "You were angry."

"I was afraid. And not just last night. Ever since you moved to this town. I have plans for my daughter, and I thought you threatened them. But I should have trusted Libby.

And what she sees in you." He nodded at Gideon. "Thank you, son."

Even though Gideon looked away, Libby could see that, for a second, his eyes grew glossy. "Thanks, sir."

"I'm just glad you were there —"

"It wasn't me." Gideon glanced at Libby. "Actually, I lost her. But . . . well, maybe it was God or something, because just when I needed to, I saw them." He squeezed Libby's hand. "Libby keeps telling me that there's no such thing as fate. I guess I'm starting to believe her."

"I'd say that's a good start." Libby's father smiled at her. "I'll wait in the hall."

"Sir?" Gideon cast a look at Libby. "I don't suppose this is a good time to ask if I can . . . maybe . . . date your daughter?"

Her father smiled. "I suppose we'll see you at church when you're up and about?"

"You will, sir."

He looked at Libby and nodded.

Gideon watched him leave, then turned to Libby. The look in his eyes made her fall in love with him all over again. She did love him, as much as she knew about love. And like her dad said, that was a good start.

"I think your dad likes me," he said softly.

"Yeah. Him and a lot of other people."

Gideon brought her hand to his mouth,

kissed it, then held it to his chest as he closed his eyes, a smile on his face.

CHAPTER 20

Stefanie didn't want to blame Lincoln. Not after he'd been a hero, not after he'd paid Gideon's hospital bills, and not after he'd hired a lawyer to reduce the charges of auto theft — apparently Gideon's stolen Impala had been marked for towing — and dismiss the counts of kidnapping, even though as Macey and Haley's brother, he had the right to sue for custody. He'd bargained for probation and community service, something that promised to keep Gideon in Phillips for at least six months. Lincoln's lawyer had even gotten the charges against the Noble family dismissed.

But because of Lincoln and his 911 call, Social Services had absorbed Haley and Macey into the foster system. Stefanie felt so hollow, she thought she might break in half.

What was worse, Lincoln Cash was bigger than ever. And beautiful, perfect Elise

Fontaine was right beside him, sharing his moment of glory.

He'd upped his hero status with his late-night pseudo ambulance run of Gideon to the Sheridan hospital. The press picture showed him with Elise, a harried look on his face, worried about one of his new ranch hands, as the press labeled Gideon. Gideon had been released two days after his surgery, and after a week of recuperation at the Buckle, he spent nearly every waking moment at the Spotlight Ranch.

From the way Gideon talked, Lincoln had become his big brother. He so clearly adored Lincoln that it became harder and harder for Stefanie to stay angry at the man.

Especially since he'd made an attempt to apologize. He'd left countless messages on her answering machine, but after two weeks, they'd started to peter out. Hopefully he'd get the hint, pack his things, and return to Hollywood, where he belonged. It was starting to get difficult to find a parking place in Phillips since Lincoln's announcements about the scholarships the American Film Institute was handing out to prospective filmmakers had made every supermarket rag as well as *People* magazine.

Maybe she should move. She couldn't if she hoped to get Haley and Macey back.

Currently, however, Social Services wasn't taking her calls.

She should be thankful she wasn't in jail, perhaps. Gideon had seen the girls once — they were staying in a group home in Sheridan. He mentioned, with a hitch in his voice, that Haley had reverted to her silent mode.

Stefanie feared what Macey might be doing to cope.

Gideon held out little hope for his sisters to be released to him, despite the grace from the court system. However, his rescue of Libby had made him a town hero of sorts, and Stefanie couldn't help but note the way Pastor Pike had greeted him this morning as Stefanie and Gideon arrived at church, right ahead of Piper and Nick. It seemed that maybe the pastor was giving Gideon a fresh start.

Stefanie watched with a kind of sisterly pride as Gideon stood in the front row, singing from his open hymnal.

Of course, she had to have somewhere to look, because like a glutton for punishment, her gaze kept returning to Lincoln on the left-hand side, fourth pew from the front.

Stefanie tried not to choke on the words of the hymn. She closed her eyes against a wave of shame. If Lincoln wanted to worship God, she shouldn't judge him. Even if a throng of reporters presently camped outside church made the entire thing seem like a publicity stunt.

When the congregation finished singing, Stefanie sat down. Piper reached over and squeezed her hand.

Their conversation last night over a very quiet and lonely dinner rushed back at Stefanie.

"Tell me again why you aren't marching right over and telling Lincoln exactly how you feel about him," Piper had said.

"Because he doesn't love me. And I don't expect him to. He has a much different life than I do, and I can't barge into it."

"He had no problem barging into yours."

"Piper, I'm serious. I don't fit into his world. And frankly he doesn't fit into mine. Can you seriously see me jetting off to hang out on his movie sets or hanging on his arm at fancy premieres?"

"Yes. I think you'd look great on the red carpet in some fancy dress. You could ask Kat if you could borrow some of her outfits."

"Stop. It's more than that. I'm just his neighbor."

"I don't think he meant that."

Stefanie only had to stop and remember

the look on his face when Elise had asked him who Stefanie was in his life. Right then, her world teetered on a precipice, and even as she held her breath, she'd known. Lincoln needed his fame. His women. His cars, his movies, his tabloids. He needed them to keep himself from hiding in the dark and letting his fears, the truth of his condition, consume him. Deep down, he was still the little boy hiding in the junkyard, waiting for E-bro to haul him out and pummel him. To prove he was weak before the entire world.

What hurt the most was that she had believed, *truly* believed with everything inside her, that he was stronger than that. Or maybe she'd only seen what she wanted to.

Oh, how Stefanie suddenly missed Lewis.

Because after she had left the hospital, after she'd made it home and cocooned herself in her comforter, after she'd let the pain of losing Macey and Haley pour through her, she'd realized what Lincoln had been afraid of all this time.

He was afraid that she couldn't love him if she met the real him.

Lewis was the man he'd been trying to hide. Although he thought Lewis was someone to be ashamed of, Lewis was the man she'd begun to love.

As Stefanie sat in church, watching half the congregation watch Lincoln, a wave of sadness swept through her. They weren't so different, she and Lincoln, she and Lewis. Never sure of who they were or where they belonged.

After the service, she waited for Gideon outside in the churchyard. Lincoln stopped and shook the pastor's hand amid a serenade of flashes and questions from the press about his relationship with Elise.

Stefanie shook her head. Even if the rumors were true and he and Elise were an item, a person had to be blind to miss the look of annoyance on Lincoln's face as he told them not to get ahead of themselves.

She shouldn't make any assumptions either. But it was hard not to. Lincoln looked magnificent today, in a gray shirt, black suit pants, and silver aviator sunglasses, a slight wind blowing his recently trimmed hair. He'd look great for this week's cover — or wherever his picture ended up. But perhaps only she noticed the way he gripped the railing of the stairs as he made his way down.

Leave him alone. The thought panged inside her. She put on her sunglasses before he could see her watching him.

"Can you believe all this hype about Lincoln?" Gideon said, walking up to Stefanie. She noted Libby beside him, grinning, her hand in his. Gideon seemed to be on the mend, although he still walked gingerly. Libby still wore a haunted look around her eyes, but it faded when she was with Gideon.

"Yes, I can believe it." Stefanie opened the truck door. "Maybe it'll convince the town to pave the church parking lot. Ready to go?"

"Uh . . ." Gideon held up Libby's hand, giving Stefanie a strange look. "Pastor Pike invited me over for dinner and . . ."

Looking at Libby, Stefanie wondered if she'd ever worn such a happy expression as she saw on Libby's face now. Certainly not with Doug . . . but with Lincoln?

She didn't want to go there. "Of course, Gideon. Have fun."

She watched them walk away, but it was long after they'd vanished into the crowd that she realized her gaze had landed on Lincoln as he'd gotten into his pickup and driven away with her heart.

Lincoln had made a mess of everyone's lives and he knew it. The quaint town of Phillips had gone from lazy and quiet to a beehive of activity. The Buffalo Saloon had never had so many cowboy wannabes riding the mechanical bull, and a deputy from Billings had taken up full-time residence outside the bar to head off drunk drivers. For a couple of days, there'd been photographers sleeping in their cars, and Missy's diner at dawn resembled an LA club on a Friday night.

He had turned the town into a three-ring circus. Lincoln had the strange urge to apologize everywhere he went. Especially to Stefanie Noble.

He drove back to the ranch, wishing Stefanie had at least raised her hand in greeting this morning at church. He'd gotten so used to seeing her in working clothes that the long floral skirt and yellow blouse under a jean jacket had thrown him right off his game. Especially when she wore her hair down, and all he could think of through most of the service — much to his chagrin — was the memory of winding his hands through her hair. Of holding her in his arms. Of the way she smiled up at him, her eyes shining, after he kissed her.

His ears did perk up, however, when Pastor Pike began his sermon. These last two weeks, it seemed as if the minister had designed his words for Lincoln — talking about grace and strength. Lincoln had ordered a Bible online so he could look up the verse in Hebrews he and Pastor Pike had talked about at the hospital.

He especially clung to God's words in Hebrews 13: "I will never fail you. I will never abandon you." It felt like too much promise for a man like Lincoln, who'd done exactly that to God. Still, although Lincoln couldn't name the sizzle inside him, sometimes he thought it felt a lot like hope.

Elise was lounged on the back deck of the porch reading a magazine when he got home. She didn't look at him, just raised her voice. "Don't you think that going to church is a little overkill?"

He walked out to the deck and stood watching a few of his homely herd grazing in the field. "You have something against God?" She wore sunglasses that swallowed half her face, a pair of black stiletto boots, low-rider cargo pants, and a bejeweled tank. She might as well be wearing a sign that read Walking Sin.

"No. I used to go to Sunday school. I know the Ten Commandments. But I just don't know what's gotten into you in the past couple of weeks." She put down the magazine, stood up, and ran her hand down his arm. "This is the first time we've been alone. I feel like you've been ignoring me. And today, when Dex had to go into Sheridan, you leave me for *church*."

Lincoln moved away from her. "I'm not ignoring you. Dex has me taping interviews and evaluating scripts and . . ." And he wasn't interested in anything Elise had to offer. Not anymore. In fact, the idea of holding anyone other than Stefanie in his arms made his stomach knot.

Elise sat down in a huff. He glanced at her. Yes, there was probably something wrong with him to turn down a woman like Elise.

His brain said he needed Elise if he wanted to stay on top of the game. Dex liked her, and she had *megastar* written all over her. Besides, Stefanie obviously didn't want him. He felt like he had when he first started knocking on doors in the film industry.

Shut out.

Invisible.

Seeing Stefanie today had only raked up every hidden, forgotten, ridiculous hope that they might have a future together. What had he been thinking anyway? Stefanie had a life here — one firmly rooted in her land, her horses. He was mucking it up.

And not just with the press people who parked in the high school football field and clogged the only road between Phillips and the Silver Buckle. Lincoln still hadn't tracked down who had poisoned Clancy and driven his four-wheeler off the road. He'd hoped for a confession from JB and Luther. In fact, he had offered to go down to police HQ and offer some assistance in that area. However, although JB had turned on Luther and claimed the attack on Libby had been payback for Gideon's part in getting Luther fired, both men denied any involvement in the other two incidents. As much as Lincoln wanted to believe it was them, he had to agree that neither JB nor Luther had any clear motive to kill Stefanie's dog. Thankfully, they wouldn't get away with hurting Libby. Both men had been shipped to Sheridan to wait for their court date.

Then there was the issue with Lincoln's dead new truck. Gideon had discovered a broken right headlight when he'd had it hauled into town for repairs. But Lincoln knew he hadn't run into anything, especially with the truck sitting in the garage. Worse, after he'd had the truck checked out, even the mechanic couldn't explain the short between the engine computer and the starter.

He couldn't escape the sense that someone had tampered with his vehicle in hopes of running him off the road.

Lincoln had started sleeping with his bedroom door locked, just in case Luther was innocent and Gina had somehow tracked Lincoln to Phillips. With the premiere of *Unshackled* scheduled for next weekend and a slew of critics and cast members flying in to attend, Lincoln would have to double security to get any sleep.

He glanced at Elise, who had picked up her magazine again and was pretending to read. Maybe he *had* been ignoring her.

With everything going on and after the dust cleared from the nightmare with Gideon and Libby, the one person he most wanted to talk to was Stefanie. He missed her smile and the easy way she had of listening and moving with his moods. She read him better than anyone did, and even when he wanted to be left alone, she wouldn't let him. He needed that most of all.

Left to his own devices, he filled his world with . . . things that only accentuated what he didn't have.

A real friend.

A friend who knew his secrets and cared for him anyway. A friend who knew what he really needed, what his deepest prayers might be.

A friend with whom he could talk about

how it felt to hope that maybe God was answering his prayers, just as she'd suggested.

"Strength is in who you are."

He hoped so. Because, like the pastor had said today, quoting from 2 Corinthians 12, " ' *"My grace is all you need. My power works best in weakness." . . . For when I am weak, then I am strong.' "* Contrary to Elise's insinuations, Lincoln wasn't going to church to avoid her — he desperately wanted to believe that God could make him strong, even through this disease. That it didn't have to overtake him. That maybe God could answer his prayer.

And he needed that hope from Stefanie because the last two weeks his body felt as if he were walking through sludge, every step a struggle. Even Dex noticed his afternoon naps and the way he took his time moving up and down the stairs. Enough that when Dex handed him a new script, he told Lincoln, point-blank, that this time, he'd be using a stuntman. Lincoln knew he'd probably have to come clean to Dex soon.

Lincoln had been about halfway through the script — an action-adventure about a mountain climber — when he realized that Dex was right. This one would be way above his abilities.

"They're all caught in a time warp," Elise said, cutting through his thoughts. She lowered her glasses onto her nose.

"Who?"

"This town. These people. By the way, I saw your neighbor. The one with the long black hair. The horse girl."

The horse girl? He tried to hide a bitter-sweet smile. Yeah, *his* horse girl.

"Did you see what she was wearing? Hello, Calamity Jane." She giggled and crossed her long, slim legs.

"Be nice, Elise. Stefanie is a friend of mine."

"A friend?" Elise touched his arm, still smiling. "Sure she is. Who is she, anyway? You said she wasn't the help, but I can't figure out what you see in her, so . . ."

"She's not the help." He kept his voice low, real low, because he didn't want her to hear how he suddenly wanted to throw her out of his home, his state, his life. "She's . . ." What? The woman he loved? He wasn't exactly sure about that, but he knew she was . . . his best friend. The words curled through his chest, followed by an explosion of truth that took his voice.

Stefanie had never treated him, not even once, with pity. With anything less than the expectation that he could be her hero.

"Don't tell me. . . ." Elise's smile vanished. Then, as if to give voice to the expression he knew he wore on his face, she said, "You can't be saying you . . . like her? Lincoln, be serious. She's a country girl. A hick."

Elise was staring at him as if he'd just run over a pack of kitties. And then he saw it, written in Elise's eyes. The reason Stefanie had so easily, so quickly, so finally, walked out of his life.

Elise didn't think Stefanie was good enough for him — no surprise there — but Stefanie had *agreed* with that judgment.

The wind went out of him. He thought back to the picnic under the beautiful sky, listening to Stefanie, really listening, like he should have when she told him about Doug Carlisle. *"He* had *made plans. . . . Except not for us. Or rather, not with me."*

He winced and rubbed his forehead.

"Are you okay?" Elise gave him a disgusted look.

He'd treated Stefanie — at least in her mind — like Doug had treated her. He hadn't only been a jerk to Gina and women like her. He'd been a jerk to Stefanie. She'd trusted in him, in their friendship. And even if he hadn't meant it that way, she felt as if he'd thrown her away.

Just like Doug had thrown her away.

No wonder she wouldn't take his calls.

"What was I thinking?"

"What?"

He turned to Elise, watched her pale as he said, "Stefanie is much, much more than a friend, and you need to know that."

Elise's jaw hardened.

Lincoln left her there, slamming the door to the house behind him as he stalked to his office. But she was right. And he had to figure out exactly how to tell Stefanie that he was sorry.

CHAPTER 21

Apparently, since Stefanie wasn't answering her telephone, Lincoln had decided to use the postal service.

And the florist.

Stefanie stood in the kitchen staring at the dozen lilac roses and the box of chocolates. Everything inside her sank. What was Superhero trying to do to her?

Stefanie had moved back into the house after Macey and Haley left, but last night they'd had the dreaded talk — the one about Nick and Piper's need for a bigger place. With Stefanie's permission, Nick had chosen to dismantle her room, thanks to the pink walls. Even she agreed it would make a perfect nursery.

Stefanie had lain in her bed last night, looking at the pink wallpaper, thinking about Haley and Macey sleeping in the group home in Sheridan. She'd asked to be considered as a foster parent, but with Nick and Piper's coming addition, the Silver Buckle was lacking adequate bedrooms. And she was sort of on the naughty list with Social Services.

To add salt to her wounds, the social worker had refused to let the children talk to her. But Nick had been able to find out that the girls were being taken back to South Dakota.

Where she'd probably never see them again.

Gideon was beside himself with frustration, and Stefanie wouldn't put it past him to bust them out again. She nearly offered him her truck.

Casting another glance at the untouched boxes on the table, Stefanie grabbed her jacket and marched out to the barn.

She bet that Elise Fontaine had never touched a manure shovel, but it fit so well into Stefanie's hand, as if she'd been born with it. And that oh-so-lovely smell was probably embedded in her skin — eau de manure.

She led the horses into the corral and fed and watered them. Then, grabbing the rake, she began to muck out the stalls. She was really good at that.

Not so good at trusting people, though. Really good at letting the bold and the beautiful twist her brains into a knot. Not so good at guarding her heart.

She took off her gloves and wiped her tears, hating that just when she thought he was gone from her system, Lincoln sent her flowers.

She wondered if Elise knew about his condition. And if she would stay with him . . .

She stopped raking and closed her eyes. That wasn't fair. Elise might be beautiful and poised and perfect, but maybe she wasn't that shallow.

Stefanie hoped.

She left the barn, watching the tumbleweeds rolling across the windswept grasses, now pale green as they flowed over the hills of Silver Buckle land. Here and again, wild iris and Wyoming kittentail edged the gullies that had been furrowed out of the earth by God's creative force. She usually forgot to see it. Forgot to notice as spring swept in, as summer made its lazy creep into their lives. Forgot to smell the air as it changed from crisp to scented, to watch as the calves began to leave their mothers and play in the fields. She had simply melted into the days, letting the work overtake her.

"You belong here, Stef." Her father's

words after she'd returned home from college sounded a faint echo in her memory. He'd stood beside her at the corral and simply said, *"You belong here. You're in this land."*

Maybe, instead of seeing that as second best, she should see it as a blessing. This was what God had given her. This life. This family. This job.

And for a time, these kids.

She saw Macey in her memory, that last day as she'd followed her to the barn and stood on the bottom rung of the corral, watching the horses. She had parted her hair into two ponytails and washed her face clean of makeup. Stefanie had spotted the real color of her hair, a lighter brown, beginning in a swath across the top of her head. Stefanie liked it so much better than the jet-black dye. She wore a pair of Stefanie's old pants and a pale pink shirt, and it reminded her of the day Macey had said pink wasn't for her.

Stefanie smiled. Maybe Macey had just never let herself consider that she might be a pink girl.

Just like Stefanie never let herself consider that she might be right for Lincoln. But maybe, for the time he needed her, she had been.

Still, it didn't make his rejection any easier.

I miss you, Lewis.

A horse nickered, one of her new ones, and she reached into an alfalfa bag along the corral fence for a treat. *"Listen, Dances with Horses, not everyone can talk to the animals."* Oh, how she missed his corny nicknames for her. Missed the way they made her feel like she mattered.

Stefanie heard the door slam and looked up to see Nick coming down the steps. She wiped her tears and headed back to the barn.

"The postman was looking for you earlier."

"I saw the packages." Stefanie said, not stopping.

"Stef, slow up."

She sighed, halted at the door of the barn, and dredged up a smile. Nick had always been intimidating, big and a little frightening, although his rebel behavior had taught her that even big brothers could mess up, and bad. But Nick had put his life back together and in the past two years had become every bit as huge as he'd been when she was eight and he was thirteen and the Buckle's roping champ.

"What?" she said, already on guard.

421

Nick said nothing more, just reached out and pulled her tight against him.

"What are you doing?"

He didn't let go. "What I should have done a long time ago. I'm telling you that if you want me to beat him up, I'll do it."

Stefanie managed a smile and disentangled herself. "No, that's okay. I'm over —"

"Gimme a break. You were crazy about him, and the guy broke your heart." Nick put his gloves on. "I'm serious about beating him up." This time he didn't smile.

"Thanks, Nick. But I don't think that's necessary."

He nodded. "Well then, I've got something to say." He glanced toward the house. "Piper told me about the guy who hurt you years ago."

"Oh."

"And I think I figured out why you came back to the ranch and never left."

"Someone had to run it —"

"Stop. Dad had Dutch, and he could have hired on help. But because you were here, he depended on you, and you let time tell you that's where you belonged."

"It is where I belong."

"Of course it is. But not because you don't fit into the lives of men like Lincoln Cash.

422

Don't let what other people expect of you tell you who you are or where you belong. And most of all, don't let your own defeats brand you. I did that. All I heard was my guilt and shame, and they kept me from ever making things right between Dad and me." Nick wore his grief on his face, and for a moment, Stefanie couldn't speak.

He closed his eyes and swiped off his hat, blowing out a breath. "You're an amazing person. I look at you and it makes me proud to be your brother."

Stefanie looked away, unable to keep her emotions from her eyes.

"But I think fear, or maybe hurt, has kept you from seeing that. From seeing yourself the way you are. I said not to let anyone else tell you who you are and where you belong — and that includes you. I know this guy from your past hurt you and I know Lincoln hurt you, but sometimes I wonder if the Noble genetic predisposition to be our own worst enemies hasn't affected you too." He reached out and touched her arm. "You're not going to find out who you are until you listen to the only One who knows."

"And who might that be?" she asked, a smile on her lips.

He wasn't smiling. "God. He knows you better than you even know yourself. And I have it from a good source that He's crazy about you."

Stefanie clenched her jaw, turned away.

But Nick caught her and pulled her against him again. "Sis, there's only one name you should be calling yourself. And that's God's Beloved."

She ached to believe him, to hear his words.

"I'm sorry I wasn't here when you needed me," Nick said softly. "I should have been the big brother you needed."

Oh, Nick. She let herself relax in his embrace, leaning her head on his chest. "You're the bestest biggest brother a girl could have," she said in a little-girl voice.

He laughed. "And in case you're getting the wrong impression, I really do need you around here."

Stefanie smiled at him as he headed for the barn to fetch his horse. *Beloved.* How she longed to let that word soak through her.

Lord, I want to be Your Beloved.

"Watch out that no poisonous root of bitterness grows up . . ."

Maybe the worst root of bitterness she'd nurtured had been her unforgiveness of herself. She'd forgiven Doug. And she could even forgive Lincoln. But she hadn't forgiven herself for loving so easily, for giving herself away without a thought to the future, for derailing her dreams in a moment of weakness. Over the years, she'd let her self-condemnation fester, let it weave through her dreams, choking them, strangling her ability to see all God had given her, all the ways He called her His Beloved.

No wonder she was never content. Because she never believed that God would give her the best after what she'd done.

She paused just inside the barn door, closing her eyes. *Lord, I want to forgive myself. Help me forgive myself. Help me see myself the way You see me and to hear Your voice.*

The sound of a truck driving into the yard broke into her thoughts. Stefanie came out of the barn as Piper emerged on the porch. They stared at the brown cargo truck.

A man in brown shorts climbed out of the open door carrying a large white box. "UPS delivery," he said to the two women.

Neither moved.

The deliveryman stood there, wearing his dark sunglasses, under the full heat of the morning, glancing between them. He looked at the label. "For Stefanie Noble."

"That's her," Piper said, pointing. She cocked her head and smiled.

"I've never seen a UPS man before,"

Stefanie said with a soft smile.

He handed her the box. "Had to drive up from Sheridan. Pretty country," he said as he got into the truck.

"Another delivery?" Piper said, following Stefanie into the house.

The cool air from the kitchen whisked over Stefanie's sweaty face. Or maybe the heat in her face came from seeing so many gifts piled on the table.

"Open them," Piper said, taking a seat. "And please start with the chocolate."

But Stefanie stared at the loot, unable to move. "Why is he doing this?"

"Apparently you're the only one who thinks you're 'just a neighbor.' Open the presents."

Stefanie sat down on the chair. *Why?* "Maybe only the card," she said.

Lincoln had his own stationery, of course. Very masculine, yet refined, with a big *LC* written in black ink on a white-on-white card affixed to the big white box.

"What does he say?"

Stefanie opened the card. She wasn't prepared. Maybe because she'd thought he hadn't been listening that day when she'd told him her dreams about having her own ranch, or maybe because she'd hoped he'd forgotten how pitiful she'd been, laying her heart out for him. Nevertheless, there it was, written in black and white.

Dear Horse Whisperer,
Please come and watch a movie with me.

Lincoln

A formal invitation inside gave the date and time of tonight's *Unshackled* premiere.

Stefanie looked at the box. There was no name on the box to indicate a department store. She put the card down and made a fist to stop her hand from shaking.

Just a neighbor.

She closed her eyes. No, she was his friend. And he was her friend. Even if that was all it was, maybe she could still open the box and enjoy that.

Inside was the most beautiful dress she'd ever seen.

"Oh, my goodness — is that for you?"

"I . . . guess so." But, oh, how she hoped so, in a wild, fantasy-come-true kind of way.

The dress, made of burnished gold satin, had a beaded corset bodice, appliquéd with tiny pink and red flowers along the neckline and up the spaghetti straps. Stefanie pulled it out and held it up to herself. The skirt fell just above her ankles, and a flimsy organza overlay fluttered the rest of the way to the floor.

It was the most exquisite thing she'd ever seen. Like wearing a piece of caramel.

Stefanie put it back into the box. Stepped away from it. Stared at it. Touched it.

"For heaven's sake, Stef, it's not a rattlesnake. Try it on."

"No!"

Piper put down the box of chocolate and wiped her hands. Then she riffled through the dress box and produced a pair of gold strappy sandals. "At least try these on."

"I can't possibly . . ." But Stefanie couldn't stop the wash of feelings — delight and surprise and a bit of indignation, but that was quickly doused by more delight.

"Yes, you most certainly can." Piper stood up and shoved the sandals into Stefanie's hands. "C'mon. We have a lot of work to do in the next couple of hours."

But Stefanie backed farther away from the box, then sank into a kitchen chair. "Who is he trying to fool? I'm going to look stupid. There will be a hundred actors and special guests there, ones who get paid to look good. What is Lincoln thinking?"

Piper picked up the invitation. "I think he's asking you out."

"I can't go out with . . . Lincoln Cash."

"Why not? Because the entire world will see? Because you might end up on the cover of a tabloid?"

Stefanie winced at the headlines running through her mind.

"And what's so horrible about being seen with Lincoln?"

"Because when he's tired of —" She covered her mouth with her hand. "He was listening. All that time, he was listening."

"I think it's more than that. I think he's trying to tell you that he wants you in his life. Look at this dress. Lincoln is a man of taste, and he picked this out for you." Piper picked up the corset. "It's bold and strong yet delicate, and the color . . . he picked that out too."

Stefanie touched the flowers on the dress. "It's gold."

Gold.

"Go to the premiere, Stef. Go in this dress of gold and see what love story might be waiting for you."

Lincoln knew he shouldn't be surprised that Dex had pulled it off. Not that Delia hadn't helped — well, her and a slew of party planners who camped out at his home in the newly constructed guest bunkhouse that stood on the former John Kincaid homestead. Now his ranch looked more like a frontier hotel preparing for a wedding. Enormous white tents had been erected in the yard, and the smell of barbecue ribs from the grills the caterers brought in had everyone salivating. A red carpet had been run out from the theater and a perimeter erected for the press, enforced by an army of private security, all of whom had Gina's picture in their breast pockets.

Lincoln had ordered a pair of snakeskin boots made for the event and paired it with a silk shirt and black tails. Elise wore a scoop-neck, princess-cut red ball gown and black past-the-elbow gloves, her hair piled high on her head.

His assistant, Delia, who had flown in two weeks ago, looked stunning in a black dress that accentuated her dark skin and flashing brown eyes. She had the party well in hand, and even as Lincoln sat in his office, leaning against the desk and watching the crowd and the chaos outside, he could hear her barking orders.

Where was Stefanie?

"Knock, knock," a voice said.

Lincoln motioned for John Kincaid to enter. At over six feet tall and cowboy to the bone, John had shocked the world when he revealed his identity as a Western romance

430

author. But no one minded when his book hit the best-seller list for twenty-six weeks straight. He hadn't ditched his cowboy roots tonight either, despite the black silk suit. Under it he wore a shiny gambler's vest.

"It's the height of arrogance to bring the crowds to you, pal," John said, holding out his hand. "And what did you do to my ranch?"

"A few improvements. Indoor plumbing, electricity — you know, the works." Lincoln dodged a fake punch, laughing. "I think you'll like what I did to the barn." The fact that John had owned the land with his family for fifty-plus years should have left Lincoln worried about the changes he had made, but John had washed his hands of the ranch when he moved last year, taking with him his best souvenir from his life in Phillips: his beautiful wife, Lolly. Lincoln looked past John, searching for her. "Where's your inspiration?"

"In the kitchen, of course." John shook his head. "She's going crazy with too little to do. I think we're going to open a restaurant."

John and Lolly had moved to LA last fall, right after their quick wedding in Hawaii and after selling Lolly's railroad car diner in Phillips to Missy Pike. But the way Lolly could put together a pie, Lincoln could easily see their place being the hottest eatery in Pasadena.

"I've been catching up with the locals. Sounds like you've made your mark here." John walked over to the window, staring out. "And I met Gideon and his sisters. Nice kid, even if he did burn my house down."

Lincoln smiled at the kindness in John's face. The fact that Macey and Haley's caseworker had allowed them to attend the premiere only made this day more spectacular.

That was, if Stefanie turned the day from dark to sunny with her arrival.

Please, Stefanie, show up.

Please believe that I am different than Doug Carlisle. Give me a chance to prove myself. And if things didn't turn out the way he hoped, he still wanted to see her smile when she saw Macey and Haley decked out in their fancy dresses. Even Gideon had agreed to wear a tux.

"I saw Nick outside. And Piper. She looks like she's going to pop any second," John said.

"I sincerely hope it won't be tonight. I need a nice calm party without any action scenes or drama."

"Speaking of drama . . ." John turned

away from the window and smiled as the limousine driver who transported people from the parking area down by the gate to the house opened the door for the latest passenger.

Stefanie had come. Wearing the dress.

Everything inside Lincoln turned to liquid.

Her hair was down and curled in dark rich waves past her shoulders. She wore makeup — brown around her eyes and a pink mouth that now gave a tentative smile. And the dress — Stefanie shimmered in all that gold, her figure perfectly outlined in the corset top, the flow of the skirt. He'd told Delia exactly what he wanted, and she'd sent him a list of samples from his favorite designers. He'd finally found the right one, the one that told Stefanie exactly how he felt about her.

She came up the porch steps, and suddenly it hit him. He loved her. That realization was carried in on a breath that felt at once cleansing and new. Of course he loved her. Not the kind of love he'd uttered so many times in the movies and not the love that Elise offered. But a love that wanted only the best for her, wanted to see her laugh and shine, a love that needed her and knew that was okay. Those feelings bunched up right below his breastbone so he could hardly breathe with the fullness. He swallowed, aware that his mouth had dried, and he felt as if he might be falling, even as his thoughts whirred.

A living description of everything Nick had predicted.

"She's here," Lincoln said.

If John responded, Lincoln didn't hear it as he strode from his office to meet Stefanie on the porch.

Bathed in the light of camera flashes, he took her hand and smiled down at her. "Wow. You look incredible."

"Thank you. I . . . like the dress."

He stood on the porch a moment longer, her hand in his, and hoped the cameras caught every nuance of delight on his face. "Me too." He slipped his arm around her shoulders. "Come inside."

He wanted to take her in his office and tell her exactly what he'd been thinking and feeling, but Lolly met Stefanie as they went inside and swooped her into an embrace. Lolly looked like a woman who knew herself in a sleeveless gown of hot coral with a mock turtleneck top that accentuated her shoulders and regal neck. She had her blonde hair pulled behind her ears with a pair of diamond clips.

"Can you believe all this?" She looped her arm through Stefanie's. "When John said Lincoln bought his ranch and was remodeling it, I had no idea he really meant *remodeling* it."

Stefanie glanced at Lincoln. He couldn't read her eyes when she said, "I know. He's full of surprises."

He wanted to remove her from Lolly's grip and pull her into his office and kiss her. More than that, he wanted to tell her . . . that . . . Oh, the words clogged in his chest. He even winced under the pressure. He'd never told a woman he loved her before. Not . . . really. Not when it meant reaching inside his chest and giving her the opportunity to walk away with his heart, leaving him hollow and broken.

But she'd shown up in the dress. Did that mean she'd forgiven him?

He followed the women out to the back, where Lolly was already introducing Stefanie to her new Hollywood friends.

"Stefanie!" The young voice came from the porch.

Lincoln was right behind Stefanie, heard her gasp as Haley ran up and launched herself, pink fluffy dress and all, into Stefanie's arms.

Stefanie twirled the little girl around,

435

laughing, then set her down. "What are you doing here?"

"Lincoln did it! He even bought me and Macey our dresses!" Haley stepped back and twirled like a ballerina for Stefanie. Even more beautiful was the way she giggled, her sweet voice, not confined by her sadness.

"You are beautiful, Haley!" Stefanie said, looking at Lincoln. Her shining eyes told him he'd done well.

Macey came up behind Haley. "There you are! I was looking all over for you!"

Lincoln had to admit, he'd been nervous picking out Macey's simple black long-sleeved dress, but with the group home director's help, he'd found one that was cool enough for Macey. She looked so elegant that he had a difficult time remembering the girl in ripped jeans and black eye makeup.

Lincoln stood on the deck and watched his favorite girls shimmer.

The dinner lasted for over an hour, with speeches and ribs and music, courtesy of a country musician who'd agreed at the last minute to detour his tour, thanks to Dex's promise to use him in an upcoming film. Lincoln had arranged for Stefanie and the Kincaids, the North kids, Libby and Pastor

Pike, and Nick and Piper to all sit at the same table. He appreciated Karen's special attention in serving them. She, as much as Delia, deserved a bonus for her hard work.

Lincoln's seat was between Dex's and Elise's, but he made a point of working the crowd, mostly because he didn't want a shot of Elise and him to make the front cover.

He was secretly holding out hope that his smile at Stefanie would be the hot news of the night. Maybe if she saw it on his face, she'd guess the truth and he wouldn't have to . . .

Why was it suddenly so difficult to tell a woman he loved her?

Maybe because it was the first time in his life it wasn't a well-delivered line but the truth.

He watched her from over the heads of his guests, laughing and having a good time with her family. She glanced his direction, as if she'd known he was watching her, and he didn't look away. He was rewarded with a shy smile.

The cicadas came out as the music died down, and the guests started to move toward the theater. Lincoln hung behind, waiting for Stefanie.

She glided through the crowd like someone magical, and he was caught by the sight of her, even as Elise wrapped her hand around his arm. "Coming to the theater?"

He put his hand over hers, starting to disentangle it, just as Stefanie came near. She looked at Elise, then at Lincoln, and everything on her face seemed to shut off. Her mouth tightened, and her gaze slid past him as she followed the crowd to the theater.

"You did that on purpose," Lincoln hissed at Elise. He threw her arm off his and glared at her.

She looked at him as if she hadn't a clue what he might be talking about. Then, to his horror, her eyes started to fill. "You don't get it, do you?" She looked after Stefanie, and for the first time, he saw something like jealousy cross Elise's face. "She has a life here. But we only have now and what we make of it." Elise ran a finger under her eyes and forced a smile, the actress she was. "I'll see you in there."

He didn't watch her go. She was right. Lincoln only had now, as long as the crowds loved him.

But maybe Lewis had forever. In fact, *that* was the answer.

Lincoln and Elise did belong together. But *Lewis,* the man inside, needed Stefanie. It had been Lewis who cried out for help and Lewis whom God had answered.

Because Lincoln didn't need God. But Lewis so desperately did.

And Lewis belonged here in Phillips. With Stefanie.

She refused to be hurt. She refused to be hurt. *She refused to be hurt.*

Oh, who was she kidding? Stefanie smiled with the best of them as she walked past Lincoln, her gaze forced off the way Elise had him by the arm. He hadn't talked to her once all night. Hadn't crouched by her chair to ask about her food — which tasted delicious — and hadn't escorted her to the movie.

Even if he had brought Haley and Macey to the party, outfitted them in beautiful clothing, fed them delicious food.

Even if he'd told her she looked incredible.

Through it all, a verse pulsed right behind all the glitter: *"I have learned how to be content with whatever I have."*

The words, so incongruous with the surreal world around her, made her feel sorry, deeply sorry, for the people who determined their self-esteem by headlines. No wonder Lincoln had panicked, had felt lost.

The thought panged inside her. Wasn't that exactly what she had done? Based her identity on who she wasn't? Or, worse, who other people decided she was?

Ranch Hand. Defender of the Oppressed. Horse Whisperer. Leading Lady. As she stood there next to Macey and Haley, it hit her. These were God's words of love to her. All these names told her what she had — a family, friends, a gift with animals, even the ability to care for someone. She was all these things . . . and more. These names, blended together, gave her life meaning and purpose and told her she was exactly where she was supposed to be. *Who* she was supposed to be.

She put her hand to her throat, watching Nick lean over and take Piper's hand, watching Haley pull Gideon down to whisper in his ear.

Lord, I'm sorry I thirsted for something more when You've given me so much — all I needed, all I dreamed of, right here. I'm sorry I didn't hear Your voice. Please forgive me. Thank You for calling me Beloved, whether I'm in jeans . . . or a golden dress.

And with or without Lincoln.

She glanced at him. Tonight he had the world in the palm of his hand, not a hint of his disease showing. He looked like a bona fide hero with those wide shoulders and tailored suit. His whiskers were a perfect

440

two-day growth, his smile whiter than she'd ever seen it.

He took her breath away, and as she watched the press shower him with questions, she understood the truth. She'd probably never get over Lincoln Cash. She'd always, in some small way, or maybe a large way for a long while, pine for him.

His friendship, however, had made her see what she had. Had made her look at her life, at her friends. While she didn't for a second believe that Lincoln loved her, being courted for a moment by someone as amazing as Lincoln Cash had made her find herself again. He'd made her see that she was beautiful and special, and tonight, he'd showed her she could belong in both worlds.

And prefer hers.

Prefer the slow, honest work of training her horses, of tending the land, as she eked out a life each day with her family. Lincoln had shown her the other side of the fence, and it had been a gift because she realized how much she liked it on her side.

The press lined up along the red carpet. Stefanie waved and smiled as she walked into the theater, following Macey, Haley, Gideon, and Libby. Music from *Unshackled,* a country song, played over the speakers as she took in the cool air of the theater. Gideon was just scooting into his row of seats, his hand on Libby's back, when Stefanie's stomach began to twinge.

"You okay, Stef?" Libby asked as she sat down.

"I don't know. My stomach is queasy."

Gideon nodded. "Mine too." As if to confirm it, he shifted in his seat. "I'm actually starting to feel nauseous."

"Should we go?" Libby asked, disappointment so clear on her face that Stefanie's heart went out to her.

"Maybe I'll go up to the house. Lie down for a while." Gideon leaned over and spoke to Macey, who glanced at him with concern. Then he stood up and scrambled out of the row.

"I'm going with you," Stefanie said. She winked at Libby. "No worries. I'll bet we can talk to the theater owner and get another showing."

Piper and Nick sat down beside Libby. Piper didn't look so hot either.

"You okay, Piper?"

She nodded, but her expression didn't reflect her words.

Gideon led the way from the theater, through the crowd. As he and Stefanie waited in the lobby, he looked ashen. She didn't blame him. She suddenly felt as if someone had taken a scalpel to her insides.

"What was in those ribs?" Gideon said, his voice tight.

"You guys okay?" Lincoln had approached, as if he'd seen her and followed her out. "Are you not staying for the show?" The light dimmed in the lobby as one of the attendants closed the inner doors to the hall.

"Something we ate, maybe," Stefanie said. She looked at Gideon. "You go ahead to the house. I'll be right there."

He didn't need further permission.

And then Stefanie was standing there, alone with Lincoln. If she didn't know him better, hadn't seen him radiant and confident and knowing that he could act his way out of a ring of armed terrorists, she'd think he was nervous. He swallowed, watching Gideon leave, and every ounce of his confidence seemed to follow the kid right out the doors.

He turned back to her. His mouth moved a few times before words emerged. "Thank you for coming."

"I had this cute outfit I was dying to wear somewhere," she said, allowing a smile to creep into her face.

He actually looked more in pain. "Yeah.

But you look pretty great in your jeans and Stetson too."

She flushed but pressed her hands against her stomach, pretending it might be her illness.

Concern flashed across Lincoln's face. "What's the matter?"

"I have an upset stomach. Maybe from supper. Or . . ." She lifted a shoulder. "Nerves. I've never had my picture taken so many times."

"You get used to it."

Do you, Linc? Do you get used to smiling, hiding the man inside? "I think I'll sneak up to the house and lie down, if that's okay."

He nodded with an expression that looked like relief. Until she turned and he touched her arm. "Wait —"

"Lincoln, we're starting." Dex stood at the door of the theater, and Stefanie saw frustration pass over Lincoln's face.

"Okay." He lifted her hand and kissed the back of it, probably influenced by all the swooning heroines in the movie posters around him. "I'll be up to check on you in a while."

The timing couldn't be more perfect if she had sent engraved invitations. Her audience was here, waiting, including the press. No

444

one recognized her; no one even expected her.

No one would stop her.

And she would give them the story of a lifetime.

She stood on the porch of Lincoln Cash's beautiful home, watching him disappear into the ostentatious theater, and waited.

Her star would come to her.

CHAPTER 22

Lincoln sat in the air-conditioned theater, watching himself onscreen, or rather ignoring himself, and thinking of Stefanie.

He'd experienced a slight panic when he saw her get up and start to leave. All he could think of was how he'd let her go, without telling her how he felt.

Only . . . despite the dress and the way she'd said she believed in him, right here in this theater, despite the way she flushed tonight when he told her she was beautiful . . . what if she didn't want him?

With a whoosh, he realized it was this exact thought that kept the words glued to his chest. *I love you* should be freeing, not paralyzing. But maybe it took a special kind of strength to rip those words from inside, to lay out everything he wanted to be with her and let her write the ending.

If he didn't tell her right now, he might never find that strength again. If she responded with even the faintest of smiles, he'd sort out the rest later. He wanted her with him. On Spotlight Ranch. Even as that truth sank in, another followed it. He wanted Haley and Macey and Gideon here too. And horses, lots of them, and someday little dark-haired cowboys of his own.

He wanted it so badly, it loosened the words from the hard place inside him and they floated to the surface.

But what about his MS?

Lincoln watched himself on the screen, saw the smile that always seemed too brilliant, the stunts he knew were fake, and heard Stefanie's words: *"You bring to life all the dreams and hopes of your characters so well that it makes us feel that we know you and that we can be like you. You make us feel that we, too, can overcome those things in our lives that scare us."*

Maybe it was time for Lincoln Cash to step off the screen and into life. To tell the world about the real-life challenges facing him and thousands of others every day.

"But God used the man's blindness to bring him to Jesus. To healing. And He'll do the same in our lives." Pastor Pike's words from that first sermon filtered back to him, accompanied by the soundtrack on the screen.

God had used Lincoln's disease — not to

destroy his life but to make him stronger. To make him need God. Because, like the Bible said, when he was weak, that's when God was strong inside him.

What had Libby said about doing good? *"The only good we do that counts with God is the good we do in faith, in cooperation with Him."*

Lincoln smiled. He wanted that — to do something good and eternal.

Something that would make him respect himself.

And he'd start by being honest. With himself. With Stefanie. With his heart.

He closed his eyes, blocking out the dialogue, the music. *God, I see now that Stef was right. You've been answering my prayers for years. Maybe even now this is an answer — to show me that I can't be strong without You, but in my weakness, You can use me, make me the man I'm supposed to be. Please forgive me for forsaking You — thank You for not forsaking me. Please use this disease — my triumphs and my defeats — for good in my life and others'. And —* he opened his eyes, smiling at the man he saw on the screen — *help me tell Stef I love her.*

Now. He felt the press of urgency even as he prayed the words.

Now . . . yes. He loved her, and he wasn't

waiting another minute to tell her.

Getting up, he moved past Dex out of the row and ducked his head as he walked up the aisle. Piper and Nick were shuffling out of their row also. Piper had her hand on her stomach. Lincoln followed them into the lobby.

Nick looked like a man just taken out by a bull, pale and sweaty. "She's in labor. We gotta get to Sheridan."

"Oh." *Good one.* He scrambled for a better response. "Do you need help?"

Piper grabbed his arm. "Find Stefanie. Tell her to meet us there at the hospital."

He nodded as Nick led his wife toward one of the waiting limos. Lincoln opened the door. "Sheridan hospital," he said as if he might be talking to a cabbie in NYC.

Nick helped Piper into the backseat and crawled in beside her.

Lincoln closed the door on Piper doing deep breathing. Someday maybe he'd be the one sitting next to a pregnant wife. He nearly ran to the house. "Stef?"

He knew Delia had gone to the movie, but he expected to see Karen in the kitchen amid the population of caterers in white attire as well as another troupe in the backyard. "Anyone seen Karen?" he asked, thinking that she might have put Stefanie and Gideon upstairs.

He fielded a few negatives, then decided to check himself. The upstairs bedrooms were empty.

Returning to his office, he sat down at the desk. Stefanie had felt pretty bad. . . . Maybe . . . He lifted his phone and let the line at the Silver Buckle ring until he finally put down the receiver.

He dialed again.

She must have been either really sick or sleeping. He guessed an hour had passed since the start of the movie.

He wasn't sure why, but he tasted a surge of panic. He picked up the phone and dialed the chief security officer. According to him, Stefanie and Gideon hadn't left. He also reported that he hadn't seen anyone resembling Gina.

The cell phone on his desk trilled, indicating a voice mail. He picked it up, hoping to hear Stefanie's voice. But as he listened to the voice of his private investigator, Lincoln felt his heart begin a slow drop to his knees. Gina had been on a jaunt to Vegas and had returned to her home in LA last night.

Maybe Karen had seen Stefanie and Gideon. Lincoln passed the kitchen and climbed the stairs to Karen's apartment. When he knocked on the door, it cracked open to reveal darkness. "Karen," he called, feeling like a thief for the way he crept into the room. "Karen?"

He stood there, his heart thumping. Where had she gone?

Crossing to stand at the window, he looked out over his ranch. Dark shadows enveloped the hills, and he could barely make out the curve of the land from the sky.

He was about to go back to the theater when his gaze fell on a scrapbook, wedged behind the Queen Anne chair next to the window. Remembering all those times when Karen had clammed up about her past, he picked it up.

He turned on the light by the chair. Obeying the sick feeling of panic inside, he sat down and invaded her privacy.

Wedding pictures. Karen and her husband, a good-looking man with a thin face and rectangular wire-rimmed glasses. Taken in the nineties, based on Karen's Jennifer Aniston haircut. More pictures showed a honeymoon and a first house. Five or six pages later showed Karen with a pregnant belly.

What had happened to this happy couple to produce the quiet, sullen Karen who cooked a mean Denver omelet?

He found his answer near the end of the scrapbook, contained in a series of newspaper articles . . . about Gideon.

Gideon and his role in the accident that had killed Karen's husband and child and put her in the hospital.

Lincoln shut the book, clicked off the light, and let the ice slide through him.

What was she doing here?

Their conversations rattled him as he remembered bits and pieces from the last couple months.

"I don't have a family."

"I needed a job, and this is what I was looking for."

"I fixed up the leftovers for Stefanie to take home to that nice boy who lives with her."

Karen had fixed the plate of food the night Stefanie came to dinner. For Gideon.

The vet said that Stefanie's dog had been poisoned. . . . Could Clancy have eaten poisoned food meant for Gideon?

And the map of the ranch . . . *"Could I keep it? Just in case I might want to go exploring someday?"*

Lincoln stood, dropping the scrapbook onto the carpet with a soft thud.

"I've always wanted to write a screenplay, maybe be a filmmaker."

He walked over to the tiny desk, pulled

open the drawer, riffled through the papers. The script titled *The Last Ride* lay buried beneath receipts and scraps of paper. He remembered reading it. Rough at best, it had spooked him with its violence, the hopelessness of a story starting with a man driving his car over the edge in a fiery death. An edge like Cutter's Rock?

Oh, please, let me be wrong.

But ten years of reading movie scripts based on real-life horror stories told him he wasn't. *Please, God, help me get there in time. Please . . .*

"Call security!" he shouted to the army of caterers as he hustled down the stairs and outside. The movie was still in full swing, a few photographers milling around. He stood at the base of his porch stairs, waiting, but no one came. He grabbed a caterer. "Tell security to meet me at Cutter's Rock. Hurry!"

He raced to his four-wheeler and gunned it, praying that God would give him one more chance to save the girl.

"This is really kind of you, Karen. Thank you." How Stefanie could talk with her stomach rampaging like a bull inside her seemed a miracle, but at least she'd had the good sense to take Karen up on her offer to

453

drive her and Gideon home. After discovering him sprawled on Lincoln's sofa, she realized that they might as well suffer in their own house.

Lincoln probably wouldn't notice her absence much anyway.

Okay, that wasn't fair. He had come out after her and said he'd check on her. He had even told her she looked beautiful. In a Stetson and jeans.

Maybe someday they could be friends. After her heart figured out how to be in the same room with him without breaking.

She wanted to give Karen more than a feeble thank-you, especially after seeing how her own truck was caught in the snarl of cars parked below the house. Thankfully, Karen's truck was by the service entrance of the house, and she was taking the back way through the fields to the Silver Buckle.

"No problem," Karen said. She looked tired, her hair pulled back because of her long hours in the kitchen. "I'm just sorry you're sick."

"Me too," Gideon said. He gripped the door handle and gulped air from the open window.

Stefanie stared ahead at the headlights cutting through the darkness. She couldn't believe she was missing Lincoln's premiere.

The truck went over a rut, and Stefanie braced her hand on the dash.

"I think I'm going to be sick," Gideon said.

When Karen glanced over at him, Stefanie noticed a strange look flash across her face. A . . . smile?

Gideon doubled over.

Karen hit the brakes.

"What's wrong?" Stefanie said.

But Karen didn't answer as she got out, went around to the back of the truck.

Stefanie wanted to crane her neck to watch her, but it was all she could do not to slink back into her seat and cry. She closed her eyes instead. Why, of all days, did she have to get sick today? How she wanted to see Lincoln's film. But perhaps some things just weren't meant to be.

She heard Gideon's door open.

"Get out," Karen said in a tone Stefanie had never heard from her before.

Stefanie's eyes snapped open. The pain in her stomach couldn't compare to the shock of seeing Karen holding a .308 rifle at them. Or Gideon's face as any remaining blood drained from his expression.

"I said get out." Karen was talking to Gideon, who had moved slightly in front of Stefanie. It didn't matter whom she pointed the gun at — from this range, the bullet would tear through Gideon and end up hitting Stefanie.

Stefanie lifted her hands in surrender. "Karen?"

"Get out!"

Gideon was already complying. "Calm down. I'm getting out!" He slid out of the truck, still holding his stomach.

"I don't understand —"

"Shut up." Karen tossed Gideon a roll of duct tape. "Tape her hands behind her back."

"What are you doing?" Gideon stood there as if caught in headlights, blinking.

"I said tie her up."

Gideon stared at the tape, then looked at Karen. "Why are you doing this?"

"Because someone has to make sure you get what you have coming to you."

Gideon stumbled, putting his hand out to catch himself on the door.

Karen reacted by pushing the barrel against his head. "Do that again, and I'll have to rewrite my ending. And I don't want to do that."

Stefanie couldn't wrap her brain around Karen's words. What ending?

Gideon straightened, his hands raised. "Please don't hurt her. She has nothing to do with this. Let her go."

Karen took a step back. "Tape her hands, Gideon. You condemned her the minute you walked into her house."

The look on his face as he turned to Stefanie made her weep. "What is she talking about, Gideon?" she whispered as she leaned toward the dashboard and let him tape her wrists behind her back.

"Tighter, Gideon. Or I'll make you do it over."

Stefanie bit back a cry as the tape pinched her skin. Or maybe it was just her frustration.

"I'm sorry, Stefanie. I'm so sorry."

"What's going on? Gideon? Karen?" Stefanie said as she turned and watched Karen tape Gideon's hands, then tape his mouth. She shoved him back into the truck.

Karen climbed into the driver's side and tightened a piece of tape over Stefanie's mouth before she could demand more answers. "Apparently Gideon left something out of his past when he came to live with you," she said as she tucked the gun beside her. She patted Stefanie's knee. "Gideon killed my family. And now I get to return the favor."

Stefanie glanced at Gideon. Tears rolled down his face, pooling in the tape over his mouth. She remembered Karen serving them earlier, touching her shoulder in greeting as she did it. Her mind tracked back to Karen giving her leftovers — poisoning her dog, probably like she'd poisoned them tonight. And Lincoln's accident on the four-wheeler — had that been meant for Gideon? How long had Karen been in town?

Talk about Oscar-worthy performances.

They bumped through the fields, and in a moment, Stefanie saw the familiar outline of Cutter's Rock rise before them. Darkness gathered in the ravine.

If she ever needed a superhero, it was now.

She could be every bit of a director, like hotshot Dex Graves, and a million times better than Lincoln Cash would ever be. He had money, sure, but did he have talent? or courage? Especially courage.

Like all things, opportunity was created for those with courage.

Karen hadn't expected this turn of events, for everything to line up. She'd simply wanted Gideon to pay for his crimes.

When Lincoln had announced his scholarship program, she knew fate had dealt her another chance. Just like it had the day she watched Gideon exit juvenile hall, hike out

458

to the highway, and lift the run-down Impala.

Fate had been good to her then, payback for the way it treated her the three years before and every moment after until she got out of treatment.

And tonight, fate, more than anything, had been her codirector, culminating in a production that turned out better than she could ever imagine.

Lincoln had to choose her film, *The Last Ride,* for his scholarship, especially when he discovered that the author had been living under his nose for three months. Watching, plotting, cooking, cleaning. Did he know how difficult it had been to film the story? She'd had to work backwards from Gideon's giddy smile as he met Libby and worked at the diner — that had been a sheer stroke of luck. And yes, she'd taken a few artistic licenses, like cracking his distributor cap, not once but twice, to make his car cooperate with her loosely written script.

She'd have to thank Dennis for that, too, when she gave her acceptance speech for her award-winning movie. If it weren't for her husband's car repair hobby, she would have never known how to disable Gideon's car and Lincoln's truck. She'd planned only to scare Gideon. She hadn't meant for Lincoln to get in the way. In fact, she'd thought Gideon would walk home alone, but Lincoln had nearly destroyed everything with his sudden do-gooder offer of a ride home on his four-wheeler.

She would also thank her supporting characters — Luther had played a circumstantial part in kidnapping Libby. She'd have to acknowledge him. And then the fire, the glorious fire — it had been her inspiration.

It had all come full circle, despite the mistakes. She hadn't meant to kill the dog. She'd been trying to test the amounts on Gideon, see how much poison might render him ill. How much more might then kill him.

And tonight, Stefanie Noble had been a last-minute powerhouse addition to the cast.

Power rushed through her as she finally took her life back, right here, before her eyes and on film. She held a torch, letting it illuminate her face. To her left was the pickup truck — gleaming black in the moonlight. From the gas tank trailed a rag, which she'd already soaked in gas.

She'd parked the truck at an angle, the nose pointed toward the cliff, a rope in her other hand connected to the emergency brake release. It would be a glorious crash, and she'd positioned two cameras at the bottom of the ravine, checked to confirm the angles.

A spectacular explosion would open the film, and in the editing room, she'd then backtrack to the moment, to the look on Gideon's face when he realized who she was and the fate waiting for him at the bottom of Cutter's Rock. She'd made good use of the duct tape, just like they did on *CSI*. Gideon and Stefanie would be together forever.

"I dedicate this film to Dennis and Gretchen Axelrod," she said to the camera positioned ahead of her. It would capture the truck's catapult over the edge. "Without them, this would never be possible."

Her throat tightened at that. Her husband, Dennis, still visited her — he was the one who'd given her the idea. But Gretchen gave her endurance, encouragement. Karen could still hear her baby daughter's squeals of laughter deep in the night, when she thought she was alone.

This was for them.

"Karen!"

The voice startled her, and she turned, watching as a light scraped the ground.

"Karen, stop! It's Lincoln."

She smiled. "You came!" She knew he'd figure it out. And he wanted to watch, wanted to —

"Karen, don't do this."

Her smile fell. She gripped the rope and backed toward the truck. "Don't, Lincoln — stay there."

He stopped outside the pool of light from her torch, a dark shadow that showed off his size.

"Just watch."

"Watch?"

"It's going to be perfect, I promise. You'll love it — you just have to trust me."

Lincoln seemed to be taking in the situation. "I see. And . . . I do trust you. But . . . are you sure this is the way you want the beginning to go?"

He'd read her script! "Yes, yes, don't you see? It's the explosive opening that every movie begins with, and it'll draw the viewer in."

Lincoln stepped closer. "But what about the hero? If he's dead, the viewer can't root for him. They'll already know the ending, and they'll have nothing invested in the story."

She looked at his feet, now entering the circle of her light. He had a point, but . . . "No. I planned it this way."

"So, you rewrite. You reshoot. That's what directors do — they look at the story and rebuild the plot when it suits better."

She could see his face now, and it held no blame, no guile.

"Start the story right here, right where you have it. And then bring it full circle, to this moment. With the hero staring at the end." Lincoln had nearly reached her now. "It's a great story about someone who sees what his life could have become and goes back to change it. Someone who knows that without this horrible, black moment, he would have ended up on the bottom, broken. Now the hero has a chance to go back, to make things right. To tell the people he cares about how he really feels. It's a redemption story. Critics will love it." Lincoln put so much emotion into his voice, his eyes, his body language, that Karen could only believe him.

She lowered the torch. "I like your ending," she said softly.

"Then let's put this movie in the can." He reached out and took the torch.

Lights in the distance pinpricked the darkness. She jerked. "Who are they?"

Lincoln didn't even turn around. "Your fans?"

She didn't have fans. Not yet. "No, Lincoln. They're your fans! Fans that are going to wreck this entire movie!" Then, as he lunged at her, she yanked the emergency brake release.

The truck rolled over the edge and disappeared.

"Now the hero has a chance to go back, to make things right. To tell the people he cares about how he really feels."

Stefanie knew exactly what Lincoln meant as she awkwardly tried to unwind the duct tape that held Gideon's hands together. She'd already worked free the tape over her mouth. "Linc!"

She longed to go back and tell him exactly what he'd meant to her, that he'd made her see herself in a new light. She didn't care if she sounded like a fool, if he didn't love her. The real Stefanie Noble was tired of living her life listening to the voices of fear and failure.

The truck lurched forward, began to pick up speed.

"Stefanie!" Lincoln's voice broke through her panic.

Gideon freed his hands and kicked open his door.

"Go!" She braced her feet against the floorboards. "Go, Gideon!"

But she felt his arm snake around her waist, felt herself sliding along the seat, felt herself launched into the air.

She hit the ground almost on top of him. He grunted and she rolled off him, tearing her dress, watching the truck finish its career down the ravine and crash into the empty creek bed.

At least it hadn't —

Boom! The explosion threw her back as it lit up the night.

She looked up and saw Lincoln silhouetted at the top of the ridge, his hands on his head, staring at the blaze.

"Linc!" She doubted he heard her over the roar of the fire.

Gideon was pushing up on one elbow, groaning. "I think I broke something again."

"Are you okay?" Stefanie was bleeding from a scrape on her chin, right into her dress.

"Turn around," Gideon said as he went to work on her duct-taped hands.

"Gideon, you saved my life." She looked at him over her shoulder.

He was concentrating on his work, but he shook his head. "No, Stef. I think you saved mine."

"But —"

"Stefanie!" Lincoln had finally seen her and had begun to work his way down the slope, his face lit by the glow of the fire.

She watched him stumble toward her, nearly tripping, and remembered his words to Karen: *"Someone who sees what his life could have become and goes back to change it. Someone who knows that without this horrible, black moment, he would have ended up on the bottom, broken."*

Maybe his words weren't all an act. Maybe he, too, knew what they had and nearly lost.

Confirming her thoughts, Lincoln looked at Stefanie as if his world had nearly crashed at his feet, his face white, his eyes glossy. She knew his expression wasn't part of any role he might be playing.

His hands shook as he scrabbled down to her, as he hit his knees and held her by the shoulders. "Thank You, God. Oh, thank You. . . . I thought you were dead." He had real tears in his eyes and closed them as if trying to hide his emotions. "Did you really throw yourself out of that truck?" He took out a handkerchief, pressing it to her bleeding chin.

Her adrenaline was piling up, making her giddy. "What did you call it? The Dex something —"

"The Ditch and Roll. But please, I never want to go through watching that again." He pulled her to himself and held tight. "I thought I lost you. I was so scared. I just kept praying that God would give me the right words to say to Karen, something to buy time. I kept thinking that if He just gave me one more chance . . ."

" 'It's a redemption story. Critics will love it.' "

Lincoln leaned back and put his hand on her cheek. "Listen, okay. I gotta tell you something. Probably I should have told you before, a long time ago, but I only just figured it out, and you can't interrupt, because this is for real and it's not easy —"

"You love me."

His mouth opened. "You interrupted."

"Well, I know how wordy you actors are, and I wanted to get to the point. You love me."

He nodded.

"Okay, say it." She raised an eyebrow.

"What about you? Do you . . . love . . . me?"

"Oh my, you are insecure, aren't you? Have to have adoring fans everywhere?"

"Pretty much."

"Yes, fine. I love you. I'm crazy about you. I'm the president of your fan —"

He kissed her. And it wasn't one of those sweeping, movie-music-accompanied kisses either, but a kiss of desperation, filled with emotion and what-ifs, and finally, everything she knew about him, his fears and dreams. His strength. He wrapped his hand around her neck, and it was all she could do to catch her breath.

"I . . . do love you." His voice was broken, matching hers.

"See, that wasn't so hard," she said softly.

He gave her a slow trickle of a smile. "Maybe not. Maybe because you were right all along. There is a little piece of me in every scene I play. And I've been practicing for years to get it right . . . with you. Only, this isn't a scene. It's real. I do love you, Stefanie. You see through Lincoln to the real me."

"To Lewis."

"Yeah. To Lewis. Just a guy who hopes the girl he loves, loves him back."

"I do love you." She smiled at him. "But I think you need to come up with a better line because that sounds like it's from a movie."

"Shh." He was still holding her, however. "No, that's all mine."

This time when he kissed her, she did hear the music, the swooning and the violins and the happy ending to her own, very personal, chick flick.

"When I suggested coming out to Montana,

I was kind of thinking that you'd steer clear of all the thrilling, action-adventure, edge-of-your-seat, death-defying drama. Just can't live without it, huh?"

"Funny, Dex," Lincoln said, watching as the sheriff's red lights lit up the top of Cutter's Rock. It did seem ironic that out here, in the hills where he'd looked for peace, he'd confronted his greatest challenges.

Finding himself. Finding the man who didn't need the lights and the persona to be a hero. Finding the man who could confront his fears with trust that God had a bigger plan for him.

Finally he was becoming the man he'd always hoped he'd be, and he'd had to be on his knees to see it happen.

"How are you feeling?" He had Stefanie nestled in the curve of his embrace, a blanket wrapped around them as they sat on a large rock. He was still a little weak, the memory of the truck exploding against the pane of night playing over and over in his head. He'd never been so afraid.

"All that adrenaline must have flushed whatever poison Karen gave me right out of my system," Stefanie said.

"I think that's shock talking," Dex said. "I'd get her to a hospital, Linc."

"It's next on my list. As soon as Karen is locked up."

The woman sat in the backseat of the police cruiser, having been intercepted by his security team as she'd tried to flee the scene. She'd had to be subdued, a sight that Lincoln would long remember with pain.

Whatever was in the crazy woman's head, she was also grieving.

A grief that Gideon apparently felt too, because he'd stood frozen, watching as she was handcuffed, as she screamed accusations and murder in his direction. Then he'd cupped his hands over his head and sobbed.

"What's going to happen to her?" Stefanie said.

"I would guess she'll be hospitalized," Dex said. "Was she really planning on filming your deaths?"

"The camera was running — she probably got me on film."

"I'll have to get my hands on that before the press or someone else grabs it. Don't want you ending up on the Internet."

Lincoln saw more lights, and another four-wheeler pulled up.

Libby sprang off from behind her father and ran to Gideon, sobbing. He turned into her embrace.

"He's going to be okay," Lincoln said

softly, almost to himself.

"I think so," Stefanie said. "It just might take a while."

"Maybe we're all going to be okay." Lincoln touched his lips to her hair.

She smiled at him. "How was the movie?"

"Two thumbs up!" Dex answered. "Another Lincoln Cash blockbuster."

Lincoln heard voices calling his name and realized the reporters had found them. His groan was cut off by Dex. "I'll handle this."

"Dex to the rescue again," Stefanie said.

Lincoln shook his head. He'd have to put the kibosh on any plans Dex might have to turn this night into a PR moment for the movie. "Dex is going to be upset when I tell him that I'm out of the movie business."

Stefanie turned in his arms. "What? You can't quit. The world needs Lincoln Cash movies. I thought we went over this."

"We did, but . . . I think I'm done with blockbusters for a while. I want a nice, calm, peaceful . . ."

"Drama?" Stefanie gave him a small smile.

"How about . . . life?"

Something that included Stefanie, Gideon, Haley, and Macey. His beautiful horses and his land — the space that was his, as far as his eye could see. He'd come to Montana thinking his life was imploding.

He never dreamed that it would get so big.

Or that he would find himself in the middle of it, thankful to be alive and breathing, with the woman he loved in his arms.

"That sounds like an epic to me," she said as she lifted her face.

He kissed her again and saw cameras flash in his peripheral vision. "And you're my leading lady."

She laughed softly, sweetly. "As long as I don't have to do any stunts."

EPILOGUE

Lincoln Cash had never been more invincible. At least on the big screen.

However, if he didn't give her the popcorn, he was really going to get hurt. "I'm serious, Superhero. Hand it over," Stefanie said, reaching for the tub.

But Haley had already climbed over his shoulder, diving for it even as Macey reached between Stefanie and Lincoln for a grab.

Gideon reached over both of them and snatched it out of Lincoln's grip. "Uh-uh. It's mine and Libby's. It's the first popcorn we've had together in months, so beat it." He sat down and put his arm around a giggling Libby. Although the healthy tans they'd received from the summer sun had faded, Gideon nearly glowed with happiness at having Libby back after her fall term at college in Chicago. Stefanie had no doubt she'd go back in January, and in a year, Gideon might even join her.

But he wasn't quite ready to leave his family yet. His new family. Besides, he had to stand up for Lincoln in February in a wedding ceremony on the Noble family's ranch.

"Is this the movie about — ?" Macey started.

"Shh — I haven't seen it yet!" Rafe Noble, on a well-needed rest from his bull-riding tour, sat with his fiancée, Kat — Kitty, as Rafe called her — Breckenridge. Her feet, in their signature red cowboy boots, were propped on the seat in front of her, her dark brown hair fanned out against Rafe's arm.

Down the row, Maggy St. John sat with her husband, Cole, her hand resting on her pregnant belly. Their son, CJ, was in the back of the room, running the projector.

"Neither has Alyssa," Lincoln said, reaching over to give her a sideways hug.

Stefanie watched as Alyssa smiled at him, her eyes clear and shining, even if she still thought like a child. Her occasional visits to Spotlight Ranch, along with a private nurse, had proven to be the medicine she needed to break free of her nightmares. And on this trip, her smile had finally begun to connect to her eyes. Not unlike Lincoln's, really.

"Okay, I got the gumdrops, the red hots,

and the malted milk balls," Nick said as he came through the door. "Who wants what?"

"Malted milk balls," Lincoln said.

Rafe took the red hots.

Macey grabbed for the gumdrops and opened the box, getting up on her knees in the seat to share with Haley.

Stefanie could hardly believe Macey's transformation in these last five months. She wore a long-sleeved pink shirt, and she'd cut her hair so that it hung in soft waves around her head. Her counselor spoke highly of her, but Stefanie didn't need any confirmation. Even though Macey and Haley were still living with a foster family, she could see for herself that these weekend visits to the ranch were healing the girls. And Lincoln, their hero, had already put the wheels in motion to adopt Macey and Haley as soon as he and Stefanie got married. Perhaps it would even be the start of something she'd dreamed of long ago — a ranch not only for the North kids but for others who needed a place to heal.

The fact that Lincoln had proposed to her around the Nobles' Thanksgiving table last weekend, with everyone watching, had guaranteed him a yes.

Who was she kidding? Stefanie had never felt more herself — beautiful and cherished

and capable and smart — than when looking at Lincoln's smile. The man God had
given her to call her Beloved.

"Where's Piper?" Stefanie asked as Nick
sat down in front of them.

"Feeding Ruthie up at the house. She'll
be down soon."

Stefanie leaned her head on Lincoln's
shoulder. He was having a good day today,
his last attack quelled with some fast-acting
medicine. Still, his hand trembled slightly.
She reached out and folded it in hers.

That he'd found his strength, the man he
was meant to be, through this weakness only
confirmed her words that God was answering Lincoln's prayers in more ways than
even she had imagined. Through his life as
Lincoln Cash, he'd learned to be strong.
Learned to say and do things that made him
a hero, to be the person he'd always hoped
to be.

It hadn't been an act at all. It was something he already had inside that God had
put there and was just waiting for him to
discover. And as a new spokesman for
multiple sclerosis research, as well as by
providing scholarships to help student filmmakers with disabilities find a voice, he'd
become a different kind of hero to his fans.

Stefanie was so proud of him that she

could burst. Instead she squeezed his hand.

He looked at her and smiled. The formerly smug, heartbreaking, invincible movie star who'd turned into exactly the type of hero she was looking for. Fallible yet perfect for her.

Nick handed her the malted milk balls. She poured some into Lincoln's outstretched hand. "What movie are we watching this weekend? Lincoln saves the world, or Lincoln saves the world?"

He laughed. "Hey, you're the one who said you had to see every one of my movies before you'd marry me." He rolled his eyes in mock annoyance. "You must like watching me save the world."

"Maybe I just want to confirm that you're hero enough for me," she said and winked at him.

"I saw you and Aunt Stefanie on TV last week, Uncle Linc," Haley said. She had a sweet voice, and when she spoke, everyone seemed to light up. "They said she was your hot summer romance."

"I tried to get her to turn it off," Macey said, "but our foster mom loves E! channel. And whenever there's a Lincoln Cash sighting, she has to turn it up."

"I like Edith. She takes good care of you," Lincoln said. "But you shouldn't believe everything you hear."

Stefanie looked at him, pouring as much indignation into her expression as possible.

Lincoln grinned. "Hot, yes. Romance, yes. Summer? Not on your life." He leaned over and kissed her. "This is forever."

"Can we watch the movie now?" Alyssa said in a voice that spoke impatience.

"Roll it!" Stefanie yelled to CJ.

As the lights went down, Lincoln settled back in his seat, his arm around Stefanie, tucking her in close.

Stefanie smiled. He might have come to Montana to hide, but instead, God had used him to help *her* come out of hiding, to find herself, her life, her future.

To tell her that He loved her.

Maybe this was what it felt like to be invincible.

No, this was what it felt like to be called Beloved.

A NOTE FROM THE AUTHOR

Writing this book couldn't have come at a more difficult time. I'm not sure why, but I always seem to back myself into my schedule, turning around just in time to see it crashing down over me like a wave. If I'm well-balanced, I keep my feet and can ride the wave to shore. However, often the wave knocks me over, and I'm left scraping the ocean bottom, wedging sand in my teeth and gasping for air when I surface.

The spring of 2007 hit me like a tidal wave. I was homeschooling three of my children in fourth, sixth, and ninth grades. I had speaking engagements every weekend for three months, and I was trying to write Stefanie Noble's story. I thought I might lose my mind.

My husband sensed that I was overwhelmed — perhaps because of the way I mumbled in my sleep — and he came to me with a plan. He would cook supper.

Every night. For three months. Maybe some of you have husbands who cook. Mine is a fabulous cook, but I'm the primary chef in the family. And when you're feeding a family of six, four of whom are men, you have to cook a lot. I could have cried at his feet with relief.

But his generosity didn't stop there. Not only did he cook — he cleaned, carpooled, fixed my car, and occasionally brought supper up to my office. And he prayed for me.

He was God's gift of strength to me.

So much of the time, heroes in stories are alpha males, able to leap tall buildings and swim through hurricane waters to save their heroines. However, in today's world women are strong and often don't need that kind of hero. Stefanie Noble was one of these. A woman accustomed to working with animals, she knew how to handle herself. But she needed someone who would stand beside her, believe in her, and encourage her. She needed a different kind of hero.

I have a good friend who is one of the strongest women I know. She is beautiful and poised, talented and wise. She's raising three children, two of my favorite teenagers and a delightful toddler. From the outside, one would never know her challenges —

namely, her wonderful toddler has Down syndrome and needs extra eyes on him as he explores his world. And her husband had MS. From her demeanor and smile, people might think her life was easy. I know differently. I also know how much she has loved her husband, and how she appreciated that when he couldn't be physically strong, he was strong in ways she needed him to be.

Watching my friend in her struggles made me wonder what it would be like to be someone strong — like action hero Lincoln Cash — then have your body betray you. I wondered how he might feel and if he could see God using him to be heroic in a different way.

I love strong heroes, but I love strength of character in a man more. Especially when he surrenders his heart to the One who gives strength. This is the theme I brought to *Finding Stefanie.*

Lincoln also helps Stefanie see her world and herself through new eyes. As a mother, I remember those early days when I'd look up from my daily routines — helping with homework, doing laundry, cooking supper — and wonder, how did I get here? Last time I looked, I was newly married and about to conquer the world as a super missionary. Did I blink?

I'm sure my friend wonders this also. How did she get here, with so much on her shoulders?

I know that she wouldn't trade her life for anything. Neither would I. But I know what it feels like to be discontent, believing there is something more. Like when I was living in Siberia, without heat, chasing down roaches. Or when we were homeless for four months and lived in our garage. I have come to believe that contentment is a mind-set, a submission to all God is doing in my life. His call is for me to be obedient to the life He's given me and to embrace it with a tender heart — no matter what the circumstance. When I do, He has a way of making me see it with new eyes. Life doesn't always turn out the way we expect. But it can still be good. Very good.

My friend taught me that too. And those are the lessons I wrote into this book.

"Fill my cup, Lord. . . . Come and quench this thirsting of my soul. Bread of heaven, feed me till I want no more. Fill my cup, fill it up and make me whole!"

God can fill your cup with strength, contentment, and wholeness. I pray that today you find Him your hero in every way.

Thank you for journeying with me

through the Noble Legacy!

God Bless,

Susan May Warren

ABOUT THE AUTHOR

Susan May Warren recently returned home after serving for eight years with her husband and four children as missionaries in Khabarovsk, Far East Russia. Now writing full-time as her husband runs a lodge on Lake Superior in northern Minnesota, she and her family enjoy hiking and canoeing and being involved in their local church. Susan holds a BA in mass communications from the University of Minnesota and is a multipublished author of novellas and novels with Tyndale, including *Happily Ever After,* the American Christian Romance Writers' 2003 Book of the Year and a 2003 Christy Award finalist. Other books in the series include *Tying the Knot* and *The Perfect Match,* the 2004 American Christian Fiction Writers' Book of the Year. *Flee the Night, Escape to Morning,* and *Expect the Sunrise* comprise her romantic-adventure, search-and-rescue series.

Finding Stefanie is the sequel to *Reclaiming Nick* and *Taming Rafe* and the third book in Susan's new romantic series.

Susan invites you to visit her Web site at **www.susanmaywarren.com.**

She also welcomes letters by e-mail at **susan@susanmaywarren.com.**